"What if I do or s thing?" Luc said

"Henry isn't my son yet. that damages my case? What if I somehow hurt him or make a mistake with him? I couldn't stand that."

"Luc, nobody is born knowing how to be a parent. It's trial and error for everyone." Holly smiled, hoping to ease his anxiety. "Come on, Luc. You've talked about adopting Henry. Now's not the time to get cold feet. In fact, this is probably the perfect time to try the things you want to do with Henry when you adopt him. Show him what you love," she said quietly. "He'll love it, too."

"I guess that's my biggest fear," he admitted. "Maybe Henry won't like my life."

"Are you kidding? Cowboys are Henry's heroes. He's going to dive headlong into whatever you show him. But if he doesn't, you'll find something else, right? Because Henry is the son you've always wanted."

Without warning, Luc leaned forward and pressed a kiss against her forehead. "You're a good friend, Holly."

She gulped, utterly unnerved by that soft kiss and yet deeply moved that this strong, competent man needed her. It took a second to get her happy-go-lucky mask in place so Luc wouldn't see how deeply he'd affected her.

Lois Richer loves traveling, swimming and quilting, but mostly she loves writing stories that show God's boundless love for His precious children. As she says, "His love never changes or gives up. It's always waiting for me. My stories feature imperfect characters learning that love doesn't mean attaining perfection. Love is about keeping on keeping on." You can contact Lois via email, loisricher@yahoo.com, or on Facebook (LoisRicherAuthor).

Books by Lois Richer

Love Inspired

Family Ties

A Dad for Her Twins
Rancher Daddy

Northern Lights

North Country Hero
North Country Family
North Country Mom
North Country Dad

Healing Hearts

A Doctor's Vow
Yuletide Proposal
Perfectly Matched

Love for All Seasons

The Holiday Nanny
A Baby by Easter
A Family for Summer

Visit the Author Profile page at Harlequin.com for more titles.

Rancher Daddy

Lois Richer

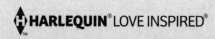

HARLEQUIN® LOVE INSPIRED®

Recycling programs
for this product may
not exist in your area.

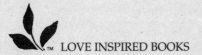

™ LOVE INSPIRED BOOKS

ISBN-13: 978-0-373-81853-2

Rancher Daddy

Copyright © 2015 by Lois M. Richer

www.Harlequin.com

Printed in U.S.A.

Let Him have all your worries and cares,
for He is always thinking about you and
watching everything that concerns you.
—*1 Peter* 5:7

This book is dedicated to children young and old who have ever felt abandoned, alone and unloved. You are not. God loves you with a love so deep no human love could touch it. If you let Him, He will fill your heart and soul so that you never again need to feel you're on your own.

Chapter One

❦

Holly Janzen loved her early-morning ride home after a night shift on the hospital's pediatric ward. Especially now that spring had crept into the valley where Buffalo Gap nestled in the foothills of the Alberta Rocky Mountains. With the sun just cresting, the town lay bathed in the rosy hue of May's promise. The best part was that morning signaled a fresh start, untouched by the horrible memories of her past.

Holly gaped at the twenty-foot photo of her own face pasted to a huge billboard in the center of town, her heart sinking as she read,

Holly Janzen. Buffalo Gap's citizen of the year.

Why did they keep doing that? Several times a year Mayor Marsha Grant and the town council did something that featured Holly as the town's poster child for success. Years ago they'd granted Holly, the girl voted most likely to succeed, a scholarship to earn her nurse practitioner credentials in Toronto. The mayor and the rest of the town never heard the truth about those years down east and how un-poster-child-like she'd behaved, because nobody in Buffalo Gap ever saw past the good-girl image of her childhood. To them Holly Janzen was a role model they wanted their own kids to emulate.

As if!

Tired of the never-ending guilt that memories of those years in Toronto always brought, Holly shoved them away and focused instead on the sight of the newly renovated hotel that now housed Family Ties, an adoption agency two friends had set up to help kids who needed homes. But unlike most days, this morning Holly gave the place more than a yearning glance.

This morning a child sat on the steps that led to the front door.

A horn sounded behind her, a short beep, just enough to let her know someone didn't appreciate her pausing in the middle of the street. Holly identified the rusty brown half-ton truck in her rearview mirror and smiled. Luc Cramer, aka Mr. Just In Time.

Luc had come to her rescue many times but especially during her father's illness and after his death three months ago. He'd continued as Holly's ranch manager leaving her free to focus on her work as the community's nurse practitioner which often meant she helped pregnant moms deliver healthy newborns. A side benefit of that was that she got to work with moms-to-be at Family Ties.

Holly mostly accepted what Luc suggested in regard to the ranch and so far it was working out great. The only negative side was that whenever Holly voiced her concern that Luc wasn't benefitting as much as she was from the arrangement, he brushed her off.

Now Holly thrust her hand out of her car window, pointed to the boy on the steps then steered hard left, crossing the street to pull into an angled parking spot in front of Family Ties. Two seconds later Luc's truck pulled in beside hers as she jumped out of her orange jeep.

"Holly, you can't just stop in the middle of the street and then pull across it like that," he began in that quiet but pained tone he sometimes used, which carried a kind of big-brother resignation.

"What are you doing in town so early, Luc?" she asked.

"Just coming home from Calgary." He smiled at her arched eyebrow. "No, I wasn't partying, I was trying to help a friend who's going through a messy, painful divorce."

"That's nice of you." She tilted her head in the boy's direction. "Who's this little guy?"

"No idea. Let's find out." Luc followed Holly as she hurried forward. She was aware of him but her focus centered on the little boy in worn-out jeans and a tattered red hoodie sitting in front of Family Ties. Big black glasses made him look like a wise owl.

"Hi, honey," she said in a soft voice, crouching down to meet the child's gaze. "What's your name?"

"Henry." He blinked huge brown eyes at her then his gaze shifted to Luc. "Are you a real cowboy?" he asked in awed tones.

Holly turned to see Luc's slow, easy grin slash across his handsome, tanned face.

"Real as they get, partner," Luc said in a drawl that reminded her of some Hollywood star in a bygone Western movie. When he hunkered down beside Holly, his elbow brushed her arm, sending an electric charge up it as he thrust out a hand to shake Henry's.

Holly noticed the contact with her hunky foreman because it caused her stomach to do that shaky dance. But she couldn't figure out why that was. Luc was a friend but nothing more. That was the way she wanted it.

"Pleased to meet you, Henry. I'm Luc and that's Holly." Luc smiled then quietly asked, "What are you doing here?"

"Waiting." The boy reached up to touch the brim of Luc's jet-black Stetson, the one Holly had only ever seen Luc remove for church and funerals. But this morning the cowboy took off his hat and set it on the boy's head. Henry's eyes widened. "I wish I had one of these."

"Maybe one day you will." Luc shot Holly a look that asked for help.

She nodded. They needed to find out more about this boy so they could figure out what to do next.

"Are you waiting for someone special, Henry?" Holly asked.

"Uh-huh. The people who work here." The boy jerked a thumb over one shoulder. "They find families for kids. I want one."

Nonplussed, Holly glanced at Luc, who stared right back at her, his brown eyes crinkling at the corners with his lazy grin. That was Luc—laid-back, comfortable in his skin and always in a good mood. When she arched an eyebrow at him he simply shrugged. Obviously he was waiting for her to continue the investigation.

"What's your last name, Henry?" she asked.

"Brown. Henry Brown." His little chest puffed out. "I'm five and three quarters."

Five and three quarters. He was almost the same age as her baby... Holly gulped at the memories of that tiny innocent child and instead concentrated on what Henry was saying.

"Last night I stayed with this lady—Ms. Hilda." Henry's big brown eyes narrowed. His lips pressed together as he scrunched up his nose so his glasses would move back in place. "She snores."

"I see." Holly shot Luc a look meant to stifle his snort of laughter. She guessed Henry was one of the many foster kids from Calgary for whom Mayor Marsha often agreed to find temporary care.

Holly considered phoning the mayor but hesitated. Marsha was still recovering from complications after her second knee surgery. Maybe Abby Lebret, owner of Family Ties, would be a better choice. But it was barely 6:00 a.m. and if Abby's young twins hadn't yet woken her, she wouldn't appreciate an early-morning call, either.

"I want a family," Henry said with a glance over one shoulder, his voice and face as serious as a little old man.

"Me, too. Are you hungry, Henry?" Luc's grin flashed at Henry's emphatic nod. "Hey, me, too."

"Well, what's new about that?" Holly grumbled, irritated that her ranch manager didn't seem to be taking the situation seriously. "You're always hungry, Luc."

"Sounds like maybe you are, too, Miss Cranky," Luc teased, his eyes as warm as his smile. "Long shift, huh? What say we go get some breakfast?"

"Luc, you can't just take him—"

"Can I have pancakes? I love pancakes," Henry asked, his voice beseeching.

"Pancakes it is." Luc straightened. "We can come back here, Holly. When Family Ties is open," he added when she frowned.

"Well, all right," she agreed. "But we'd better phone Hilda first. She might be missing Henry."

"She's prob'ly still snoring." Henry's tone was utterly serious.

Holly had to turn away to hide her smile. When she did she bumped into Luc. He grasped her arms to steady her, which set her heart on a gallop.

"Whoa there, little lady. You must need some food if you're swaying on your feet." His hands dropped away but his gaze never left her face. "Did you forget to eat your lunch again?"

"I ate an apple around midnight," Holly said, avoiding his gaze. "I can take care of myself, Luc."

"Oh, I know that," he said, nodding, though his next words belied that. "But you do forget to eat when you're on night shift. Come on. Let's go to Brewsters." He swung his arm around Henry's shoulder. "They have the best breakfast," he said in a low voice.

"They have the *only* breakfast at this time of the morning," Holly corrected, noticing how easily Henry and Luc had bonded. Feeling left out, she dialed Hilda's. When there was no answer, she left a message on the machine then followed the two males while wondering how Luc knew she usually forgot her lunch.

He knew because he was always there for her.

Luc's being there had started the day he'd purchased the land adjoining her dad's Cool Springs Ranch. It continued after Holly's dad got a terminal diagnosis and elected not to fight his lung cancer. Marcus Janzen had chosen instead to live out his days at home. Since her mom had long since abandoned her daughter, husband and Cool Springs Ranch, Holly was the only one Marcus had left. Because she loved her dad dearly she'd focused her time and efforts on making his final days perfect, with Luc's help.

Marcus and Luc had become fast friends the day after Luc moved in to the neighboring spread three years ago. He'd shown up at Cool Springs that evening to ask Marcus about a sick steer. He'd come a hundred times since, eager to learn all he could about ranching from Holly's very knowledgeable dad.

Maybe that's why it had seemed normal for Luc to "help out" as he put it, when Marcus fell ill. Luc did the chores her dad couldn't, sold the cattle Marcus wanted to part with and even sheared the sheep Marcus had just begun raising. After Marcus died, Luc kept coming back, kept helping out. And Holly had been glad of it, especially after Family Ties opened and, as the local nurse practitioner, she was called on to assist with several births.

"You must be daydreaming about something wonderful," Luc whispered in her ear when she passed through the door he held open. "Your smile couldn't get bigger. Something good happen?"

"Yes." She sank into a booth across from Henry. She smiled at him then faced Luc. "This morning I made a decision. I'm going ahead with the renovations on the house. I intend to make the extra bedroom into a full-blown sewing room."

She'd decided to go ahead because this morning the very thought of always having to clear off the dining table so she could sew the baby clothes she sold online seemed daunting. The extra bedroom was the perfect space; it just needed a few modifications.

Holly grimaced. Was it her good-girl image that made her try to gloss things over? Truthfully, that room needed a lot of modification if it was going to help her grow her business.

But Holly didn't tell Luc that. Nobody in town knew about her business and that's the way she intended to keep it. Getting dumped the day before her December wedding had generated enough gossip in Buffalo Gap to last a lifetime. She sure didn't need the town thinking she was so heartbroken and desperate to have a child that she now poured her soul into making baby clothes for other moms because she'd lost her chance to be a wife and mom.

"Holly?" Luc's touch on her arm roused her from her introspection. "Pancakes and sausage? That's what Henry and I are having."

"No, thank you." Holly made a face. "The very last things I want are heavy, syrup-drenched pancakes and sausages before I go to sleep. I'll have dry rye toast, two scrambled eggs and tea, please," she said to Paula Brewster. They shared a smile before Paula left to place the orders.

"Pancakes are good," Henry told her seriously. "Way better than eggs or cereal." He lost his serious look for a moment when Luc held out a hand to high-five him. But the gravity returned almost immediately. "When do I get my family?"

Holly didn't know how to answer. It would be nice to say "not long," to reassure the boy, but the truth was that neither she nor Luc knew anything about Henry and whether or not Family Ties could help him.

"That's a hard thing to answer, Henry," Luc said seriously. Holly liked the way he didn't brush off the boy's concern or make promises he couldn't keep.

"Why?" Henry's big brown eyes looked into Luc's trustingly, waiting for an answer.

"Because families are hard things to build,"

Luc told him. He grinned. "Look at me. I don't have a family yet."

"Don't you want one?" Henry thanked their server for his glass of milk, took a sip then leaned back in his chair to hear the answer.

"Definitely." Luc nodded. "But finding a family isn't easy. I grew up without my own family. Instead, other families took care of me."

"Did you like that?" Henry asked.

"Mostly I did. I was safe," Luc said after a moment of thought. "I had a place to sleep, good food to eat and nobody hurt me. It was okay."

"I want a family to love me." Henry's earnest tone matched his solemn face. "I prayed to God for it."

"That's the best thing you could do, Henry." Holly waited until Paula had served their food before she continued. "God loves us. He wants to give us what we most want. You just keep praying for a family."

"Do you have a family?" Henry studied her seriously.

"Not anymore," Holly explained quietly, setting down her fork as she spoke. "My dad died three months ago. He was all the family I had."

No way would she include her mother as family. Since the day she'd walked out, Holly barely gave the woman a thought and certainly not in terms of motherhood.

It struck Holly then that she'd done a much

worse thing than her mother had done. The familiar burden of guilt that always accompanied thoughts of her baby settled on her spirit once more.

"I'm sorry." Henry reached across the table and enfolded her fingers in his. "I'll ask God to get you and Luc families, too."

"Thank you, Henry," Holly said, greatly humbled by his strong faith. "You'd better eat your pancakes while they're hot."

While Henry dug into his food, Luc bombarded her with questions about the changes she wanted to make to the farmhouse where she'd been born.

"Be more specific. What exactly do you want?" he pressed.

"I want more electrical outlets for one thing," Holly specified. "I want wide countertops to cut out fabric. I want better lighting so I can work at night if I'm on the day shift. I want lots of storage space and room for my quilting frame. If I get called in, I want to leave my sewing as is and pick up where I left off when I return."

"Shouldn't be hard." He shrugged.

"Good, because the dining table doesn't cut it anymore," she told him with a grimace. "I'm tired of making do."

"So am I," Luc said in a low-throated tone. "I'm really tired of that."

Holly stared at his serious face, confused by

his words. But before she could ask him to explain, her phone rang. Mayor Marsha, who knew everything that happened in town, had already talked to Hilda about Henry. Pushing off her need for sleep, Holly agreed she and Luc would bring Henry to meet Marsha in the mayor's office in half an hour. Luc nodded when she told him then picked up their earlier conversation.

"I've never seen whatever it is you spend so much time sewing." He studied the green scrubs she still wore from her shift at the hospital, his gaze resting on the label on the chest pocket. "Not those, I'm guessing. Are you helping with more quilts for Family Ties? I heard the intent was to give one to every woman who uses the services of Family Ties to adopt out her child."

"I am helping with that." Holly wished he wasn't so curious. "But that's not exactly what I want a sewing room for."

It was silly trying to evade the question because Luc never let anything go until he had an answer. That was the way he'd been the whole time he'd been learning ranching from her dad, and Holly doubted he'd ever change. His curiosity was innate. He was one of those people who asked and probed until he received a satisfactory answer. She thought Henry had the same trait.

"I could understand if you were still making your wedding dress." Luc squinted out the window, watching the town come to life. "But you don't need that anymore, do you?"

"Even if I did, it's too late," she told him defiantly. "I cut it up the day Ron dumped me."

"But you could use it someday," he protested.

"I am not getting married, Luc. Even if I were, do you honestly think I'd wear a wedding dress I chose to marry someone else? I assure you, I would not. But I repeat, I'm not getting married. Ever." She crossed her arms over her chest.

"Ever? That's pretty harsh." Luc raised an eyebrow then inclined his head toward her plate. At her nod he picked up the last slice of her toast and smeared jam over it. "Surely one day—"

"Never," Holly repeated. "I'm too independent." She glanced at him through her lashes as she fudged the truth. "I prefer to be single."

He shot her a look that questioned her statement.

"Don't worry. I put that wedding dress to good use. There are some really nice curtains in the living room at Family Ties." She burst out laughing at his startled look, hoping to hide the hurt that snuck up on her occasionally, ever since the day Ron had told her he wouldn't marry her.

That's what comes of keeping secrets.

"You're a good sport, Holly. I like that about you. Though I can't say I have such high regard for the man you chose to marry." Luc's voice tightened. "Ron Simard was a first-class jerk to walk away from you like that."

"He had his reasons." If Luc knew what she'd kept hidden from her fiancé until a few days before her wedding, Holly was pretty sure he'd have agreed wholeheartedly with Ron's decision to turn tail and run.

Luc had lost his family and frequently spoke of his desire for an heir. How could he ever understand her decision to give away the infant she'd birthed while she was in training?

"So your new sewing room doesn't have anything to do with Ron?" he pressed, nudging her from the past with its guilty secrets.

"Not at all! Sewing is my hobby, Luc, a way to be creative and a total change from my work," she explained. "It lets me achieve some of my dreams. Aside from the cost of the renovation, it shouldn't impact the ranch budget too much. Okay?" She stared at him, one eyebrow arched.

"If you're asking my permission, I certainly think it's okay if you make a sewing room out of your extra bedroom," he said, pushing away his empty plate.

"I wasn't asking your permission," she shot back, irritated that she'd felt compelled to explain but even more annoyed that she'd let him get to her. He knew it, too, judging by the smile flickering at the corner of his lips.

"If that's what you want. I might even offer to help you do the renovation."

"Really?" She frowned. "I thought you'd be too busy with ranch stuff. You keep asking if I've done it yet, but you've never actually offered to help me clean out Dad's trunk."

"That's different." Luc had the grace to look embarrassed. He turned, grabbed a napkin and wiped Henry's syrup-spattered cheeks. "I don't want to push in on your personal affairs," he muttered.

"Luc, you already know everything there is to know about Cool Springs Ranch," Holly pointed out, surprised by this sensitivity.

"There might be something personal in there that you don't want to share. Did you ever empty it?" He did look at her then.

"Not yet." Holly couldn't shake the feeling that Luc was hiding something. "I'll get to the trunk. Eventually."

"Good. Anyway, renovating is different than going through personal stuff. Sort of." He nodded then shook his head. "Or maybe not."

"Definitive answer," she teased as she studied him, confused by his response. Luc was never uncertain. "You'll help me with the renovation and I suppose you'll expect me to help you with something in return. What?"

"I'm not sure yet." He tilted his head just the tiniest bit to the left where Henry sat silently watching them. Holly frowned, prepared to push for an answer but Luc shook his head.

She shrugged. Let him have his secret. Goodness knew she had her own and she hated it when anyone tried to push her into saying something she didn't want to.

"Can we get my family now?" Henry asked.

"It won't be that simple, Henry," Holly warned. "It's a long process to find a family. Besides, we've got another fifteen minutes before we're supposed to meet the mayor." His sad expression touched her. He must be very lonely. With a spurt of inspiration she asked, "Where did you live before, Henry?"

"In Calgary. In a shelter. My brother took care of me." For the first time the boy's composure fractured. A big tear plopped onto his cheek. "Finn can't take care of me anymore because he's in prison. He told me he didn't do it but I think he did steal the money from the store and it's my fault."

"How could it be your fault?" Luc asked, touching the boy's shoulder gently.

"My teacher said I need new glasses. But I shouldn't have told Finn because he didn't have any money to buy them." Henry's voice dropped to a whisper. "I asked him anyway."

"You couldn't know what Finn would do," Holly said, hugging Henry close for a moment. "It's not your fault."

When Luc didn't add his voice to the comment, Holly glanced up and found him staring at her and Henry, his brown eyes almost black with intensity.

"What?" she murmured, discomfited by his look.

"I just had an idea." A slow grin moved across Luc's face, accenting the handsome ruggedness. "Henry, here's some money. Could you go pay the bill?"

Delighted by this sign of trust, Henry scooted out of the booth and across the café.

"Why did you do that?" Holly liked that Luc was an open book. He didn't hide his thoughts or pretend to be anything but what he was—a cowboy. He was honest and straightforward and she knew she could count on him. So when he leaned toward her, Holly smiled, expecting a joke.

"In return for helping you with your renovations, I would like your help," Luc said.

"With what?" Surprised when he beckoned to her to move closer, Holly leaned toward him.

"With adopting Henry."

Luc winced when Holly's eyes widened then flickered with disbelief. What was so surprising about him wanting to adopt Henry? She studied him until Henry came back then turned her focus on the boy, watching as he first handed Luc the change and then began scribbling on his place-mat with the pen he'd given him earlier.

"Henry," she said softly. "Mrs. Brewster has some toys over there, in the box under the window. Would you like to play with them for a few minutes until it's time to leave?"

"Okay." Henry shifted out of the booth, paused to study them through his big round glasses. "You and Luc should make a family."

"Uh, I don't think so." Holly avoided Luc's glance until Henry walked over to the toy box. "Where did he get that idea from?" Her beautiful blue eyes now had silver sparks in them which shot his way. "Never mind. Were you kidding about adopting him?"

"Why would I?" Irritated that Holly would think he'd joke about such a serious subject, Luc clenched his hands on the leather bench. Why shouldn't he be a father to this needy boy?

Holly's glossy brunette curls, caught up in the ponytail she always wore to work, shone red-gold glints in a flash of sunlight coming through the window. She always looked lovely to him, but with the pink flush of annoyance now staining her cheeks, she was stunning. And she distracted him.

"You can't adopt Henry." Her voice had the sharpest tone he'd ever heard.

"Because?" Luc leaned back in his seat and waited, formulating arguments in his mind, ready to shoot hers down while wondering what was wrong with the usually happy Holly.

"You make it sound like it's a done deal, just because you've decided. Adoption's not that easy." Holly fiddled with her teacup.

"How do you know?" Funny how she didn't look at him now. Instead, she hid her gaze by staring at the uneaten food on her plate. Luc's radar was alerted, but he waited for her to speak.

"I've seen and heard stuff at Family Ties. There are procedures to go through. Isn't it time to leave?" Holly sounded almost desperate.

"We've still got several minutes," he said, wondering why she hadn't looked at her watch. It hung from a gold pin near her shoulder. Luc knew she did that because she'd once told him she disliked wearing anything on her wrist. He knew a lot about Holly. "What kind of procedures do I need to go through, Holly?"

"Uh, well…" She leaned back, obviously searching for an answer. "I don't know. Maybe start by learning all you can about adoptions. Check out support groups for adoptive parents or conferences where you can learn what to expect, what others have gone through, how to handle certain problems."

"Sounds like that would take a long time." There was something funny going on. Uncomplicated, straight-shooting Holly wouldn't look at him.

"Of course. Adoption is a long process," she said hurriedly. "You're adopting the child for life so it would be better to learn as much as you can before you act."

"I suppose." Luc nodded. "So what else do I need to know?"

"This isn't my specialty, Luc. I'm a nurse practitioner not a social worker." She sounded frustrated. Must be lack of sleep.

Luc knew ordinarily Holly would be tucked up in bed by now. She always gave her best at work but she worked doubly hard when she was on night shifts and especially when children fussed and seemed to need extra attention. Most mornings he watched her return home utterly wornout.

"You're tired. Never mind," he said, sorry that he'd bothered her when she was spent.

"You should talk with Abby Lebret." Her voice sounded calmer. "She's the social worker who runs Family Ties and she'd know how to proceed."

"That's a good idea." He stretched out his booted feet and bumped hers. "Sorry. I suppose someone will visit my place, make sure it's all right for a child to live there?"

"I'm sure that's part of a home study," Holly told him. "But I doubt you'll have just one meeting. It's—I mean I *think* it's more like a series of meetings and it gets pretty personal. Or so I've heard," she added, ignoring his surprised look.

"I'd expect to be investigated." Luc wondered where she got her information and then decided it must be from Family Ties. Abby and Holly were good friends. "I'd want them to get all their questions about me answered so there wouldn't be any mistakes that would mean they'd take Henry back."

"I guess that's wise. But, Luc, there's no guarantee Henry is even adoptable." Holly's smooth forehead pleated with her frown. "He might already be a candidate for some other family or it may be that he's not eligible for adoption."

"He is. I just know it." Luc couldn't explain how he knew Henry was supposed to be his son. He'd struggled for the past year trying to figure out God's will for him. Surely having Henry show up as he had, asking for a family, was a sign God's plan was for Luc to be a dad to Henry.

"I imagine Henry has a child worker assigned to him. I guess that person will be your first hurdle." Holly tried to hide a yawn behind her hand but didn't quite succeed. "I think we'd better get over to Marsha's office before I doze off."

"It's time." He waited while Holly collected Henry then walked to the door. "Are you going to stay awake through this?" he asked when she tried to smother another yawn.

"I can give you another half hour," Holly promised. "But then I am going to crash."

"Thanks, Holly. You have no idea how much this means to me." Luc reached out and squeezed her shoulder. With Holly on his side, he couldn't possibly fail to get his son.

Chapter Two

"Henry has no home. I don't see what's wrong with bringing him to my place to stay until the adoption goes through," Luc said as he took a seat at her dining table.

Holly watched as the tall, lean rancher gulped down a mouthful of the coffee she'd just poured, disregarding her warning that it was hot. Coughing and sputtering, he raced across the dining room to the kitchen sink and downed a glass of cold water. He made a series of silly faces as he tested his scorched mouth.

She tried but couldn't quite stifle her laughter at his antics.

"It's not nice for you to laugh at me, Holly," he reproved her then added, "Certainly not something the town's wonder girl would do."

"Oh, lay off that nonsense," she said, losing her good mood. "I'm not that wonderful and the town would know that if they really knew me." Sobered by his words she reminded him, "It's only been a week since you met Henry and you're still treating adoption just like that hot coffee. I warned you it was hot just as I warned you it wouldn't be easy to adopt Henry."

"I never thought it would be easy." Luc flopped back down in his chair and stretched out. "I just didn't think it would be a lesson in fighting bureaucracy."

"Please keep your boots away from that bag of fabric." Holly's warning came a second too late. "This is exactly why I need a sewing room," she complained in an exasperated tone as she freed a piece of frilly lace from the toe of his boot.

"Sorry. I know I promised I'd work on a sewing room in exchange for your help, Holly. I'll get to it soon." He took the lace from her and studied it. "What is this for anyway? A hair bow?" He peered at it then studied her head. "Since when do you wear pink? You hate pink."

"It's not a hair bow and it's not for me," Holly told him, snatching the delicate lace from his fingers. "I'm going to sew it on a gift I'm making."

"*Another* baby gift?" He leaned over to study the fabric pieces lying on the table. "Looks like a jigsaw puzzle but I can tell it's for a girl. You sure do have a lot of new moms as friends."

"I deliver babies. It's my job to know the moms. I like to give them a little gift after their baby's birth." Holly flushed and looked away.

Shame on me for fudging the truth.

But how else could she explain without telling him about her online business? And Holly didn't want to do that. If Luc knew he'd probably pass on the information and soon the whole town would be talking. She couldn't bear to hear the gossips.

Poor jilted bride. That's why she makes baby clothes, you know. Because she doesn't have any children of her own.

If they only knew that she'd once held her own precious child in her arms and then given him away to save her father's reputation.

Since it was Holly's week off, Luc had made a habit of stopping by unexpectedly for coffee, ostensibly to discuss the work he did on her ranch. Somehow the conversation always turned to adopting Henry. A couple of times he'd caught her with her work spread all over the dining table. Well, it wasn't as if she could just scoop everything into a box whenever he appeared.

"I probably shouldn't have bothered you about this again," Luc apologized. "But I wondered if you'd given more thought to selling Cool Springs Ranch?"

"Not again." She rolled her eyes. "Luc, you've asked me that a hundred times since Dad died. I told you on Monday that I wasn't interested in selling any of Dad's land. Today is Thursday and I'm still not interested."

"It's not your dad's land anymore, Holly," Luc said in a somber tone. "It's yours."

"Yes, but he worked so hard to acquire this land and his herd," she said softly. "He wanted me to have a birthright." *Which should have gone to his grandson.* "I wouldn't feel right selling off any of it."

"Okay." Luc sighed. "But when you do decide, you'll give me first dibs, right?"

"If and when," she promised.

"Good enough." He wrinkled his nose at the brightly striped fabric she was about to cut. "That looks like clown material," he said then added, "Have you got time to go for a ride?"

"Now?" Holly paused, her scissors frozen in midair. She looked up at him and frowned. This was about the ranch; it had to be important. "What's wrong?"

"I'd rather show you than explain," he said. "Then I'll come back here and you can show me exactly what you want in your sewing room."

"Fine." Resigned, Holly put down her scissors and shut off the pattern mill in her brain. If she had a bigger, more private work space, she'd be able to accept more orders and finally pay off the last of the bills leftover from her dad's illness. It was the only debt she owed him that she could repay. Nothing could ever make up for the love and care he'd showered on her all her life.

Except perhaps the grandson he'd never known.

"Holly?" Luc touched her shoulder. "Would you rather wait?"

"No. Let's go." She mentally shook off the past, knowing the guilt would return again later, when she was alone.

"It's the north quarter. We'll have to ride." Luc glanced at her bare feet and raised one eyebrow. "I think you're going to have to cover those," he jibed.

Holly glanced down and giggled.

"One of my Sunday school students gave me this polish," she said, wiggling her toes. "She said her mom thought it was too old for her."

"It's too something," Luc agreed, unable to stifle a laugh.

Holly laughed with him. Luc always had that effect on her, she thought as she pulled on her socks and riding boots. He was a very good friend who coaxed her to enjoy life. She enjoyed having him around.

They took the shortcut to the north pasture, past Luc's house. Holly slowed to a stop and squinted into the sun below the brim of her hat, waiting until he'd reined in beside her.

"What's that in your yard, Luc?"

"I'm restoring a truck and needed some parts so I had the garage tow in a couple of wrecks." He must have seen something in her face because he asked, "Why?"

"You're still determined to adopt Henry?" she asked, even though she knew he was.

"Of course. Why not?" Luc glanced at the yard then back at her. "What's wrong?"

"I think that whoever comes to check out your place will see those old cars and parts as a potential hazard for a kid Henry's age," she said gently. "You can still restore your vehicles but maybe not in front of the house."

"It's handy when I have a few minutes after dinner," he explained. "I can walk out the door and work as long as the light's good, but you're right. I wouldn't want Henry poking around where there's a lot of rust and jagged edges."

"I'm sorry," she murmured, knowing how much he loved to restore vehicles.

"Don't be." Luc twisted to look at her, his grin back in place. "That's exactly the kind of thing I want your help with, Holly."

"Did you talk to Abby yet?" she asked. "She might have some weight with the government if Henry is in the care of Family Ties. Or even if he's under other stewardship."

"Abby told me Henry's only been in foster care since his brother went to prison, but that he hasn't been able to settle in anywhere. Apparently he doesn't like foster care and keeps asking for a forever family." Luc chuckled. "His case worker in Calgary was relieved Abby agreed to temporarily oversee his care while he's staying with Hilda Vermeer."

"He's still there, even though she snores?" Holly asked, tongue in cheek.

"Apparently there is a lack of foster homes right now. When he argued about staying with Hilda, Abby said she had to be very forceful with him to get him to understand that he'd never get his family if he didn't give her time to find it. Henry then said he'd wait a little longer." Luc laughed. "He's such a solemn, determined kid."

And you already love him, Holly thought, her heart pinching at the trouble that might lie ahead for Luc. And yet, she had only to think of the joy he'd experience as a father, joy she'd missed out on, joy she'd denied her dad.

"Henry reminds me of you sometimes," she said, not realizing she'd voiced her thoughts until Luc's eyebrows arched.

"Me? How?"

"His purpose, the way he won't give in, his certainty about what he wants from life. And his eyes. Henry's eyes are exactly like yours. Are you sure you weren't married and had a child you didn't tell anyone about?" Holly teased.

Luc's face tightened. "Never married," he said firmly. "Never will. Some people, like you for instance, should be married. Some, especially if they're like me, shouldn't."

"Why not?" Surprised by the comment, Holly rode closer and tapped him on the arm. "Luc?"

He remained silent for so long she thought he wouldn't answer. She'd thought Luc simple and carefree until now. Her questions about him multiplied.

"I always intended to get married." He pulled his horse up when they came to the stream that divided their properties and dismounted. "That had been my dream since I was a kid, to someday have a wife and a family. A home. I thought with them I'd be able to make up for the family that I'd lost when my parents died in the car accident."

"And now you can't?" Holly's heart ached for the little boy he'd been and the grief he'd had to go through after losing the only family he'd ever known.

"I think maybe with Henry I can have that dream," Luc murmured thoughtfully.

Holly appreciated the way Luc held her horse's harness so she could dismount, even though she'd been riding since she was five. There was something nice about having Luc do those polite things that made her feel cherished, special.

She sat down on a rock by the creek bed and waited while Luc fastened both horses to a tall poplar tree. He pulled two cans of soda from his saddlebags and a sack of nuts.

"I thought it'd be nice to take a break here,"

he said after handing her a soda. He folded his long lean length next to her then set his Stetson on a rock. His short dark curly hair glistened in the sun.

Luc, Holly suddenly realized, was a very handsome man.

"I love this spot. It's so peaceful." His voice rumbled quietly through the little glade. "It makes me think of God."

Holly sipped her drink and waited for him to continue. She, too, loved this spot and often came here to pray for forgiveness.

"This year I let go of the marriage part of my dreams," Luc told her, his face inexpressibly sad.

"Because?" Holly could hardly contain her curiosity.

"Because it wasn't realistic." A self-mocking smile stretched his mouth. "I thought love and marriage meant forever."

"And they don't?" Holly wanted to hug him when he shook his head. His face reflected his disenchantment.

"A month ago the woman I'd just proposed to told me she didn't love me enough to leave Calgary and move out here—to the back of beyond I believe she called it." Luc said it coolly, without emotion, but Holly saw the sting of rejection in his eyes.

"Oh, Luc. I'm so sorry." Holly frowned. "You never told us you were engaged."

"You and your dad had enough to deal with. Your canceled wedding and his illness took up every spare moment." His gaze rested on her, brimming with compassion. "My problems didn't matter."

"Of course they did. If you'd told us, we would have celebrated your happiness, even thrown a party." Holly pinched her lips. Luc grinned.

"Yeah, probably not a good idea," he said. "Too much to explain when we split up."

Holly couldn't suppress an oddly disquieting sensation at the knowledge that Luc had been contemplating marriage. She looked at him now with new eyes. Luc as a husband?

"Surely one breakup is no reason to give up on love and marriage," she said.

"It wasn't just one woman," he admitted in a low voice. "But this one hurt the most. Being rejected like that takes the starch out of you. It takes a while to get your feet back under you."

"Tell me about it," she muttered drily.

She wondered why she hadn't known he was in love. Then again, why wouldn't he be? Luc was very handsome, kind and generous, with faultless manners. Any woman would be fortunate to be loved by him. "I've been having second thoughts about marriage for a while," he volunteered.

"Why?" Holly hoped he wouldn't tell her to mind her own business.

"Several years ago I stood up at the weddings of several best buddies, guys with hearts of gold who'd gladly give you the shirt off their backs." Luc fiddled with his soda can. "I'd never seen them as committed as when they married their wives. They were determined to make it work, ready to put their all into it. Later they all had kids and seemed so happy. I envied them."

Holly said nothing, giving Luc time to gather his thoughts.

"I didn't know those marriages weren't even close to perfect. Now, one by one, each is ending in divorce." Luc swallowed. "The morning we found Henry I'd just come from my friend Pete's. He's the latest casualty." His face was troubled.

"Talk to me, Luc." Holly heard a world of pain in his stark words. He needed a friend and for once she *wanted* to be the one to help him.

"When I saw him, Pete was devastated, sitting in his truck, a shell of himself. He's lost his wife, his kids, his home. The love I envied five years ago is gone." He shook his head. "It was the most heartbreaking thing I've ever seen."

"I'm so sorry." The depth of his dejection touched her. "But that doesn't mean your relationships will fail. You just haven't found the right woman yet."

"I don't think love has to do with finding the right person, Holly. I'm not even sure there is a right person for me to find." Luc looked at her, his eyes dark. "Love is something you give, freely, unreservedly. How do you put your world together when the person you loved no longer wants you?"

"I wish I had the answer." Holly prayed desperately for words to soothe his stark hurt but couldn't find them. How could she help her friend?

"I'm no expert." His forehead pleated in a frown. "By everything I saw, those marriages should have worked. But my friends lost love and their dreams."

Holly felt stunned by Luc's desolation. She wanted him to expel the rejection from his heart so it couldn't hurt him anymore. As if! In five months she hadn't expelled Ron's accusations. Not yet. Not completely. "Go on, Luc."

"Sarah told me she didn't want to marry me after we'd been seriously discussing our future for several months." He shook his head as if he still couldn't believe it. "We'd even decided to get married in Tahiti because she said Buffalo Gap was too 'primitive.'"

That should have been a warning sign, Holly thought, but she kept silent.

"I agreed to almost all the conditions she set until she wanted me to sell my ranch." Luc smiled grimly when Holly reared back. "She told me she could never move here, so far from the city and her friends." Luc's face bore a pained look as if it hurt to admit the rest.

"I get the picture," Holly muttered, wishing she'd met this woman so she could have told her what a great guy Luc was.

"I didn't. Not until I insisted on keeping the ranch." His lips pinched together.

"Oh, Luc." Holly could almost guess the rest.

"She called Buffalo Gap Hicksville and hinted nothing here could possibly live up to city life. She said she wanted a husband to be proud of. She made fun of me for loving ranching, said I was wasting myself on cattle." His face telegraphed his sense of betrayal. "She said she wanted a husband to be proud of, not some guy smelling of manure, stuck in a mindless routine of chores."

"It's a good thing she broke it off," Holly burst out angrily. "Because if she hadn't, you would have. She would never have worked as a ranch wife."

"No, she wouldn't." Luc nodded. "But that's when I understood that I was just like my buddies. I gave everything to Sarah and she threw it in my face. That's when I knew that whatever I'd felt for her wouldn't survive the test of marriage. She hated everything I stood for. I made a mistake loving her."

"I'm not sure loving someone is ever a mistake. Love's not the problem," Holly mused.

"No, judgment is," Luc said. "My heart blinded me, which is bad enough. But my poor judgment is what scares me."

The sting of his admission reached deep inside Holly. Luc was one of the best men she knew. She didn't want him to hurt like this.

"I'm sorry," she whispered, knowing it wasn't enough.

"Now I know how you must have felt when Ron walked away, Holly. It's like being a kid again and having my world torn apart." His hands fisted at his sides and pressed against his worn denim jeans. "I will never go through that again."

"You can find someone else. There's nothing saying your marriage has to end like your friends' marriages did." Holly wished she knew how to help him.

"There's no guarantee it wouldn't. Sarah fit all my requirements for an ideal wife. That's why I started dating her. But I saw the outward beauty and missed what was inside. If we'd married and then split, it could have cost me the ranch…" His voice trailed away.

Love had cost Holly a great deal. She had no advice to erase the wistful sadness on Luc's face.

"I've accepted that I'm never getting married so it's a moot point now. But I refuse to give up all my dreams," he said sternly. "I am going to have a son. That son will be Henry."

"Luc, I—" Holly stopped when his fingertips covered her lips.

"Don't say it, okay?" he begged, his voice soft, intense. "I need this dream so badly."

Holly frowned, wanting to understand.

"You don't know what it's like to suddenly lose your home, your family, everything. You're a little kid that no one cares about." Luc's intensity grabbed her heart. "I made do, I pretended, I fit in as best I could and concentrated on getting through."

Holly could see him in her mind's eye, a little boy, like Henry, pretending all was well, not making a fuss in case the family he was with asked to have him removed. And then at night, after the lights went out and he was alone in his bed, she could see him tear up, yearning for someone to say *I love you, Luc. I'm here for you. I'll always be here for you.*

That was the legacy her father had given Holly after her mother had left without saying goodbye. Pain stabbed her heart that Luc had lost that security. How could he not want to adopt Henry as his son and begin building his family?

"Dreaming of having a child was the one thing that kept me going through five very rough years in the oil fields." His face tightened. "I did some things, accepted some dangerous jobs on the rigs so that I could earn enough money to buy my ranch. I want to make a legacy, to reinstate the

Cramer name as something to be proud of. I want to pass something on to Henry. He is the son I've longed for. I can't let go of this dream, Holly."

As his hand slid away from her face, Holly blinked at the loss rushing through her. She was heart-sore for this kind, generous man who only wanted simple things—a family, a home. Things other people took for granted.

"Then if that's your dream we'd better make sure there's no reason to deny appointing you as Henry's guardian, hadn't we?" she said finally. Her heart thudded at the joy exploding across his face.

"Thank you, Holly." Luc's smile made Holly's breath catch.

Why did she suddenly have such a strong reaction to him? Because she'd seen past the carefree persona he presented, to the man inside.

Luc was her best friend. Neither of them was willing to trust enough to love again. What they had in common only heightened their friendship. It was good to know nothing between them had changed.

And yet somehow it had. Holly now understood what drove Luc, comprehended his intense desire to make his ranch into a home, to adopt Henry. Luc would never walk away from that relationship. Somehow Holly knew he was trustworthy as surely as she knew her own name. Luc was a man of honor. In her life Holly had only ever known one man whom she'd found truly honorable and that was her dad. But Luc came in a close second.

Suddenly, unbelievably, Holly rejoiced that Luc had not married Sarah. She didn't deserve him.

You can't get close to this man, her brain warned. *Not unless you're willing to share your secret with him.*

That inner voice unsettled her. "I guess we'd better go see what's bugging you up north," she said, needing to do something to escape her thoughts.

"Okay, but I'm warning you," Luc said as he rose and held out a hand to her. "Next time we come back here, I'm getting in that water." He nodded to the creek. "And I'm bringing Henry one day, too. Next to raspberry pie, swimming is my favorite thing."

He drew her upward too fast. Unprepared, Holly bumped her head on his chin. Good thing. She needed to snap back to reality because for a moment she'd seen herself in the picture, splashing Luc and Henry in the creek, as if she belonged there.

"I don't think I've ever known anyone who cooks like you." Luc held up one macaroni, bloated and tinged pink. "Who taught you to cook the tomatoes *with* the pasta?"

"Dad." She smiled at him, her sun-tinted face uplifted. "Don't criticize until you taste."

"Right." Luc popped the pasta into his mouth then held up his hands. "I stand in awe of you, Holly. You manage to make everything taste great."

"For your information I draw the line at cooking liver. I don't care how good they say it is for you." She giggled at his gagging motions. "I see we agree on that."

Luc nodded. "We agree on a lot of things."

"Like what?" she asked.

"We both like to eat." He snatched a radish from the salad.

Holly swatted his hand away but truthfully he thought she'd enjoyed the camaraderie they shared today. Luc wasn't sure he should have dumped his sad story all over her, but he needed her help with Henry and to get that, he'd felt compelled to explain his reasons for wanting to circumvent marriage. Maybe he'd let her see a little too far into his heart but he knew he could trust her. Holly was like a soul mate.

"So what will we do about those missing cattle and the ruined fences you showed me?" she asked after she'd said grace.

"I'll go up into the hills tomorrow and find those cows if it takes all day. But I need to figure out something to take the place of those fences where that steer was injured." He took a large helping of the macaroni and two pork chops, his stomach rumbling as he inhaled the delicious aromas.

"I guess it's been ages since Dad installed that fence."

Holly showed surprise when he told her the date he'd found in her dad's ranch notebooks. "That long?"

"Yes. They've been repaired once too often. We need something else. There are coyotes in those hills and our cattle are too valuable to serve as their food." He paused. "Unfortunately, building a more solid fence means I'll have to cut down some of those gigantic spruce you planted with your dad."

Holly rose to get the teapot. When she returned to the table a tear glittered on the end of her lashes. Luc knew she was remembering happy times she'd shared with Marcus, and missing him. How he hated causing her pain.

"Don't worry, I'll fix it, Holly."

"You always do, Luc. Thank you." Her gaze locked with his and in that instant he wondered if he should have embraced her. That's what Marcus would have done, and Luc had promised him he'd make sure Holly was taken care of. "You're a good friend."

Friend. His heart sank a little. Was that all he was? Some kind of long-distance acquaintance who never made it into the family circle?

Luc chided himself. Holly and Marcus Janzen had always made him feel a valued part of their lives. From the moment he'd stepped onto their Cool Springs Ranch, Luc had felt at home. What more did he want?

More.

"What's that funny face about? Does my cooking taste that bad?" Holly asked in a worried tone.

"It's delicious," he reassured her. "I thought your dad was a good gardener but you're even better. Lettuce, onions, radishes—that's good for early June."

"I'm not just the town superstar you know," Holly teased with a self-mocking grin.

"Apparently not. What else have you got planted?" As far as Luc was concerned, Holly was as pretty as cotton candy, inside and out. He figured any man should be more than happy to forgive her for anything. Her fiancé obviously hadn't seen it that way. Again Luc wondered what had gone wrong between them.

Holly talked about gardening for a while. As she did, Luc studied her. She'd changed from her jeans and shirt into a pretty blue sundress that brought out her eyes. Her orange-tipped toes were bare again in a pair of comfortable-looking sandals. Her hair wobbled in a topknot that he expected to tumble down over her shoulders any second. She looked like the perfect rancher's wife. For somebody.

Though Luc could envision Holly as a wife, he couldn't settle on which of the available local guys would be the best candidate for her husband. Any of them would be lucky.

"You deliver a lot of babies," he blurted. "Have you ever thought about having your own?"

Holly's hand paused halfway to her lips. Her head went back and she gaped at him as if he'd asked where she'd buried her secret treasure.

"I didn't mean to offend you," he apologized. Why hadn't he kept his mouth shut? "I just thought that you'd naturally dream about your own kids and—"

"I'll never marry, Luc. I told you that." Her voice sounded hoarse as she set her fork back on her plate.

"You don't have to marry to have—"

"I'll never have children," Holly cut him off for the second time, exhaled and forced a smile. "I'm one of those women who don't have the motherhood gene."

"Not true." Luc speared a noodle and held it up for examination. Something was wrong. "I've seen you with your Sunday school class. Pretty sure you're what they call a born mother."

Holly said nothing. A moment later she jumped up from the table and began making tea.

"I'm sorry. I guess your mom probably turned

you off motherhood, huh?" he guessed, coming up with a reason for her jumpy behavior.

"My mother?" She turned to frown at him. "She never stuck around long enough to make much of an impact on me. It was Dad who was most hurt by her leaving."

"Really?" Unsure whether or not to continue, Luc pressed on, curious about her response. She was hiding something or else he didn't know this woman at all. "You were what—seven?"

"Almost eight. So what?" Holly returned to the table, completely forgetting the tea. She leaned her elbows on the table and crossed her arms as if to put a barrier between them. "She wasn't around here much even when she was supposed to be. Dad was the one who met me when I got off the school bus. As I said she didn't have an impact on me."

"Holly, it's okay to admit it." Why was she so adamant? "I imagine all kids would miss their mother if she suddenly wasn't there."

"Well, I didn't miss her. Her absence never mattered because I had Dad. I always knew I could count on him." Her shrug signaled the end of that topic. "I drew a rough sketch of what I want in my sewing room. I'll show you after dessert."

"Dessert? Why didn't you tell me? I wouldn't have eaten so much." Luc let it go for now, but was determined to find out what kept Holly from admitting she missed her mother.

"I think it's very doable," Luc said after examining the bedroom she wanted renovated. "The costliest stuff will be the cabinets and countertops you put in."

He'd barely stopped speaking when Holly's cell phone rang.

"Hey, Abby. It's late for you to still be at work." Holly waited for her friend to explain. "He what?" She glanced at Luc and frowned. "Yes, I'll go look right now and I'll get Luc to help, too. I'll call if we find anything."

"Look for what?" Luc asked when she'd hung up, following her into the kitchen.

"For whom and it's Henry," she said as she kicked off her sandals and pulled on her boots. "He left Hilda a note."

"A note? Can Henry write?"

"It's kind of a picture note. Did you invite him to come to your place?" Her heart sank at his nod. "Well, apparently he decided to do that this afternoon, against Hilda's specific instructions. Some kids on their bikes saw him heading out of town earlier. He never came home for dinner. Hilda's frantic." She grabbed her jacket. "I'll saddle up Melody and ride her cross-country."

"Why cross-country?" Luc asked in confusion.

"Because the kids I mentioned told Henry the shortest way to your place was through Parker's Meadow." Holly watched Luc's face blanch. "What?"

"I put Ornery Joe in there yesterday," he said very softly. "That bull is mean. If Henry goes near him…" His words died away. They both knew the little boy didn't have a chance if the bull decided to charge.

"Let's go," Holly said.

"It wasn't an outright invitation to Henry," Luc said as he followed her outside. "It was just an offhand invitation like, 'You'll have to come see me.'"

"He's a little kid, Luc. He takes everything literally." He looked so upset Holly touched his shoulder. "Pray. Hard."

"I need to do more than that." Luc's face was tight with strain. He slapped his Stetson on his head. "How can I help?"

"Take my vehicle and go by road. Your truck can't handle the deep ruts as well as mine can," she explained, forestalling any argument. It was funny how they seemed able to anticipate each other. "Maybe Henry stuck to the road and didn't go for the shortcut. I hope. And, Luc?"

He'd been walking toward her jeep but now he stopped and turned, a question on his face.

"If you find him, you call 911 immediately so

they can call off the search teams. Not me, not Abby but 911. Okay?"

Luc nodded, a perplexed look on his face. "Of course."

"Good. Pray hard, Luc." Holly didn't take the time to explain. Instead, she raced across the yard to the barn where she saddled Melody and galloped across the fields, scouring wooded nooks and crannies for a little boy in a red-hooded sweatshirt who just wanted a family.

"Henry is Luc's dream," Holly prayed as she rode. "Luc's a good man. He's trying hard to be Your child." The reminder of Abby's words this afternoon sent a frisson of fear up her spine.

The case worker from Calgary is suggesting that Luc coaxed Henry out to his ranch after Hilda insisted they both wait for the visit till the weekend.

"Luc wouldn't do that. He's a wonderful man. He'd make a great father for any child," she whispered. "Please keep Henry safe and work this out so Luc won't be blamed. He was only trying to help Henry."

Holly spurred Melody to go faster. She had to find Henry; she had to make sure Luc didn't suffer for his eagerness to have the little boy in his life. As the wind dragged through her hair, Holly took shortcuts she hadn't used since she was a girl. Luc's words, filled with pathos, rolled through her mind.

Sarah said she wanted a husband to be proud of.

Silly woman. As if Luc wasn't that man! Fury spurred Holly on but she couldn't escape the echoed intensity of his words.

Henry is the son I've longed for. I can't let go of this dream, Holly. I just can't.

In that moment Holly decided she'd do whatever it took to help Luc realize his dream. She would never have another child, but Luc *was* going to adopt Henry if she had anything to do with it.

Chapter Three

He'd left his phone at Holly's!

Heart in his throat, Luc climbed the fence and moved forward while speaking constantly to Ornery Joe. From the corner of his eye he saw Holly arrive, slide off her horse and creep from tree to bush, edging ever nearer Henry who sat crying atop a big stone, the bull directly in front of him.

"Come on, you miserable grouch. Move over here. Leave the boy alone." Ornery Joe cast him a disparaging look, dug in one hoof and snorted before his gaze returned to rivet on Henry. For the first time since he'd become a Christian, Luc clung desperately to his faith. "God, we need Your help here."

Every so often the wind tossed Holly's words to him.

"You stay there, Henry. Don't get down. Don't even move," she said in a calm, even voice. "Luc and I will get you out of here but you have to stay still."

"I don't want to stay here," the boy sniffed. "I don't like that old cow."

"That's not a cow." Luc could hear amusement thread Holly's tone. "That's a bull. It's a boy cow."

"I still don't like him." At least Henry's voice had lost some of its sheer terror.

"He doesn't like you much, either," Holly told him. "Or me," she added when Ornery Joe lurched to his feet and lumbered around Henry's stone to take after her. Fleet-footed Holly scooted across some open ground and climbed a tree. "He sure doesn't like me at all. Get out of here, you grumpy old man," she yelled to the bull.

Luc had found nothing in Holly's jeep with which to entice the bull, except for a half-eaten package of chips. He rattled the foil bag now to draw Ornery Joe's attention.

"Here, boy," he called. "Here's a treat for you." He scattered the chips on the ground then looked toward Holly. "When he comes toward me, take Henry and run."

"What about you?" she called, her gaze intent on Ornery Joe who was watching them, swinging his big head from side to side.

"I'll be fine. You take care of Henry." Luc crackled the bag again then held it up, hoping the breeze would carry the smell of the chips to the animal. Sure enough, Ornery Joe lifted his head, sniffed then began to walk toward him. "Go," he said to Holly, hoping she'd hear him since he kept his voice low to avoid distracting the bull. "Go now."

In a flash she'd jumped down from her perch, picked up Henry and raced across the pasture to the gate.

Seconds later, certain she and Henry were safe on the other side, Luc backed up as Joe advanced. When the animal lost interest in the chips and glared at him, he turned and bolted, vaulting to freedom before Ornery Joe could get up enough speed to charge.

"You okay?" Holly called.

He nodded. "Just another pair of torn pants," he told her. "I caught them on a nail when I went over the fence."

"I'll mend them." Holly dialed 911 and said she was bringing Henry to town. Then she made another call. "We found him, Abby. He's fine. We'll meet you at Hilda's." Seconds later she slid her phone in her pocket before hunkering down to stare at Henry. "I'm mad at you," she said sternly.

Henry's eyes widened.

"Since when do you disobey the lady who's taking care of you? Poor Hilda's worried sick," she scolded. "That's rude and also wrong when she specifically told you she'd bring you to visit Luc on the weekend."

"I didn't want to wait," he said with a pouty look.

Interested to see how Holly handled this, Luc remained still and listened.

"Do you think Luc wanted to wait to have you for a visit? He didn't but he knows you can't always have what you want when you want it." Holly studied Henry, her severe look not dissipating. "Sometimes you have to be patient, Henry. Otherwise you end up in a heap of trouble, like you just did. That bull is very dangerous. You could have been hurt and all because you couldn't wait."

"I'm sorry." Henry's lower lip trembled and he ducked his head.

"I hope so. Luc risked his life to get you out, do you know that? If Ornery Joe had been really angry, he could easily have charged Luc or me." Holly paused a moment to let her words sink in. "Ms. Hilda knows about Ornery Joe. I'm sure that's why she wanted you to wait until she could take you to Luc's."

"I didn't know that." Henry sounded the tiniest bit belligerent. That didn't faze Holly.

"Of course you didn't and you didn't ask, either, did you?" When Henry shook his head, Holly made a clicking noise. "That's the thing, Henry. We all know you want a family and we're

trying to help you, but you have to trust us."
Holly brushed the hank of hair off his forehead.
"We can't always tell you every single thing
that's happening. You need to believe we're
doing our best for you and be patient. Okay?"

He nodded slowly. "Are you still mad at me,
Holly?"

"A little. You scared the daylights out of me."
She pulled him into her arms and hugged him
tightly. "Don't do it again, okay?"

"Okay." Henry hugged her back, his face
wreathed in smiles.

"I think you owe somebody a big thank-you,"
she whispered just loud enough for Luc to hear.
Her blue eyes glistened as Henry walked to Luc.

"I'm sorry I got in trouble," he said. "Thank
you for helping me." He thrust out his hand.

Luc did the same. He looked at Holly, struggling to suppress his grin.

"You're welcome," he said as he shook Henry's
hand. Then he scooped the boy into his arms, rel-
ishing the feel of holding this wonderful child.
"But what are we going to do about my torn
pants?" He set Henry down and showed him the
tear in the back of his jeans. "These were my best
ones, too," he mourned.

"Holly can fix them," Henry said with a grin.
"Holly's good at everything."

"Not him, too," Holly muttered. Luc smiled.

"You should ask her to sew your pants," Henry advised.

"I'll do that." Luc shot a sideways glance at Holly who was looking anywhere but at him. "Something wrong?"

"Melody. She must have gone home. Guess I'll have to hitch a ride. But first we're taking Henry to Ms. Hilda's as promised. Let's go."

Luc waited, wondering if Holly would prefer to drive her own vehicle, but she waved him to the driver's side.

"I'm still shaking so much I'd probably crash us. He doesn't seem any worse for wear, though." She nodded toward Henry, who'd climbed into the back of the vehicle.

"You looked unflappable." He held her door. As Holly passed him, he murmured, "You were wrong, you know."

"About what specifically?" Holly gazed at him, her expression curious.

"That you don't have the motherhood gene." He saw a look of fear flicker through her gaze before her chin lifted. "I think you're a born mother."

"You're wrong, Luc." She stepped past him and into the vehicle. "I'm not the kind of mother any child needs."

Luc climbed in on the driver's side and drove to town. But all the way there he wondered why Holly was so sure she wasn't the mother type.

The way she'd reprimanded Henry, firmly but gently, ending it with a hug, easing his fear but imparting the lesson of patience, was pure mothering. Surely she could see that.

Was there something in Holly's past that made feel she wasn't motherly?

Luc really wanted to find out.

"Thank you for finding Henry," Abby said as Hilda ushered the little boy away for a late supper. "I'm sure my call took you away from something important."

"Nothing's more important than keeping Henry safe," Luc said.

Holly felt his scrutiny, his earlier words replaying in her mind. Why hadn't she just let his comment about motherhood go? She'd only made him more curious. She also knew Luc well enough to know that he wouldn't stop until he'd figured out what was behind her comment. Stupid to have said so much.

But she was so tired of pretending. People in Buffalo Gap thought she had it all, that she never blew it or regretted anything. They only saw the perfect girl she'd tried to be so as not to disappoint her father, as her mother had.

But they didn't see the real her. Nor did Luc. Holly knew she was far from the perfect mother candidate. Perfect mothers didn't give away their newborn babies to save themselves shame or embarrassment. They certainly didn't forget about them once they'd given away their children.

But then Holly realized that despite her best attempts, neither had she forgotten. With every birth she assisted, every delivery, every prenatal class she taught she wondered, *Did my baby look like this? Is my baby happy? Where is my baby?*

There wasn't and never could be an answer to those questions. That's the way she'd wanted it. No shame or recriminations that her father would have to live with. At least that's what she'd told herself when she'd given up her son for adoption.

"Holly?" Luc was looking at her oddly. So was Abby.

"Sorry. Just thinking about Melody. She's still loose. I need to get home." And away from Luc's piercing stare.

"I'm sure you do. I just wondered if Henry had said anything to you about going to visit Luc." The speaker was a woman named Shelly whom Abby had introduced as Henry's case worker from Calgary.

"He didn't, but we did talk about what kind of things happen on a ranch," she said. "Henry asked how things worked and since I've lived on the ranch my entire life, I explained as best I could."

"Was your friend Luc there at the time?" Shelly asked, her gaze narrowed.

"No. I'd taken Henry out for a soda one afternoon, with Hilda's permission," she added. "He never said anything about visiting Luc then but kids get lots of spur-of-the-moment ideas and often act on them. Luc didn't tell Henry to come on his own if that's what you're insinuating," she insisted, disgruntled by the case worker's suggestive attitude.

"You're defending him." A smug smile tilted Shelly's lips.

"I don't have to," Holly said, disliking her more with every word. "He hasn't done anything wrong." She turned to Abby. "I really do have to leave. I can't afford to lose my horse."

"Yes, you and Luc go ahead. And thank you for your help. I don't know how we'd have managed without you." Abby hugged her and Luc.

"You do realize the police were called out," Shelly said to Luc.

"But that's what you do when a child is missing, isn't it?" he asked, a confused look on his face. Holly wanted to hug him.

"Come on, Luc. I need a ride back to find Melody." Holly tugged on his arm, relieved when he finally followed her from the house. She got in the driver's seat without thinking, started the engine and turned onto the highway toward home.

"Can you slow down a bit?" Luc asked in a mild voice.

"That woman! She was intimating that it was your fault Henry took off."

"I know." He smiled. "It was nice of you to defend me, but I didn't coax him to come."

"Well, *I* know that but Shelly doesn't. She seemed a little too ready to put a black mark against you." Holly sniffed. "I've seen workers like her before. So suspicious."

"I suppose she has to be when she's protecting a child who has no one else to do it for him." Luc sounded unruffled. "It's important to know that the people to whom you give the care of a kid like Henry won't abuse that trust."

"I suppose." Holly leaned back in her seat and took a deep breath. Thinking about the past always unsettled her. But she could hardly tell Luc that.

"Can I ask you something, Holly?"

"I guess." She twisted to look at him. The last vestiges of daylight were almost gone, leaving only the vehicle's dashboard lights to highlight his reflection.

"Before your fiancé," he said hesitantly. "Was there someone special in your life?"

What could it hurt to tell him? It had happened long ago. It was in the past.

"I can't imagine what prompted that question," she said, giving him an arch look.

"Humor me." Luc kept watching her.

"When I was going through my medical training I met a resident. Troy." Holly exhaled. "I thought I was in love with him but I was wrong."

"How did you come to think you were wrong?" Luc said quietly. "Did he decide that or did you?"

"He did, okay?" Talking of that time, remembering the decisions she'd made and questioned ever since hurt. She wanted Luc to let it go. "He told me he had plans for his life and they didn't include me. Then he walked away. I never saw him again."

Holly didn't tell Luc that Troy's plans also hadn't included the baby she was carrying. That was her secret and she intended to keep it that way. Luc was her best friend but as she'd learned to her cost, keeping your friends meant you didn't share absolutely everything.

Especially to a man like Luc who was desperate to have a child.

"It's good to get rid of that ugly wall board," Holly said right after she'd tossed a sheet of the offending stuff into the back of Luc's truck.

"Wood paneling isn't your favorite?" He was glad to see the smile on her face. For the past three days, ever since the Henry incident, Holly had been introverted, obviously stewing about something yet she refused to share the burden with him.

"It's dark and depressing. I don't know why Dad ever chose it. Or maybe my mother did. That would explain a lot about what went wrong in their relationship." She made a face at him then walked back inside her house. "Want some lemonade? I made it fresh this morning."

Luc nodded. He'd enjoyed these past few days they'd spent working on her renovation. Holly was fun to be with, full of great ideas and eager to implement them. She also didn't fuss about things like broken fingernails and dust as Sarah had on the four occasions she'd visited his ranch.

Luc sat next to Holly on the deck outside, savoring his drink and the warm spring afternoon. "Can I ask you something?"

Immediately, her eyes darkened and her face got what he termed her worried look. "I guess."

"Why is there an umbrella in your garden?" He watched her shoulders sag in relief.

"To shelter my pumpkin plant, of course." Holly's grin teased him as did her wink.

"Okay. That certainly explains it." Luc knew she was waiting for him to ask. "Why does your pumpkin need sheltering?"

"I just transplanted it. I'm trying to make sure it doesn't dry out before it gets established or get broken in a strong wind so I shelter it for part of each day until it's hardy." Holly sounded like a worried mom.

"Must be an important pumpkin." Luc watched the sparkle return to her eyes.

"It is. It's a gigantic variety. I'm hoping to

enter it in the fair in August and win." When Holly was excited like this, Luc couldn't take his eyes off her. "First prize is five hundred dollars. I'm also entering a baby quilt. First prize for that is another five hundred. That would go a long way toward a new sewing machine."

"Great minds think alike. I'm hoping to win a prize with the old truck I'm restoring." Luc grinned. "And if I could win another five hundred for being best historic entry in the parade this summer, I'd be able to fix up the '55 Chevy I've got stored in my barn."

"So we're both out to win." Holly chinked her glass against his. "Good luck to us."

"What is it about sewing that gets to you?" Luc asked curiously.

"What is it about fixing old cars that gets to you?" She shrugged. "I pick up a piece of fabric and I see how it could be used. I have to make it. Now you know how weird I am."

"Not weird at all," Luc told her. "That's how I am with old vehicles. I think I got that from my dad. I don't remember him much but I remember he loved old cars. I think he lived every moment of his life, like you." He smiled at her blush. Holly always tried to deflect praise. "Is it tonight Henry's coming for your wiener roast?"

"Uh-huh. And Abby and her family and Hilda and whoever else shows up. I kind of left the invitation for a spring picnic open." She chuckled at his raised eyebrows. "Well, it's really hard to know where to stop. This is the kind of place where everyone drops in. At least they did when Dad was alive. I don't want that to end."

"I wonder if Henry's ever had a wiener roast," Luc mused aloud.

"You haven't talked to him since the Ornery Joe incident?"

Luc shook his head. "No."

"Why?" Holly asked with a frown. "Have you changed your mind about adopting him?"

"No way. I want to adopt Henry very much." Luc couldn't come up with the right way to say it so he blurted it out. "I felt like you thought I should stay away from him."

"What? No." Holly's eyes narrowed. "If you'd asked I'd have suggested you keep seeing Henry as much as you can. You need to build your relationship so that the two of you will grow comfortable with each other."

"But—" Luc shook his head. "That's not the impression you gave that night we found him with Ornery Joe."

"I was worried, Luc. I thought that Shelly was looking for a reason to give you a black mark and I think I was right. Abby confirmed privately that Shelly suggested to her that you coaxed Henry to visit you, thereby superseding the authority figure she'd chosen—Hilda. But I don't think you need to worry about Shelly anymore."

"Why not?" He loved the way her face glowed when she was excited or trying to keep a secret. "What happened?"

"Abby told me today that Henry's case has been transferred from the Calgary social worker to Family Ties. Abby's the case worker now thanks to Mayor Marsha's daughter in Calgary who is credited with getting the case moved here."

"And that means?" he asked, one eyebrow raised.

"That you don't have to worry about Abby because she'll give you a fair shake."

"This town," he said in pretended disgust. "You have to be in on the rumor mill to find out anything." In truth he loved that aspect of small-town life. Well, most of the time.

"Yep. Sometimes being the town mascot is good," she joked.

"The good citizens of Buffalo Gap do not think of Holly Janzen as a mascot," Luc scoffed. "More like a goal every child should strive to attain."

"I hope nobody tries to be like me," she said, her voice harsh. She fell silent for a while, her thoughts on something he couldn't share. But after a few moments, she snapped out of her bad mood to smile at him. "Now you need to solidify your case. Abby won't go against you, but she will take into account the efforts you make to get to know Henry. She'll probably be the one to do your home study, though I don't think that will happen for a while."

"That's a relief. I'm not finished with the spare room yet."

"Redecorating is a good idea." She sipped her lemonade. "It'd be different if you were adopting a newborn, but with an older child, I think placement officers will like the idea that you're making a special place for him, that you're preparing your world for him to be part of it."

"I don't know where you get all this knowledge," he said, studying her. "The internet?"

"Um, yes." Holly seemed startled by his question. "And Abby." She paused for a moment. "You should ask her lots of questions. She loves to explain."

"I don't think I can ask Abby how I'm supposed to mesh with Henry." Luc had thought adoption would be straightforward, but he kept coming up against more and more uncertainties. He hadn't realized he'd have to prove himself capable of fatherhood in so many ways. "She'd expect me to know."

"So?" Holly's blue eyes widened. "What's the problem?"

"The problem is that I don't have a clue how to mesh with Henry," he said, feeling inept.

"Sure you do." She rose. "You talked about taking him swimming when it got warmer.

Maybe he'd like to fish. Or learn how to ride. What did you like to do as a kid?"

"Marbles." He followed her into the house, almost bumping into her when she suddenly stopped and turned to look at him.

"Marbles?" One eyebrow arched and she gave him a look that said "stop teasing me."

"I played marbles all the time," Luc told her. "And usually won, though I don't have a trophy for every time I excelled, like some people." He grinned when she groaned.

"Stop it, will you?" Holly said, her voice cool. "I don't have that many trophies."

"Are you kidding me?" Luc snorted. "Lady, I just moved boxes of them from your spare room. Horsemanship, curling, baseball, friendship leader, junior citizen of the year, debate team, valedictorian, highest science test scores—to name a few." He stopped ticking them off his fingers and faked a sigh of exhaustion. "Is there anything you didn't win a trophy for?"

"Dealing with men who promised to renovate my spare room then ended up talking too much," she shot back pertly.

"Low blow." Luc clutched his chest and pretended to swoon.

"Can we get back to Henry? Maybe he'd like to learn to play marbles." Holly stored her drinking glass in the dishwasher with his and checked the clock. "I think we could get the rest of the paneling out before I have to start putting together dinner for my guests."

"How hard can it be to put together a few hot dogs?" Luc knew the minute he said it that it was the wrong thing to say. She glared at him then plunged her hammer right into the middle of a sheet of the despised paneling. "Um, I could help you with—whatever," he offered.

"I'd appreciate it, but let's finish this first. Then we'll see how much time we have left." Holly's no-nonsense tone told him she wasn't ready to forgive his comment.

Luc liked the way they worked together, each anticipating the other's moves. In no time the room was stripped, except for her father's big trunk in the corner. He looked from her to the trunk and back again, eyebrows raised in an unasked question.

"You have an obsession about that trunk." She scowled at him. "I'll sort it out."

"Just not today, right?" He shrugged. "Fair enough. How many more days off do you have?" he asked as they hauled out the last of the trash and threw it in his truck bed. He'd get rid of it later.

"Only two and that's if the hospital doesn't call me in." Holly sighed. "And then there's Family Ties. Abby phoned to tell me a new girl arrived yesterday. Seth Treple was called in to examine her and he feels she's close to her due date so I'm on call."

Seth was the local GP who'd agreed to handle Family Ties' patients, both mothers and children when Holly couldn't.

"Seth can't deliver the baby?" Concern tugged at Luc as he noted the weary lines around Holly's eyes. It didn't seem as if she was getting the rest she needed. "You've been covering for him a lot. I know that as a nurse practitioner you're more than qualified to do most things he does, but you've been logging a lot of hours lately. You deserve your days off."

"Babies don't fit a schedule. Besides, Seth needs a couple of days off to visit his sick mother in Calgary." She shrugged. "It's fine."

It wasn't fine that she was almost dead on her feet. Maybe this demolition was too much for her, on top of everything else in her life, But he noticed Holly admiring the empty area.

"Soon all this will be sewing workspace." She sounded enthusiastic.

"Hopefully." Luc checked his watch. "I'm guessing we have about an hour until your guests will arrive. What do you need to do to get ready?" There was no point in telling her to relax for a minute. Holly did what needed to be done. Tiredness wouldn't stop her but maybe he could ease her load.

"To get a few hot dogs ready?" She shot him

a look. Apparently not prepared to let him live down his earlier comment. "I've got to haul the tables from the shed and set them around the lawn. Spread out some chairs. Build a fire. Assemble the snacks. Change clothes and set out the food and—"

"Okay, stop. I'll do the outside stuff. You change and get the food ready." He loved the way her smile spread across her lips right up to her lovely blue eyes.

"Really? You're sure you're not too tired?" She threw her arms around him and hugged him. "You're an answer to my prayers, Luc." One more hug and then she raced into the house.

Luc stood where he was, taken aback by her hugs, but even more astonished by how much he'd enjoyed them.

"Something wrong?" Holly called, her head stuck out the door.

"No. Just planning." He walked toward the shed, touching his cheek with his forefinger where her lips had rested if only for a nanosecond. In all the time he'd known Holly, she'd never hugged him.

He'd only managed to set up one table when Abby and Cade Lebret arrived with their twins and Ivor, a foster boy they'd adopted. Cade and Ivor helped Luc lug out tables and chairs while Abby took the twins to the house. Ivor begged to start the fire so Cade hunkered down and showed him how to start one with shavings then tinder then sticks and logs. Luc stood watching, thinking that soon he'd be able to do the same thing with Henry.

As others began to arrive in the yard, Holly emerged from the house. Luc caught his breath. Her skin glowed against the aquamarine top she wore with slim black jeans. Her dark curls tumbled loosely over her shoulders. His heart raced like a steam engine when she smiled at him and thanked him for setting up.

"You've done a great job," she praised him. "All that's left is to bring out the food. Would you mind helping with that, too, or would you rather visit?"

And miss another of her embraces?

"Lead on," was all Luc could say as he followed her inside the house.

"There's a ton of stuff." She pointed to a lime-green bin Luc figured weighed nearly fifty pounds. "Table coverings, cutlery, candles, et cetera in that one."

"Okay." He watched her pick up another bin. "Is that as heavy as this one? Somebody else could carry it."

"Hey, I'm no weakling." Her blazing smile did funny things to his pulse. "Don't worry. This one has paper plates and plastic glasses. It's light but thanks for your concern." She hurried out the door in front of him.

Luc followed, wondering why lately his knees went so rubbery whenever he was close to her. Once he'd set the box down, Holly took over, spreading plastic cloths and directing him as they loaded the table with everything they'd need. A few minutes later he noticed Hilda's car trailing dust as it headed toward Cool Springs Ranch.

"Okay, let's get the food." Holly hooked her arm through his and drew him toward the house. "Isn't it a perfect evening?" she enthused.

When they returned with food trays, Luc noted that Cade and some of the other men had cut roasting sticks for the wieners. The fire blazed. A moment later he heard Henry yell.

"Hi, Holly. Hi, Luc." Henry shoved his glasses up on his nose right before Holly threw open her arms and the boy rushed into them.

Holly giggled and laughed as she spun him around in a circle of joy. Then she set him down and said so quietly Luc almost missed it, "Luc's been waiting for you to arrive, Henry."

Henry seemed suddenly shy. He stood where he was, staring at Luc who grinned at him and stepped forward.

"Hey, Henry." The boy held out a hand to shake but Luc needed more than that. As he scooped Henry into his arms, he glanced up and found Holly watching, a wistful look on her face. It seemed as if she should be in the circle with them but suddenly she moved away.

Her voice emerged a little tight as she called everyone to join hands before Mayor Marsha said grace. Somehow Luc ended up with Henry on one side and Holly on the other, her hand clasped in his.

As if it belonged there.

But Luc was pretty sure that wasn't God's plan for his life.

Chapter Four

On a balmy June evening, Holly pulled up to her home on Cool Springs Ranch with a sigh of relief.

"Thanks for the safe trip, Lord," she said after she'd switched off her car. "Sometimes I forget You're with me all the time, even when I get stuck in past memories."

Determined that tonight she would not get dragged down to that place of guilt and regret from the past, she climbed out of her jeep then began unpacking the results of her shopping day.

"Can I help?"

Holly squealed in surprise and whirled around, bags flying.

"You scared me half to death, Luc," she told him with a groan. "What are you doing here so late?" She wrapped her arms around the parcels he handed her and smiled her thanks when he unloaded the rest from her vehicle.

"I had a few spare hours and I thought I'd get started on drywalling your room. You did say to come and work even if you weren't here," he reminded.

"I said it and I meant it." She started toward the house. "It's just that you mentioned branding the new calves today and I thought you'd be busy with that."

"Finished before noon." He grabbed the screen door and held it open for her.

"Thanks." Unable to corral her packages any longer, Holly let them drop on the dining room table. "You can put those here, too," she told Luc.

"I'm not sure they'll all fit. What did you do, buy out the store?" he joked then did a double take at the look on her face. In a hesitant tone, he said, "Holly?"

"I received a phone call last night from my favorite fabric store in Calgary. They were holding a one-day sale today. Fifty per cent off everything." Her shoulders sagged as she sat down, slid off her shoes and flexed her toes. "So I went. And I bought. A lot."

"Is that all? I thought maybe something bad had happened."

"That *is* bad, Luc," she moaned. "I overspent. A lot."

"But you needed this fabric for whatever you're sewing, right?" He waited for her nod. "So you weren't wasteful or spending for spending's sake, right?" He waited for her nod. "So why should it bother you that you got a good deal?"

"I hope this doesn't come out the wrong way," she said finally, "but your Sarah was an idiot to let you go. I've never heard another man approve a woman's overspending on shopping."

"I am truly a man among men," he said with a grin.

"Now I've fed your huge ego." Holly shook her head then leaned down to rub her foot. "All that shopping has given me an awful cramp in my foot."

"Neither you nor Sarah has any idea of just how wonderful I am." He preened. "I happen to know all about foot-itis."

Luc sounded as if he'd begun to shed some of his hurt over Sarah and she was glad. But when he snagged a chair leg with one foot then drew it near so he could sit in front of her, Holly stared. Then he lifted her foot onto his knee.

"Uh, what are you doing, Luc?" She wiggled her foot, trying to free it.

"Hold still and you'll find out," he ordered. When she'd settled he explained. "One of my foster moms used to get terrible leg cramps after a day of work. The first thing she taught me after I moved in was how to help her. Relax, Holly."

Holly wasn't sure she *could* relax with Luc's strong fingers pressing and kneading her sensitive foot. Every time he touched her it was like a spark shot through her. But after a few moments she had no doubt he knew what he was doing. She closed her eyes and let him work the kinks out of her toes. She'd almost drifted off when he gently set her feet on the floor.

"Better?" he asked quietly.

"Much," Holly breathed. She blinked her eyes open and smiled at him. "Give me your foster mother's name. I want to send her flowers. Maybe Sarah, too. Her loss is my gain."

Luc chuckled, his dark eyes bright with laughter. "I'd better put away my tools and get out of your hair. Then you can admire your purchases."

"Do you ever just go out and splurge, Luc?" Holly asked, unable to contain her curiosity.

"I splurged when I bought my ranch," he said thoughtfully. "I'll be paying for that for a while. I need to set aside money to raise Henry, too, so I can't afford too many splurges." He walked toward the spare room. "But if I did, the last thing I'd buy would be frilly fabric."

"Ha-ha. Did you eat supper?" Holly could tell from the look on his face that he hadn't, though he neither confirmed nor denied it. "I have a steak thawing in the fridge. I'll share it with you in exchange for the foot rub. Deal?"

"Of course I accept." Luc's grin stretched across his face. "My foster mothers didn't raise a dummy."

She liked the way he was so at ease with his

past. A lot of men wouldn't have been able to accept losing their parents let alone joke about being raised in foster homes. Luc was so comfortable with who he was but then he didn't have to live up to a whole town's expectations.

"Give me ten minutes then you can grill the steak on the barbecue," she promised.

"I'll finish up what I was doing." Luc disappeared into the bedroom. Seconds later the sound of a drill echoed through the house.

Holly scooped her purchases into her bedroom closet, changed into her favorite jeans and T-shirt and hurried back to the kitchen. When she'd finished baking the potatoes in the microwave, made a salad and fired up the grill, she went to find Luc.

"I can't believe you've made so much progress." She surveyed his work from the doorway. "Except for that wall." She frowned at the unfinished studs.

"That's the wall where the new outlets will go," Luc explained. "I'm waiting for the electrician."

"Oh." The room looked huge. When it was finished she'd have tons of storage, a functional work area and a great view of the hills through the new window he'd installed. "I can't thank you enough for doing this, Luc."

"It's going to be a good work space," he said with a nod. "And I'm getting a great exchange with you helping me with Henry." His eyes twinkled. "I took him for a milkshake after school today as you suggested. With Hilda's permission," he added with a wink.

"How'd that go?" Holly's heart bumped when he flashed his amazing smile at her. He looked handsome and proud and thrilled.

"Great." Luc's smile grew. "Henry's got a slew of new knock-knock jokes for you."

"I can hardly wait." It was obvious he'd enjoyed every moment of his time with Henry. Holly chided herself for feeling envious of the affection he lavished on the boy. She *wanted* Luc and Henry to bond, so where did that emotion come from? Not willing to search for an answer, she changed the subject. "Time to grill," she told him.

"My favorite way to cook."

Holly sat outside on a lawn chair, sipping a cup of the coffee she'd just brewed, while Luc barbecued. Before she'd always been at ease around him, like anyone would be with a good friend. But this evening that comfortable feeling eluded her. She felt the need to fill the silence gaping between them.

"When I stopped in town for gas on the way home I heard that James Cooper is looking for a partner to buy the old McCready homestead." She didn't understand his frown. "Buying it would be a way to enlarge your ranch, wouldn't it? The land adjoins yours."

Luc flipped the steak like an expert. But then he did most things competently. And he was so easy on the eyes that Holly kept watching him.

"James phoned and offered me a partnership but I turned him down," Luc said.

"Why? You're always going on about adding land to your spread." His refusal perplexed her.

"I want to buy Cool Springs Ranch." He turned to glance at her. "Not the McCready place."

"Again, why?"

"The McCready ranch is too rocky for one thing and the low parts are subject to spring flooding," he explained. "Besides, I want to own my land, not share it. I can wait for yours."

"But, Luc, I may not be ready to sell Cool Springs for a long time." Holly was aghast that he would put his plans on hold indefinitely. She felt guilty and somehow responsible for staying here and thereby denying him his dream.

"I know. I'll wait," he repeated. "Meantime I'll save my money, so when you do decide to sell I won't need a big mortgage."

Though he tossed her that warm, easy grin, Luc's words troubled Holly.

"But what if I never sell?" Luc couldn't just sit and wait for her to leave Cool Springs Ranch because Holly had no plans to do that. Despite the pressure the locals put on her, this was where her friends and neighbors were. This was *home*.

"You won't stay here forever, Holly," Luc said imperturbably.

"I won't?" She blinked, curious yet hesitant as to why he said that. The warmth in his dark gaze made her feel cherished, protected, as if Luc truly cared about her and her future.

"Holly, it's obvious despite your denials that you're meant to be a wife and a mom."

"I told you—"

Luc stopped her by simply raising his hand. He scanned her from the ribbon that held her hair tied at the top of her head, to the toes of her feet, now snuggled into comfy moccasins. That scrutiny made her skin tingle.

"You love babies and kids, Holly. That's why you chose the career you did. One day you'll meet some guy and fall in love with him." His voice was very quiet. "You'll get married, move to your husband's place and I'll buy Cool Springs from you."

"I've told you. I am not getting married. Ever." Irritated, she rose, tossed out her coffee into the flower bed and walked through the patio doors.

Two minutes later, Luc followed her with the steak sizzling on the platter she'd left by the barbecue.

"I wasn't trying to annoy you, Holly. I was just telling you what I believe." He set the platter on the table then studied her, his head tilted to one side. "Forgive me?"

"There's nothing to forgive." She wasn't going to discuss it anymore so she motioned him to sit down, brought the potatoes from the microwave and carried the salad over. "You want to say grace?"

"Sure." Luc closed his eyes and bowed his head. "Thank You, Lord, for this day and for Holly's good food. Bless her and me as we share this meal. Amen."

He was even comfortable saying grace, Holly mused. Funny that only now after he'd revealed his relationship with Sarah did she truly realize what a remarkable man Luc was—utterly kind and likeable. She cut a small piece of steak for herself and left the rest for him, puzzling over this increasing appreciation of him.

"You're spending a lot of time on my project," she said. "I hope it's not making you ignore other chores?"

"Are you asking me if your foreman—me— is shirking?" The corners of Luc's eyes creased with his amused grin. "Would I do that after learning how to ranch at your father's knee?"

"You think Dad didn't slack?" Holly chuckled. "Maybe you weren't paying close enough attention. Dad often rushed through his most demanding chores, sometimes left others undone so he could inspect his beehives."

"I never understood why bees fascinated him," Luc said thoughtfully.

"*Fascinated* is the word. He used to say they had secret lives and that only God knew what they did all day." Holly laughed out loud. "When I was little he'd tell me stories about a character named Benny Bee and how he was buzzy doing God's will."

"Buzzy?" Luc smiled. "Now I think of it, Marcus did use the word *buzz* a lot."

"Remember he used to tell you to buzz off when he got tired of answering your questions?" She giggled at his sheepish grin.

With Luc across the table, her plain fare tasted delicious. There was a lot to like about sharing a meal with a friend like him. Holly hadn't realized how much she'd missed sharing relaxed moments like these with her dad. She closed her eyes and let the memories swamp her. When Luc cleared his throat she smiled at him through her tears.

"I miss him."

"Me, too," Luc said. He reached out and squeezed her hand. "He loved you very much."

"I know." She swallowed the lump in her throat and changed the subject. "As I remember it, Dad also had a lot to say about God's will."

"That's a topic I wish I could quiz him on now." Replete, Luc leaned back in his chair.

"Oh?" Holly poured them each a cup of coffee as she waited for him to continue.

"I didn't just work on your room this afternoon," Luc admitted. "I spent about an hour on the phone with my buddy."

"Pete, the one whose marriage is breaking up?" she guessed, wincing at the sad look in Luc's eyes.

"Yes. He hasn't been a Christian for much longer than I have. He has a lot of questions about God's will that I can't answer." He looked at his hands as if he was embarrassed by his own ignorance. "Learning God's will is something I've also been struggling with. Got any ideas I could use and also share with him?"

"I'm not really good at giving spiritual advice," Holly said, feeling like that was the understatement of the year. Lately, guilt had almost convinced her she'd failed at being a Christian but she kept up her faith despite the way she'd botched her past. But now she couldn't ignore the pain in Luc's words. "I've heard lots of sermons about God's will. If you want to share what's bothering you I'll listen. Maybe I'll remember something that will help you."

"Thanks." Luc played with his fork for a few moments before he looked directly at her. "How do I figure out what God's will is for me, Holly?"

"You don't ask the easy stuff, do you?" She took her time arranging her thoughts. "I think it depends how you mean the question. If you're talking generally then God's will is for you to accept that His son died for you and live as His child."

"I'm trying to do that every day," he said with a nod. "But it's the specific details, what God intends for me personally in my future that I can't figure out."

"That is hard to know. I've questioned that, too. 'Does God want me to do this or this?' It would be nice if there was a bolt of lightning that pointed the way, wouldn't it?" She sighed. "But I've never seen God work that way."

"How do *you* understand His will?" His desperation reached into her heart.

Holly didn't like revealing details about struggles in her faith journey. It seemed too personal, opened up a part of herself that she'd always kept hidden. And yet, Luc wanted her help. She couldn't brush him off. She whispered a prayer then inhaled.

"I start by studying the Bible," she began. "I believe that's where God has put the answers we seek. Of course it would be easier if He would thump us over the head with His will, but I think learning what He wants us to do is supposed to be a journey of discovery."

"Really?" Luc looked skeptical.

"Really. Think about it. My dad could tell me twenty times over how to saddle a horse, but until I figured it out for myself it wasn't meaningful." She grimaced. "Falling off because I'd forgotten to tighten the cinch personalized it in a way his words could never do."

"How could Holly the perfect rancher's daughter ever forget a thing like saddling a horse?" Luc chuckled, his dark eyes dancing with teasing.

"I never claimed I was perfect." His words put a damper on her spirit. There were those expectations again.

"*Perfect* is what everyone in town calls you," Luc shot back.

"I know." She made a face. "I tried so hard as a kid to make up for my mother's leaving, to never have my dad be ashamed of me. Too hard, apparently." Luc's uplifted brows made her hurry to explain. "My dad was devastated by her departure. I saw that and thought he'd forget her and love me more if I achieved. I wanted to be a daughter he was proud of."

"Your dad would have been proud of you no matter what, Holly," Luc said softly.

"I didn't understand that. I thought I could heal his pain. I didn't understand till years later that nothing I did could take her place for him. Back then I kept pushing to be the best I could be." She swallowed hard, amazed that the memory of that confused, painful time still had the power to hurt. "It's my own fault nobody sees the real me," she murmured. "All they ever knew was the image I projected, still project I guess. Holly the overachiever."

Holly hated the gush of hurt that always swamped her when she admitted to herself that she lived a lie, that ultimately she'd failed to be the exemplary daughter she'd striven so hard to be. She was the local golden girl tarnished by a major mistake. She'd given away her child, let someone else raise the grandchild her father never knew because she hadn't wanted her dad to be ashamed of her. Worse, she hadn't wanted the town to realize how far she'd fallen from the pedestal on which they'd placed her. She'd never realized that what others thought would never make up for the loss that now plagued her.

That was why she couldn't open that trunk. She didn't want to hear her father's praise and know she wasn't worthy of it. She'd tried to accept that the only important opinion was God's, but she'd failed Him, too. It was a burden she couldn't break free of. How could God ever forgive or forget her sin?

Holly studied Luc's face, suddenly curious to know what he'd think of her if he knew the truth about her. Luc was all about children, a heritage, a legacy. Deep down inside she knew he'd never countenance giving away a child she should have loved and protected. His reaction would mirror Ron's. Luc would be disgusted by her willingness to abandon her principles to maintain a charade, to protect herself.

That's why she'd never tell him or anyone else in town about her baby.

"Holly?" He urged her from her reverie. "God's will?" he nudged.

"Sorry." She regrouped and continued. "If the answer I'm looking for isn't clear, I pray for a specific answer, like asking God to do something special so I'll know I'm in His will."

"But I've done that and I'm still unclear," he said with a frown.

"I'm sorry, Luc." She smiled, but her heart ached for his confusion. "Sometimes it's a matter of moving ahead with the information we have and trusting that He will guide us where we should go. Maybe that's where you are at," she suggested.

"But what if I misjudge what He's saying?" His eyes bored into hers with an intensity that made Holly shift uncomfortably.

"That's how we learn. We start over and try to do better." Saying those words made Holly feel like a hypocrite. How could she possibly start over from her mistake?

"You don't sound convinced," he teased. "But then given your dad and the home you had, I doubt you've ever made any serious mistakes."

"You'd be surprised." Exceedingly uncomfortable with the turn of the conversation, Holly rose and began clearing the table.

"I'm sorry." Luc's hand covered hers. When

she turned to glance at him, his face was mere inches away. "That wasn't very sensitive. I'm sure you've had lots of struggles, Holly. I didn't mean to diminish them."

"I've struggled with being in God's will for years," she admitted quietly before moving away from his touch.

"Really? But you know your future. You have a great career. You're there whenever someone needs you." Luc paused. "What is there to question? You're *in* His will."

"If I am, then why didn't I know my fiancé wouldn't be able to accept—" She stopped before she blurted out her secret to Luc. He was too good a listener. "When I didn't know he wouldn't be able to accept what I told him? That was a humiliating mistake to make." She was utterly embarrassed to discuss this with him.

"At least you didn't marry the wrong guy." Luc touched her shoulder and turned her so he could look into her face. The sympathy she saw there soothed the stinging hurt inside her heart. "God saved you from making that mistake, Holly."

"I wish He'd chosen a less public way," she mumbled. "Everyone in town…and everyone at any wedding…they look at me with pity. I hate that."

"I doubt anyone pities you," Luc said. "If there is pity, it's for Ron. He has no idea what he missed out on by dumping you."

"That's nice of you to say." Holly turned away to load the dishwasher, trying to hide her blush at the depth of sincerity in Luc's voice.

"It's the truth. Any man would be proud to have you for his wife, Holly. Don't let Ron turn you off marriage."

"It's not just that." She poured two fresh cups of coffee and set them on the table along with the tarts she'd bought that afternoon. She waited until Luc was seated, too. "You're talking about God's will."

"Yes." He waited patiently for her to organize her thoughts.

"I don't believe I'm supposed to be married." Before he could speak she hurried on. "That's not a reaction to my canceled wedding, it's *because* of it. I think God has something else in store for me, so that's why I'm confused about His will. I don't know what that something is."

Luc wasn't exactly sure why he hated hearing Holly reject marriage. In his mind's eye he could see a little girl with Holly's turned-up nose and bouncing curls running across the field after a baby lamb. The movie in his mind widened to include Holly, her bubbling laughter floating on the breeze as she chased after her daughter. She scooped up the little girl and hugged her close, whispering "I love you."

She was so meant to be a mom.

"Luc?"

He blinked back to reality. "Yeah?"

"Can I ask you something?" Holly waited for his nod. "When you talked about Sarah, you said you two broke up because she wouldn't move here."

He nodded, wondering where this was leading.

"In hindsight, do you think that if she had agreed your marriage would have been a success?" She stared at him, waiting for an answer he didn't have.

"I don't know." Looking at Holly, Luc realized he could barely recall Sarah's features. He only knew she'd never looked as pretty as Holly did now, the lamplight bathing her in its glow.

"I don't think it would have," she murmured, her face pensive as her gaze held his.

"Because?"

"Your problem wasn't that Sarah wouldn't come here." Holly pinned him with that needle-sharp look that couldn't be evaded. "Could it be that you thought having her come here was some kind of guarantee of her commitment?"

"I never thought of it that way, but I did think that once she moved she would have settled in." He made a face. "That was before she called Buffalo Gap Hicksville."

"But, Luc," Holly persisted. "You could have found work in the city if you really loved her. You could have given up your ranch." She nibbled on her bottom lip for a minute, a sure sign Holly had something else to say.

"Go ahead. You won't hurt my feelings," he said.

"I think you wanted Sarah to move here because you thought that would mean she really loved you," she said very quietly. "Maybe you didn't quite trust her."

Luc frowned, not liking what he heard but finding a grain of truth in Holly's words. "Why do you think that?"

"Because I made the same mistake." Her voice brimmed with sadness. "I hung on to my secrets until the last possible moment before I told Ron. That's not how trust works between people who love each other."

"You're saying you didn't really love him?" Luc found himself holding his breath as he waited for her answer and wondered why it mattered to him so much.

"I didn't love him enough to marry him." Holly's blunt admission surprised him. "First Corinthians 13 says that if you love someone you will be loyal to him no matter what the cost. You will always believe in him, always expect the best of him and always stand your ground in defending him. I couldn't do that for Ron."

"So another man will come along one day—" He stopped because Holly was shaking her head.

"No, I don't think it will be different with

another man." Holly's lips tightened. "That's why I think God's plan is for me to remain single."

Luke was astounded by his need to scream "no." By the certainty that loving, motherly Holly deserved to marry and be the mom he knew she would be. By the urge to take her in his arms and assure her that God would never have created such lovingness in her if He hadn't intended her to share it with a family. Luc opened his mouth to object, but his response was cut off by the ring of the telephone.

Holly answered, listened for a moment then slowly hung up. When she turned to him, her face was ashen.

"That was Mayor Marsha. Henry's been hurt. He's at the hospital and he's asking for you."

Luc froze as fear grabbed him and held on.

"Come on, I'll drive you there." When he didn't, couldn't move, Holly grasped his arm and nudged him forward. "Come on, Luc. We need to go to Henry."

"But—" He could not voice all the things that could go wrong, that could steal this precious child from him. Fortunately, he didn't have to. Holly understood.

"Pray," she said quietly. "Pray and trust knowing that God's will is to do what's best for Henry."

As Holly drove him to the hospital, she talked about Henry's little foibles, the fun they'd had together and things she planned to do with him in the future.

"We need to take him on that fishing trip we promised," she said. "Maybe not tomorrow if he's injured, but we do have to make it happen, Luc. And we should also teach him to ride. Every kid should know how to ride a horse. And I want to make cookies with him."

Holly's list of activities kept him so busy during the drive into town that he almost stopped imagining the worst about Henry.

"Henry's going to need you to be strong for him, Luc," Holly said as she pulled up to the hospital.

"He's going to need you, too," Luc said. And that's when he knew that he wanted Holly there when Henry finally visited the ranch. He wanted all three of them together, safely enjoying this world God had created.

Holly and Henry were part of his life now.

And he couldn't lose either of them.

Chapter Five

"You had us so worried, Henry." Luc's pale, tense face bore witness to his words.

Holly grasped his arm and squeezed it to let him know she was there to support him, but also to help him calm down because she could see worry building in Henry.

"We're so glad you weren't badly hurt, Henry," she added. "Is your arm very painful?"

His bottom lip trembled as he shook his head, but he winced as the on-duty nurse pushed his sleeve up to bandage the razed skin.

"I'm okay," he said bravely.

Since they'd already heard from Mayor Marsha that he'd raced into the street to save Hilda's cat and been bumped by a passing car, neither she nor Luc asked for more details. It was clear from the way Henry had latched on to Luc and not let go since they'd arrived that the boy had been badly frightened.

"There we go." Nurse Dora Cummings taped the last bit of gauze in place then handed Henry a sticker. "Good job, little man. In a day or two we'll take that off and put a small bandage on it. Pretty soon you won't even remember it was there."

"I appreciate the extra fussing over him, Dora," Holly whispered as they stood together near the door while Luc and Henry chatted.

"He's a cute kid. I think the worst damage he did was to scare himself. He'll be fine." The nurse frowned. "Say, did you check over that young girl that showed up at Family Ties?"

"Alice Something?" Holly shook her head. "Doc Treple did when she first showed up."

"No, she delivered yesterday. This one is Petra, Petra Stark."

"Never met her." Holly knew Dora was an excellent nurse. If her radar was up, there was good reason. "Something wrong?"

"I was at Family Ties today and I only saw her for a few minutes, but since I did something's been niggling at me. One of the other nurses did the workup that Abby always asks for before accepting a client at Family Ties. I checked it." Dora hesitated. "On the form Petra said she was thirty-six weeks along in her pregnancy."

"You think that's wrong," Holly said, understanding immediately.

"I think she's very close to giving birth but

she's trying to hide it and I can't figure out why. You're better at getting patients to confide than I am." Dora's big smile stretched across her face. "I can never worm out all the details like you do. I thought maybe you could stop by, talk to her."

"I'll try." She thought for a moment. "I drove in with Luc and I'm not sure if he's in a hurry to get back, but if I can't see her tonight then I'll stop by tomorrow," Holly promised. "I have a couple of quilts to drop off anyway."

"I heard you'd volunteered to do quilts for each child Family Ties arranges adoptions for. That's generous. I love your baby quilts. I hope I get to see your latest one before it's gone. One is more adorable than the next."

"Thank you. But don't worry, I'll have pictures. I'll probably bore you to tears," Holly said, basking in the compliment.

"Your quilts would never bore me. I'm going to hire you to make me one if I ever manage to get pregnant." For a moment a flicker of uncertainty washed through her eyes.

"You will. At the right time." Holly wrapped an arm around Dora's shoulder and squeezed. "And you won't hire me because I'll give you one for a baby gift. Any special orders?"

"Anything you make will be perfect. Thank you, Holly." Dora glanced at her patient. "Tell Hilda the doctor says to keep Henry quiet tonight. He bumped his head and I think he still feels a bit woozy, though he won't admit it. There's no concussion and he should be fine by morning." After a wave for Henry she hurried away to tend to another patient.

As Holly turned she noticed Hilda emerge from another part of the emergency ward. Her face was pale and she was holding her hand to one hip. Before Holly could ask, Hilda explained that she'd hurried after Henry, tripped and injured herself. She was clearly weepy and began fussing over Henry's care.

"What if he needs me in the night and I can't get up those stairs?" Hilda said in a fretful tone.

"That would be awful," Holly agreed. She waited a moment then said, "Maybe, just for one night, Henry should go for a sleepover at Luc's." She waited with bated breath for Hilda's objections. None were forthcoming. In fact, Hilda looked relieved. "I don't know Luc's plans, but we could ask him. If you'd like?"

"I think I would like that," Hilda said with a heavy sigh. "And maybe Henry could stay two nights. I believe I'll need that long to get myself truly mobile."

"No one wants you to overtax, Hilda. Let's go see if Luc can manage it." Holly linked her arm in the older woman's and led her to Luc. She explained the situation, stifling a smile as she noted the joy now lighting his eyes and how quickly it spread to Henry who clung to his hand. "So we were wondering, do you think you could manage a couple of nights? Today's Friday so maybe until Sunday?" She waited for Hilda's nod.

"I'd be very glad to help you out, Hilda. Do we need to check with Abby first?" Luc politely waited for Hilda's response but Holly could see his anticipation.

"I've already phoned her to meet me here. She'll want to know about Henry's accident." A worried look filled Hilda's tired eyes. "I just hope she doesn't think I'm too old to handle him. I know I should have gotten to him sooner but..."

"Things happen with kids, Hilda. You know that." Holly hugged her. "You're doing a fine job of watching Henry. Abby will tell you that, too," she said as the owner of Family Ties hurried toward them.

After an explanation, Abby agreed Luc was the perfect answer in this situation. So half an hour later Holly and Luc were helping Henry load an overnight bag into Holly's jeep.

"Would it be okay if you two stop for a milk shake while I visit someone at Family Ties?" Holly asked them. Huge grins told her the two males would have no problem with that. As she watched them enter the café, a wistful thought flitted through her heart.

Luc would have Henry. But who would she have?

Holly knew of no way to soothe the ache inside except to pray for God to heal it. Then she walked into Family Ties to see the newest guest Dora had mentioned. Petra Stark sat in the living room. Holly fiddled around rearranging the quilts as she studied the girl and her movements. Petra certainly looked like she was further along in her pregnancy than thirty-six weeks.

"Hi," Holly greeted her, introducing herself and explaining her role. "I'm the nurse practitioner for Family Ties. We haven't met yet but I wanted to stop by and say welcome. I'll come to see you officially on Monday. We can chat then."

"About what?" Petra asked in a guarded tone.

"Anything you like. I'm here to help with whatever you need." Holly studied the young blonde while mentally assessing the tiny stress lines around her eyes. "Finding it hard to sleep?"

"Yes. The baby seems to be kicking me constantly. I can't sleep much at all." Petra nodded after Holly made some suggestions. "I'll try that," she said.

"Good. Here's my card. You call me if you want to talk or for any other reason and we'll set up a time to meet. If the baby starts coming, you call me right away."

"Oh, that won't be for a long time," Petra said, but her gaze didn't meet Holly's.

Holly walked out the door of Family Ties with a troubled heart. How could she help this girl if she couldn't get the truth?

"Is everything all right?" Luc rose from his seat on the top step. "You look concerned."

"I always am with a new patient and this one seems disinclined to tell me the truth. It's hard to help when someone won't trust you." She sighed then frowned at him. "You look worried, too. Where's Henry?"

"He finished his milk shake fast and needed something to do so I taught him to play a game on my phone. He's in the car," Luc said, pointing to Henry's dark head barely visible through the car window. "He's fine. It's not that." Luc raked a hand through his short hair, his dark eyes brooding.

"What is it then?" she asked, pushing back the weariness that swamped her.

"It's kind of embarrassing to admit," Luc muttered. Then he looked her straight in the eyes, dots of red coloring his prominent cheekbones. "I spent so long trying to figure out how to get him to my place. Now that he's coming, I don't know what to do with him. I'm scared, Holly."

"You can't be scared of Henry." She laughed but smothered it immediately as she realized how serious Luc was. It was odd to see the big rancher so unnerved by a little boy, but it was also endearing, and somehow sweet that he cared so much. "What's bothering you?"

"What if I do or say the wrong thing?" he said hesitantly. "Henry isn't my son yet. What if I do something that damages my case? What if I somehow hurt him or make a mistake with him? I couldn't stand that."

Luc looked so miserable that Holly had to reach out and pat his shoulder.

"Luc, nobody is born knowing how to be a parent. It's trial and error for everyone." She smiled, hoping to ease his anxiety. "I tell my prenatal classes that if you love the child and keep his best interests at the forefront of your mind, you won't go far wrong."

"I know but—" He hesitated before he continued. "Could you come over tomorrow morning and have breakfast with us? That might ease things."

"Sorry. I can't." She drew her hand away, wishing with all her heart that she could be there to watch Luc form tighter connections with Henry. "I just got a text and agreed to reschedule two prenatal appointments for tomorrow morning. I won't be free till noon or so."

"But what will I do with him until then?" Luc said in a panicked voice.

"What kind of things did you envision doing with your son?" She smiled at him, coaxing him to remember, hating to see this strong man so vulnerable. "Come on, Luc. You've talked about adopting Henry. Now's not the time to get cold feet. In fact, this is probably the perfect time to try the things you want to do with him when you adopt him. Show him what you love," she said quietly. "He'll love it, too."

"I guess that's my biggest fear," he admitted in a soft, hesitant tone. "Maybe Henry won't like my life. Sarah didn't."

"Are you kidding? Cowboys are Henry's heroes. To him you're the best thing since bubble gum." Holly shook her head at him. "You just wait, Luc. He's going to dive headlong into whatever you show him. But if he doesn't, you'll find something else, right? Because Henry is the son you've always wanted."

Luc nodded. Then without warning he leaned forward and pressed a kiss against her forehead. "You're a good friend, Holly."

She gulped, utterly unnerved by that soft kiss and yet deeply moved that this strong, competent man needed her. It took a second to get her happy-go-lucky mask in place so Luc wouldn't see how deeply he'd affected her.

"Stop worrying and concentrate on the fun you'll have. This is what you prayed for. God's answered your prayer. Enjoy it." She smothered a yawn and thought how often she did that around Luc. He was going to start thinking of her as a doddering old spinster.

"Come on," he said. "You need to get home. I'll drive you back to the house and pick up my truck."

"Yes," she agreed. "Then you can take Henry

home and tuck him up in that spare room you fixed up especially for him." She knew Luc had recently painted and installed new carpeting.

"I'm looking forward to that," he admitted in a soft voice that brimmed with yearning.

"You've got two whole days with Henry." Holly smiled at him. "You asked about God's will. Well, He's in control of everything so why not relax and enjoy this time with Henry and leave the future to God."

As they drove home, Holly decided that she was going to take her own advice, even if she had to sneak time from her sewing to spend it with Luc and Henry. She could sew anytime, but spending time with these two special guys was not to be missed.

"So we can have scrambled eggs with toast or pancakes," Luc offered. "Which one sounds good?"

"Scrambled eggs with toast and ketchup *and* pancakes," Henry decreed.

"Excellent." Though the boy showed no sign that last night's injuries still bothered him, Luc had decided to go with less ambitious activities today. He just hoped he could keep Henry interested.

He had barely begun cracking eggs into the hot pan when a knock on the door made him pause. His heart gave a bump of relief when

Holly stepped through the door. He'd wished she'd show up but didn't want to get his hopes up. Funny how with Holly on hand he felt less likely to botch the job of entertaining Henry.

"Have you eaten?" he asked. "We've decided on scrambled eggs and pancakes." Then he remembered. "I thought you had appointments this morning?"

"I did. Listen, lazybones, I was up way before you. I've been to Family Ties, had some cancellations at my office and now I have the rest of the day to myself." She grinned at him as if this was the best place she could imagine being on a sunny spring morning, then leaned down to tweak Henry's nose. "Hi, buddy."

When Holly turned her head and smiled at Luc, her joyous smile made his stomach clench. Belatedly, he realized smoke now filled the room from his overheated pan.

"I'll take an egg and some toast since you're offering," she said, wrinkling her nose. "But I prefer my toast *not* black."

"Ha-ha. I didn't hear your car." Luc glanced out the window. The palomino gelding she'd named Babycakes stood placidly under a poplar tree, munching on freshly sprouted grass. "Oh, you rode."

"You talked about teaching Henry to ride, so I thought I'd be ready in case that's what you'd planned. Babycakes is always good to go."

"Really? You're sticking with that dumb name for that magnificent animal?" Luc made a face then got on with his cooking.

"He's a big baby, Luc. The name suits him." She chucked Henry under his chin and mussed his hair. "How're you feeling?"

"I'm good." Henry's eyes widened. "You mean we could ride a *horse*?"

"Yes, a horse." Holly giggled. "You're sure not going to ride Sheba," she joked, petting Luc's dog who rested under the table. "She's expecting puppies."

Luc had planned something else but if riding was what Holly wanted, that's what they'd do. Why was it she only had to look at him and he'd do anything she asked? He knew the answer. He'd promised Marcus he'd do his best to keep Holly happy and he had no intention of reneging on that promise.

"How about if I make toast while you cook the eggs and pancakes. And Henry can set the table." Holly waited for his nod then got to work.

Luc's kitchen filled with her laughter at Henry's newest knock-knock jokes. She told him a couple of her own and answered his endless questions with patience and humor. Mom Holly at her best.

Luc managed not to scorch the eggs or the pancakes, but it wasn't easy. His attention kept drifting to Holly with her glowing face. She didn't need cosmetics to make her more beautiful. She was already the most gorgeous woman he'd ever seen and it wasn't just a skin-deep beauty.

Though Luc didn't know what drove Holly to keep sewing, he did know how much she loved it. He could hardly have missed the mounds of fabric cut out in odd shapes piled on her dining room sideboard. He'd carefully avoided the quilt frame hogging a big corner of her living room, too. Holly was a woman with plans. She had things to do.

Yet she'd given up her beloved sewing to be here for him, to help him with Henry. That touched a spot deep inside him and Luc felt a rush of...something. Unwilling to define that feeling right now he slid the pile of fluffy golden eggs onto a plate and called the others to sit down. After a short grace, Luc leaned back and watched the pair dig into their breakfasts before his stomach rumbled and he attacked his own.

Henry was still gorging on pancakes when Holly pronounced the meal delicious and pushed her half-empty plate away.

"If it was so delicious, why did you pour a cup of ketchup on your eggs and then leave some?" he asked, delighted to see a flush of red staining her cheeks. She always seemed so in control.

"Me 'n Holly like ketchup," Henry explained, the red sauce smeared all over his face next to the syrup. "On everything."

"Except chocolate ice cream." Holly winked at Luc. "I don't like ketchup on that."

When Henry giggled, Holly joined him. A certainty filled Luc. This was going to be a wonderful day because of Holly. Out of the blue, a thought struck him. If he was looking for a wife, Holly would be the standard he'd use to measure her against.

But of course he wasn't getting married.

Once the dishes were in the dishwasher, Luc conferred with Holly because her advice was always good and because she had medical experience.

"Henry doesn't look to be hurting." Luc used his quietest voice while the boy lavished affection on Luc's dog. "But just in case, maybe he should ride in front of me to the stream?"

"Excellent idea," Holly agreed. "I wore my swimsuit just in case you'd planned to go there. The water might be chilly but—"

"Might be chilly?" Luc said drolly and arched one eyebrow.

"Okay, it will be frigid." She shrugged, unable to suppress her grin. "So?"

"Yeah, we're tough ranch people." He flexed a biceps, trying to look manly. "We can handle a little chill." He growled and bent over like a football player intent on sacking the quarterback.

He was acting silly. But Holly didn't seem to mind. In fact, she was growling, too, and encouraged a freshly-washed Henry to do the same. That was what Luc had always admired about Holly. No matter what the game, she always joined in.

"Let's go saddle up, pardner," he said to Henry, whose eyes stretched wide.

"What's a pardner?" Henry asked as they walked to the horse barn. "Is it like a partner?"

"Exactly the same," Luc assured him. "It's just a different way of saying it."

Henry hesitated in the barn doorway.

"What's wrong, bud?" Luc crouched down, saw the confusion in Henry's dark brown eyes.

"I don't think I can be your pardner." Henry's round face brimmed with misery.

"Why's that? Don't you like it here?" Luc voiced his worst fear. "Don't you like me?" He hated asking but it was better to get it said out front, though saying those words made him cringe. What if—

Lord, help.

"It's not that," Henry rushed to reassure. "I love you and Holly. You're the nicest people I know." He glanced up at Holly and tried to smile but it was a poor effort. "I wish I could stay here forever."

"Then what's the problem?" Luc glanced at Holly and shrugged, trying to tell her without words that he was at a loss to understand what was going on.

To his dismay, Holly said nothing. She simply watched him for a moment then her glance strayed to her horse. Something in Luc's brain clicked.

"Henry," he said quietly, taking the boy's small hand in his. "Is it the horses? Are you afraid of them?"

Henry's head bobbed once.

"There's nothing to be afraid of. Horses are very gentle." Luc squeezed Henry's hand but the look on the boy's face told Luc it would take more than a few words to soothe his fears. He glanced at Holly again but she simply smiled and nodded, as if to encourage him.

"Can't we do something else?" Henry asked in a plaintive tone.

"Well, we could. But I really think you'd love our little creek. Holly's been going there since she was a kid." Luc saw a new frown appear.

"But I can't swim!" Henry wailed, looking ready to cry.

"Are you kidding me?" Luc touched his cheek then shook his head. "Henry, everyone can swim. They just have to learn how."

"Will you teach me?" Half-worried, half-excited, Henry shifted from one foot to the other.

"Maybe. If the water's warm and you want to. Or we could fish. What do you think, Holly?" he asked, trying to draw her into this. "I've been wanting a good feed of fish for ages."

"Either one sounds good to me." She crossed her arms and tilted back on the heels of her cowboy boots.

Luc tossed her a frustrated look then turned his attention back to the boy he hoped would one day be his son. Maybe by then he'd be better at figuring out this kid. "Do you like to fish, Henry?"

"I don't know. I never did it." Worry had overtaken Henry's excitement. "Maybe we should stay here."

"I'll tell you what. Let's ride up to the creek and see if you like it. You don't have to ride a horse on your own," Luc explained, interrupting his objections. "We're pardners. You can ride in front on me on my horse. Dillyboy is a great horse. Very safe and gentle. He and I have gone lots of places together."

"Dillyboy?" Henry frowned. "You said Holly's horse had a silly name but Dillyboy is silly, too."

"I know. I bought him from a little girl." Luc made a face then pretended to sneak a look at Holly before he leaned close to Henry and whispered, "Her name was Dibby."

"Dibby and Dillyboy?" Henry's grin spread.

"See what I mean? I should probably change his name," Luc said, immensely relieved that Henry was no longer frowning. "Come on, I'll introduce you."

Very aware of Holly trailing behind them, Luc

led the boy into the barn and to Dillyboy's stall. With great hesitation Henry touched his fingers to the stallion's crest and let them rest there a moment while he gathered his courage. Then he climbed on a bale, slid his hand upward, past Dillyboy's poll and between his ears to his forehead.

The horse whinnied and bent his head lower for a good rub which, when he understood, Henry willingly gave. His grin stretched wide when he touched Dillyboy's muzzle and the horse neighed his appreciation. But when Dillyboy dipped his head lower and nudged it against Henry's chest his smile drained away.

"He's going to eat me." Henry pulled back.

"No way. He's checking your shirt for carrots. He loves them." Luc walked over to a box where he always kept a few carrots. "Want to feed him?"

Henry thought about it for a moment then tentatively agreed. He took the carrot and held it out. Dillyboy couldn't reach and immediately stamped his foot.

"He won't hurt you, Henry," Luc explained. "But he can't reach the treat you're offering and he doesn't like that. Just hold it in the palm of your hand and he'll scoop it up."

Henry did and crowed with delight when the horse snatched the carrot and gobbled it up. Without asking the excited boy raced to the box, grabbed another carrot and repeated the action. After the third one, Luc called a halt.

"We don't want to stuff him. We need Dillyboy to give us a ride, remember." Slowly, patiently, careful to make sure Henry understood, he showed him how to prepare the horse for a ride. "You can sit here, in front of me, and I'll ride in the saddle."

"We're too heavy," Henry worried.

"No. Dillyboy has a silly name but he is very strong." Luc tightened the cinch the last millimeter, patted his horse's flanks then turned to Henry. "Ready?"

"I—I guess." He looked dubious when Luc swung up into the saddle but bravely accepted Holly's help to get settled on the horse in front of Luc.

Henry's face stayed tight and tense for several moments, until Luc had walked the horse out of the barn. He squealed when Luc nudged Dillyboy into a slow canter and squealed again when they drew to a stop by Holly's horse.

"Okay?" Luc asked him, sharing a look with Holly who gave a thumbs-up.

"Can we go faster?" Henry wanted to know.

"One step at a time," he cautioned, loving Henry's enthusiasm. "Hey, I forgot something. Stay here for a minute." He dismounted and handed the reins to Holly. "I'll be right back."

"We'll be here," she said, winking at Henry. "And, Luc?"

He stopped, turned back to her.

"Good job." A soft smile curved her pretty lips. "You'll make a wonderful father."

"Thanks." Luc strode back into the house to retrieve the picnic lunch he'd packed earlier. His heart sang with joy at Holly's words. He could do this. He could be a father.

As long as Holly was around to nudge him forward.

What would he do without Holly?

Chapter Six

"Thanks for letting me tag along today, Luc. It's been a long time since I've had so much fun." Holly's sides ached from laughing. She collapsed on a rock by the creek.

"Thanks for coming," Luc said.

She studied him, savoring the sheen on his face, clearly visible since he'd removed his Stetson.

"I thought I was in shape," he said, huffing as he sat down. "But clearly chasing a little boy all through this glade never figured in my fitness routine." He grimaced. "Henry, on the other hand, seems to be suffering not a whit from his accident yesterday. He's like one of your dad's buzzing bees."

"Kids recover amazingly well. You were great teaching him to swim." She was so proud of the way Luc accepted Henry's many fears and worked through each one.

She knew it hadn't been easy for Luc to overcome Henry's fear of actually immersing himself in running water, but she'd watched the cowboy draw on his incredible patience. Even though his lips pinched in frustration a couple of times, he'd pushed it back, inventing little games to get Henry used to the water until he'd finally managed to float a short distance on his own.

"I persisted because of something from my childhood," he said in a low voice.

"Oh?" Holly appreciated Luc's awareness of Henry standing fifty feet away, skipping pebbles over the water. He'd modulated his voice so the boy wouldn't hear.

"I saw another foster kid die when he was twelve because he couldn't master his fear of the water." Luc's face tightened. "It was such a needless thing. All kids should know how to swim and what to do if they get into trouble in the water."

Holly noted his fervent tone, surprised by it. She'd never have labeled Luc as passionate about things; he was always laid-back and comfortable. She liked this other side of him, admired his stance as a champion for kids. A lot.

"I've been thinking of what we were talking about." Holly smiled at his puzzled look. "God's will."

"Oh, yeah." His wry grin touched her heart. "We've talked about so many things I didn't connect for a minute. Did you come up with any answers?"

"No answers, but I remembered something." She paused, startled to realize that he was right. They did talk about a lot of things. As friends did. "It was a sermon I heard a long time ago, when I was in training." She deliberately looked away from him, not wanting to release too much information about her time in Toronto.

"Oh, yeah?" Luc's gaze was on Henry, making sure he was all right.

"The pastor said that if you were unsure about God's will for you and couldn't get the answers you needed, the best thing was to prayerfully keep moving forward with your plans." Holly squinted into the sun, trying to remember the exact words. "He said that if God wanted you to move in a different direction, He'd show you a new way."

"Makes sense." Luc pulled the stem off a blade of grass and worried it between his teeth as he gazed up at the clouds that floated past. "So you think I should keep on with my plans to adopt Henry and if God doesn't want that, He'll make it so I can't adopt?"

Holly nodded, but in her heart a bubble of fear grew. Luc had so much invested in Henry. His heart primarily, but he'd also planned, worked and now reached out to host the boy. If the adoption didn't go through, both he and Henry were going to be heartbroken.

That was where she came in, Holly decided. As his friend, her job was to help, maybe even protect Luc as much as she could.

"I had a phone call this morning," Luc murmured. When he didn't look directly at her, Holly frowned. "From Sarah."

She tamped down the immediate rush of anger. Luc wanted her friendship, not her judgment. For all she knew, he might still love her.

Listen, Holly. That's all he wants from you.

"Oh," she said, trying to sound noncommittal. "Is everything okay?"

"Not really." Luc threw away the stem he'd been chewing and sat upright. After congratulating Henry on a great stone throw he said, "She apologized for what she said. Apparently she'd had a big disappointment at work and says she took it out on me. She wants to come visit the ranch. She hinted about us maybe getting back together."

"Oh." Holly gulped, filled with loathing at the idea of Luc being tied to what sounded to her like a selfish woman. But she was there as his sounding board, she reminded herself again. "Is that what you want?"

"No." He shook his head to emphasize his rejection. "I'm not leaving my ranch and I don't want a part-time wife who lives miles away.

I don't want to get together on weekends and holidays. And where would kids fit in?"

"It could work, Luc. You could make it work if you wanted it enough." *Please don't want it.*

"Maybe, but I keep thinking about my buddies. If their marriages didn't work when they were together, both working on it, how good a marriage could it be when the couple doesn't share their everyday world?" He froze. "Hang on a second."

Holly watched him rise and jog over to Henry. He hunkered down beside the boy and said something that had Henry nodding agreement. Luc pulled a roll of candy out of his pocket, and Henry sat down on a big rock to enjoy his treat.

"Sorry. I figured he was about to take off after that squirrel." Luc sat back down. "Where was I?"

"Compromise," Holly told him.

"I don't want to compromise." Luc held her gaze, his own dark and intense. "I realized as I was talking to her that I don't want to sink everything I have into a relationship that I think is already doomed to failure. Ever since our breakup I've struggled to focus on not settling."

"So you told her no?" Holly fought to keep her voice even, striving for impartiality though inside she was cheering his decision.

"Yes." He frowned. "I don't want to hurt Sarah. I just don't love her anymore, if I ever did. And I'm beginning to doubt that. I think it's a blessing we broke up. I'm not the guy she needs. I love ranching. I don't want to do it part-time. And I do want to adopt Henry."

"Are you sure, Luc?" She wondered if he'd regret his decision later, especially if the adoption didn't go through. "Maybe if you thought about it a little more—"

"No. I'm certain." Luc heaved a sigh. "I've realized a few things since we split up, things you've helped me see more clearly."

"Me?" Holly squeaked.

"Yes, you, Holly Janzen." He reached out and brushed the end of her nose with his finger. "You take a no-holds-barred approach to life. You press through the tough parts, like your dad's passing and Ron's departure, and you don't settle. And then there's your sewing thing."

"My sewing 'thing'?" she repeated and wrinkled her nose at him.

"I don't know what else to call it." Luc grinned when she rolled her eyes. "But anyway, I watch you keep pursuing that. You're passionate about it and you don't let things like lack of space or anything else stop you from doing what you love."

"There's a difference between sewing and marriage," she said, surprised and pleased by his comments.

"Is there? The Bible says to press toward the

mark of the high calling. It doesn't say settle for compromise." He crossed his arms over his chest and leaned back. "Breaking up with Sarah really hurt, maybe more because she's not the first one who's rejected me because I live on a ranch and horses are my life."

That was news to Holly but she decided not to ask him about it, not right now anyway.

"I don't want to open myself up to that rejection again, Holly." His voice emerged low with an ache underlying the words. "It's like being gutted. All the things I love she hates. No matter how I compromise I won't ever feel like I'm enough."

"Then you're right to refuse her." She saw Luc almost every day yet she hadn't realized what he was going through. He'd been there for her so often. But when had she been there for him? Friendship was supposed to work two ways.

"Is that the way you feel about Ron?" His quiet, hesitant voice made her look at him.

"I expected too much of Ron," she said softly. "I realize that now."

Silence fell between them as they watched Henry throw larger and larger stones into the water, laughing at the splash they made.

"He's wonderful," Luc murmured. And Holly agreed.

"I learned something new about adoptions," she said, hoping he wouldn't think her nosy.

"Tell me." Luc shifted slightly, alert as Henry moved near the horses, picking wildflowers.

"An article I read said it makes a big impression on the powers that be when you know the child's routine and have already made adjustments for it," Holly told him. "Like knowing his favorite games—"

"Checkers," Luc shot back in a dry tone. "I don't know where he learned to play, but he's very good at it."

"Oh. Good," she said, startled that Luc had already gained this information. "It also said that if you talk to his caregiver and find out what his normal routine is you will be better prepared to make adjustments."

"I spoke to Hilda while you were helping Henry pack to come here." Luc held up his hand and began to tick off items on each finger. "I know he sometimes wakes calling for his brother and that he likes a snack before he goes to bed. His favorite color is blue. His favorite food is French fries and his best memory is of him and his brother biking in a park."

"Ah, that explains the blue bedroom." Luc was miles ahead of her, Holly realized as she returned his smile. But she wanted to alert him to everything she'd learned. "It also said you should have a financial plan in mind for his future."

"I set up what I call my adoption fund for that purpose," Luc told her. "I've been putting a little extra in it since I met Henry because someday I'd like to invite his brother out here. Nothing's carved in stone, I just thought that maybe when Finn gets out his being here might help Henry, though I'm not sure exactly when that will be."

"You've thought of everything." She was in awe of his foresight.

"The debacle with Sarah taught me to consider every angle." He shifted uneasily and made a face. "You know, I've been meaning to talk to you about something. Abby gave me a document with a whole list of questions to answer. I'm supposed to have it done by Monday but I haven't even started."

"Why not?" Holly could see how difficult the admission was for him. "Tell me," she said quietly.

"I'm scared to answer them. It feels like some kind of trap. If I answer wrong, I could lose Henry." He looked at her, his brown eyes shadowed. "Adopting him means so much. I can't lose him because I didn't answer a question the right way."

"Oh, Luc." She moved closer and laid her hand on his. "Have some faith. This little boy needs a home. You have a home. And you have a lot of friends in Buffalo Gap. One of them is Abby. She's not going to trick you. She's just doing her job so that when you get Henry, nobody will be able to undo that. And you've got God on your side, remember."

Luc studied her for a long time. When at last he spoke, Holly saw past the words to his sincerity and tried to keep from blushing.

"How do you stay so positive, Holly? Don't you ever get overwhelmed by everything?" He answered his own question with a shake of his head. "No, I guess you don't. Even during your dad's illness and after he died, I never saw you at a loss. You always seemed confident things would work out."

"I'm not always confident," she said, half-annoyed that he saw her as some paragon of virtue. "But I don't see the value in repeatedly voicing the direness of my situation. Maybe it's my profession. Nurse practitioners are trained to deal with issues and move on."

"It's not only that. It's more that I see a confidence inside of you," Luc said. "An assurance that God is in control and He'll work things out."

"Isn't that what the Bible promises?" she asked in exasperation. She was so tired of this perfect image. But if anyone knew how far from perfect she was, maybe they'd doubt her ability to do her job.

"I need to emulate your faith," he said.

"No, you don't," she said in exasperation. "I'm not perfect, Luc. I get as down as anyone else, mess up as badly as anyone, have as many doubts as anyone else. But in the end, God *is* in control, even when it doesn't seem like it. I try to remember that."

Suddenly Holly noticed that Henry had been watching them. She was pretty sure he'd overheard them because he was now walking toward them.

"Are you an' Luc fighting?" A frown marred Henry's smooth forehead.

"Nope, we're not." Luc smiled. "We're discussing. That means we're trying to find out what the other one thinks."

"Oh." Henry considered that for a moment before nodding. "Maybe you need Ms. Hilda's verse."

"Maybe we do." Holly shot Luc a sideways look then smiled to encourage the boy. "What's the verse, Henry?"

"I'll try to remember." Henry scrunched up his face. "'I leaned on You since I was borned...' I forget the rest." He sighed. "Ms. Hilda says it's from a song in the Bible."

"A psalm?" Holly asked, hiding her smile.

"Maybe." Henry shrugged. "It means God's been with you since you were a baby."

"It's a great verse. It does help our discussion." Luc's face beamed as he lifted a hand and smoothed it across Henry's brow. "Thank you very much."

"Welcome." Henry leaned against Luc's arm. "I'm hungry, Luc."

"Again?" Immediately Luc's face dropped. "But we've eaten everything I brought for lunch. I didn't realize— I should have known—" He stared at Henry, clearly blaming himself for not planning better.

"I had a hunch all that swimming and riding might make you hungry," Holly said. She grinned at Henry. "I've noticed that boys and men can eat a lot."

"That's 'cause we have to be strong, right, Luc?" Henry proudly flexed a puny bicep.

"Right." Luc studied Holly with a calculating look. "What's in your saddle pack? No, wait. I think I can guess. S'mores?" He gave a triumphant hoot when she nodded.

"And lemonade," she said.

"You just can't give up the chocolate, can you, Holly?" Luc's gaze felt like the sun, warming, cherishing her.

"Be glad about that," she said with a teasing growl. "Or I might not share."

"What's a s'more?" Henry asked.

"Oh, my boy, you have a real treat coming if you've never had a s'more." Luc jumped up, held out a hand to Holly and when she grasped his, tugged her upright. "You and I are going to build a fire in that pit over there," he said to

Henry. "And then Holly and I will introduce you to s'mores. You'll love them."

Henry studied Luc's every move, mirroring each action with one of his own. Slowly the two males built a tiny fire inside the metal rim of a tractor tire that Holly's dad had brought here when she was a small girl.

A pang shot through Holly's heart as she watched the two heads nearly touching as they fed the fire. That bittersweet moment stung so much she had to turn away and busy herself spreading the snacks over the makeshift table she and her dad had fashioned out of a tree stump when she was just a bit older than Henry.

She touched her fingers to the *HJ* carved into the corner of the top and suddenly the memories were too much. She tried to stop them, but in spite of her best efforts, a tear slipped down her cheek.

"What's wrong?" Luc murmured. She hadn't even seen him move and yet he was suddenly in front of her, tipping up her chin so he could look into her eyes. Without saying a word he gathered her into his arms and held her close, whispering words of comfort.

"He gave me such a wonderful childhood," she said through her tears, soaking Luc's shirt and not caring. "I never realized how hard he worked to be both mom and dad to me. I miss him so much."

"I know. But Marcus is in your heart and your soul." Luc's breath skittered across her skin, ruffling nerve endings that trembled at being so close to him. "Your dad will always be with you."

"Just like Jesus," Henry said, standing just beyond them, his gaze intent as it rested on them. "He said He'll always be with us, too."

"Yes, He did." Luc pulled back and peered into Holly's face. "Are you okay?" he asked softly.

"I'm fine. Just being a bit of a crybaby." She dashed away her tears and smiled at Henry. "Thank you for reminding me, sweetheart."

"Can we make the s'mores now?" Henry asked. "'Cept I don't know how."

"First Luc needs to make us some sticks to roast our marshmallows." She found his gaze unnerving and quickly veered her focus back to her supplies on the table.

Luc was her very good friend. But he'd never held her before. Not even after her father's funeral. It felt like something in their relationship had changed, become more intimate. And that scared Holly.

She watched as Luc showed Henry how to choose the perfect roasting stick from a nearby poplar tree. When Henry had selected his, Luc quickly whittled down the twig and began shaping the point with his pocket knife while Henry watched and, as usual, asked questions.

It wasn't that Holly hadn't liked Luc's arms

holding her, lending support. She had. Maybe too much. But she couldn't allow herself to dwell on how right it had felt. She couldn't afford silly girlish dreams about a cowboy on his horse because this wasn't a dream. Luc had told her time and again that he wasn't getting involved. His focus was on Henry.

So when the pair returned, she forced herself to smile as she slid the giant marshmallows onto their sticks and watched them roast the confections to a toasty brown. She had squares of chocolate on graham wafers ready and scooped up Henry's marshmallow before he lost it to the fire. She managed a carefree laugh with Luc when the boy tasted his treat and his eyes grew huge before he quickly asked for a second. And when Luc insisted she accept his marshmallow for her own treat, Holly thanked him, just as she always had done.

But deep inside the feeling that she'd soon be left out lingered like a blister. It wasn't anything the others did. It was more seeing how Luc and Henry bonded over the snack and later fishing that made her feel like a third wheel.

By the time the sun had sunk below the foothills, Henry drooped wearily. Holly just wanted to get home and mull over the day in private. That's when Luc's phone rang.

"Hi, Mayor… You do?… Oh." He paused, lifted his head and started at Holly. "Um, I guess

I could though I don't know anything about hosting that kind of thing." Suddenly his eyes brightened. "Yeah, you're right. I could ask Holly. Okay, I'll do it. Bye." By the time he'd pocketed his phone Luc was grinning.

"You could ask Holly to do what?" A flicker of worry built inside her. She'd hate to say no to Luc, but she needed to put some distance between them to sort out her feelings.

"The mayor says that each month someone involved with Family Ties hosts a potluck supper. Since I'm a volunteer and hopefully soon-to-be a parent, she suggested I hold the next potluck, probably next week." Excitement shone in his brown eyes then dimmed. "But I don't know anything about potlucks. Marsha said I should ask you for help."

"The potlucks are fun," she said without thinking. Her mind raced with ideas. "I always thought a theme party would be fun. Maybe a birthday theme? That could be a lot of fun. You sure have enough yard space."

"How would I do it?" Luc gave her that beseeching look that she never could resist. "Help me, Holly."

She'd gone and done it again, gotten herself involved when she was trying to opt out. She had a ton of sewing orders due, but they couldn't compare with the thrill of sharing hosting duties with Luc.

"Let's talk about it on the way back," she said, noticing how Henry dragged his feet. "Time to saddle up, Henry."

Moments later their horses were ambling toward Luc's ranch as Holly spouted potluck ideas left and right.

"You could print out birthday invitations," she said. "Specify birthday food so people will know what to bring. And you could supply dessert, which could be a big cake to celebrate everyone's birthday."

"Holly, I can't make a cake!" Luc cried, so loud that a sleeping Henry roused in the saddle in front of him.

"I made a cake with Ms. Hilda," Henry mumbled. "We could help you."

"A very good idea," Holly murmured. "Building bonds and all that." Luc frowned then nodded. "You could decorate the yard with balloons and make it look like a real party. People will love to bring their children because they won't have to find sitters."

"I'd need activities for the kids then." Luc frowned at her. "I don't think I'm much good at that."

"No time to learn like the present. After all, you're going to be a father," she reminded him with a wink.

They brainstormed all the way back. Only when they finally rode into the yard did Holly notice that dusk had crept across the ranch. By then Luc was really getting into the idea of hosting this party.

"I could have a bonfire and we could roast hot dogs," he mused aloud as he lifted Henry down and held the sleeping boy cradled in his arms. "Or do you think a fire would be too dangerous with kids around?"

"Why not discuss it with Abby? She'd be able to give you the best advice." Holly lifted his saddle packs off the horse and carried them into his house, noting how Henry's arms had automatically moved to circle Luc's neck.

The sweet sight of this big gentle man cradling the little boy made Holly sigh.

"He's beat." She could hear Luc's fondness for Henry in his voice. "I'm going to put him straight to bed. He can shower in the morning."

"I'll leave you to it then," Holly said quietly, needing to be alone to decipher her unusual feelings. "Thank you for a wonderful day. I had so much fun. Thanks for sharing Henry with me."

She smiled at Luc but his answering smile did odd things to her stomach so she brushed a light hand across Henry's cheek before kissing it then hurried out the door before Luc could coax her to stay.

Holly rode home quickly, her horse comfortable on the familiar paths. Her brain kept replaying moments throughout the day, special moments she'd tucked away to savor, moments when Luc had seemed like the soul mate she'd once hoped Ron might be.

How wrong she'd been about Ron. Everything she thought she'd known, everything she thought she'd loved had been mistaken. And now, as she pondered the day she'd spent with Luc, she thought perhaps she understood why.

She hadn't really loved Ron. She'd never felt the peculiar, catch-your-breath reaction with Ron that she'd felt this afternoon. Nor had she felt it with the father of her child. Infatuation, yes. But how could she have thought that was love?

Holly had always known her mother hadn't loved her father. Otherwise, why would she have left? Maybe that was why Holly craved that solid, steadfast, there-no-matter-what love in her own relationship. Other people found it. Abby had it with Cade. So why couldn't she find it?

With Luc?

The question nagged at her as she curried the horse and put him away for the night.

Did she want a relationship with Luc? He was her good friend, but he'd never been more than that. She'd never wanted him to be. Did she now? Was that the reason behind these unusual reactions to him?

Holly stepped inside her house. Her spirit dropped at the piles of fabric littering the dining room and the dream dissipated. Of course she didn't want a romantic relationship with Luc. She'd accepted that it was God's will for her to remain single so why was she asking herself these silly questions when she had tons of orders to sew and ship?

She brewed herself a cup of coffee and set to work finishing the late orders, muttering to herself as she sewed an incorrect seam and had to pick it out from the delicate lace dress meant for a baby dedication.

Wait a minute! This was work that had always lifted her spirit, made her happy. So why did it feel like a chore?

"This is what you do, Holly," she lectured out loud. "You make one-of-a-kind things for other people's kids. It's what you *love*," she emphasized.

That didn't help. A hank of glossy white satin lay sprawled across the sideboard. She rose and walked toward it, sliding her sensitive fingertips down the length, luxuriating in its weight and richness. Perfect for a new baby at a family event where friends and loved ones gathered to support the baby's parents as they promised to raise their child to know God.

A well of longing erupted inside. Holly could not deny it. She wanted the husband, the family, the friends *and* the child. She'd tried to suppress it, pretended she didn't crave what everyone else had. But those yearnings wouldn't stay neatly tucked inside.

Okay, she could never have the child she'd birthed. That child had another family, another mother now. She'd made that decision knowing full well it was final.

"But I was just a kid. I didn't realize—"

There was no point in going over it all again. Nothing had changed. She was still alone. Luc was her friend, but he didn't want marriage. He'd made that very clear. She'd tried to find happily-ever-after with Ron, but he hadn't been able to excuse her behavior. What God-fearing man could forgive a woman for giving her baby away in order to save her reputation?

For a while today Holly had let herself get caught up in the idea of her own romance but it was just a mirage, not reality.

Holly took another sip of her coffee then set it aside and began sewing, forcing everything from her mind but the work she needed to complete to pay for her father's medical supplies and eventually the renovations for her sewing room.

God didn't intend for her to be a wife or a mother. It was time to put those dreams away.

Chapter Seven

"I've already made a potato salad and a garden salad, but are you sure I can't help with something else for your potluck tonight?" Hilda asked Luc as she rebuttoned Henry's shirt where he'd left a gap.

"Thanks, Ms. Hilda, but I have about a hundred lists. I've checked and rechecked and I think I—" Luc grinned at Henry. "I think *we've* got it covered."

"Well, okay then." Hilda smoothed Henry's cowlick then stepped back and nodded in approval before turning to study Luc. "I do think this 'birthday' potluck is such a wonderful idea. We who volunteer for Family Ties have never done a birthday theme before. It's going to be a fun night tonight, especially for Holly."

"Why Holly?" Luc asked, slightly confused.

"Because her birthday is tomorrow." She frowned at him. "Don't tell me you've forgotten the shenanigans Marcus went through to celebrate her special day?"

The thing was, Luc had forgotten.

"I remember when Holly was just a wee thing and her dad wanted to surprise her with a pony." Hilda chuckled. "The whole town was in on getting that little pinto pony to the ranch and hiding it so she wouldn't find it till morning."

"Her birthday is tomorrow." Luc checked his watch to confirm the date and frowned. How could he have forgotten? More to the point, what was he going to do to make it especially nice for Holly, not the least because she'd been there helping him prepare?

"You didn't remember?" Hilda frowned at him as if she suspected he was addled by the sun.

"How could I forget?" Luc said with a laugh, as if he'd known all along. With sudden inspiration he asked, "Ms. Hilda, you don't have any strings of those fairy lights folks use at Christmas, do you?"

"Why, yes, I do. I have several boxes. I intended to put them up last Christmas but then I went on that trip and didn't have time so they've never been used. Why?" She inclined her head like a curious bird.

"May I borrow them? For the potluck tonight?"

"Well…"

It took a little explaining but finally Hilda approved his newest idea. Luc loaded the lights in his truck, thanked her for them then headed over to the bakery to add a birthday cake to his order and tell them Abby would pick it up. He wasn't taking any chances of making a cake that could ruin his party.

"You sure have a lot of errands." Henry trotted hard to keep pace as Luc led him through the five-and-dime store for balloons, some multicolored streamers and a bag of candy.

"Yes, I do. Hey, there's Mayor Marsha. I need to talk to her." Luc handed him the items and gave him ten dollars to pay for it while he explained his change of plans to Marsha. "It's Holly's birthday tomorrow so I thought we'd turn tonight's potluck into a surprise party, if that's okay with you."

"Sounds like a fantastic idea," Marsha enthused. "It will make Holly's birthday less sad for this first year without her father."

"I know the town has some kind of phone list where one person calls the next. Could you use it to send some calls around so folks know we're celebrating her birthday?" Luc asked.

"Something special for Holly." Marsha gave Luc a knowing glance. "Leave it to me." She waggled her fingers goodbye before hurrying away. Luc stared at her disappearing figure, confused by that look.

"Here's the change," Henry said, tugging on

Luc's pant leg to get his attention. "What's this candy for?"

"I'll explain later. Now we need to go to the florist." Once he picked out the flowers and arranged for them to be delivered to Holly tomorrow morning, Luc drove back to his ranch mentally reviewing the tasks still to be done for tonight.

"What's my job?" Henry demanded when they arrived at the ranch.

"You fill this with the candy." He showed Henry how to ease the candy through the hole in the rainbow piñata he'd bought earlier. "While you work at that, I'm going to hang Ms. Hilda's lights."

"But you told Holly you weren't going to hang any lights for the potluck," Henry said. Looking suddenly bashful he added, "I heard you say that at church on Sunday."

"I wasn't going to hang them," Luc said, feeling a little bashful himself.

"So why are you?" As usual, Henry was full of questions.

Luc really liked his inquisitive side. Henry's desire to learn was refreshing, but Luc wasn't crazy about explaining his change of heart regarding the lights. Mostly because he hadn't yet figured out himself why it mattered so much. Judging by the look on Henry's face, he wasn't about to leave the subject without getting an answer.

"Holly loves fairy lights. Since her birthday is tomorrow, I think we should do something extra special for her." Luc paused in unpacking the lights to glance at Henry.

Those big brown eyes held a steady bead on him. "You like Holly, don't you?"

"Yes," Luc admitted. "We're good friends."

"Holly has lots of friends," Henry said.

"She sure does," Luc agreed, thinking how true it was.

"Know why? 'Cause she makes people feel better." Henry returned to stuffing candy into the piñata.

"You mean with medicine?" Henry shook his head. Curious to hear his response Luc asked, "Why, then?"

"She makes them feel better inside." Henry patted his chest. "In here. She always smiles and says nice things and tries to help."

"Yes, she does." Luc couldn't smother his own smile as he draped the tiny lights from tree to tree, creating what would become an arbor of light after dark.

Holly certainly made him feel better inside but that was friendship. It didn't mean anything more. Slightly unsettled by the turn of his thoughts, Luc mentally listed all the reasons there could be nothing more than friendship between them.

Remember the hit to your ego when Sarah

dumped you? Remember how hard it was to get back your self-esteem? Remember that hollow sick feeling in your stomach every time you went to some activity at church and realized you didn't fit in the couples' groups or the married groups anymore? That again you were a single man in a church full of families?

Luc remembered all of it. Too well. He could close his eyes and it would all come back, that feeling that he wasn't enough, that he had no pictures of his kids to proudly show off like other men, that he couldn't make teasing jokes about his wife.

But he didn't want a relationship, certainly not that stomach-turning reaction on realizing that the woman he'd trusted completely hated everything about him. It all rushed back like a tidal wave. No way would he risk going through all that misery again.

Yet, in a way, Luc didn't want to forget any of what he'd gone through because he didn't want to make the same mistake. He had no desire to pour his love into a relationship only to be dumped all over again.

At first he'd seen the breaking of his engagement as something terrible, but now he realized that it'd been a blessing. At least it had saved him from the same fate as his buddies. So did that mean his broken engagement had been part of God's will?

"You're not eating all those candies, are you, Henry?" he called, suddenly aware of the silence.

"Just two peanut butter ones. I love peanut butter." Henry's lips smacked. Luc squinted and saw streaks of chocolate and peanut butter smeared across his face, especially around his lips.

"Henry, it's not good for you to eat too many—" He cut off the reprimand when Henry tossed a candy at him.

"You like peanut butter, too." Henry selected another candy for himself with a sneaky grin.

"Yes, I do." Luc grinned and popped the chocolate in his mouth, almost laughing aloud at Henry's wit. "But that's enough. We don't want to spoil our supper."

"Just one more, okay?" The candy was in Henry's mouth before Luc could protest.

Luc gave the boy a stern look, and Henry went back to stuffing the piñata. Luc returned to stringing another set of lights. A tickle of laughter burst out as he envisioned Holly's surprise when she saw the lights twinkling above her tonight. He started to whistle and then paused. What was all this bubbly feeling about?

"Where are you going to hang the rainbow?" Henry asked.

"I don't know." Luc climbed down from his ladder, surveyed his work and nodded. It looked good and until they were switched on,

Holly would never even guess he'd put them up. "Where do you think the piñata should hang?"

"Is it just for kids?" When Luc assured him it was, Henry surveyed the yard then pointed. "Over there. Then they won't hit anyone if they miss."

"Excellent choice. Can you hold it while I hang it?" A few minutes later the rainbow gently waved in the warm afternoon breeze. "Good job, Henry."

"Is it gonna rain?" Henry asked, scanning the sky.

"No, that's not a rain sky. One day I'll teach you about clouds." Luc smiled at the very thought of such a delightful future. "Anyway we can't have rain on the night of our party for Holly," he chided as he tickled Henry under his ribs and then swung him in a circle. And surely nothing could stop his plans to adopt this precious boy.

They collapsed together on the ground. The feel of Henry in his arms, the sound of his giggles in his ears brought a lump to Luc's throat. Was there anything more blessed than a child's laughter? Wanting to enjoy every ounce of pleasure with Henry while he was here, Luc collapsed on the grass and lay back, pointing out the cloud formations to the almost-son pressed against his side.

It should have been perfection, but some

niggling part of Luc wished Holly was here to share these moments with Henry and him.

"I hope I get to live here soon." Henry lay with his head tucked under Luc's arm.

"I hope so, too, Henry. I hope it more than anything." Luc sent up a prayer before he hugged him close. For the hundredth time he assured himself that adopting Henry had to be God's will.

"Do we have chores before the party?" Henry sat up when Luc nodded. "Should I change into my work clothes?"

"You know where they are?" Luc asked.

"In the closet in *my* room." Henry jumped to his feet. "I'll race you to the house."

"No rush," Luc told him, but he doubted Henry heard as he took off running to the room Luc had painted blue because Henry loved the color.

"I'm ready." Henry returned to the kitchen a few moments later proudly dressed in the baggy overalls and red plaid shirt Luc had bought him. He danced from foot to foot, clearly impatient. "Hurry, Luc. We don't want to be late for the party."

"How could we be late? It's going to be held here," Luc grumbled, dumping out his coffee after only a taste. "We can hardly miss it."

Truthfully, Luc felt the same excitement as Henry, but he couldn't decide if it was because of

Henry's presence in his home or because Holly was coming. Probably both, he decided then thrust away the tiresome warning his brain kept offering about getting too close to Holly. How perfect that Henry seemed to love helping with jobs around the ranch.

They worked together companionably with Henry asking his usual plethora of questions. When chores were done they went inside to shower. Luc went first while Henry enjoyed one last candy that somehow hadn't made it into the piñata. Then it was Henry's turn to shower. When his squeaky tones warbled from the bathroom all the way to the kitchen where Luc was polishing his boots, Luc sat still and let the sound of it penetrate to his heart.

This is what I want, God.

He realized the only other time he'd felt this burst of joy was when he was with Holly. Luc's world came alive when Holly stopped by just as it did when he was with Henry.

"Lord, I love this kid," he said, his heart full. "Please let him move here soon. If that's Your will," he added after a second's thought. But how could this not be God's will? Henry needed a home and Luc needed Henry. And Holly would be there for both of them.

Luc was savoring that thought as he smoothed

down Henry's cowlick when Holly drove into the yard.

"Remember what I said, Henry," Luc murmured.

"I know. It's a surprise." Henry grinned at him then took off running to meet Holly.

The exuberance and affection in their reunion brought a wave of emotion that made Luc gulp. Holly, clad in formfitting jeans and a white shirt, scooped Henry into her arms and swung him around. Luc's gaze was riveted on her face. Pure unadulterated joy rested there as she clung to Henry. Then she murmured something in his ear and leaned back to smile at his response.

Henry seemed just as enthralled with his arms wrapped around her neck. Holly tossed Luc a grin as she set Henry on the ground. That smile made Luc's evening suddenly brighter.

"We're going to have so much fun tonight," Holly said tweaking Henry's nose.

"I know." Henry's little chest puffed out with pride. "I helped Luc get ready."

Luc admired the way Holly crouched down to listen with rapt attention as the boy enthused about the things he and Luc had prepared. Holly could deny it all she wanted, but she was a natural mother.

Once or twice Luc opened his lips, ready to intervene when it seemed Henry would give away the secret. But Henry stopped in time, gave him a smile and changed the subject.

"What's going on?" Holly asked when Henry rushed off to greet a friend from school.

"He's excited about tonight. What did you bring for the potluck?" Luc couldn't tear his eyes off her. She glowed, her cheeks pink, her blue eyes shining and her curls bobbing behind the white ribbon that held them off her face.

"I baked some fresh rolls. I hope they taste all right." Holly pointed to the big tray of golden buns she'd already set on the table.

"Why wouldn't they be okay?" he asked, suddenly realizing how hungry he was.

"Right in the middle of mixing them I got called into town for a delivery. Maxine Mallory had her baby this afternoon." She made a face, and he knew exactly what it meant.

"I'm guessing that was more of a production than the usual birth?" Luc smirked when she rolled her eyes.

"Everything is more of a production with Maxine." She gave him a wry look then shook her head. "They now have another son, which makes four. A darling sweet child that yelled once when he arrived before settling into his mother's arms. Seven pounds seven ounces. Healthy and happy."

"That's the outcome you like," he said, knowing it was true.

"Yes," Holly agreed haltingly. "It was just a

bit disconcerting that Maxine had such a short labor, especially when her due date is still two weeks off and there's nothing in Seth Treple's notes to indicate he thought she would be early. I don't like surprises like that."

The tightness of Holly's voice told Luc she'd been worried for her patient. He required no explanation for her expressions. A breathless sigh meant Holly was tired. Tiny frown lines on her smooth forehead told him she'd probably been chastised by the very vocal Maxine. The slump of her shoulders said she'd given her best for mom and baby. The twinkle in her eye meant she was thrilled she'd been there to help deliver the baby and was now looking forward to a relaxing evening.

Luc blinked. When had this communication without words happened? Could Holly read him as easily?

"What can I do to help, Luc?" She ruffled Henry's hair when he returned.

"Me 'n Luc already did it all," Henry told her, stretching tall. "It's for you to relax."

Luc had never been more proud of his would-be son.

"Really?" Holly glanced from Henry to Luc.

"Henry's right. We've done most of it." He shrugged at her surprised look. "Now what we need is a hostess to make everyone feel welcome."

"I'm your girl." She shrugged as if that was

such a little thing to ask. Holly was a born hostess. "But if you need something else, ask."

"Your work is about to begin." Luc inclined his head toward the road. "Isn't that Cade's truck?"

"Meeting and greeting is exactly what I feel like doing tonight." She tossed him a smile before hurrying toward Abby to take one of the twins. "These two are growing like weeds," Luc heard her say. "I don't suppose they'll fit the outfits I made for very long. I better get sewing again."

Was he the only one who glimpsed the rush of longing filling Holly's face as she held the baby? A second later that look was gone, hidden behind her ever-present smile, leaving Luc even more curious about the sewing that filled her life.

"You're using my kids as an excuse to sew something new," Abby teased as she set the twins in a playpen Cade set up.

Certain the children were settled and happy with their toys, Holly touched Abby's arm.

"Do you have a moment? I've been meaning to talk to you but it's been so hectic."

Luc exchanged greetings with Cade who was quickly drawn away by Henry who wanted to show him the piñata. Concerned by the intensity of Holly's voice, Luc lingered to listen in on the conversation.

"I've been trying to get Petra to confide in me, but it's not going well." Holly rubbed the back of her neck. "She's hiding something about her pregnancy and I'd prefer to know what before she goes into labor."

"You think she's that close?" Abby asked.

"Pretty sure." Holly nodded. "I saw her again today. The baby's dropped."

"But she keeps telling me she has almost a month to go." Abby sighed. "Running Family Ties isn't as easy as I thought it would be. I appreciate your help, Holly."

"Anytime. Family Ties is making a real difference to moms who have nowhere to go to have their babies. I'm really glad you decided to make sheltering them a part of the Family Ties ministry. It takes a lot of stress off the mother when she knows she has a safe place to stay until the birth." Holly handed Abby a glass of the punch Luc had made earlier. "Or would you rather have coffee?"

"This is great." Abby drew him into the conversation. "Luc, your place looks wonderful. I see you've added a tree swing for Henry."

"And a sandbox. Isn't that cover ingenious?" Holly enthused with a wink at him. "Luc built it so it keeps the sand clean and dry when Henry's not using it."

"He's a lucky boy." Abby's gaze tracked Henry's progress as he raced around the yard pretending to be an airplane. "He's certainly loosening up."

"Does that mean the adoption will go through?" Luc asked, wishing he didn't sound so needy. He knew Holly worried he was investing himself too deeply in an outcome that might not happen.

"Things are progressing very well," was all Abby would say. "We have three new boys to find homes for," she told them. "But they're babies. Are you interested, Luc?"

"I want to adopt Henry," he said, meeting her gaze and holding it. "I have to see that through."

"Committed, I see. Good for you. Oh, here comes Hilda. And Mayor Marsha." Abby turned away to speak to her friends.

"I'm always intimidated by that woman," Luc said to Holly in a low tone.

"Who? Mayor Marsha?" Holly chuckled. "She's been a real blessing to Abby with Family Ties. She got town council to approve so many things to make the adoption agency possible. Hi, Mayor," she said.

"Good to see *both* of you." Mayor Marsha winked at Luc then patted Holly's shoulder. "Good work with Maxine," she said. "Couldn't have been easy. I could hear her yelling at you from my office."

"Now, Mayor." Holly's cheeks wore an interesting shade of pink. "You know that we never hold anything against a woman who's in labor. It's hard work to have a baby."

Luc gave Holly a lot of credit for that answer.

From the look on her face earlier, he'd guessed she'd been irritated by Maxine as she coached the woman through labor, but if so she wasn't willing to put down Maxine publicly.

It was their little secret. He liked sharing it with her. Too bad she wasn't as open with him about why she was always sewing. They couldn't all be baby clothes, could they? Buffalo Gap didn't have that many newborns.

Luc also wondered if she'd opened her dad's trunk yet. He'd hinted six ways through Sunday that Holly might find something important inside, but she never seemed to take the bait. Marcus had made him promise that when Holly had mourned enough, Luc would get her to look inside. Luc intended to keep his promise.

Now he moved through the crowd, noticing how well he and Holly meshed as they welcomed new arrivals and invited the guests to set up their chairs around the big iron tractor rim he'd placed on bare ground to contain a campfire.

Moments later Mayor Marsha rapped her cane against the table leg to get everyone's attention. After she'd issued strict warnings to the excited children about going too near the fire pit, Luc lit the tinder he'd laid earlier. He'd been worried about having a campfire but as he looked around, he saw that each parent monitored their children.

"Pastor Don's going to say grace for us and

then we'll dig into this delicious food," Marsha said. "Thank you for hosting us, Luc."

Luc nodded then edged through the crowd to squeeze in next to Holly. Just before he bowed his head he felt someone's stare. He glanced up and saw Marsha watching him with a knowing smile. In a flush of embarrassment that she'd caught him trying to get close to Holly, Luc bowed his head, listening to the words of gratitude as he savored the pleasure of rubbing shoulders with Holly. She'd been right to encourage him to host this potluck. A sense of overwhelming pleasure flooded him that all these people had come to his home. Maybe soon he'd have a son and host another celebration.

When the grace ended, a line formed at the food table. Luc was relieved to note there were plenty of choices that offered something for everyone. When the children had eaten, Hilda and Henry provided the makings for s'mores. Soon all of the kids and some of the adults were sticky with marshmallows and chocolate.

"Smart idea to put out basins and water pitchers for wash stations throughout the yard," Holly whispered as she passed by. "You're a natural host."

Feeling ten feet tall after such praise, Luc made sure everyone had what they needed before grabbing his own plate of food. He deliberately sat next to Pastor Don in a spot away from the others because he wanted to pose some questions to the minister.

"I've prayed and prayed but I still don't have a strong feeling about God's plan for me, Pastor," he explained.

"Knowing God's will isn't like putting a quarter into a machine and getting an answer out, Luc." The pastor smiled. "Sometimes we wish it was that simple but the truth is, just getting answers to your prayers isn't enough. The point of prayer is to develop a friendship so you can talk with God. It takes time and patience to understand God, and even more to really hear what He wants to say."

"But I thought God had a plan for my life. Why doesn't He just tell me what it is?" Luc persisted even though he felt slightly foolish for asking.

"Of course He has a plan." Pastor Don nodded. "But that doesn't mean God will dump the complete job description on you like in one of those action movies. I believe that learning our purpose is more of an unfolding that causes us to grow, like a plant that gets rain and sunshine and wind, and slowly matures through all of it."

Luc frowned, not totally clear.

"The way I see it, maybe today God's purpose was for you to host this potluck, which is delicious by the way." Don set aside the bones from his fried chicken and smiled at Luc. "Maybe tomorrow His purpose for you will be something far harder."

"That sounds ominous." Luc frowned.

"It shouldn't," Don said. "The point is to listen and be ready. God never asked you to do great things for Him, Luc. What He asks is for you to allow His greatness to shine through you."

"You're saying that learning God's will isn't necessarily a 'Paul on the road to Damascus moment' that will tell me my future," Luc said, feeling his way. "It's more about being available and communing with God so He can tell me my purpose for today?"

"Yes. It's not always for us to know the big picture but the more we're in tune with God, the more we'll find out His will." Don rose. "Don't get frustrated. Be patient. Talk to God. Let Him speak to you. Read Romans 8, especially verses twenty-six to twenty-eight. Then come and talk to me again."

"Thanks, Pastor." Luc grimaced. "I'm sorry to interrupt your dinner."

"You didn't." Pastor Don chuckled. "Let's go see if there's any of that strawberry pie left. I love strawberry pie."

"We're going to have birth—er, cake, too, so leave some room." Luc moved around the group, picking up discarded plates and cups. He looked for Abby, found her next to Cade, each holding a baby and a bottle. He walked over.

"I guess you're looking for the birthday cake," Abby said in a low voice. "It's in the back of the truck. Want me to help you?"

"No, you're busy. I'll do it. Just make sure you lead us in the singing," he reminded.

"What are you two whispering about?" Holly appeared at his side, a quizzical look on her face.

"I was going to ask Abby's help with something but she's busy. Care to take her place?" He waited, puzzling out how to do this and still surprise her.

"What do you need?" Holly asked.

"Could you clear a space on the table and have some plates and forks ready? I'm going to get a special dessert I ordered." He watched her face, loving the way she bit her bottom lip to stop from asking him what it was. Luc knew how hard that was for curious Holly.

"No problem," she agreed.

"Now I need— Ooh, there you are." Luc chuckled when Henry suddenly appeared. "Come on, partner."

"But what about the piñata?" Henry asked.

"Okay," Luc agreed sighing inside at the delay. "We can do that first."

Henry dragged Holly with him to watch the kids take turns hitting the rainbow. She cheered as loudly as anyone when it finally spilled candies all over the ground.

Pockets and cheeks bulging, Henry grinned

at Luc while Holly and the other ladies helped clean up the remains of the piñata.

"Now we can get the cake," he whispered with a sideways glance at Holly.

"Not that you'll be able to eat any of it after stuffing yourself with that candy," Luc said with a chuckle.

Henry simply grinned.

At the truck, Luc found the cake and took off the lid. A box of candles lay tucked to one side, as the bakery had promised. He let Henry stick all twenty-seven candles in the cake then carried it to the table.

"Happy birthday a day early, Holly," Luc said while Henry drew her forward.

Immediately, Henry burst into the birthday song with Abby's swift support. The guests joined in. Holly stood wide-eyed, trying to smile despite the wetness on her lashes.

"I thought this was supposed to be a community birthday party," she scolded when the song was over.

"It is. But since your birthday's tomorrow, we wanted to make it a special day for you." Luc savored her pleasure.

"Blow out the candles," Henry demanded. "They're melting all over the cake."

"Smart boy," Hilda praised as she patted Henry's shoulder. "Blow, Holly."

"There are way too many candles," Holly joked.

She puffed up her cheeks so the kids laughed then blew out all except one candle.

"That means you've got a boyfriend." Henry's grin stretched wide as he called out to the other kids. "Holly's got a boyfriend." Then Henry looked directly at her and said in a voice loud enough for everyone to hear, "Is it Luc?"

Luc wished he could melt into the dirt of his ranch as embarrassment turned Holly's cheeks hot pink. He should have counseled Henry but it was too late to worry about that now. He needed to do something to get the focus off her.

"Of course I'm her friend," he said, swallowing his own embarrassment as everyone gawked at them. He grabbed a plate and held it out as Holly cut the cake. "Come on, folks. Let's see if we can make a dent in Holly's birthday cake."

Thankfully, the group eagerly moved forward. Holly cut large slices that had most of the women groaning and most of the men smacking their lips. When the last guest was served, Luc insisted she enjoy a slice of her cake.

"It was nice of you to do this, Luc." Holly spoke softly so the others wouldn't overhear. "But you didn't have to."

"We all wanted to make your birthday special, even if we are a day early." For some reason he didn't comprehend he didn't want her to know he'd been the instigator. He touched her hand so she would look at him. "I'm sorry if Henry embarrassed you." Her skin felt warm against his.

"It was a nice kind of embarrassment," she murmured before Mayor Marsha called for order.

"Don't worry, folks," Marsha said when someone groaned. "Our only official business tonight is to celebrate Holly's birthday." She chuckled. "So let's visit and enjoy this lovely evening God's given us. A toast to the birthday girl."

There was a loud cheer and a crackly tinkling of plastic glasses. Luc stood in the shadows of the trees savoring the look on Holly's face as folks handed her one gag gift after another. But his biggest pleasure came when he connected the fairy lights and her face lay bathed in their ethereal glow.

Holly paused in reading a card and looked up. She seemed to delight in the delicate glow then lowered her head and scanned his yard, not pausing her search until her gaze met his.

Thank you.

The silent message hit him loud and clear. Luc nodded and mouthed, *You're welcome.*

Someone, probably Henry since he'd helped Luc set things up, started the boom box and soft dreamy music filled the area. Children who had fallen asleep were wrapped in warm quilts and left to rest while their parents danced in a slow rhythm to the dreamy music. Luc wondered who had chosen such romantic music. He jumped a little when he heard a familiar voice in his ear.

"Are you going to dance with me, Luc, on my almost-birthday?" Holly held out her arms, her smile faraway.

"Of course." He slid his arm around her narrow waist and laid his palm against hers before leading her in the mesmerizing beat of the song.

Swaying together as one, they danced under the fairy lights and into the shadows. They danced through friends' laughter and the occasional cry of a fractious child. Luc didn't know how long they danced; he only knew he wanted it to go on forever.

"Did you notice?" Holly's breath feathered over his ear. "They've left and we're all alone." She drew away the length of his arms, her beautiful eyes gleaming. "It was a wonderful birthday evening, Luc. Thank you."

Holly leaned forward and pressed a soft, sweet kiss against his lips. Then she eased from his grip and pointed to a note left on the table that had held the potluck dishes.

Henry's with me. See you. Hilda.

"I'll help you clean up." Holly began gathering leftovers but Luc put his hands on hers.

"No, don't do that."

Holly smiled a funny little smile. "Are you sure?"

He nodded. "I'm sure."

And he was. He was sure that it was time for Holly to go home and past time for him to step back. Being with Holly so much lately had made him emotionally vulnerable. At this moment all Luc wanted to do was keep her in his arms, maybe return that kiss she'd laid on him.

But that wasn't going to happen because he knew too well that fairy tales didn't always end happily ever after and neither did most marriages.

"Go home, Holly. Enjoy tomorrow. You deserve it."

"Oh." She looked confused but eventually turned toward her car. "Okay. Good night Luc," she said, turning back once to say, "Thank you."

"Happy birthday, Holly."

Luc watched until the faint red of her taillights disappeared into the night. Then with a sigh of acceptance he unplugged the lights, gathered the remaining debris and poured water over the fire. That was what he needed to do to his strange feelings, because nothing could come of them.

Tomorrow he'd find out Holly's schedule and work out one of his own so he could finish her renovation when she wasn't around.

"You were a lucky man, Marcus," he muttered as he restored the kitchen to its usual neatness. "Holly is a wonderful woman. I'll do my best to help however she needs me, but I won't let her become more than a good friend. I can't."

Chapter Eight

A few days later Holly drove home after a consultation with Abby, preoccupied by the young girl so close to giving birth.

"Petra's afraid of something," Abby had insisted.

"Or someone. The question is who or what?" Holly mused aloud. "So far she's resisted all my efforts to find out. But I'll keep trying."

"I wish she'd realize we only want to help." Abby had waved off Holly's offer to stay, insisting she'd spent far too many hours at Family Ties already.

Now as Holly drove into her yard, she noticed Luc's truck parked under the big poplar tree she and her father had planted on her fifth birthday. For a moment the tree-planting memories marking each year of her life overtook Holly and she paused to let them roll through her mind.

"I miss you, Dad." She took a bracing breath

and brushed her fingers across her eyes to erase evidence of her tears.

Odd that Luc was still here. Ever since the night of the potluck he'd avoided her, and Holly was fairly certain she knew why. Because she'd kissed him. If she'd thought twice she wouldn't have done it. But it had been so sweet of him to painstakingly hang those lights just for her.

The town grapevine still buzzed with talk about all the work Luc had gone to in order to make the night before her birthday special. She'd been embarrassed to walk away and leave him with the mess, but he'd been so insistent she go. And truthfully, it had hurt to realize her kiss had left him unmoved.

Not that Holly was looking for anything romantic with Luc, but the way he'd held her, danced with her—it seemed to Holly there'd been something growing between them, something deeper than the casual friendship they'd shared earlier.

"Is something wrong?"

Startled by the voice she'd been imagining, Holly jumped and let out a squeal. "Stop creeping up on me!"

"Really?" Luc lifted one eyebrow then glanced down at his cowboy boots. "Creeping? In these?" He shrugged. "Sorry." He turned and walked toward his truck.

"Luc." Holly had blown it and she knew it.

She climbed out of her jeep and hurried toward him. "I'm sorry. It's just that you caught me at a bad moment."

"Oh?" He looked at her with those eyes, and it was like being x-rayed, as if he saw right through her.

"I drove into the yard and noticed that tree." She ignored his dubious look. "I got caught up remembering when Dad and I planted it and, well, I miss him."

"I miss him, too, Holly," he said in a quiet tone. The stern lines that had kept Luc's face impassive a mere moment earlier now dissipated with his soft smile. "Marcus left a big impact on a lot of people."

As you have, Holly thought.

"I was going to tell you that I've about finished with your room." He frowned. "I still have the floor to do but I can't do that with your dad's trunk shoved in the corner. Aren't you ever going to empty it?"

"What is it with you and that trunk?" she asked with asperity. "Can't you just shove it into the dining room or something?"

"I guess." He shoved back his cowboy hat to rub his eyebrow. "But I think you should deal with it. Why keep ignoring it?"

How could she tell him?

"I'm afraid to open it. I don't know what he

has in there and…" She couldn't finish, couldn't reveal what was at the root of her hesitation.

"You think he was keeping some secret from you?" Luc frowned again. "That doesn't sound like your dad."

"Yes, it does." She managed a laugh to cover her nervousness. "It sounds exactly like Marcus Janzen to go to great lengths to keep something from his baby girl, especially if he worried it would make her sad."

"I never thought of that." Luc gave her a strange look. Before she could decipher it, he looked away. "What do you think he was hiding?" His voice sounded almost hesitant.

"Something to do with my mother maybe?" It was a relief to finally say it. "I think he always hoped I'd connect with her. It would be like him to feel that was his fatherly duty."

"So what's to be afraid of?" Luc asked.

"I have no desire to try to build some kind of connection after all these years." Exasperated that he didn't understand, Holly blurted, "She gave birth to me but there is no emotional connection. Not like I have with you or Henry."

"Maybe you could build one," he said quietly.

"I don't want to invest myself and be dumped again. Don't you understand?" She was tired of trying to explain how she felt without letting Luc see the bitterness that still festered inside over her mother's treatment of her father. So she turned and strode back to her car.

"Holly, I'm sorry." Luc caught up and grabbed her arm. "It's just that I don't want you to later regret not connecting."

"I won't." He let her go and she removed her purse and a grocery bag from her vehicle. "In all these years she hasn't made any effort to see me. Seeking her out now would be trying to force a connection that neither of us truly wants."

"Then what are you afraid of?" Luc said, his brows drawn together.

"That Dad will have left a note asking me to do just that. I'd have to do it, if he asked," she said.

"So open the trunk." Luc crossed his arms over his chest and stared at her.

"I'll get around to it." Holly walked toward the house leaving Luc standing where he was. When she reached the door, she turned. "Hilda's bringing Henry out for dinner. You're welcome to join us."

"Henry, huh?" He stood there, obviously considering her offer.

"Yes, Henry and steak and blueberry pie," she said curtly, irritated that her presence didn't seem to matter to him. "Dinner's at six. If you're not interested, fine."

Apparently startled by her brusqueness, Luc opened and closed his mouth. Disgusted with his slow response and remembering a time when he would have eagerly sought out her company and her cooking, Holly blew out a sigh of frustration that ruffled her bangs. She went inside. Good thing she'd quashed those silly romantic daydreams because Luc certainly wasn't interested in her.

"And I'm not opening that stupid trunk yet, either, Luc Cramer," she grumbled, shooting the inanimate article a nasty glare as she passed the second bedroom. She'd started toward her room to change clothes when the front door opened.

"I'd like to come for dinner with you and Henry. I'll go do my chores, change and be back by six. Thank you." After that stilted speech, Luc left.

A slow smile crept across her face.

Holly changed and prepared dinner while puzzling over his attitude. In the past week Luc hadn't sought out her advice and help once. Was that because his adoption plans were proceeding smoothly? That dismaying thought made her pause. Once Luc had permanent custody of Henry, would she be left out?

She was bothered by that thought. She didn't want to relinquish the closeness she and Luc had developed since her father's death. She'd grown accustomed to Luc's protective watch and hated the thought that he would no longer be there for her as he had been.

Perhaps asking him to dinner was a good idea that should be repeated later this week. Or maybe she should change it up with a picnic or a suggestion to accompany Luc and Henry on an outing.

"Inveigling yourself like that is pathetic," she mumbled.

But so was sitting at home sewing baby clothes for someone else when she could be with Luc and Henry. When had her beloved sewing taken such a backseat?

"I'm here," Henry announced, shoving open the door and stepping inside the house. Hilda stood behind him, trying without success to tame his cowlick.

"I didn't even hear you drive up," Holly apologized after hugging the little boy. "It's good of you to bring him out here, Hilda. Would you like to join us for dinner?"

"No, thanks." Hilda preened a little then leaned forward to whisper, "I have a dinner date."

"You look lovely." And she did with that flush of rose coloring her cheeks and anticipation lighting her eyes. "I hope you have a wonderful time," Holly told her.

"I will. Dennis Canterbury is a nice fellow." She smiled at Holly's confused look. "Dennis is the grandfather of that baby girl you delivered this morning."

"Of course. How silly of me to have forgotten." A video of this morning's delivery with friends and family eagerly awaiting the birth of a darling boy with big blue eyes and blond hair played in her memory, creating a block in Holly's throat. "Dennis has a beautiful grandchild," she managed to say around it.

If only she hadn't given her son away, her father would have had a grandchild, too.

"I'd better get going." Hilda patted her freshly set hair. "Do you think this hair color is too bold for a woman of my age?"

"I think you look nice," Henry said, his head tilted to one side as he observed her.

"So do I." Holly slid her arm across Henry's shoulders and smiled at him. "And Henry and I have the best judgment." She winked at the boy.

"Well, I don't know." A faint frown drew lines around Hilda's eyes.

"Don't fuss," Holly ordered. "I'll bring Henry home later and put him to bed at the usual time if you're not home."

"Thank you, dear. You know where the key is." Hilda reached out to smooth Henry's stubborn hair but stopped midreach. She sighed, shook her head and walked to the door.

"Bye," Holly called out at the same time as Henry. They looked at each other and Hilda and all three of them burst into laughter.

This was what Holly wanted. Friends, family. A person to share her life with. She knew she didn't deserve it, not after what she'd done.

That didn't stop the wanting, not that it would do her any good.

"Am I too early?" Luc asked through the screen door.

"Just in time," Holly told him with a smile. Because he always was.

Luc patted Holly's shoulder in his best avuncular manner. Dinner was done and he was looking forward to spending time with Henry and her when she got a phone call. Petra was in labor.

She looked around at the messy kitchen, but Luc preempted her objection.

"Leave the dishes to Henry and me. You go help that girl at Family Ties. She needs you."

"Petra sounded scared." Holly's voice brimmed with worry. "She kept telling me she wasn't due for ages but I knew better. I should have—"

"You can't blame yourself," he said. "You always say babies have their own schedules."

"True." She tucked her phone in her pocket. "What about— Scratch that. I know you can handle anything."

"Almost." Luc grinned.

Holly rolled her eyes. She hugged Henry before striding to the door then at the last minute turned. "I promised Hilda I'd get Henry to bed at her place if she wasn't home by eight thirty."

"Go, Holly," Luc said. "We'll be fine. Take

care of Petra. Henry and I will take care of that blueberry pie you made."

"Like I didn't already know that." She hurried out the door. A moment later he heard the roar of her car's motor and the crunch of gravel as she sped away.

"Okay, buddy." Luc ruffled Henry's hair. "It's up to you and me to get this place shipshape for Holly."

"Does shipshape mean cleaning?" Henry asked, his nose wrinkled in repugnance.

"Sure does," Luc assured him with a smile. "Holly made the meal. We clean up. You want to wash the dishes?"

"And get my hands wet?" Henry looked so scandalized Luc burst into laughter.

"Okay, you can dry."

They spent the next few minutes returning the kitchen to its usual immaculate condition. Henry found a domino train game on Holly's shelf. They played until Luc saw Henry's head droop.

"Time to get you back to Ms. Hilda's." Luc smiled when Henry didn't argue.

Hilda was home and waiting for her charge. She sent Henry to prepare for bed then listened to Luc's explanation about Holly.

"So if you can handle it from here, I guess I'll head home," Luc said. "G'night, Henry," he called.

Henry came flying downstairs. Luc relaxed into his hug, savoring the precious moment.

Please, God, let him be mine soon.

"I hope that Petra girl isn't playing a game with Holly." Hilda escorted him to the front door. "Something isn't on the up and up with that girl."

"How do you know that?" Luc asked, curious about the comment.

"I've been by Family Ties a few times, Luc. I've heard Petra tell Abby wild, fanciful stories. I've even caught her in a lie myself." Hilda's lips pursed. "Holly's a good girl. She our town treasure. I don't want her hurt."

"You're a town treasure, too, Hilda." Luc hugged her then ducked out the door. "Thanks for watching out for Henry."

"He's a joy," Hilda said. "I'll be sorry when he leaves."

As Luc drove through town he realized Henry had touched more than his own life. Surely God would keep him here, let him be raised among people who really cared about him.

He noticed that the light at the church was on and decided to stop. Andy, the most recent casualty in the marriage department, had called him last night to ask for help and Luc was short on answers. Maybe Pastor Don could help Luc help Andy.

Luc pulled into the lot certain of just one thing. Andy's call had reinforced Luc's certainty that he never wanted to get married. He didn't want to go through what Andy was suffering. He hoped the pastor had some answers for him about God's will. Luc had studied his Bible but still couldn't get a handle on God's plan for his life.

Nor did Luc understand the strange bloom in his affection for Holly. He did know he'd better keep these feelings for her under control because nothing could come of them. He needed to avoid getting too close. Starting a relationship could mean he'd risk ending up as wretched as his friends. No, marriage wasn't for him.

But wasn't it funny that he kept having these thoughts of Holly by his side?

"You're doing well, Petra." Holly smiled at the young girl encouragingly, wishing she'd been able to extract the name of her parents or a friend, anyone who could be here for her. But even after three hours of hard labor, Petra remained adamant. There was no one to call.

"I'm sorry I lied to you." The contraction over, Petra leaned her head against the pillow and inhaled deeply, a sheen of perspiration on her face. "I knew I didn't have long to go but I didn't want anyone poking and prodding at me every day."

"It would have helped us prepare for the birth," Holly said. There was no time for scolding as another contraction gripped the young girl.

"Breathe, Petra. Breathe just as I showed you,"

Dora Cummings ordered in a no-nonsense voice. "Come on now."

Holly was glad she'd called the nurse to assist. Dora had been invaluable in encouraging Petra to push through the contractions when she would have given up. Ever mindful of the imminent birth, Holly waited until this one was over then quickly checked the girl's progress.

Dora shot a questioning look at Holly.

"It's time," Holly murmured, knowing Dora would understand. "You're doing great, Petra. When the next one comes we'll ask you to push really hard but when I say stop pushing, you must stop. That's very important. Okay?"

Petra barely had time to nod before a hard contraction grabbed her. Thanks to Dora's support she was able to sustain a push that freed the baby's head. As usual, Holly's heart filled with awe as a fuzzy head appeared. She never tired of the wonders of birth.

"You're doing great, sweetie," Holly praised. "Now one more big push and your baby will be here."

A moment later Petra exerted the final effort and her baby slipped into the world. A tear slid down Holly's cheek as she cradled the little life in her hands. Her breath strangled her when the tiny girl wrapped one small finger around her thumb and clung. Awe exploded inside Holly as the

baby's blue eyes gazed at her with sweet innocence.

"Your baby is here," she told Petra. "A beautiful baby girl. You did very well. We'll get her
cleaned up and then you can see her."

"A girl." Petra sagged against the pillows Dora
had piled behind her. She showed none of the
relief of Holly's usual maternity patients when
labor was finally over. In fact, sadness lingered
in her gaze. "I don't want to see her. Take her
away."

No! Holly wanted to scream it. How could anyone not want this beautiful child? But who was
she to judge? With soft, soothing murmurs, she
carefully cleaned the baby, weighed her and then
swaddled her in a flannel blanket. All the while
those big blue eyes studied her. After the first
initial cry, the child made no sound. Could she
sense that her mother didn't want to hear her
voice, didn't want a memory she couldn't delete?

After laying the baby in a small bassinet on
the far side of the room behind a screen, Holly
finished attending to Petra. She gave her the
usual list of instructions after a birth and encouraged the girl to walk, with Dora's help, as
soon as she felt able.

But through it all, Holly's attention centered
on the infant she'd ushered into this world, a tiny
bit of life that would grow into a child, able to
love and laugh, to feel joy and sorrow.

The magnitude of what she'd done to a child just like this so long ago swamped Holly in a wave of regret. How could she have given away her own child? How could she now stand by and watch this precious baby be thrust into the world with no one to protect her?

In that instant the idea came to Holly, full-blown, simple, necessary. Maybe, Holly would be able to make up for the child she'd given away. At last she could atone for her sin.

Preoccupied, Holly finished her work at Family Ties. By the time she walked outside into the star-filled night, her every nerve was alive with emotion. She *could* make up for her mistake. She *could* ensure that this tiny, precious life was loved and coaxed to reach her full potential. Surely this was part of God's plan.

"Holly?" Luc's hand rested on her shoulder. "Is everything all right? The baby—"

"—is wonderful," Holly told him. She took his hand and clasped it between hers, hardly able to stop herself from throwing her arms around him. "Petra had an adorable girl, healthy and strong. Ten on the Apgar at birth and again five minutes later. She's absolutely perfect."

"That's good." Luc leaned back on his heels, a frown creeping across his face. "You look… funny," he said.

"I feel fantastic." Holly let the joy inside her escape in a smile of delight. "I've had the most wonderful idea, something I'm sure you'll support because you're doing the same thing."

"Oh?" He studied her with a worried look.

"I'm going to adopt Petra's baby," Holly told him. "And I want you to help me do it."

Chapter Nine

A week had passed since Holly's stunning announcement that she intended to adopt.

Luc still couldn't process it, couldn't even understand it. That's why he'd made this plan.

I'm going to need some help here, God.

He checked his mental list. A ride, a picnic by a campfire in the hills she loved so well, a beautiful sunset; surely all of those would help her relax. Maybe then he could get her to explain what had led to her momentous decision.

Knowing she'd be home from work by now, Luc rode quickly from his house to hers, barely sparing a moment to admire the beauty of the land now burgeoning with summer beauty. At home, stuck to his fridge was a list of tasks he should be completing. The hay crop was ready to be cut. He needed to cull his and Holly's herds and sell off the cattle they didn't want. There was a yearling in his pasture that needed breaking to halter sooner rather than later.

None of it mattered as much as helping Holly.

"Luc?" Holly stepped out of the house as he rode up, still clad in her work scrubs. It was clear she'd just arrived home because her hair was still bound in the mussed-up ponytail she favored for work. "Is anything wrong?"

"On a day like this?" He told himself to keep it light. "What could be wrong? I came to see if you wanted to take a ride with me to the hills. I need a break."

"Sure. Give me ten minutes." She returned inside her house.

"I'll saddle Melody while I'm waiting." As Luc caught and readied Holly's mare, he mulled over the peculiarities of the week just passed. "First she came up with this crazy idea she was going to adopt. Now she's late every day, her eyes are kind of glassy and all she talks about are babies and what they need."

"Are you talking to yourself, Luc?" Holly stood four feet away, her voice laced with mirth.

"Yes, I am." He handed her the reins. "That way I get the answers I want. Ready?"

"I guess." She swung up into her saddle with a lithe ease that signaled years of riding. "What's wrong?"

"Nothing." He knew she wouldn't let that go. He exhaled. "I'm worried about you."

"Me?" Her blue eyes flared in surprise. "I'm fine."

"Really?" Luc searched for a way to voice his concerns without sounding as if he was trying to interfere.

"What does that mean?" Holly frowned.

"It means you've been different ever since you delivered that baby at Family Ties last week."

"Different? How?" she snapped.

"You came out of Family Ties talking adoption the night Petra's child was born and you haven't ceased since." Luc saw anger building in her eyes and knew he hadn't started well. "I hardly ever hear you mention your sewing lately except to do with that baby."

"What's wrong with that?" Holly's chin jutted out defiantly.

"Nothing, only—" He faltered to a stop, intimidated by her glare. "Adoption?"

"You're adopting Henry." She glared at him.

"It's not the same." But Luc felt hard-pressed to explain why it wasn't.

"The child I want to adopt is female and younger than Henry. Other than that I don't see a difference." Holly reined her horse to a stop then clapped her hands on her hips. "Is this some kind of plan to get me to change my mind?"

"No." Luc saw her skepticism. Holly was so cute when she was steamed. Best not to say that. "Look, I know it's not really my business—"

"No, it isn't." The way Holly's lips pinched together told him he was botching this discussion.

"I just want to understand," he said quietly, infusing every ounce of sincerity he possessed into his voice.

"What's to understand?" Her brows met in a fierce frown.

"Holly, you said you'd never marry." How could he get this frustrating, endearing woman to see reason? "You made no bones about it."

"I'm not getting married, Luc." At least she wasn't chewing him out.

"No, but you also ruled out motherhood. You kept telling me you weren't mother material," he reminded. "Now suddenly you've done a complete reversal. I'm trying to understand why."

"I see." Holly kept staring at him with that narrowed gaze.

"I thought if we could get away for a while, relax and have a picnic supper maybe you'd be willing to explain your plan to me." Luc now had second thoughts about that idea as long seconds dragged by, passed under Holly's intense scrutiny. He held his breath, stifling all the things he wanted to say to her. *Just give me a chance, Holly. Trust me. We're friends. I only want the best for you.* He only exhaled when she finally nodded.

She chuckled as she lifted Melody's reins.

"Next time, Luc, ask me straight out instead of tippy-toeing around." She shot him a prim look then kicked Melody's sides and took off across the green meadow.

"She's mercurial," Luc muttered as he followed. "Is that the word, Lord? Or maybe I mean she's like a puzzle."

Holly rode ahead of him for a long time, letting the wind blow through her hair now that it was free of her ponytail. Luc kept his own pace, figuring she needed time to organize her thoughts. Holly was like that.

When she finally slowed down next to the creek he wasn't surprised. He'd known she'd stop at her favorite place. Luc reined in, tied his horse to a tree and began unpacking while Holly, jeans already rolled up, stepped into the water.

When Luc had his picnic and a small campfire ready, he sat down and watched her, smiling when she dipped her fingers in the water to tease the minnows, chuckling out loud when she slipped and almost splashed face-first in the creek and bursting into loud laughter when a bee chased her.

He didn't think he'd ever get tired of watching Holly. She was interested in everything: a butterfly that landed on a dandelion at the water's edge, a frog that scooted under a stone to avoid her, a robin perched at the water's edge, sipping daintily from the bubbling creek. When she finally came to sit across from him, Luc saw the turmoil in her eyes had settled.

"So what are we having?" She nodded at the cloth he'd spread.

"Ham and cheese sandwiches, chips, iced tea and watermelon." Luc prepared her paper plate, held it out then added his garnish. "With dill pickles, of course."

"Oh, of course," she agreed, her grin charming.

Why was it that Holly's smile always turned his insides to mush? Luc didn't know and at the moment he didn't care. He was content to simply be with her as the sun moved slowly over the hills. A gossamer breeze whispered across the land, tickling the lush ferns that grew beside the creek. The smell Luc could only describe as summer filled his nostrils. For the first time in many years he felt close to fulfilling his dreams.

So why didn't it seem enough?

He was building his legacy. Soon, hopefully, Henry would live with him permanently. It was what he wanted and yet— Luc crushed that thought to focus on Holly. He understood his goal but what had changed with Holly?

"Look, Luc," she murmured and inclined her head to the right.

A doe and a fawn stepped carefully into the glade on the far side of the creek. The mother deer studied them for several silent moments before she bent her head and began munching on the rich green grass. Her fawn wandered several feet before it, too, began eating.

"See how she won't let her child out of her sight," Holly said her voice barely audible. "What a wonderful mother she is." There was something wistful in those words.

While Holly gazed at the animals, Luc focused on her. Her head, with its tumble of curls, was tilted just the tiniest bit to one side. A smile tugged at the corner of her lips. Her long arms were clasped around her knees. Luc wondered if she sat like that to contain her fervent joy in life, to keep her from jumping to her feet and rushing toward the animals.

Luc didn't think he'd ever known anyone more lovely inside and out. Holly's beauty made his stomach shiver. He could watch her forever. And that scared him.

"When I delivered Leah the other day, it was like a curtain pulled back and a whole new world spread out before me," she said in a voice so quiet he had to lean closer to hear.

"Leah?" Luc asked.

Holly glanced at him once, smiled then turned her attention back to the doe and fawn.

"Leah is what I call Petra's baby, because she

reminds me of Jacob's wife in the Bible, the one he didn't want." She turned her head and made a face at him. "Jacob really loved Rachel but Laban tricked him and made Leah the bride."

"Okay." Luc recalled the story but he didn't understand the parallel.

"Can you imagine how Leah felt?" Holly asked. "The man who loved her sister was willing to marry her in order to get her sister for his wife. How hard it must have been to know she was so unloved, so unwanted."

"But how does this relate to Baby Leah?" Luc asked in confusion.

"Because that's exactly how Petra feels about Leah."

When Holly's eyes welled with tears, Luc's fists clenched. He wanted nothing more than to take her in his arms and comfort her. Instead, he forced himself to remain seated and await her explanation.

"She doesn't want Leah, Luc, doesn't even want to get to know her," Holly continued.

The sorrow and grief lacing her voice swelled the lump in Luc's throat, almost choking him.

"Petra has no idea what she's giving up, let alone how this decision will affect her future," Holly said sadly.

"But you do?" he asked, his curiosity piqued by the way she said that.

"I'm older. I—I can see what she's in for." Holly shot him a quick glance through her lashes.

Not that much older. Luc let it go, eager to hear what had changed.

"I go to Family Ties every day just to hold Leah." Her awe-filled voice dropped. "Every time she lifts her golden lashes and looks at me I feel as if she's begging me to take her home, to give her a family, to want her and love her."

"Holly, I think it's natural that this child draws you in." Luc struggled to find words that would help her. But he was keenly aware that with the lowering sun, the sheltered glade grew increasingly more intimate. "You're a loving person. You helped bring her into this world and you can't bear to think of anyone unloved or uncared for."

"You make me sound like a sickly sweet marshmallow." She stuck out her tongue but the shadows in her eyes remained. "It's more than that."

"Tell me," he murmured.

The way Holly looked now with the glow on her face and her shining eyes forced Luc to realize that what she was feeling lay deeply rooted in her heart. But it also forced him to admit that his feelings toward his amazing neighbor had strengthened to a deep caring he'd never expected to feel when he promised Marcus he'd watch out for Holly. That's what made it imperative that he remain objective, helping to ease her suffering yet still protecting her from any hasty decisions.

"You're frowning. What are you thinking?" Holly asked him.

"I'm remembering the warning you gave me when I told you I wanted to adopt Henry." He paused. "You're kind to want to rescue Leah, to draw her into your world so you can lavish all the love you have stored up inside." He hated saying this part. "But will the rush of emotions you feel now sustain you through years and years of raising a child on your own, without help?"

"Without *your* help?" She held his gaze.

"Of course I'll help you however I can, Holly," Luc assured her. "Just call and I'll be there. But in the end, you'll be the one responsible for Leah. There would be no going back. You couldn't change your mind."

"I wouldn't want to." Holly didn't blink.

Luc busied himself storing the leftovers from their picnic. He needed a few minutes to process her comments. Her intensity bothered him. It was as if she felt driven to adopt Leah by something more than mere emotion, as if she felt she needed this child to be whole. Was Holly telling him the whole story?

"Leah is part of my heart," she said simply. "How could I tear that out and throw it away?" As soon as the words left her mouth she stopped, gasped and squeezed her eyes closed. A moan escaped through her pinched lips.

"Tell me." Luc reached out and threaded his fingers with hers. "Tell me all of it."

She opened her eyes and stared at him, as if assessing his trustworthiness. Then Holly did a very strange thing. She came to sit right beside him and laid her head on his shoulder.

"Could you just hold me for a minute?" she whispered.

"I can do that." Luc slid his arm around her waist. The contact made his breath catch. A myriad of emotions whistled through him.

On one hand he wanted to draw Holly nearer, hold her closer and try to assuage whatever was bothering her. On the other hand he wanted to vault onto his horse and ride hard toward home, to escape Holly. Why? Because of the strength of his need to hold her, because of the emotions she evoked in him, because of the dreams that having her sit next to him like this engendered. Dreams he well knew he couldn't indulge.

Luc had fought off a similar dream many times this week, knowing how pointless it was to even consider allowing Holly to be that special woman in his life. There couldn't be a future for them. He'd seen over and over that relationships didn't last. They led to hurt and that was the one thing he wanted to spare Holly.

"I don't know how to explain it to you," she

whispered after a moment of silence. "From the first moment I held Leah in my arms, it was as if I knew God meant me to have her."

"Because?" he pressed.

"I did something very bad once. Something that ever since I've wished I could change. But I can't." Her voice filled with pain. "I never can. I have to carry that guilt with me."

"Holly—"

"No, let me go on." She inhaled and gave him a watery smile. "Maybe it was the way her eyes locked onto me and wouldn't let go but I could hardly stand to let go of her. When I held her, suddenly my burden of guilt rolled away."

He couldn't stop her, not when her voice grew hushed and reverent. "Go on."

"She made this little mewling sound. Not a real cry. At first I thought maybe her lungs were blocked, but they weren't." Holly's eyes glowed. "She cried when Dora took her, but when I held her again she didn't make a peep."

Luc worried that he wouldn't be able to make Holly see sense, that reality couldn't impede her dream world. But he was being silly. Holly Janzen was the most down-to-earth, practical person he knew. She took everything in stride.

So what was it about this child that had changed her? And what terrible thing had she done? Was that the reason Ron had so abruptly left her?

"Leah is like my second chance. She gives this tiny sigh when I pick her up." Holly gazed at the darkening sky, her mouth lifted in a sweet smile. "As if she knows she's safe with me, that I'll love her forever."

"But you've delivered lots of babies," Luc said. "Why *this* baby?"

"I don't know. I only know that she's given me a new awareness of life." Holly drew a deep breath. "Because of Leah my world has changed."

"How?" he demanded.

"For one thing, I've faced the truth. You were partly right, Luc." Holly smiled at him. "I do want a family. I want children who make me laugh and test me and fill my life."

"So get married. I'm sure half the guys in town would be happy to propose." Luc winced at the thought of Holly marrying any of the local men. None he could name was good enough for her. She deserved someone special.

"I don't want to get married." She shifted against him. "I'm like you. My last relationship really killed my self-esteem. Ron's rejection made it hard to consider a future. I don't think I've ever felt so unwanted in my life."

"I know that feeling," Luc muttered.

"I can't try again, get dumped again and go through the same grueling self-questioning." Holly shook her head. "I'll be left trying to figure out how to get through the rest of my life."

"I doubt that would happen." Luc wouldn't let it. "Not every man is like Ron."

"It's happened to me twice." Holly scowled. "I told you, I don't want to try romance again."

"Got it." Luc closed his eyes and relished these moments with her, knowing they couldn't last.

"But if I did," she said, her voice firm, "bottom of my list would be to get involved with a local guy. Nobody around Buffalo Gap can see past who they *think* I am to the real me. My wonder-girl image just won't go away."

"Holly, no one expects—" She cut him off.

"Face it, Luc, even if they could see that I'm not their 'local girl made good,' if the relationship broke up, I'd be in for another pity party from the entire town." Her face contorted into a mask of horror. "Dumped twice in Buffalo Gap? No way."

"For as long as I've known you, Holly Janzen, you've done your own thing, gone your own way." Luc shook his head in disbelief. "I can't believe you're worried about what folks in Buffalo Gap think."

She pulled away so she could look him in the eye. As cool air rushed between them an odd sense of loss swamped Luc. He didn't want Holly to distance herself, and yet he felt she was doing that mentally as well as physically.

Daylight had completely faded. Aside from the light given by the moon and the flickering fire, they sat in darkness. The intimacy made Luc doubly aware of how easy it would be to let the feelings that had built up inside spill out. It would be better if they remained unsaid. Imagining a future with Holly had to be suppressed.

"I don't want to get married. I want my own child, Luc." Holly's face lay mere inches from his. Her voice begged for understanding. "You're certain you can raise Henry on your own, aren't you?"

"Yes, but—" He hesitated, uncertain where this would lead.

"If you can raise Henry, why shouldn't I raise Leah?" she demanded. "Why shouldn't I give that child the love she deserves?"

Holly shifted nearer to the fire, rubbing her hands on her arms to warm them. That simple movement felt like a physical loss. A chill whispered up Luc's spine, but it wasn't only because of the cooler evening air that came between them. It was a gut-deep certainty that something else lay behind Holly's motivation that she kept hidden from him. Something drove Holly that she couldn't or wouldn't explain. All he could offer were words of caution.

"You've never spoken about adopting before. It's quite a surprise that this baby has affected you so deeply," he said. "I wonder if you've thought about this from a different point of view."

"Like what?" Her tone didn't brook meddling.

"A while ago we were talking about God's will. Do you see this as God's plan for you?" He needed her to think this through. "Are you certain that God is directing this and not your heart? Maybe you're trying to fill the hole that Ron left."

Holly stared at him long and hard before she rose, dusted down the legs of her jeans and walked toward her horse.

"Holly?" Luc followed. He touched her arm, not surprised when she flinched. His heart pinched at the sheen of tears that glossed her blue eyes. "I'm not trying to hurt you, Holly."

"You may not be trying to hurt me, but that's exactly what you've done, Luc." Holly fought back the disappointment that felt like a shroud smothering her.

"Please." Luc stood beside her, his face in shadow, his voice pleading.

"No. You listen to me." She would not cry in front of him. "I supported you completely when you said you wanted to adopt Henry. I helped you with Abby, I researched and did the best I could to help you bond with him. I've been there for you, Luc."

"You have. I'm very grateful." His tight voice bugged her.

"Silly me. I thought you'd do the same for me. Because I thought we were friends." She could hardly stomach the thought that Luc opposed her decision to adopt Leah.

"Holly, you're my best friend. I'd never want to hurt you." He hesitated then touched her cheek. "I didn't mean to make you sad."

"Then why—"

"This all came out of left field for me." Luc sighed and raked a hand through his hair. The angle of his stance allowed the moonlight to cascade over his face. He looked so strong, so handsome. So...lovable?

"I've been thinking about it a lot." Holly suppressed her wayward thoughts about Luc Cramer. This was about adopting a baby, not some silly crush on her neighbor.

"You never said anything." He sounded dubious.

"I'm sure I've been talking about Leah nonstop lately, haven't I? She's the best thing in my life right now." As Holly said it, a warm glow filled her. Surely he felt the same about Henry.

"I understand she's special to you." He nodded.

"Then why don't you want me to adopt?" A rush of bitterness boiled up inside her. "You don't think I'd be a good mother?"

"I've told you a hundred times you'd make a fantastic mother, Holly. But you've always said there was no way. Your sudden about-face is confusing. Come, sit down and explain it to me," he invited. "I'll stir up the coals to keep us warm."

"I don't want to talk anymore, Luc." Holly studied his face for a long time. Finally she shook her head. "I've told you my plan. If you can't support me then I'll look to my other friends. But if it's at all possible, I am going to adopt Leah."

She swung up onto Melody's back but kept the mare from moving, bothered by an expression on Luc's face that she couldn't quite decipher.

"Holly, I need to tell you something." Luc's grave tone caused chill bumps to appear on her arms.

"What is it?"

"I went to visit Petra this week." He held up a hand to stop her comments. "Not to do anything behind your back. I wouldn't do that."

"Then why?" she asked.

"To talk to her. To see Leah. To try and understand your decision," he said very quietly.

"And?" There was more. She could see it in his eyes—something he didn't want to say. "Tell me, Luc."

"Petra doesn't want to keep her baby, but she plans to ask Abby to arrange for a two-parent adoption." The words burst out of him.

It took Holly a moment to comprehend. She reared back as the words struck home. Luc's hand covered hers on the saddle fork.

"Petra was raised by a single mom who never

had time for her. When her mother hit tough times, she couldn't handle it, had no one to lean on. She had a severe emotional breakdown that affected Petra badly," Luc explained.

"Petra never told me." Taken aback, Holly sat there stunned.

"She's reluctant to tell anyone." Luc's eyes brimmed with sympathy. "That's why she came here. When her mother learned Petra was pregnant, that there was another mouth to feed, she couldn't take the thought of more responsibility. She's in a mental hospital."

Gutted by his words, Holly sat motionless, trying to digest everything.

"Holly?"

"It doesn't matter," she said, straightening her spine. "Leah is an answer from God for me. He'll work it out." She lifted the reins. "Thank you for the picnic but I'm going home now. I need some time to think. Alone. Good night, Luc."

Holly rode as quickly as she dared toward home, knowing Luc would stay long enough to ensure the fire was completely out. As she rode, she replayed their conversation. Devastation threatened to swamp her.

"You've come through before," she told herself. "And the way you've made it through is by relying on yourself. You can't depend on anyone except God. You can trust Him."

She could trust Leah, too, Holly decided. A

baby wouldn't betray her. Not like Luc had just done. Why hadn't he told Petra what a good mom Holly would make? Why hadn't he stood up for Holly? Why wasn't he there for her?

Because deep down Luc didn't believe Holly should be a mom.

Chapter Ten

How things could change in a few short weeks.

"A few things from Family Ties to welcome her to your family," Holly said with a tremulous smile.

Luc gulped. On the first Monday in July, he stood beside her in front of Family Ties, his heart pounding with fierce pride at Holly's generosity as she laid a gift-wrapped box in the arms of Leah's new parents. He knew the box was filled with the sweet baby garments she'd sewn when she believed Leah would soon be her daughter. With the box transferred, Holly bent and gazed at the child she'd lost.

"Bye, darling Leah."

The words were so quiet Luc might have imagined them except for seeing Holly's lips moving. Her avid gaze riveted on this blessed baby, committing to memory every detail of the child who would never be hers. When she stepped back and waved goodbye to the new family, he knew she was holding back her tears, but her composure wouldn't last long.

That's why Luc was here. That's why he wasn't going anywhere until he was certain Holly was all right, no matter how often she told him she wanted him to leave her alone.

"Can you get me out of here, please?" she asked through gritted teeth, obviously aware of the curious townsfolk watching.

"Let's get coffee at the drive-through then go drink it in the park. I doubt there's anyone using that bench by the river at this hour of the morning." Luc escorted her to his truck and saw her inside. He checked her stoic face once before starting the engine. Silent tears dripped from her chin. "Oh, Holly. I'm so sorry."

"Go, Luc. Please," she begged.

So he bought coffee, handed it to her to hold and headed for the most secluded corner of the town park, made more private by the wide circular hedge which sheltered it from onlookers. A wrought-iron bench sat next to the river. When Holly sat down he handed her a cup then sat beside her. He sipped his brew, waiting for her to open up when she was ready.

"I should have listened to you," Holly murmured, ending the long silence that had fallen between them. "That day up in the hills, I should have listened instead of trying to get my own way. I wish I had. It's just that I thought maybe Leah was some kind of gesture of God's forgiveness. Maybe if I'd listened to you it wouldn't hurt so much now."

"Don't hurt, Holly." He folded her hand in his. Though the morning was hot, her fingers against his were icy. "Think about Leah with her loving parents, safe and secure in a home where she's wanted and celebrated. God didn't mess up with Leah. He gave her a family to love her."

"I know." Pain lay buried in her voice. "I blamed you, you know. Told myself you didn't have enough faith in me."

"Well, that's wrong." Luc smiled at her. "Because Leah left doesn't mean He's forgotten you or your prayers."

"Why do you say that?" She tossed him a curious sideways glance.

"Because the Bible says that God's plans for us are good and just because there's a delay or a change in course, doesn't mean He's saying no to what we desire. It only means God has something different in mind."

"It wasn't long ago you were questioning God's will," Holly remarked in surprise.

"I guess I'm learning to trust." Luc desperately wanted to help this tender, giving woman get past her grief and see the potential in her world. "You have so much to give, Holly."

"I don't want to give anymore." She lifted

her gaze to meet his. "I want my own way. I want Leah."

"I know." He squeezed her fingers, loving her honesty. Instead of diminishing after the campfire a week ago, his emotional bond with Holly had strengthened. Her sadness was his because she was an integral part of his world.

"When will losing Leah stop hurting, Luc?"

"Maybe when you get involved with others." He grinned. "In that vein, I wouldn't say no if you wanted to help me today."

"With what?" She studied him so curiously Luc could only hope this idea worked out.

"I promised Henry that the day camp he's attending this week could come out to the ranch this afternoon." Luc faked a shudder. "I could really use some help."

"Don't play me, Luc," Holly said with some asperity. "You're trying to cheer me up by giving me a job but I know you're perfectly capable of entertaining those kids."

"I'm not—" The look she shot his way made him pause.

"As it happens I am at loose ends today and keeping busy with a bunch of kids is exactly what I need to wear me out." Her backbone straightened. "When do they arrive?"

"Half an hour. They'll stay for lunch," he told her deadpan.

"What?" For a second lovely Holly Janzen's

mouth dropped. Then she regained control, capped the lid on her coffee and rose. "Well, let's get out there. Why are you dallying here with me?"

"I like dallying with you." He doubted she knew how true that was.

"Luc." Holly walked with him to his truck then laid her hand on his wrist. "I'm sorry about—"

"No. I'm sorry." He tapped a gentle forefinger against her lips. "But the thing is, friends don't need to apologize to friends." He lifted his hand away. It was either that or smooth his fingers over her cheeks, slide them into her hair and press her head to his shoulder.

"Friends shouldn't be such jerks when other friends are only trying to help them." She held his gaze. "Should they?"

"Nope." He grinned at her.

"I should never have expected to adopt Leah," she admitted. She stared at her feet. "I should admit that when I was trying to pray about it, I knew I was really asking for my own way and not God's will. I don't deserve Leah."

"What do you mean?" Luc frowned.

"Not getting to keep Leah, that's God's punishment," Holly murmured.

"God isn't like that." Luc couldn't fathom anything Holly could do that would bring God's punishment. "God is love," he said firmly. And how could God help but love sweet, tender Holly?

"We should go. Your guests will be arriving." Holly forced a smile that didn't reach her eyes. "I'll get my jeep, drive myself and meet you there. Do you need any supplies?"

"No. I have everything I need." But as Luc watched her walk away, he knew it wasn't true. He needed Holly. But he knew he would fail at romance.

But I can be her friend. I can help her heal, find new possibilities, new ways to give from that loving heart of hers.

Luc's dreams of the future always included Holly. She would be an essential part of his future with Henry. She was the first one Luc thought of whenever a problem stymied him. Now Holly's happiness was becoming the most important thing in his world.

Is that love?

"I want her to be happy," he prayed as he drove to his ranch. "But that isn't love. It can't be."

Because falling for Holly would mean opening himself up for rejection and the one thing Luc did not want to experience with Holly was rejection.

"I'll be her best friend, God," he promised.

Somehow that felt like second-best.

"Thank you for asking me to help, Luc," Holly panted, opting out of the rousing game of dodge ball to stand by him. "This is exactly what I needed."

"We're certainly glad you came, Holly." Local teacher Georgette Finstead had again volunteered to lead Buffalo Gap's one-week summer day camp for local kids. "This class is the biggest our program has ever had. I'll take all the hands I can get. Luc's been wonderful to let us come out here."

Holly barely covered her snort of disgust as the teacher simpered at Luc who backed away as if he'd been stung. He shot Holly a look of pleading.

"If you can manage alone for a few minutes, Luc and I could sure use a break," she said to Georgette. "We ranchers get up before the sun."

"Oh, by all means." Georgette turned to correct some misbehavior, and Holly yanked on Luc's arm.

"Stop staring at her hair," she hissed.

"I can't help it," Luc muttered. "How does she get it to stay piled on her head like that?"

"I wouldn't know," Holly mumbled, feeling disheveled and sweaty beside the pristine Georgette. In the shade of a poplar tree, she poured them each a glass of lemonade and handed one to him, which he swallowed in one gulp.

"I only wondered because the wind's been strong all afternoon but her hair hasn't moved a bit." Luc shrugged. "Weird."

Why should she feel relieved that he wasn't

interested in the lovely Georgette? Holly wondered. Luc was a good man and even if he didn't want a romantic relationship, he deserved to find happiness.

Only not with Georgette.

"Did you say something, Holly?" Luc asked her.

Could he hear her thoughts? "Just that your truck looks good," she said quickly. "Is the restoration finished?"

"Not quite." His grin stretched from one ear to the other. "But rest assured I'll have it ready for the parade next month. My fingers are itching to claim that five-hundred-dollar prize."

"Mine, too." When he stared at her she reminded, "For the biggest pumpkin."

"Oh. Right." He grabbed one of the gingersnaps she'd brought and sampled it. "These are the best. When did you have time to bake?"

"Last night." She gulped and forced herself to continue. "When I still hoped maybe I'd be celebrating Leah's arrival."

"Well, it was nice of you to bring them." He popped the rest of the cookie in his mouth. "Do you think the kids had fun?"

"They had a blast," Holly assured them. "Hiring Sadie Smith as the clown was perfect. Her magic show gave them a break between games." She put her hands on her hips, leaned back and studied him. "Are you sure you haven't tried parenting before?"

"That's the best compliment you could give me." Luc grinned and suddenly Holly's heart danced light and carefree. "At least no one's complained about the mosquitoes," he said, slapping at one buzzing near his head.

"They're too busy having fun to notice the odd bug." She plucked her T-shirt away from her body. "I am going to appreciate a cool shower after this."

"Not me. I'm riding up to the creek." Luc grinned. "Want to come?"

"Oh." She closed her eyes and imagined that cool water covering her. "Yes, I do. I think this is the hottest day we've had so far this year. Swimming will be fantastic at the creek."

It was only when Georgette cleared her throat that Holly realized she and Luc had been staring at each other for a long time.

"As you see, we're getting ready to load the bus and return to town, but the children want to thank you, Luc." Georgette linked her hand through his arm, her doe eyes fawning. "As do I. It's been a wonderful afternoon."

"My pleasure." Luc tried to ease his arm free, but Georgette wasn't letting go, so he winked at Holly and caught her hand in his other arm. "Thank Holly also. I couldn't have done it without her help."

Holly chided herself for the smug satisfaction she found in Georgette's grimace. How could she have doubted Luc's friendship?

"It's to be expected Holly would help make this afternoon a success. After all, she's the town's goodwill ambassador. So thank you, Holly," the teacher said.

It should have been a compliment but in Holly's eyes it was just another expectation people placed on her.

"No thanks needed, Georgette." Holly eased away from Luc, unsettled by the reaction his touch brought. She liked Luc holding her arm a little too much. She waited until the kids had performed their goodbye song then found Henry and gave him a hug. "Did you have fun, honey?"

"Tons," he said between chewing the last piece of watermelon. "Only I wish I could have showed the kids my room here."

"Maybe next year, when you start first grade," she said, ruffling his hair.

"Yeah. When me an' Luc are a family. And you'll be here, too, Holly." Henry grinned then gave her a sticky hug. "See ya, Holly."

"See you, sweetie." She stood and waved away the busload of children while thinking about Henry's comment. She'd be here, too, he'd said. But would she? Where did she go from here? What did God want for her?

"It seems so quiet," Luc said from behind her.

"Not that I'm complaining. That was a whole lot of kids at one time." He flung an arm across her shoulders and led her back to the party remains. "You're not leaving me with the mess this time."

Holly marveled at the wealth of odd feelings whirring inside her. She felt light, almost care-free after such a difficult start to her day. But when Luc removed his arm, some of her pleasure evaporated. Why?

"Do you have to work tomorrow?" Luc began clearing off the table where they'd served a snack.

"Two whole days off. Why?" she asked.

"Because I don't want to come back from the creek until I'm good and cooled off." His gaze narrowed. "I'm going to be late."

Holly stared at him, knowing that with Luc's help she could get through the hovering sense of dejection waiting to engulf her. She'd keep seeking God's will even though the cloud of guilt lingered. Luc would help her. He wouldn't let her down.

Holly grabbed the end of the paper tablecloth and rolled it toward him, bundling the whole thing into his arms. Luc had been there for her this morning when she thought she'd betray herself to Leah's parents. He'd supported, encouraged and helped her all these months since her dad's death. Maybe, just for a little while, she'd depend on him.

"What I'm saying is that I don't intend to rush home." Fun danced in his dark eyes. He was so good-looking. "Any objections?"

"Nope. No objections at all," she said and meant it.

"Well, glory be. Miss Holly Janzen is going to let loose in the creek," Luc teased.

"You know," Holly said slowly. "I think I just might." *But only with you, Luc.*

"Watch this!" Holly ordered.

Luc was pleased to do so. She looked so lovely with the sun glossing her wet hair as she danced from rock to rock across the creek, her cutoff shorts revealing her tanned limber legs.

"You'll slip," he warned then caught his breath when she did. He half rose to go rescue her but she recovered her balance, twisted her head and winked at him. "Show-off."

"Of course," she said in a dry tone, flopping down beside him. "After all I was voted Buffalo Gap's girl most likely to do everything, achieve anything and generally become a role model to emulate," she said with a wink.

"And you have." Luc handed her a soda from the cooler he'd brought along. "Haven't you?"

"No." She leaned back and let the sun take away the chill of the water.

"But you're very successful in your work." He saw the way she shifted uncomfortably and wondered what was bothering her. "Abby told me you were offered a very nice position in Calgary's biggest hospital this morning."

"Which I promptly declined." Holly shrugged. "Not that they accepted that. They've given me a month to 'think it over.' As if I need to."

"There's no upside to that job?" Luc asked.

"Not enough. I like knowing my clients, watching the babies I deliver grow up. I like living in Buffalo Gap and I love being involved in Family Ties." A sad look flitted across her face before she chased it away and grinned at him. "So don't go thinking you're going to buy Cool Springs Ranch anytime soon 'cause I'm not selling."

"Duly noted." Luc nodded. "So what are your hopes and dreams for the future, if that's not being too nosey?" He saw the way she caught her breath then tried to cover her discomposure.

"At the moment I don't have any." Holly spread her arms wide. "I'm going to relax, enjoy the summer and wait for God to show me what's next."

"Not a bad idea," he said with a nod. "Anytime you want to talk, remember I'm just a call away."

"Thanks, Luc, but what about you? We're always talking about me," she said in a guilty tone. "What's happening with you and Henry?"

"As far as I know, everything is progressing

well," he told her. "One of these days I'm going to take him to see his brother."

"In prison?" Holly sounded surprised.

"Yes. Henry keeps saying how much he misses Finn." He frowned. "I want to adopt Henry but that doesn't mean I want to exclude the only family he has."

"Good for you," she praised, looking slightly stunned.

"His parents are dead. Finn's all the family he remembers." Luc turned to study Holly. No matter where or when he saw her, she always looked lovely. "Want to come with us?"

"I'd love to. Just tell me when." She nodded then narrowed her gaze. "But you seem preoccupied with something. If not Henry then what?"

Luc hesitated. It was one thing to try to help your buddies. It was something else entirely to share their personal problems with someone. But he trusted Holly and she had good instincts about people. Maybe she could give him some ideas of how to help his friends.

"Luc?" She laid her hand on his, a concerned look darkening her eyes.

"Remember I told you my friend is getting a divorce?" When she nodded, he turned his palm so his fingers could mesh with hers. "Actually it's not only Pete, it's three of the most devoted men I've known trying to work through marriage breakdowns. I've tried but I don't feel like I'm helping."

"Maybe it's not up to you to help," she said after several moments' pause.

"But I'm the one they turned to," he spluttered.

"I know. You've been a great friend and spent hours letting them speak their hearts. You must have spent time searching for godly ways to advise them." She smiled. "I'm guessing they've exhausted your suggestions?"

Luc nodded, curious as to where this was leading.

"What's the next step?" Holly's fingers tightened on his.

"I'm out of suggestions. All I can say is keep trying, for the sake of their family." He hated that. How could relationships as intense as his buddies' had been just be over?

"Maybe it's time for them to let go." At her words, he jerked forward. Holly held up one hand. "Don't shoot me down yet, Luc."

"But what you're saying is unacceptable," he insisted.

"Is it?" She squeezed the hand he still held then drew away. "Or is it the failure of their marriages that is unacceptable?"

"I— I—" He couldn't find the right words.

"You're a good man, Luc. When you make a commitment, you make it for life. That's the way it should be," she said. "But life doesn't always turn out that way."

"You're saying I should tell them to walk away?" He couldn't wrap his mind around that.

"No, I'm saying that maybe it's time to step back and assess." He could tell she'd given the subject some thought. "These men—their situations are sad and hurtful but unless their wives change, there's not really any way to revive their marriages, true?"

Luc nodded, hating to admit what was clearly true.

"So perhaps it's time to think about how to manage this new dynamic so they keep close to their children. Maybe it's time to let go and wait for God to show them a new path for their lives. That's what I'm going to do." Holly jumped to her feet and beckoned him. "Time for another swim."

"You go. I'm still shivering from the last one." Luc watched as Holly raced to the edge of the creek and then slid down into the frigid water with a choked-off scream.

Let go and wait for God to show them a new path. Not bad advice and equally applicable to his own life.

Luc's heart thudded with pleasure as he watched her float down the creek, eyes closed, face tilted upward. Holly was part of his world, part of his life. A day without Holly in it was empty. The next few weeks without Leah would be rough for her, but he'd be there.

He'd always be there for Holly. But that wasn't love. That was pure friendship.

Somehow Luc would need to be content with that.

Chapter Eleven

"Come on in, Luc. Help yourself to iced tea. I'll finish this seam and I'll be ready to leave."

At his agreement Holly started her machine and zipped down the seam, glad for the air conditioning that made the late July heat bearable. With a sigh of relief she laid the receiving blanket across her new work surface and paused a moment to admire her embroidery work.

"I'm finished." She glanced over one shoulder to smile at him. "Hi."

"You never told me why you're always sewing baby clothes." Luc's gaze locked on the small pink, blue and green striped boxes stacked on top of her father's chest. "Those can't all be for friends' babies."

"They're not." She swiveled in her chair to face him and decided it was truth time. "I'm running an online business, Luc. I sell baby clothes made to order. I needed a way to pay off all those things I bought to make Dad's last days easier."

"But couldn't you have sold that stuff and recouped some of the money?" He scratched his head. "Instead, you donated everything."

"Because somebody else might need them and not be able to pay for them." She shrugged. "Anyway, I like sewing."

"You must if those are all orders you've filled." Luc looked without success for a place to sit. "How come nobody in town knows?"

"Because I've taken special pains to keep it quiet. I go to the next town to mail the packages. I have a mailbox there, too, just to make sure nobody finds out when I pick up the supplies I order online." She couldn't avoid his stare.

"Why go to such lengths?" Luc said.

"The truth?" She chided herself for not trusting him.

Luc nodded, leaned against the door frame and waited.

"After the thing with Ron, everybody in town felt sorry for me. It was horrible. Then I couldn't have Leah. If they also knew I was making baby clothes, can you imagine what they'd say?" She shuddered. "'Poor Holly. No marriage, no children so she consoles herself making baby clothes.' No way do I want that."

"Did anyone ever tell you that you worry too

much about what other people think?" Luc shook his head. "What is it with you and this hang-up about being the town's good girl? Nobody's watching you to see if you mess up, Holly."

"Aren't they?" She cringed at the memory of the discussion she'd overheard at Maxine's baby shower. *Holly, these outfits are so cute. When are you going to have your own kids to sew for?*

"Are they?" He frowned. "I haven't heard anything."

"Sure you have. Georgette hinted as much." When he didn't remember she repeated, "'Holly's the town's goodwill ambassador.'"

"Isn't that a good thing?" he asked.

Luc didn't get it. Well, how could he? He was a relative newcomer to the area and Holly knew that to clarify would make her sound like a whiner. For reasons she couldn't explain to herself right now, she didn't want Luc to see her in such a negative way.

"I'm ready to go if you are," she said as she rose. "I gather we're picking Henry up as we go through town. Is he excited about seeing his brother?"

"I'm not sure." Luc followed her out of her house, waited while she locked the door then walked beside her to his truck. "I tried to explain everything that would happen but he hasn't said much. Hilda says he hasn't talked to her, either. I'm thinking he probably hasn't processed everything yet."

"Or maybe he's afraid of going to the prison," Holly suggested as they bumped down the gravel road that led to town.

"Maybe. We'll just have to help him through. Okay, partner?" he asked, grinning.

"Deal." How she liked that word, *partner*.

Henry was indeed subdued when they found him sitting on the front stoop with Hilda. He told her goodbye then with Luc's help, climbed into the truck to sit beside Holly.

"How are you, Henry?" Holly asked, slightly worried by his solemn look.

"Okay, I guess." His hand slid along the seat and curled it into hers.

"I bet you're excited to see Finn. It's been a while, hasn't it?" Her worries mushroomed at his monosyllabic response. "Honey, what's wrong? Luc and I will be there the whole time. You don't have to be scared."

"What if Finn doesn't want me to be 'dopted?" Henry finally said. "He's my brother."

"It doesn't matter what happens, Henry," Luc said. "Finn will always be your brother. That's never going to change. Brothers are forever."

"Oh." The boy's brow cleared immediately. His eyes began to glow with excitement. "Could Finn come to the ranch sometime and see my bedroom? And I'd show him the horses and the tire swing that you made for me and the place where I feed the cows."

Holly looked over his head at Luc, with a what-do-we-do expression.

His smile charmed her, before he looked at the boy. "You know, Henry, I think you and Finn should discuss that. You could tell him that you'll write him a letter and he can write you back and let you know if he wants to come for a visit."

"I'll be in first grade soon," Henry said thoughtfully. "I'll be able to write really good, won't I?" Once they'd assured him, Henry borrowed Holly's iPod and settled down to listen to music she'd recorded for him.

"That's very generous of you to have Finn," Holly said, impressed by Luc's settling of Henry's fears.

"Family is always family. Henry and Finn should remain close," he said.

How generous Luc was. He was accepting Henry lock, stock and convicted felon brother. Which was as it should be, of course. It was just that Holly didn't know many men who'd insist on retaining a familial connection like that. Luc's determination to embrace Henry unconditionally sent her esteem of him even higher.

With the radio quietly playing in the background, Holly got lost in her thoughts about the man she called her best friend. Lately Luc stopped by for coffee a lot if she was off work.

They'd gone twice more to the creek for a swim. She'd helped him arrange a treasure hunt for Henry on the ranch and the three of them had worked together to clean his restored vehicle and prepare it for the upcoming parade.

What Holly hadn't done, despite Luc's repeated reminders, was open the trunk her father had left. She'd finally realized her father had tasked Luc with getting her to look in the trunk. And she would. One of these days when it didn't hurt quite so much to see it and remember all the stories her dad had told her about the trunk's travels with him through Africa where he'd bought it.

"Are you asleep, Holly?" Humor threaded Luc's voice. When she looked at him, he smiled. "We're here."

Holly wasn't sure what to expect. All she knew was that she had to keep a close eye on Henry and soothe his fears. So when they entered the prison she held on to his hand, even though she knew he thought he was too old to need such attention.

The three of them were shown into a small room where they waited for only a few minutes before a young man entered.

"Finn!" Henry tore his hand free, raced across the room and threw himself into his brother's arms.

"Hey, Henry." Finn, an older version of Henry,

gathered the boy close, closed his eyes and savored the joy of holding his brother. "Long time no see, buddy." Pure joy radiated across his thin face. His eyes, mirrors of Henry's, took in every detail. "Your hair is different. It looks good. Are you behaving?"

"Uh-huh." Henry grinned. "This is Luc and this is Holly. They're my friends."

"Nice to meet you, Finn. Luc Cramer." Luc held out his hand, waiting until Finn finally extended his and shook it. "I've heard a lot about you from Henry. He says you like to work with wood."

"Yeah." Some of the hesitancy vanished from Finn's face. He dug in his pocket and pulled out a small animal. "I heard you were staying on a ranch so I made you this horse, Henry."

"Thanks." Henry grinned adoringly at his big brother then reverently took the horse from Finn's hand. "You made it look just like Holly's horse. He's called Babycakes."

"For real?" Finn asked wide-eyed.

"For real. I'm Holly Janzen." She shook Finn's hand. "Luc and I are ranching neighbors but Henry lives with Ms. Hilda." She knew Finn was almost eighteen but was surprised by how young he looked. "I'm glad to meet you. A brother of Henry's has to be very special."

"Thanks." Finn gave her an embarrassed smile then his attention returned to Luc. "I was told you want to adopt my brother." He watched Henry gallop his horse around the room.

"Yes, I do. I want to give him a home. Henry's a very special boy and I love him dearly," Luc said quietly.

"So do I." Finn's look challenged Luc, but Luc didn't take the bait.

"I know you do, Finn." He didn't retreat from the confrontation in the brother's eyes but kept his tone friendly. "Henry's told me all about how you looked after him. You did a great job of raising him."

"He's a good kid," Finn muttered.

"Due to your influence," Luc agreed. "I hope when you get out you'll come and see us at the ranch. Henry talks about that a lot."

Holly's heart melted at Luc's gentle tone as he tried to reassure this big brother that he had no intentions of cutting him out of Henry's life. It was a brilliant way to ensure Henry's adjustment to Luc was made even easier. Luc's big heart was as large as his ranch, Holly thought fondly. He made her world and Henry's and Finn's a better place. How she loved him for it.

Wait a minute. *Loved* him? That couldn't be.

"Right, Holly?"

"Huh?" She blinked, found Luc frowning at her.

"What's wrong?" he asked.

"Nothing." She blushed at Finn and Henry's curious stares. "Just thinking."

"I was telling Finn that if he wants to look for a job near Buffalo Gap there's always someone hiring." Luc gave her a funny look.

"That's true," Holly agreed, trying not to show that Luc's proximity had such a strong effect on her. "If that's what you want. What are your interests, Finn?"

Finn spoke of his love of carving. Moments later he and Luc were bent head to head discussing wood.

"I'll find out if I can send you some hickory," Luc promised when the guard told them the visit was over. "I've heard that it's great for carving."

"Thanks a lot." Finn shook his hand, his face now relaxed. "And thanks for caring about Henry. I appreciate it."

"It's entirely my pleasure," Luc assured him.

"I don't want to go." Henry leaned against Finn's leg as he gazed at his brother. "I don't want to leave you here. I missed you, Finn."

"I missed you, too, Henry." Finn lifted the boy on his knee and reminded him of some of the fun things they'd shared. They laughed together, each adoring the other. "I'm sorry I messed up, Henry. I did a bad thing by stealing. I shouldn't have done it. That's why you had to go live with someone else. Because I made a mistake."

"Luc says everybody makes mistakes," Henry

said, cupping his hand against Finn's cheek. "You have to ask God to forgive you," he said earnestly.

"I already have," Finn told him quietly. "And I know He heard me because He sent you to some very nice people. God sure does care about you, Henry."

"He cares about you, too," Henry said a little tearfully.

"When I get out of here I'll come and see you," Finn promised, holding the boy tightly. "Maybe I'll even try sitting on one of Luc's horses."

"Really?" Henry asked. Hope filled his face, and Holly's heart squeezed tight. "You won't do anything bad again? I know I made you do it."

"No, Henry." Finn's stern voice surprised the boy. He shifted but Finn hung on to his shoulders and waited until Henry looked at him. "Nothing that happened to me was your fault, Henry. Understand? *I* did something wrong and now I have to pay for it."

"But I told you the teacher said I needed new glasses," Henry said, his voice brimming with contrition. "If I hadn't told you—"

"Wasn't I old enough to know not to steal?" Finn shook his head. "You didn't do anything wrong, Henry."

"Sure?" Henry saw Finn's nod but apparently that wasn't enough. He looked to Luc who also nodded then to Holly who did the same. "Okay," he said at last with a big sigh.

"We have to go now, Henry," Luc said quietly. "But we can come back another time. If you want to."

"I want to," Henry said, his chest thrust out proudly. "Finn's my brother. We hafta stick together."

"Exactly the way it should be." Luc said goodbye to Finn, waited for Holly to do the same then ushered her outside the room, giving Finn a moment with his brother.

"That kid is one of the good guys," he said, his voice thick with emotion. "I'm going to ask Abby to do some investigation and see if the court will grant Finn early release if he's under my supervision."

What a guy. Holly could no more have stopped herself from throwing her arms around Luc and pressing a kiss against his cheek than she could have stopped breathing. When she stepped back, Luc blinked at her as if he'd survived a whirlwind.

"What was that for?"

"For being a wonderful, caring, generous, sweet man," she said.

"Sweet?" His nose wrinkled.

"Yes." She linked her fingers with his. "Do you know how much I admire you, Luc Cramer?"

"They're just kids trying to raise each other,"

he said, brushing off her compliment. But he didn't let go of her hand. "I want them to be together."

"You deserve to be a father," she whispered as Henry came out of the room.

Together they walked to Luc's truck. Then he drove them to an ice cream stand and bought the biggest cones they offered. As they sat in the hot sun licking their ice cream, Holly offered a silent prayer.

Lord, I do love this man. I love him more than I ever dreamed I could love Ron, miles beyond the love I thought I had for my baby's father. Luc stands head and shoulders above every man I've known except Dad.

But how could an honest, decent man like Luc care for the real Holly Janzen? Not the local girl everyone thought always did the right thing, but the girl behind the mask, the one who'd given away a child she'd carried for nine months right next to her heart because she didn't want anyone to know she wasn't the shining example they thought?

Holly wasn't worthy of Luc. A man like him, gentle, sincere, trusting—how could he possibly understand what she'd done? Luc deserved the best life had to offer. The best was not Holly Janzen, though she dearly wished it was.

Chapter Twelve

"I've only ever ridden in a parade before on my horse." Holly waved at bystanders as Luc drove the route. "It's more fun riding in your truck, especially knowing you won first place."

"Don't forget I also took first place for the best historic entry with this baby," Luc bragged, patting the steering wheel. "But I couldn't have done either without you and Henry to help." He glanced over his shoulder and grinned. "Okay back there, Henry?"

"Yes." That was all Henry had said since the moment Luc had lifted him into the restored truck. Dressed in a Western shirt Holly had made for him, jeans and the cowboy boots Luc had provided, he clung wide-eyed to a black Stetson, smaller but identical to Luc's.

The band behind them struck up another number so talking was, for the moment, impossible. That was okay with Luc. He couldn't put what he was feeling into words anyway. Or maybe he could. One word. Perfection.

These past weeks he, Holly and Henry had done everything together from creek-side picnics, hay rides with Henry to just generally enjoying God's creation. Studying his Bible seemed so much easier now that he'd laid off trying to instruct his buddies and instead met with them one evening a week to talk about God and pray. Every day Luc felt he learned a little more about the Father to Whom he'd given his life.

He'd also given up, at least for now, trying to figure out the master plan for his life. Instead, he'd settled in to taking one day at a time, doing the best he could and waiting for God to show him the next step. Most of those steps he'd taken with Holly at his side. She fit perfectly in his world and Luc could not imagine life without her sweet smile and charming laugh.

This summer had been the best of Luc's life. That was because of Holly. She made every day such fun that the days she couldn't join him and Henry to play seemed dull and long. Luc had finally accepted that he was falling for his boss.

And yet he was bothered by the fear of being emotionally tied, even to a wonderful woman like Holly whom he trusted more than anyone. A part of him feared his soul-deep longing for her because lately he'd begun to wonder if he knew the real her, the one she said no one ever saw.

Since Leah's departure, Holly had grown less jovial, more introspective, or perhaps the word was *contemplative*. At first Luc thought she'd finally opened her father's chest and that something in it troubled her. But he'd seen that chest sitting in her sewing room just this morning, still locked tight. So it wasn't that.

What if she isn't who I think she is, Lord?

"Be still and know that I am God." The verse from Psalms filled his head, chasing away the doubts for a moment.

But then Luc saw the way she gazed with longing at an infant in its mother's arms, and his concerns came rushing back. What if he took the risk, told her of his feelings and Holly didn't reciprocate? Worse, what if something later came between them?

Was a relationship with Holly God's will?

"We turn off here, Luc." Holly drew him from his introspection by touching his arm.

Luc nodded and made the turn as he made his decision. He wasn't going to say anything yet. Not until he'd totally thought this through. He'd stick with the status quo. For now.

"You're parking here?" Holly arched her eyebrows as she glanced around the empty field next to the fairgrounds. "We'll have to walk forever to get to the exhibits," she complained.

"Should I drop you there?" He flushed when she stared at him. "I don't want anyone to ding my door if they park too close," he confessed. "I just refinished it."

"Well, Henry." Holly grinned at the boy. "Guess we're taking a walk."

"Can I put my own shoes on?" Henry asked plaintively. "These boots hurt my feet."

Luc helped Henry change shoes, then they walked hand in hand to see if Holly's pumpkin had won a prize.

"It's ginormous," Henry whispered, gazing at the massive orange pumpkin.

"But it doesn't have a blue ribbon," Holly said, sounding a bit let down.

"It has a red one. You won second place and two hundred fifty dollars," Luc told her. "That's not bad for a first timer. Let's go see how your quilt did."

Holly held back a little, and Luc knew why. She didn't want to see that the quilt she'd crafted specially for Leah had received second place, or worse, no award at all. Holly was still emotionally bound to Leah.

"Be positive." He took her hand and led her to the area where quilts of all sizes and colors hung across the hall. "Look, Holly."

Holly's quilt lay spread against a section of the brown paneled wall where its delicate pink, blue, gray and yellow blocks joined together to become a meadow where wildflowers bloomed around a child.

"It's so pretty," Henry said. "Like a picture."

"A very beautiful picture," Luc agreed. He drew her forward to study the tag. "And it's taken first prize with a recommendation to be entered in the national quilt show in Vancouver this November. Congratulations, Holly."

Amazing work, incredible craftsmanship. One of a kind. As Holly read the words on the tag the judges had affixed, a tear tumbled down her cheek.

"Aren't you happy?" Henry asked, his face puzzled.

"People are going to see this beautiful quilt and applaud the talented woman who created it." Luc threw an arm across her shoulders and squeezed.

"No, they're not." Holly swiped away her tear and smiled at him. "This quilt isn't going anywhere except into a box for my friend Dora. She just found out she's pregnant."

Which was nice, but also meant that if Holly gave the quilt away she wouldn't have to look at it anymore and be reminded of Leah. Luc's heart melted.

Please, God, Holly's such a special woman. She deserves to be happy. Please help me bring some joy into her life.

From that moment Luc devoted himself to making it a day to remember. He insisted Holly help him persuade Henry to try every ride in the children's area, especially the miniature ponies. He paid for Holly to try her hand at a water gun gallery, but when she lost, Luc took over and won a huge teddy bear. They both cheered when Henry won a rubber duck.

They sampled burgers and fries and hot dogs and Luc fed Holly onion rings. They stopped by the local Rotary booth for a piece of homemade pie. They watched chuck wagon and chariot races. Luc couldn't stop laughing when Holly's abysmal choices continually came in last.

And finally, with the sun sinking into the western sky, Luc sat with his arms around Holly and Henry as they rode the Ferris wheel. And that's when he knew for sure that this was what he really wanted. A woman, Holly, to love and to cherish, and a son, Henry, to encourage and support. A family.

"He'll never manage the walk back to your truck." Holly smiled as Henry yawned when Luc lifted him down from the ride.

"Won't have to." A moment later Luc lifted the boy atop his shoulders. Even with all their winnings to carry, Luc managed to capture Holly's hand and hold it. "Did you have fun?"

"It was a wonderful day." The midway's multicolored lights reflected on Holly's face, enhancing her sweet smile. That did funny things to his breathing. "I think Henry enjoyed himself. It was a great send-off for his week away at church camp. It was kind of you to pay for that."

"I heard some kids at church talking about camp. When I asked Henry about it he seemed very keen as long as he could come back to Hilda's after." When they reached the truck, Luc lifted the sleeping boy off his shoulders and into the backseat, then did up his seat belt. Henry barely blinked.

"He's not our little waif anymore," she whispered for Luc's ears only.

"I hope he'll move to the ranch soon. It seems like I've waited forever."

"I'm praying for that." Holly smoothed a hand over Henry's warm sticky cheek, brushing away a fluff of cotton candy.

"Thank you." Slightly surprised that Holly would pray for him, Luc helped her into the truck. "Let's get him home," he said then drove to Hilda's.

Since Hilda was entertaining a friend, Holly offered to put Henry to bed. Luc was only too happy to help.

"Thank you, Luc and Holly," Henry whispered on a big yawn.

"You're welcome, darling. Sleep tight." Holly brushed a featherlight kiss against his brow. Luc copied her actions then paused to gaze at the sleeping boy.

My son. Soon, Lord?

A moment later Holly urged him away to give Hilda some privacy. Then they were on the road to Holly's.

"Thank you for spending today with me." Luc reached across the seat, holding out his hand for her to grasp.

"It's been my pleasure." She clasped his hand between hers but her gaze was directed out the side window where, now that they'd left town, the stars were clearly visible in the dark sky. "Luc, could I ask you a favor?"

There was a hesitant tone to the question, as if she wasn't quite sure she should have asked.

"Anything," he said quickly. "What do you need, Holly?"

"A friend." She turned and looked at him, her blue eyes filled with shadows. "A really good friend. Please?"

"I'm right here."

As he pulled into her yard, Luc had a sense that tonight would change everything between them.

Maybe it was a dumb thing to do.

Holly knew she should have opened that trunk months ago and gone through what her dad had left for her on her own. But somehow it always seemed too daunting and she'd put it off. Tonight, with Luc's help, she was going to face whatever was in there.

"Are you sure, Holly?" Luc sat with a glass of iced tea, his gaze intense.

"I'm sure," she whispered. Sitting on the floor in front of the trunk, she crossed her legs, inhaled a breath of courage and leaned forward. Tenderly, she caressed the battered wooden box her father had loved. Then with a swift move she removed the lock, lifted the lid and whispered, "Okay, Dad. What is it you wanted me to find?"

A moment later she was crying.

"Holly—" Luc's hoarse whisper drew her attention. She smiled at him though tears blocked her vision.

"It's okay." Carefully Holly lifted a tiny white infant's dress for Luc to see. "It's mine. Can you imagine he kept it?"

"You were the most precious thing in his life, Holly." Luc came to sit on the floor beside her. As she turned the dress a small blue velvet bag slid out, which he caught. "Look."

Luc upturned the bag. A baby's fragile necklace with a filigree pendant tumbled into his hand. On the back was inscribed *Daughter* with Holly's birth date. Tears burned her throat but Holly swallowed them. There was so much left in the trunk. She couldn't break down now.

"Pictures," she said, pulling out albums she'd never seen before. "I've seen some but—" Her words died at the sight of a woman by her father's side. Her mother. "I must have been about three when they took this. They look happy."

Holly took a sip of her tea and pressed on. Once she'd finished looking at the pictures that followed her all the way through high school, she pulled out the next album. This one featured pictures of every trophy, every award, every achievement she'd ever attained. She had to laugh.

"What's funny?" Luc asked.

"I don't think many of these are worthy of preservation." She chuckled at the photo of herself sitting in a cow paddy, a calf clasped in her young arms.

"I've never seen you look better," Luc teased.

Holly scowled at him before setting the album aside. Next was a copy of the local newspaper. *Holly Janzen wins Buffalo Gap's first full scholarship.* Her chest felt like it was caving in. *Oh, Dad.*

She set that aside with pictures from her high school graduation. *Not much more to go through now,* she told herself. *Nothing to fear.*

"Want to take a break?" Luc asked. When she shook her head, he refilled her tea and waited till she'd taken a sip. "It's not as bad as you thought, is it?"

But a second later it became infinitely worse.

"Toronto Medical College," Luc read from the pamphlet in her hand. "That's your alma mater."

"Yes." Why did her dad have it?

Holly removed a stack of pictures including one of the apartment building where she'd stayed. But her father had never been there. Confused, Holly picked up a brown notebook from the bottom of the box and stared at it. She couldn't read it. Not with Luc here. She was too afraid of what it said. She set it on the floor.

"Holly? What's wrong?" He reached out a hand. Thinking he'd take the book and begin reading, Holly grabbed one corner. A dozen pictures flew across the floor.

Horrified, Holly's gaze slid over them. Guilt covered her in a blanket so thick she almost smothered. But she couldn't stop staring at one tiny beloved face and wondering how her father came to have it.

Luc picked up that picture and studied it for several moments before he frowned at her. "This baby—whose is it, Holly?"

"Mine." She cleared her throat then released the festering secret. "I met a man, Troy, at the church's singles group. I fell in love with him."

"You don't need to tell me, Holly." Luc's arm drew her against his side, his warmth chasing away the chill that crept toward her heart.

"I have to." She clung to the image of her child. "Please, Luc. Can you listen? I've needed to say this for so long."

"Go ahead." Luc tipped up her chin to look

into her eyes, his own dark and filled with something soft and wondrous. "I'll listen to whatever you want to tell me. I'm your friend, Holly. I won't judge you."

He would when he heard the whole story. Nevertheless, Holly spoke.

"Troy proposed, said we'd get married after he finished medical school, when he could make enough to buy us a home. I didn't tell Dad. It was so new and—" Holly hung her head as shame suffused her. "I was so gullible. We were getting married. What did it matter if we didn't wait?" She prepared for Luc's condemnation.

"I see." That quiet acceptance meant a great deal to Holly but it didn't expunge her guilt.

"I dumped everything I'd believed in for my entire life to be with this man." She dashed away her tears angrily. "How could I have done that for someone so unworthy?"

"You made a mistake." Luc drew her closer, as if to protect her from herself.

"I sure did. The day I told him I was pregnant, Troy walked out, but only after telling me he thought someone in my profession would have more brains than to get pregnant. I couldn't believe it." She relived her confusion and horror. "A baby, a beautiful blessed baby—and he didn't want it. Or me. He wanted me to have an abortion."

Luc muttered something nasty then. "He was a fool."

"No, I was." Holly caught her breath and poured out the rest. "I knew I couldn't come home or tell Dad."

"But why?" Luc asked, clearly puzzled. "Marcus would have—"

"Been so disappointed in me," she finished wearily. "I was supposed to be an example to kids here that you could have your dreams. I'd received a big scholarship from the town. Everyone knew where I was going and why. They expected me to finish my training and come back, work here, help someone else achieve their dream."

"Holly the local hero." Luc's lips pursed.

"Yes. I couldn't come back with a baby in tow. Besides—" Holly hung her head, unable to say the words.

"They would have known you'd betrayed your Christian principles?" Luc asked.

"Yes." Too ashamed to look at him, she kept her head down. "And that would have reflected badly on Dad as well as me."

"Was your father your primary concern?" Luc's voice held such gentleness.

"Back then I told myself it was, but when I looked back on it, I was protecting myself, too," she admitted. "I didn't want to be the local bad girl. I didn't want anyone gossiping about me or saying nasty things to Dad about me."

"That's natural." Luc's lips rested on her hair for a moment. "So how did you manage?"

"I finished school during my pregnancy. In the summer I told Dad I had to pick up a special course I'd missed, that I'd be home by August." Her heart ached for the lies, half truths, for the phony life she'd led. "I had my baby and I took great pains to make sure he had good solid Christian parents. Then I came home."

"You never told anyone except Ron," he guessed, watching her face. "That was, what— five years later?"

"Yes, about that." Shame weighed her down. "He said he could never be with someone like me who lived a lie. He said I should come clean with the people who believed in me."

"As if that would help anyone." Luc snorted his disgust. "As if he'd have stuck around when the gossip started."

"Ron was right. I should have told them all. It would have been infinitely easier than keeping my secret to myself." Holly gazed down at the tiny innocent face in the picture she held. "But I couldn't do it. I couldn't stand to see Dad's disappointment. He would have been so ashamed of me."

"Marcus Janzen would never have been

ashamed of you." Luc shook his head when Holly twisted to stare at him. His arm tightened around her. His voice was strong when he said, "I think you should read that notebook, Holly. Read it now and learn exactly what your father thought of you."

Holly held her breath, half afraid to know what it said yet needing love so badly.

"Finally, at last, find the truth, Holly," Luc said.

Nodding, she lifted the notebook and began to read. The entire time Luc sat beside her, holding her, encouraging her without words. When she'd gone about a third of the way through the book, she closed it and let the tears stream down her face.

"He came to see me," Holly told him. "He says he was lonely and worried something was wrong."

"That was Marcus." A smile hid in Luc's words.

"He stopped by my apartment and heard that I was in hospital." Holly squeezed her eyes closed. "Someone told me I'd had a visitor," she remembered. "I thought it was Troy, that he wanted our baby. But he'd already left town."

"And your dad?" Luc pressed.

Holly read a little more, groaned and shook her head. "Dad saw his grandchild at the hospital. He said he felt it was my decision and he didn't want to interfere. He was able to give his blessing before the baby was given to his adopted parents. He thanks God for that."

"Marcus saw his grandson, Holly." Luc sounded as shocked as she felt.

"Yes, a perfect little boy whom I could have loved, cared for and taught Dad's values." She closed her eyes as the impact of his words sank deep. "With Dad's support I now know I could have weathered anything Buffalo Gap shot at me, but I gave away that chance. That's why God can't forgive me."

"What?" Luc's fingers tightened on her arm. "Holly, God forgave you long ago."

"How could anyone forgive that?" she asked bitterly.

"Your dad did and so has God. I'm sure if you read further, Marcus never blamed you for your mistake or your decision," Luc insisted. "God has infinitely more compassion to forgive than even your loving earthly father."

"You don't understand." Guilt threatened to crush Holly. Not only had she cheated herself of mothering her child, she'd cheated her father. Her sweet, loving father who'd never said a word about what he'd learned. He'd simply gone on loving her.

"Listen to me." Luc forced her to look at him. "I'm going to adopt Henry, right?"

"Yes." Holly felt confused by his words. "What does that—"

"Let me finish." He cupped her face in his hands, his breath whispering across her face as he spoke. "We both know that sometime in the future, without meaning to, I'm going to make a mistake in raising Henry."

"I think you'll be an awesome father," she said.

"Thank you, darling friend." He pressed a kiss to the end of her nose. "But I'm human. I'll mess up. Do you think God will be able to forgive me for it?"

Holly blinked. "Of course."

"Anything?" Luc pressed. "Will He forgive me anything?"

She thought about it then nodded. "Yes."

"The Bible says He remembers our sins no more. So, my dear Holly, God can forgive me for my mistakes but He can't forgive you for giving away your baby?" Luc shook his head, his eyes tender as his thumbs brushed away her tears. "How big is your God, Holly?"

She'd never thought of it like that. After a moment, Luc released her and shifted to crouch beside her.

"Think about God, Holly. Think on His wonder and His love. God sent His son to die for your sins. All of your sins." Luc stared into her eyes for a long time.

Then he leaned forward and pressed his lips to hers in the sweetest kiss she'd ever received.

"I think you need to read the rest of your father's notebook by yourself. Good night, sweet Holly."

She caught his hand just before he left.

"Thank you." She gathered her courage, feeling her way to the words she wanted, needed to say to him. "You've always been there for me just when I need you most. You're the best friend I've ever had. I love you, Luc."

Luc's dark eyes flared wide. It took him a moment to regroup. He touched her cheek with the tip of one finger and opened his lips as if to respond. Instead, he simply smiled and walked away.

Holly sat far into the night, cradling her father's notebook, reading slowly and reliving the past. Then she bowed her head.

"I told Luc I loved him and he walked away, Daddy." Hot bitter tears burned her cheeks. "How can I ever be enough for him to truly love?"

Chapter Thirteen

I love you, Luc.

Those words had swirled through Luc's brain for days and he still didn't know what to do about them. With Henry away at camp he'd had plenty of time to think about Holly's proclamation and his own response. But thinking didn't help.

"It isn't that I don't love Holly," he spoke aloud as he herded the cattle toward fresh pasture. "I do. I've never been more sure of anything in my life."

Why did he love her? He'd come up with a thousand reasons, but the reason that stuck with Luc most was Holly's gritty determination to protect her father from shame. He loved her for caring so deeply for the man who'd loved her.

"It also makes everything much harder," he told a stubborn steer who wouldn't follow the herd. The steer tilted his head sideways as if he didn't quite understand.

"Don't you get it?" He nudged his horse against the wayward animal. "Something from her past or anything else could come between us. What if she found the baby—it could happen, and then what?"

The very thought of loving Holly and then losing her because of something he hadn't foreseen sent shudders down Luc's back.

"I love her so much. I'd give her every bit of love I have to give," he whispered. "But if it wasn't enough, if something happened, I'd never be whole again."

It sounded silly and overly dramatic but experiencing love with Holly only to later lose it would be his mortal wound.

That would be unbearable.

Satisfied that the herd was now safely ensconced in a new feeding area, Luc rode home. He prayed for courage to accept this love and leave the future to God, but his fear drowned out his prayers. Did that mean God intended for him to concentrate on his goal of building his ranch? Was that God's will?

Luc had barely unsaddled his horse when a noise alerted him to someone else's presence. Holly stood by the barn door still clad in her work scrubs, her face pale but brimming with determination.

"Do you have time to talk?" she asked in a quiet voice.

"Sure. Come on in, I'll make coffee." Luc modulated his too-jovial tone. "How are you, Holly?"

"Confused." Instead of going into his house, she sat down on the old willow bench under a huge birch tree whose leaves trembled in the breeze.

"Oh?" he pretended nonchalance.

"I've been trying to understand why you've stayed away." Her troubled gaze held his. "You're probably disgusted by what I told you but—"

"Holly, stop." Luc sat on the grass in front of her and took her hands. "I'm not disgusted. I'm only sad you had to go through it all."

"Oh." Was that relief on her face?

"You don't deserve punishment. You've punished yourself enough." Luc squeezed her hands then let go of them because the contact caused too much inner turmoil and he needed to concentrate on what he had to say. "God doesn't hold grudges. He's forgiven you. The past is over. It's time to move on."

"But I told you—"

"I can't love you, Holly." Her shoulders sagged and her eyes misted, and for a moment Luc wished he'd never said those words.

"Why?"

"Because at heart I'm a coward. I refuse to risk loving and losing." Luc hated revealing his weakness but he needed her to stop believing there could be anything between them.

"Can you explain that?" Holly asked, and when he didn't immediately respond she leaned closer. "Please? I need to understand."

He'd give anything to erase the pain from her eyes.

Anything but love.

"I couldn't take it in when my parents died," Luc began. "I had no relatives to soften the loss. My world crashed and nobody explained anything to me." He still felt the fear lingering in the deepest recesses of his soul. "Everything was bewildering. I'd been happy at home, but, suddenly that was gone. My parents were gone. My life was gone and all I knew was that it would never be the same again."

"Oh, Luc." Her empathy forced him to continue.

"The social workers tried," he said, "but I ended up being shunted from place to place with no say about where I stayed, with whom or for how long."

"That's why you identify with Henry," Holly said.

"I guess." Luc shrugged. "Anyway, one thing kept me going." He felt his body tense as he prepared to reveal his own dark secret. "I had this dream that one day I'd make a place of my own, control my own future. Then I'd finally be home and safe."

"So you bought your ranch." The way Holly said that made it sound so easy.

"I did. But it took a long time and a lot of determination." He fell silent, loath to replay what he'd endured to make his dream live.

"Tell me, Luc." Her soft, cajoling words drew the past from his lips.

"I needed a lot of money so I chose the oil fields. Labor is always in demand there and they pay well, if you can stick it out. I did." He tried to conceal his shudder by shifting on the grass. "I chose the least favorite, highest paid shifts, I accepted the dirtiest job with danger pay and endured the most abusive bosses to earn top dollar for every hour. I dragged myself to bed every night wondering if I'd make it up again in the morning and then rise wondering if anyone would notice if I didn't."

Holly watched him without saying a word. She'd crossed her legs beneath her, huddling against the bench as he spoke.

"But I couldn't make money fast enough." Luc squeezed his eyes closed. "I craved a place of my own. That's why I started fighting. For money. A lot of money."

"Oh." Holly blinked as if she didn't quite understand. "You never said this before."

"It's not something I'm very proud of." He forced a smile. "I want to make my mark, Holly. I want people to know I was here on this earth. I wanted to create a legacy for my child so that he would never have to feel as lost and alone as I did."

"There's nothing wrong with that," she defended.

"Maybe not but I got consumed by my goals. So every weekend off I headed to Calgary and took on another competitor. And every time I won. I was willing to risk any injury if it meant more money. I kept going to build my savings account no matter what." Did she think that was silly? She who'd always belonged?

"You were hurt?" she asked. Luc nodded.

"Many times. Sometimes I almost didn't make it to work. I didn't care. I just kept punching my way to enough cash to finally leave the rigs and the fighting." Luc looked away but somehow he needed to see Holly's reaction so he lifted his head and stared at her. "I have a lot of scars from those years and a lot of bad memories. Like you with your baby, I don't talk about it."

She nodded, her eyes brimming with understanding. Luc had never loved her more.

"Now I have my ranch." He couldn't look at her now, not when he was going to refuse her love. "This is the only place I've felt secure since my parents died."

"And loving me puts that at risk?" She frowned at his nod. "How? We could combine our ranches, make something truly spectacular that we could both be proud of. If you could let go of your fear, we could trust God to give us a wonderful future."

Holly went on, listing opportunities Luc yearned to develop, suggesting ways that together made them stronger.

"I love Henry as much as you do, Luc," she said. "I think I could be a good mother."

"You would be a fantastic mother." He said it without hesitation, a mental image of Holly and Henry laughing together filling his mind. For a moment he wavered. Maybe it was possible. Maybe they could...

Luc's cell phone rang. He glanced at Holly, who smiled.

"Go ahead and answer it. I'll wait."

"Thanks." His heart sank at the sound of his buddy Andy's voice. He'd just received divorce papers. "Can I call you right back?" Luc asked. He hung up, glanced at Holly. "I'm sorry, Holly. I wish I had it in me to take a chance on a future with you, but I just can't jeopardize my future. What's happened to him—" he inclined his head toward his phone "—could happen to us and it terrifies me. If I could marry anyone, Holly, it would be you. But I can't risk it."

"You mean you won't." She rose, her back very straight.

"Yes."

"If you really believe that placing our faith in God to help us keep a relationship together would be a risk then you shouldn't do it," she said, her voice cool and calm. "You've talked a lot about finding God's will for your life. I'd never say I'm God's will for you, but I do believe that you will never discover His plan for you until you free yourself of the fear that loving someone means your world will come crashing down around you."

Luc knew she was hurting. Because of him. He rose slowly, held out a hand. "Holly, I wish—"

"Don't wish anymore, Luc. You've been granted your wish in this ranch. Soon you'll have Henry, too. I hope you enjoy both." She walked away from him in a dignified stride, head held high.

Luc watched her ride away, his hands clenched. Every cell in his body wanted to run after her, to gather her in his arms and hang on forever. But he couldn't do that.

He'd just have to learn how to be content with his life without Holly.

Somehow.

* * *

"I'm sorry, sweetie, but I don't know how to help you." Three weeks later, Abby hugged Holly. "Luc has to find his security in God's time. You can't force it."

"I know. It's just so hard, living so close. How am I going to go on seeing him every day, pretending we're only friends?" Holly sipped the hot strong coffee Abby had served and tried not to envy her friend her happy marriage, darling twins and adopted son, Ivor. Abby's life was full while Holly's felt so empty.

"You're going to leave Luc to God. He's the only one who can work it out." Abby smiled. "Maybe it's time to try something new."

Holly thought about Abby's advice all the way home. There she surveyed her workroom with its shelves now stocked full of many sweet outfits, just waiting for online orders. Try something new, but what? All she wanted was Luc.

She made herself a salad then later took Melody for a short ride, careful to avoid areas where she thought Luc might be. Though August's wane and the shift to September's autumn was her favorite season, Holly found little solace in the ride. All she could think of was that now the freedom she'd always found on Cool Springs Ranch was gone. From this point on it would be very uncomfortable to work with Luc as her foreman.

His declaration still haunted her. Gentle Luc a fighter? She couldn't wrap her mind around it. It had been so unexpected. So had his rejection. Now she felt exposed and on edge whenever she was in town, worried she'd run into Luc. When she didn't get that glimpse she craved, she was certain her feelings for him were obvious to everyone. Her situation became more untenable when Mayor Marsha and others asked questions about their relationship.

"Luc and I are friends, Mayor." Holly laughed in her most carefree voice. "Always have been. You know that."

She didn't want friendship. Holly wanted his love, which he wouldn't give. Day after day she champed at the bit, increasingly unsatisfied by a job she'd always loved. For weeks she prayed for a way to find peace until one night she sat on the deck studying September's full moon and relinquished her dreams.

"Okay, God," she huffed at last. "I give up. I can't do anything about Luc. You are the only one who can heal his past. I love him but I'm leaving him up to You. I can't change my mistakes but with Your help I'm letting go of the guilt and my struggle to be perfect Holly. Please show me *Your* plan for my future."

It felt good to say those words, to stop striving to be what she was not. It also hurt beyond belief to accept that God's will might not include a relationship with Luc.

Chilled by the night air, Holly returned inside the house to clean up the kitchen. Maybe that would keep her mind busy. While wiping the counters a piece of paper fell on the floor. Holly bent to pick it up. Her eyes widened.

Suddenly she knew what to do. She made the call that would change her life and take her away from Luc Cramer.

Though he was a wonderful man, he just wasn't for her.

Feeling dog-tired, Luc slid off his horse, onto a stone by the creek and exhaled. These past weeks he'd thrown himself into work from the earliest morning hours to far beyond midnight, trying to chase away the memory of Holly's shattered face. It didn't work.

Every waking moment he saw again her disappointment in him. In between, he remembered the sad looks she gave him when she thought he wasn't watching. If they occasionally met, she thrust out her chin and held his gaze, but Luc saw the pain lurking in those beautiful blue eyes.

Henry was their buffer. With Henry, Holly almost returned to the smiling woman Luc had always admired. With Luc, Holly was cool and businesslike.

"Why doesn't Holly like you?" Henry kept asking.

She loves me. But I'm afraid to love her.

Since Luc couldn't say that, he changed the subject. But often Henry's dark eyes rested on him, brimming with questions. All Luc wanted was the old Holly back, the one who carried her heart on her sleeve.

The one he'd hurt.

"Luc?"

He startled, almost dropped the soda he'd pulled from his saddle pack. Holly stood in front of him, eyes shadowed by her white Stetson.

"Holly." His voice came out hoarse. Luc cleared his throat before asking, "How are you?"

"I need to talk to you." She looked so lovely with the sun blazing down on a shirt that perfectly matched her eyes. He wanted to—

"Go ahead." He waved to a nearby stone but Holly shook her head.

"Are you still interested in buying Cool Springs Ranch?" she asked in a chilly not-like-Holly voice.

Luc's jaw dropped. Never in a million scenarios had he envisioned this.

"I'm moving to Calgary," she said, filling the gap his lack of speech left. "I've accepted a position at the hospital there. I'll be leaving next week."

Luc couldn't take it in. It didn't make sense. Holly loved the ranch, treasured every square mile of the place her father had cared for.

"Why?" he asked.

"Because I've spent too many years trying to be something I'm not. Because I've let guilt for giving away my baby steal years of my life." Her voice, which had started out strong and defiant, gave way to a wobble. She cleared her throat. "Because I won't waste any more time wishing you would take a chance with me on love."

"Holly—"

"I'm starting fresh in Calgary. I intend to find new ways for God to use me. I refuse to be anyone's role model or pretend to be anyone but who God created." Finally, she added, "I can't stay in Buffalo Gap anymore."

"But your dad worked years to build up Cool Springs just for you." Luc shook his head. "How can you just walk away?"

"That was his dream. Besides, he'd understand my decision." Her voice softened as she looked across the land. "He only ever wanted me to be the best I can." Her gaze shifted to Luc. "Dad's in my heart, meshed in my memories."

Luc marveled at the determined undertone in her voice.

"The ranch is just a thing. It's the people in my

life who are important." She waved a hand. "I'm offering a lease with the possibility of a sale. I want to concentrate on where God's taking me. I won't have time to fret about this place."

Holly said the words but Luc could see the effort it cost her.

"I'm not the town mascot or its ambassador or any of those other silly things I've tried to live up to. I'm Holly Janzen and I love you, Luc Cramer." Her blue gaze met his with unblinking directness. "But I refuse to hang around here pining over what will never be. This is your chance to complete your empire. You'll finally have your dream."

Luc struggled for words and failed. Holly smiled as if she understood.

"All I ask is that you keep the sale quiet until I've left town. You can talk to my lawyer about the details." She waited for him to respond, but Luc was still processing. Holly stepped forward, brushed her lips against his cheek and said, "Goodbye, Luc."

Then she swung onto Melody and rode away.

And took Luc's heart with her.

Chapter Fourteen

Holly shoved her dad's beloved trunk into her vehicle then surveyed the ranch one last time. She'd already said goodbye to her horses, her friends, Henry, her life. There was nothing left to do but leave.

"You would have understood, wouldn't you, Dad?" she said as she drove the familiar road away from what had always been home. "Just as you wouldn't have been ashamed or hurt by my baby. You would have forgiven me and welcomed my child into our family. I should have known that."

She should have known her friends would have done the same. She should have trusted them enough. Regrets that she'd lost her baby still stung. They probably always would. But thanks to her father Holly had the precious baby pictures to help her heal. She'd also found ammunition against her guilt. The knowledge that her baby was in God's hands and He was the best father any child could have. Her job was to walk the new path He'd set her on.

And yet the future looked bittersweet to Holly. Until she remembered the promises she'd read this morning from Isaiah's fifty-eighth chapter:

The Lord will always lead you. He will satisfy your needs in dry lands and give strength to your bones. You will be like a garden that has much water, like a spring that never runs dry.

"Yes, I will, God," she said firmly.

There was the old maple tree in whose crook Luc had found her the day Ron dumped her. And there was the paddock where he'd helped her rescue Henry from Ornery Joe. There was the hill where Luc had lit fireworks last New Year's Eve because her father was too sick to do it and the meadow where she'd hoped they would both teach Henry barrel racing and gymkhana. Holly drove slowly, savoring every detail.

This was where she'd found love and lost it.

"Thank You for these precious memories," she whispered. They were dear—that's why she couldn't stay here, couldn't see Luc every day and know he didn't love her enough to overcome his fears. "My heart hurts, God, but I trust You to work all things to Your good."

This was the hardest day of trust she'd ever had.

* * *

"I don't want to go to the creek," Henry said, a mutinous look in his eyes. "It's not fun without Holly."

No, it wasn't. Nothing was, Luc freely admitted. Nothing had been fun since Holly had left two weeks ago.

"What *do* you want to do today?" he asked, regretting his own grumpy tone.

"Nothin'." Henry slumped down, not even interested in Sheba's puppies.

Luc's fingers itched to call Holly and ask her advice. In fact, he even pulled out his phone but never dialed, fear stopping him. A second later it rang.

"Is it Holly?" Henry asked eagerly when Luc answered.

Luc shook his head then told Abby to continue. What she said made his blood run cold.

"I don't know how but Shelly has managed to convince her supervisors that Henry is not thriving here. They have rescinded his case from me back to Shelly," Abby said, obviously disgruntled. "Shelly advised them that Henry will be better off in a family with two parents rather than with a single dad. She's already found an interested couple."

"Meaning?" Luc needed Abby to spell it out.

"At this point, your adoption of Henry is off."

Luc listened blankly to her reassurances, said the right things and eventually hung up.

No, God, his soul cried, but he could say nothing. Shelly had insisted Henry was not to know until she told him.

"What's wrong, Luc?" Henry asked as if sensing his world had just shifted. His small hand slipped inside Luc's. He whispered, "I won't be cranky anymore."

"Oh, Henry. I love you." Luc hunched down and gathered this beloved child into his arms while his heart screamed "Why?"

"I love you, too, Luc." Henry hugged him back but after a moment wiggled free. "Too tight."

Luc laughed though his heart was breaking.

"Let's roast some hot dogs for lunch," he said, knowing that would please Henry. "Then we'll have to get you home. Ms. Hilda's going to get you some new clothes for school."

"'Cause I'm getting big," Henry boasted, his chest puffed out. "I wish Holly could see me growing."

"I do, too, son." The endearment stung. Henry was never going to be his son.

Luc did his best to make the meal fun for Henry but as he drove home from Hilda's later a pall settled over him.

Hoping to shake it, he saddled his horse and rode the ranch hills. All this would be his. It was the legacy he'd worked for but now it was meaningless. It was just land, a house, a ranch. There was no security here. Life had side-swiped him and he was alone. There was no way to protect himself.

This is your chance to complete your empire. You'll finally have your dreams.

Holly's words rang in his ears. But his dream hadn't been to own land. That was just the path he'd chosen to attain what he most wanted—to belong, to love and be loved.

For the second time that day Luc's phone rang.

"Hey, buddy," said his friend Andy. "I'm at your ranch. You said we'd have a steak barbecue tonight, remember? Where are you?"

"On the way." Luc turned his horse and headed for home, dreading the thought of entertaining tonight. He had nothing to offer Andy or anyone else.

As it turned out, Andy was good company. He talked a lot about his kids and though that hurt Luc because he couldn't stop thinking of Henry, it didn't seem to bother Andy.

When dark had fallen they sat outside by the fire pit, coffee mugs in hand as they stared into the coals. The fire encouraged intimacy so Luc finally asked the question that had plagued him for months.

"Are you ever sorry you got married?"

"Are you kidding?" Andy showed his astonishment. "I'd have missed everything. Being a husband, loving a good woman, being a dad. I could never regret that."

"But you've been so hurt," Luc pointed out.

"So? I was hurt when you fought me, remember? But I never regretted the pain when I made that hefty house payment." Andy leaned back, a tiny smile lifting his lips.

"Which you've now lost," Luc pointed out.

"Nope. It's still protecting my family. Besides, I'm not sure all's lost. I believe God's working since I stopped trying to force things and let Him be in control. Finally figured out all I have to do is take the opportunities He gives me."

"Things are better for you, then?"

"We're talking is all. But that's a big step from two months ago." Andy glanced around. "Hey, where's Holly? I thought for sure she'd stop by."

"She moved to Calgary." Suddenly, without meaning to, Luc was pouring out the whole sad story. When he finished, he waited, hoping for some sympathy, maybe a little advice. He didn't expect derision.

"Are you nuts?" Andy gaped at him. "This gorgeous, smart, funny woman tells you she loves you and you chicken out from life?"

"You only met her once," Luc reminded. "In passing."

"So? I recognize quality when I see it," Andy shot back. "Do you love her?"

"Of course, but—"

"There are no buts, buddy. My marital problems have taught me one thing. Love is what life's about. People die, disappoint or leave. Love is the only thing that endures." Andy waved a hand. "One day this place will be gone and you'll be forgotten by everyone but the ones who loved you. Who will that be if you don't reach out and accept when love is offered you?"

"I can't," he said forcefully.

"You can't what? Take the love God offered you for an amazing woman who would share every aspect of your life on this ranch?" Andy shook his head. "Do you know how rare real love is? Instead of opening your heart to such an incredible gift, you let fear take over. You chose your ranch over her. What else is she going to do but pack up and leave?"

"I never thought about it that way," Luc mumbled.

"So think about it. You've got this magnificent spread, your dream. But Holly's gone and Henry will be soon. What's left? What good is your beloved dream if you can't share it?"

There was nothing to say. Andy was right and Luc knew it. But how could he be sure he wasn't making a mistake?

"All this time, I should have taken my own advice because you're not qualified on love, Luc." Andy was only half joking. He rose and dumped out his coffee. "Think and pray about it, buddy. This is a turning point in your faith journey. You've got to trust God sometime." After a slap on the shoulder and a "thanks for supper," Andy left.

Luc sat alone in the darkness with only the faint wail of coyotes.

"So what do I do? What is Your will?"

But he knew. Inside he knew God's will.

God had gifted him with love for Holly and Henry. Whether or not that love would flourish into something he'd only ever dreamed of was not the question. The question was whether or not he'd throw it away.

"What in the world?" Holly blinked groggily. Two thirty in the morning and someone was banging on her door as if there was a fire.

The banging stopped for two seconds then resumed even louder.

"I'm coming," she called as she tied the belt of her robe. "Please stop making that racket," she begged as she dragged open the door then gasped. "Luc? What's wrong?"

"Everything." He leaned against the door frame, tall, lean and incredibly handsome even in the greenish glare of a cheap light fixture. "I need to talk to you."

All down the hallway doors opened and necks craned to see the cause of the commotion. Holly knew that tomorrow she'd get a call from the super to complain about the noise. How she hated this compacted living; she missed the freedom of Cool Springs Ranch.

"You have to talk to me in the middle of the night?" she snapped, irritated by the lack of privacy from curious onlookers. "Well, you can't stand out here to do it. Come in." She latched onto his arm and tugged him inside her apartment. "Now," she demanded, hands on her hips, "what is so important that it couldn't—"

Luc's lips covered hers in a kiss that reached into her heart and pulled her into the circle of his strong arms, right where she'd longed to be. Holly kissed him back, her lips molded to his, her arms sliding around his neck as she wordlessly told him what lay in her heart. How could she not? She'd lived, prayed for this moment. Now she asked no questions, simply gloried in the relief of expressing her love for this magnificent, attractive, delightfully frustrating man.

At last, breathless, Holly eased back to study Luc's beloved face, so glad he kept his strong muscular arms tight around her waist.

"I love you, Holly," Luc said, his voice hushed, reverent. "I have forever but I was afraid to say it. You are what gives my world meaning. You give me strength and support. Without you nothing matters and that scares me a whole lot more than loving you. Come home where you belong, Holly. Please?"

Her smile began with his first words and grew wider the longer he spoke. When he finally finished, she couldn't hide her joy any longer. It spurted out of her in a bubble of laughter.

"Oh, Luc. You really are Mr. Just In Time, aren't you?" She pressed her lips against his mouth once more then broke off the kiss to draw him forward.

"I asked you a question," Luc said with a frown.

"Which I intend to answer. Come and sit down, darling, and I'll explain."

"I like the darling part," he murmured in her ear before following her across the room. Once he was seated on her knobby sofa, Holly sat beside him, deliriously happy when he lifted his arm to draw her close against his side. She left his embrace for one second to lean forward and lift a paper from the coffee table.

"What's that?" He broke away from caressing her neck to stare curiously at the paper.

"This, my darling Luc, is a deal I made with God." She smiled at his mystified look. "It's a lease agreement. You had until tomorrow, technically today," she reminded him, "to contact me before I sign it for a year's lease on this place. For saving me from that alone you deserve many thanks."

"So thank me," he said with a twinkle in his dark eyes. So Holly thanked him as best she could in a kiss that came from her heart and needed no words to explain. "Surely you wouldn't have stayed here?" he asked sometime later with a disapproving glance around. "It's so—" he paused, searching for the right word.

"Ugly?" Holly supplied, hiding her smile.

"Exactly. And this sofa is about as comfortable as the rocks at the creek."

"How I've missed that creek," she told him.

"Then let's go." Luc rose and reached out for her hand.

"Luc, we can't go to the creek now." Holly let him draw her into his arms anyway.

"Work?" he asked, brushing his lips across her forehead.

"No, I'm off tomorrow but—"

"Come on, Holly," he murmured before kissing her once more. "At least come for a ride with me. Please?"

How could she withstand that loving, tender voice? She couldn't. Five minutes later she was changed and riding toward Buffalo Gap in his restored truck. The moments seemed too special, too precious to spend talking so Holly sat next to Luc, silently savoring the joy of having this beloved man of her dreams so near. It seemed mere moments before they arrived at Cool Springs Ranch.

"You've saddled Melody," she marveled when he helped her from the truck. Luc cupped his hands, offering her a step to mount the horse. Then he swung up onto his own.

"Let's go," Luc invited. Holly nodded.

The September night was clear with a blazingly bright full moon that lit their way up the hills to the spot Holly treasured most. She'd never thought to return and now caught her breath at the beauty of the silver-sparkled water, the milky white stones glowing in the moonlight and the murmur of bubbling creek water.

"Look, Holly," Luc whispered, one arm around her waist while the other waved to the panoramic view before them. "This is our land. This is our home."

"Yours," she corrected.

Luc shook his head.

"Ours." He helped her sit on the largest boulder then knelt in front of her. "Before he died, your father made me promise that I'd make sure you were happy. I haven't done a very good job of that. I'd like to make amends starting now."

"Oh, Luc." She loved his hands covering hers then linking their fingers together.

"I love you, Holly. Without you, nothing else in my world matters." Luc's voice betrayed no pause, no hesitation. "I'm sorry I never told you that. I'm sorry I didn't make sure you knew that you are my security, my meaning, the one I trust above all others."

"I love you, too, Luc," she whispered. "So much."

He smiled but placed a finger against her lips letting her know he needed to say this.

"This love for you is the most precious gift God's ever given me. It allows me to face the future with you with no fear, because God will be behind us. It means I can handle anything as long as God is with us."

Holly studied his dear face with misty eyes and a heart full of praise. Once again God had proven his love for her by sending her this beloved man.

"What I'm asking you for, Holly, is a life partnership, a non-breakable promise that I will hold you to," he warned, his voice tense. "I need you to love me as much as I love you."

For a moment the world around them stood still, breathless, waiting. Then,

"Will you marry me, Holly Janzen?"

"On one condition," she said through her tears.

"Name it." Luc held her gaze, hands and voice steady.

"You can't rescind it," she said, tenderly cupping his face in her hands. "You can't ever take it back. I love you, Luc Cramer. Since that's not going to change, this has to be a lifetime commitment."

They solemnly shook on it, laughed gleefully

then sealed the deal in the most satisfactory way possible—a kiss. When Luc finally released her, Holly asked about Henry.

"The adoption's fallen through," Luc told her, holding her tight as if to stave off the pain. He explained what Abby had told him. "He's not going to be our son."

"You're going to have to be tougher if you intend to stick with me, Luc." Holly held him close. "We have God on our side and He is faithful. He led the three of us together that first morning when we found Henry. He's not going to abandon us now. This is our first hurdle and we'll trust God. Agreed?"

"How could God have blessed me with such a smart intelligent woman?" Luc asked after he'd sealed their agreement with a kiss.

"Because He's God and He knew you needed me," she shot back with a grin.

"Thank You, Lord." They sat side by side on the rocks, talking, sharing everything in their hearts as the first streaks of daylight turned the sky peach.

"I meant to tell you, Holly. I'm not buying your ranch." Luc smiled at her immediate protest. "Now who doesn't have faith?"

"Tell me your plan." She leaned against him and listened.

"We'll run them as equal partners," Luc told

her. "That's if you want to come back to the ranch. What about your new job?"

"I'm supposed to work a month before deciding but I'd already decided to give notice. I realized it's not where God wants me." She chuckled. "I was waiting to learn His next step but I didn't think I'd find out in the wee hours. Now I know it's with you and Henry. Want to hear *my* plan?"

While the sun crested over the hills, Holly laid out her plan to adopt Henry and then to take online training so she'd be able to help more women.

"I'm going to ask Abby to let me add a counseling service to Family Ties to help those ladies who need us." She raised an eyebrow for Luc's input.

"Just keep some time free for your husband," he said to which she readily agreed.

Chapter Fifteen

"Luc, you're not going to make it back in time for our wedding," Holly wailed into the phone one late-October morning.

"You're not getting out of marrying me," he said, puffing slightly. "Even if I was late, you know very well it would be worth it."

"So what happened?" she asked, breathless with anticipation at the way her life was changing.

"Your judge heard we're getting married today, asked me about Shelly's petition then told me how much he'd appreciated your nursing ability when he had his heart attack. I told him about our great relationship with Henry and Finn and that we are the best couple the two of them could ever have as parents." He chuckled. "He told me how grateful he was to have you when he was in hospital, and—"

"Luc, get to the point," Holly said with a quick glance at the clock in her bedroom.

"He signed our adoption petition. We are Henry's parents."

Unable to contain her joy, she let out a scream. Then she heard the sound of the phone falling and a faraway squeak of dismay coming from Luc.

"Luc?"

He was going to be late coming back from Calgary. Holly just knew it. And then the release of the birds would be off, which would annoy Mayor Marsha whose idea it was. And that would annoy the school bandleader who wanted his group to perform a "bird" song as Marsha's birds took flight, which in turn would—

"Holly? Holly, are you there?" Luc was back on the phone. "You're worrying again, aren't you?"

"I can't help it, Luc. I love them all but they've taken our simple wedding in the meadow and turned it into some kind of Buffalo Gap circus. And now you're going to be late."

"Impossible. I'm almost to your place. You better be ready to go. I love you, Holly." Luc hung up.

Holly sniffed, clicked off the phone, adjusted her Stetson and the white wedding dress she'd made and decorated with her favorite lace then went to open the door. In the distance she could see dust trails from Luc's restored truck. He'd pick her up then they'd ride to the meadow where they'd be married in front of anyone from Buffalo Gap who wanted to attend. Which by now was probably every one of them.

"'This is the day that the Lord hath made,'" she recited between calming breaths as Luc finally pulled up. She slid into his arms for a reassuring kiss. "Darling, your truck looks magnificent with those ribbons."

"That was Hilda's idea. She wants to make wedding knots or something. I sure hope she doesn't leave any scratches." Luc leaned back to survey her. "You're beautiful, Holly. A credit to the town, best bride Buffalo Gap's ever seen, symbol of everything—" He had to stop because Holly put her hand over his mouth.

"In about ten minutes, if you don't delay, I will be Holly Cramer and I'll never have to pay attention to what anyone says about Holly Janzen again," she told him. "Now let's go."

"Huh." Luc helped her into the truck then climbed in beside her. "Is my name the only reason you're marrying me?"

"Not even close," Holly assured him with a smug smile.

After a very satisfying embrace, which delayed the wedding a little longer, they drove to the meadow where Henry waited impatiently.

"What's around your neck, Henry?" Luc

asked, shooting Holly a surprised look. She shook her head.

"I'm the ring bearer, right?" Henry glanced at them, waiting for reassurance.

"Right." Holly bent and pressed a kiss against his cheek. "Everyone will know that because you're carrying a pillow with our rings."

"Yeah. And everybody knows Luc. But you went away," Henry said to Holly. He shoved his glasses up his nose with one hand, his little face as serious as could be. "So me an' Tommy, my buddy from school, hafta make sure all these people know who you are."

"Good idea." Luc winked at Holly.

"So we made a sign to tell them." As Henry shifted a sign swung from his back to his front. "We did it at school. Teacher helped us to not spell it wrong."

Here comes the bride.

Holly wasn't sure whether to laugh or cry. All she knew was this precious boy and man were hers to love forever. Because God so loved her.

"All right now." Luc's arm slid around her waist. "Are we ready to get married, Holly?"

Just then Ornery Joe stuck his head through a nearby grove of trees. Holly glanced at Luc.

"Really?"

"A lesson in getting softened by love would do him good." Luc kissed her nose. "Don't worry, he can't get out."

"Make that a three-ring circus," Holly muttered.

"Which you love." Luc leaned toward her. "Ready?"

"Absolutely."

Luc signaled to Hilda, who attached the rings to Henry's pillow then urged him down the makeshift aisle, his sign bumping from knee to knee as he walked. Luc hurried around the side of the assembled townsfolk to the arch in front and waited beside Pastor Don for Holly.

Holly paused to take in the blessings God had showered on her. Everything in her life had led her to this moment. She could not regret any of it.

"I love you, Dad," she whispered inside her heart. Then she took the next step to the rest of her life.

* * * * *

Dear Reader,

Welcome back to my fictional town of Buffalo Gap where cowboys roam as freely as their herds. I hope you enjoyed Holly and Luc's story. Holly is trying to live up to the town's high expectations and Luc has never quite been able to let go of the loss of his family and security. Neither is ready to let go of the past and move into what God has specially planned for them until they relinquish their lack of trust in the Father who is love. Their story reminds us that none of us stands alone, each of us requires God's grace, leading and forgiveness before we can truly live as His children. Henry is a reminder that though life is rarely simple it can be filled with simple joy if we will trust.

I love to hear from readers. You can friend me at facebook.com/LoisRicherAuthor, via email at loisricher@yahoo.com or through loisricher.com. For those who prefer snail mail, you can write to me at Box 639, Nipawin, Sk. Canada S0E 1E0.

Till we meet again I pray you'll feel the intense, never-ending, gloriously motivating love of our Father God in every aspect of your life.

Blessings,

Lois Richer

REQUEST YOUR FREE BOOKS!
2 FREE WHOLESOME ROMANCE NOVELS
IN LARGER PRINT
PLUS 2
FREE
MYSTERY GIFTS

✻✻✻✻✻✻✻✻✻✻✻✻✻✻✻✻✻✻✻✻✻✻✻✻✻✻✻✻✻

HEARTWARMING™

✻✻✻✻✻✻✻✻✻✻✻✻✻✻✻✻✻✻✻✻✻✻✻✻✻✻✻✻✻✻

Wholesome, tender romances

YES! Please send me 2 FREE Harlequin® Heartwarming Larger-Print novels and my 2 FREE mystery gifts (gifts worth about $10). After receiving them, if I don't wish to receive any more books, I can return the shipping statement marked "cancel." If I don't cancel, I will receive 4 brand-new larger-print novels every month and be billed just $5.24 per book in the U.S. or $5.99 per book in Canada. That's a savings of at least 19% off the cover price. It's quite a bargain! Shipping and handling is just 50¢ per book in the U.S. and 75¢ per book in Canada.* I understand that accepting the 2 free books and gifts places me under no obligation to buy anything. I can always return a shipment and cancel at any time. Even if I never buy another book, the two free books and gifts are mine to keep forever.

161/361 IDN GHX2

Name _____ (PLEASE PRINT) _____

Address _____ Apt. # _____

City _____ State/Prov. _____ Zip/Postal Code _____

Signature (if under 18, a parent or guardian must sign) _____

Mail to the **Reader Service:**
IN U.S.A.: P.O. Box 1867, Buffalo, NY 14240-1867
IN CANADA: P.O. Box 609, Fort Erie, Ontario L2A 5X3

* Terms and prices subject to change without notice. Prices do not include applicable taxes. Sales tax applicable in N.Y. Canadian residents will be charged applicable taxes. Offer not valid in Quebec. This offer is limited to one order per household. Not valid for current subscribers to Harlequin Heartwarming larger-print books. All orders subject to credit approval. Credit or debit balances in a customer's account(s) may be offset by any other outstanding balance owed by or to the customer. Please allow 4 to 6 weeks for delivery. Offer available while quantities last.

Your Privacy—The Reader Service is committed to protecting your privacy. Our Privacy Policy is available online at www.ReaderService.com or upon request from the Reader Service.

We make a portion of our mailing list available to reputable third parties that offer products we believe may interest you. If you prefer that we not exchange your name with third parties, or if you wish to clarify or modify your communication preferences, please visit us at www.ReaderService.com/consumerchoice or write to us at Reader Service Preference Service, P.O. Box 9062, Buffalo, NY 14240-9062. Include your complete name and address.

HW15

YES! Please send me **The Montana Mavericks Collection** in Larger Print. This collection begins with 3 FREE books and 2 FREE gifts (gifts valued at approx. $20.00 retail) in the first shipment, along with the other first 4 books from the collection! If I do not cancel, I will receive 8 monthly shipments until I have the entire 51-book Montana Mavericks collection. I will receive 2 or 3 FREE books in each shipment and I will pay just $4.99 US/ $5.89 CDN for each of the other four books in each shipment, plus $2.99 for shipping and handling per shipment.*If I decide to keep the entire collection, I'll have paid for only 32 books, because 19 books are FREE! I understand that accepting the 3 free books and gifts places me under no obligation to buy anything. I can always return a shipment and cancel at any time. My free books and gifts are mine to keep no matter what I decide.

263 HCN 2404   463 HCN 2404

Name	(PLEASE PRINT)	
Address		Apt. #
City	State/Prov.	Zip/Postal Code

Signature (if under 18, a parent or guardian must sign)

Mail to the **Reader Service:**
IN U.S.A.: P.O. Box 1867, Buffalo, NY 14240-1867
IN CANADA: P.O. Box 609, Fort Erie, Ontario L2A 5X3

* Terms and prices subject to change without notice. Prices do not include applicable taxes. Sales tax applicable in N.Y. Canadian residents will be charged applicable taxes. This offer is limited to one order per household. All orders subject to approval. Credit or debit balances in a customer's account(s) may be offset by any other outstanding balance owed by or to the customer. Please allow 4 to 6 weeks for delivery. Offer available while quantities last. Offer not available to Quebec residents.

Your Privacy—The Reader Service is committed to protecting your privacy. Our Privacy Policy is available online at www.ReaderService.com or upon request from the Reader Service.

We make a portion of our mailing list available to reputable third parties that offer products we believe may interest you. If you prefer that we not exchange your name with third parties, or if you wish to clarify or modify your communication preferences, please visit us at www.ReaderService.com/consumerschoice or write to us at Reader Service Preference Service, P.O. Box 9062, Buffalo, NY 14269. Include your complete name and address.

MMLPBPA15

STEPHANIE
BOND

32607 BODY MOVERS:
       3 MEN AND A BODY   ___$13.95 U.S. ___$13.95 CAN.
32484 BODY MOVERS: 2 BODIES
       FOR THE PRICE OF 1   ___$13.95 U.S. ___$16.95 CAN.

(limited quantities available)

TOTAL AMOUNT $ _____
POSTAGE & HANDLING $ _____
($1.00 for 1 book, 50¢ for each additional)
APPLICABLE TAXES* $ _____
TOTAL PAYABLE $ _____

(check or money order—please do not send cash)

To order, complete this form and send it, along with a check or money order for the total above, payable to MIRA Books, to: **In the U.S.:** 3010 Walden Avenue, P.O. Box 9077, Buffalo, NY 14269-9077; **In Canada:** P.O. Box 636, Fort Erie, Ontario, L2A 5X3.

Name: _____
Address: _____ City: _____
State/Prov.: _____ Zip/Postal Code: _____
Account Number (if applicable): _____
075 CSAS

*New York residents remit applicable sales taxes.
*Canadian residents remit applicable GST and provincial taxes.

MIRA | HARLEQUIN®
www.Harlequin.com

MSB0611BL

REQUEST YOUR FREE BOOKS!

2 FREE NOVELS
FROM THE ROMANCE COLLECTION
PLUS 2 FREE GIFTS!

YES! Please send me 2 FREE novels from the Romance Collection and my 2 FREE gifts (gifts are worth about $10). After receiving them, if I don't wish to receive any more books, I can return the shipping statement marked "cancel." If I don't cancel, I will receive 4 brand-new novels every month and be billed just $5.74 per book in the U.S. or $6.24 per book in Canada. That's a saving of at least 28% off the cover price. It's quite a bargain! Shipping and handling is just 50¢ per book in the U.S. and 75¢ per book in Canada.* I understand that accepting the 2 free books and gifts places me under no obligation to buy anything. I can always return a shipment and cancel at any time. Even if I never buy another book, the two free books and gifts are mine to keep forever.

194/394 MDN FDC5

Name	(PLEASE PRINT)

Address	Apt. #

City	State/Prov.	Zip/Postal Code

Signature (if under 18, a parent or guardian must sign)

Mail to the **Reader Service:**
IN U.S.A.: P.O. Box 1867, Buffalo, NY 14240-1867
IN CANADA: P.O. Box 609, Fort Erie, Ontario L2A 5X3

Not valid for current subscribers to the Romance Collection
or the Romance/Suspense Collection.

Want to try two free books from another line?
Call 1-800-873-8635 or visit www.ReaderService.com.

* Terms and prices subject to change without notice. Prices do not include applicable taxes. Sales tax applicable in N.Y. Canadian residents will be charged applicable taxes. Offer not valid in Quebec. This offer is limited to one order per household. All orders subject to credit approval. Credit or debit balances in a customer's account(s) may be offset by any other outstanding balance owed by or to the customer. Please allow 4 to 6 weeks for delivery. Offer available while quantities last.

Your Privacy—The Reader Service is committed to protecting your privacy. Our Privacy Policy is available online at www.ReaderService.com or upon request from the Reader Service.

We make a portion of our mailing list available to reputable third parties that offer products we believe may interest you. If you prefer that we not exchange your name with third parties, or if you wish to clarify or modify your communication preferences, please visit us at www.ReaderService.com/consumerschoice or write to us at Reader Service Preference Service, P.O. Box 9062, Buffalo, NY 14269. Include your complete name and address.

MROM11

STEPHANIE BOND

Baby, DRIVE SOUTH

MIRA®

MIRA

Recycling programs
for this product may
not exist in your area.

ISBN-13: 978-0-7783-2944-2

BABY, DRIVE SOUTH

Copyright © 2011 by Stephanie Bond, Inc.

For questions and comments about the quality of this book please contact us at Customer_eCare@Harlequin.ca.

www.MIRABooks.com

Printed in U.S.A.

*This book is dedicated to every person
who has ever lived in "the country"...
and to those who long to.*

ABOUT THE AUTHOR

Stephanie Bond was raised on a farm
in Eastern Kentucky where books—
mostly romance novels—were her number one
form of entertainment, which she credits with
instilling in her "the rhythm of storytelling."
Years later, she answered the call back to books
to create her own stories. She sold her first
manuscript in 1995 and soon left her corporate
programming job to write fiction full-time.
Today, Stephanie has over fifty titles to
her name, and lives in midtown Atlanta.
Visit www.stephaniebond.com for more information
about the author and her books.

Prologue

Marcus Armstrong gaped at his two younger brothers sitting on the other side of his desk, unable to believe his ears. "Is this a joke? The last thing we need in this town is *women!*"

Middle brother, Kendall, averted his gaze and wiped his hand over his mouth. But their younger brother, Porter, always the hothead, leaped from his chair.

"This isn't a joke, Marcus, and you're being an idiot!"

Marcus planted his hands on his desk, then pushed to his feet. "Watch your mouth, little brother. I can still pin your ears back if I have a mind to."

Porter's chin went up. "I'd like to see you try that."

Kendall stood and positioned himself between them, hands up. "That's enough, you two. Let's sit down and discuss this like businessmen—and brothers."

At Kendall's calming tone, some of Marcus's anger defused, replaced by a twinge of guilt. Kendall had been playing referee all of their lives. Marcus conceded it was the only way the three of them had gotten as far as they had rebuilding their hometown of Sweetness, Georgia, which had been leveled by an F-5 tornado ten years ago.

By the grace of God, no lives had been lost. But with the infrastructure of the dying, remote mountain town obliterated, residents had abandoned their property and fled to safer and more prosperous ground. Of the three of them, only Porter had been around when the tornado had struck. After seeing their widowed mother settled in with her sister near Atlanta, he'd returned to the Armed Forces, like his older brothers. Scattered to far ends of the world, they each had fulfilled stints of active duty in different branches, then, fortuitously, their tours had ended within a few months of each other and they'd returned to civilian life.

While working in the Air Force on reconstruction projects after natural disasters, Kendall had learned of the U.S. government's interest in "green-town" experiments. He proposed they apply to the program to rebuild the town of Sweetness on the burgeoning industries of alternative energy and recycling. The recycling had made sense because there was a ton of debris to clear before they could lay out roads and set the boundaries of the new town. They were given a grant and a two-year window to meet minimum requirements—otherwise the land designated as the city limits of Sweetness would revert to the government. Three months into the enormous undertaking, they were making progress and Marcus was pleased by the fact he and his brothers were seeing eye to eye on the reconstruction efforts…except, apparently, on one critical topic.

"Kendall," Marcus said, "surely you don't support Porter's cockamamie idea of bringing women here."

Kendall looked pained, then lifted his shoulders in a shrug. "The men are getting restless, Marcus. They're young and…"

"Horny," Porter supplied.

"Right." Kendall sighed. "They want some female companionship, or at least some feminine scenery."

"There's Molly at the dining hall," Marcus said.

"Molly is a fine woman," Kendall replied, "but she's old enough to be a grandmother to most of these men."

"Except she was a colonel," Porter added drily. "So she's not exactly the warm and fuzzy grandmotherly type. The other day she clocked me with a wooden spoon because I couldn't finish that gruel she calls oatmeal."

"We're lucky to have her here," Marcus said. "How else would we feed the men?"

"Marcus, she runs that place like a mess hall. And the food is *terrible*."

"It's…edible," Marcus said in her defense. "And it's good that she keeps the men in line."

"Molly is a blessing," Kendall conceded. "But surely you understand the men are more interested in having eligible, young women around."

Marcus scoffed. "These are mostly military guys— they're used to being without female company."

"Sure, when they were in Iraq and Afghanistan!" Porter blurted out. "But now that they're back on American soil, they want to see some American beauties."

"We're only a few hours from Atlanta," Marcus remarked.

"*Four* hours," Porter reminded him.

"The men don't seem to mind the drive when they caravan into the city on the weekends."

Kendall made a thoughtful noise in his throat. "But invariably, some of them don't come back Monday morning. They're either in jail or in love."

Marcus pulled on his chin. Ten crews of twenty-five men each was the minimum number of bodies they needed to keep things moving forward. Admittedly, it *was* getting harder to recruit new workers to replace the men who went AWOL every week.

A commotion outside the office trailer caught their attention. Kendall looked out the window, then bolted for the door. "It's another fight."

Marcus cursed and followed his brothers outside where a few hundred yards away, two men rolled in the red mud, fists flying, while other men stood around egging them on. Kendall and Porter rushed forward to pull the men apart, but wound up getting dragged down in the mud with them instead. Marcus rolled his eyes, then reached for a water hose coiled nearby and turned a stream full force on the fighting men. "Break it up!"

The men separated enough for Kendall and Porter to drag them to their feet and shove them in opposite directions.

"He started it!" one man yelled.

"That's bullshit!" the other man yelled.

"Enough!" Marcus roared. "One more word and your pay will be docked!" He turned to address all the workers. "The next man who wants to fight will be fired on the spot, got it? Now get back to work!"

The men grumbled, but everyone made their way back to the mountainous pile of tires that were being sent through an industrial shredder, cleaned and bagged as mulch. It was their first viable commercial product. Porter, a natural salesman, had convinced several state parks and botanical gardens to switch from natural wood mulch to their reclaimed product that would last for de-

cades. Everything was moving forward as planned...
except for the constant fighting among the men.

Kendall and Porter walked toward Marcus, slinging
mud from their arms. "It's only going to get worse,"
Porter said. "These guys are together all the time, with
no way to blow off steam."

"I have to agree, big brother," Kendall offered, picking up the hose to wash off the worst of the sticky red
mud.

"C'mon, Marcus—having women here will help the
town grow faster," Porter urged. "We're going to need
retail stores and teachers and nurses—"

"And lawyers and doctors," Kendall broke in, giving
Porter a chastising squirt with the hose.

"I don't care what they do for a living," Porter said
with a grin, "as long as they bring skirts and high heels
and perfume. I don't blame the men—I'm tired of being
around a bunch of sweaty, ugly guys, too. And that in-
cludes you two."

Marcus pursed his mouth. "So this is really about
you, Porter. You want us to import women for your own
entertainment."

"No." Then Porter shrugged sheepishly. "But I don't
plan to sit on the sidelines, either. Unlike you, Marcus,
I don't hate women."

Marcus gritted his teeth. "*I don't hate women.* I just
know that bringing a bunch of females into this town
prematurely will be a disaster of epic proportions." He
gestured to the barren red-clay expanse of ground extending to a distant tree line. "Where are they supposed
to live? In the men's barracks?" The utilitarian rectan-
gular building sat at the end of the work site, adding
little to the landscape.

"We could build a boardinghouse across from the dining hall," Kendall offered, handing off the water hose to Porter. "It could be the start of our downtown."

"What about our dire water situation?" Marcus asked, jerking the hose out of Porter's hand and turning it off before he could rinse himself.

"We'd need to repair the water tower sooner rather than later," Kendall admitted.

"But the sooner we make this place civilized," Porter piped up, "the sooner we can bring Mother back home."

A pang struck Marcus in his chest—Porter knew his soft spot. Their mother's pining for her hometown had fueled their decision to rebuild Sweetness. With the whiff of defeat in the air, Marcus pulled his hand down his face. "And how do you propose we go about attracting women to a place where drinking water is at a premium, and the nearest mall is a helicopter ride away?"

Porter's teeth were white in his mud-covered face. "I volunteer to go to Atlanta and start recruiting right away."

Marcus frowned. "At strip clubs and bars? No, thanks."

"You have a better idea?" Porter asked.

"I think it's a bad idea all the way around!" Marcus shouted, then glanced at Kendall, who was, as usual, standing poised to jump between them if necessary.

"*But*...I'll go along with it," Marcus announced, then silenced Porter's shout of victory with a raised hand. "*If* you'll handle the logistics, Kendall."

Kendall's eyes widened. "Me?"

"Yes, you. Porter can get the men started on building

a rooming house and repairing the water tower while you figure out how to import the kind of women we'll need to grow Sweetness."

Marcus turned and strode back toward the office, his muscles tense. A palpable sense of impending doom overwhelmed him.

"Where are you going?" Kendall called behind him.

"To take cover," Marcus yelled over his shoulder. "Because you boys are about to unleash another natural disaster on this town."

1

Porter Armstrong stepped off the metal ladder onto the platform of the newly restored, white water tower soaring over the resurrected town of Sweetness, Georgia. "Town" was a generous description of the expanse of stark land beneath him—fields of bare red clay stretched as far as the eye could see, hemmed by stands of stunted hardwood trees that still bore the ravages of the tornado that had obliterated the small mountain town a decade ago.

Porter had happily united with his older brothers, Marcus and Kendall, in their efforts to rebuild Sweetness. With an army of strong men, they'd made great strides in clearing debris and establishing the basis for the recycling industry they hoped would provide an economic foundation for the fledgling town. One too-tall, too-perfect pine tree in the distance was actually a camouflaged cell tower erected by a communications company turned partner, eager to get in on the ground floor of the green experiment.

The project of which the brothers were most proud—the newly paved road containing recycled asphalt—was a neat black ribbon leading from the horizon into what

had been established as the town center. Granted, downtown Sweetness was more of a vision than a reality since it currently consisted of a dining hall and the boardinghouse that had been built in preparation for impending visitors. But the brothers were optimistic.

Or, according to some, crazy.

Colonel Molly MacIntyre at the diner was one such person. She ruled the men and their dining hall with an iron fist, and did not cotton to the idea of, in her words, "a bunch of flibbertigibbet females" taking over the town.

Porter shrugged out of his work shirt and folded it over the railing to enjoy a rare cool June breeze. The summer heat had been brutal already, with the temperature and humidity sure to get worse before getting better. He pulled a bandanna from his jeans pocket and wiped the sweat dripping down his neck as he scanned the horizon, hoping for a glimpse of movement—anything that might indicate a response from the ad Kendall had placed in the newspaper. The ad had run in a northern town hit particularly hard by the economic downturn, and had stated their need for "one hundred women looking for a fresh start." Kendall had reasoned women were more likely to come and stay if accompanied by friends and if they relocated from a good distance. Women in nearby Atlanta, his brother had insisted, would be too likely to hightail it back home when the going got rough.

Whatever. It wasn't as if Northern women were any different from Southern ones.

The ad had hit the newspaper in Broadway, Michigan, a week ago, and Porter had climbed the water tower sev-

eral times a day in the hopes of spotting a car or moving van headed their way.

Their eldest brother, Marcus, who had grudgingly agreed to the plan to import women, belly laughed every time Porter returned to their office and gave a thumbs-down. Porter dreaded going back to face his gloating big brother again. Marcus was convinced no eligible woman in her right mind would come to their remote mountain town despite the lure of lots of strapping, single Southern men.

For his part, women who weren't in their right mind were just the kind of women Porter was *hoping* would answer their ad. Reckless, ripe and ready for the picking. He hadn't bedded a woman in…

He cursed under his breath as he unclipped a pair of binoculars from his belt. If he couldn't remember when he'd last had a woman's legs wrapped around him, it had been way too long.

Porter adjusted the lenses to bring the distant landscape into focus, zeroing in on the brand-spanking-new road. Due to cost and labor, the brothers had decided to wait to add yellow striping until enough cars arrived to warrant two-way traffic control. For now, the most frequent travelers of the road—rabbits, skunks, opossums and armadillos—didn't seem to mind the omission.

Porter skimmed the view for any signs of human life. In the old days, the water tower had been a lookout for lightning fires and other natural disasters. The metal box on the side of the tank held tornado sirens. By a bizarre twist of fate, the tower from which the mammoth tornado had been spotted to allow an alarm to be sounded had been the only structure spared in the ensuing destruction. Tornadoes at this altitude were rare, and this

one had been monstrous. Every resident had survived, but every man-made thing in the storm's path had been leveled. To the tiny town already dying a slow economic death, it had been the fatal blow.

His brothers hadn't been in town when it happened, but Porter had been home on leave from the Army and vividly remembered climbing out of a root cellar after the twister had passed. Ground-level pictures and television footage couldn't quite capture the utter obliteration of homes, schools, businesses, churches. Only aerial photographs of the flattened debris showed the enormity of the loss. Those gut-wrenching pictures were branded on Porter's brain—their own homestead and all its contents had simply vanished from its concrete footer. Hauntingly, the black metal mailbox left standing at the end of the driveway was the only proof the Armstrongs had ever lived on that spot.

His mother had cried for weeks over her missing wedding ring. Even after their father had passed away, she'd worn the gold filigree band every day, but had taken it off moments before the storm hit to do chores. Porter had scoured their property with a metal detector for days before relenting that the ring, like all their other worldly possessions and those of their neighbors, had been lost to the four winds.

When the Armstrong brothers had returned to Sweetness a few months ago, the decaying main road had been overtaken by weeds and fallen trees. Animals had taken up residence in the piles of splintered wood and crumbled brick where houses and businesses had once stood. Porter had taken one look at the remnants of the town, choked with thick kudzu vines, and had been overwhelmed by the magnitude of the task before them.

If either of his two brothers had balked at that moment, he would've gone with them. Kendall had taken in the wasteland before them in heavy silence; but characteristically, Marcus had simply jammed his hands on his hips and said, "Let's get to work, boys."

What lay ahead had been countless hours of back-breaking work for them and the men they'd recruited, most of whom had served with Marcus in the Marines, with Kendall in the Air Force, and with him in the Army. In the beginning, they had all been too tired by the end of the day to think about the fact that their beds were empty. But now...

Porter spotted movement in the distance and jerked the binoculars back to focus. At the sight of heat rising from the dark asphalt in an undulating haze, his heart jumped to his throat—a vehicle was approaching...a *large* vehicle. Porter squinted, trying to make sense of what he was seeing. When realization struck, he almost dropped the binoculars.

It wasn't a large vehicle...it was *several* vehicles approaching. No—

Dozens.

A bumper-to-bumper caravan was headed straight for Sweetness! And from the looks of the arms and heads and long hair lolling out of convertibles and rolled-down windows, the cars were jam-packed with women. Hot, eager, willing women!

Porter slapped his thigh and whooped with joy. He waved his arms, knowing the chances of anyone noticing him at this distance were slim at best. But the ad had worked—he couldn't wait to tell Marcus! He rushed toward the ladder, returning the binoculars to his belt while fumbling for his cell phone. With one hand he

began to scramble down the tall, narrow ladder, using the other hand to speed-dial his brother, half-wishing he could be there in person to see the look on Marcus's face.

Porter suddenly realized he'd forgotten his shirt and in his hesitation, his foot slipped off a rung. The weight of his body broke his one-handed grip. His gut clenched in realization of just how far a fall off the tower ladder would be. He flailed in midair for a few seconds before conceding defeat and tucking into a roll to help absorb the certain and nasty impact.

As he plummeted through the air, Porter released a strangled curse. Just his rotten luck that carloads of women were finally here…and he'd be lying at the bottom of the water tower with a broken neck.

2

The flat-back landing jarred every bone in Porter's body and drove the air out of his lungs. He lay there for a few seconds and waited for the initial pain to subside before daring to breathe. When he had no choice but to drag air into his body, he registered gratefully that his lungs hadn't been punctured. He only hoped the rest of his internal organs had fared so well. The sweet tang of wild grass and the musty scent of soil filled his nostrils. His ears buzzed with more than the noise of the insects in the weeds around him.

He opened his eyes gingerly and saw the water tower looming over him at a seemingly impossible height. The fact that he was alive was a small miracle.

"Porter? Porter?"

At the sound of his name, he blinked, then realized the distant voice was coming from his cell phone lying near his head.

Marcus.

Porter twisted to reach the phone, but when pain lit up his lower left leg, he shouted in agony.

"Porter?"

He made another attempt, gritting his teeth against

his body's rebellion, and finally closed his fingers around the phone. He brought it to his ear. "Yeah, I'm here."

"What happened?"

Porter winced again, contrite. "I was on the water tower."

"And?"

"And...I have good news and bad news."

Marcus's sigh crackled like static over the phone. "Give me the good news."

"There's a caravan of women headed into town."

"If that's the good news," Marcus said sourly, "I don't think I want to hear the bad news."

"The bad news is I fell off the water tower and I think I broke my leg."

Porter held the phone away from his ear to spare himself the litany of curses his brother unleashed. When Marcus quieted, Porter put the phone back to his mouth. "Are you going to come get me, or do I have to crawl back to town?"

"Are you bleeding?"

Porter lifted his head and scanned his dust-covered body. "I don't think so."

"For all the good you'll do me now, I might as well let you lie there," Marcus growled, then let loose another string of expletives. "I'll get Kendall. We'll be there as soon as we can." Then he disconnected the call.

Porter laid his head back in the deep grass. Marcus was right—they were already short-handed. If his leg was broken, he'd be laid up for at least a few weeks, a liability to his brothers.

And damn, women were coming! Just when there

was a good reason to be up and moving around, he'd be relegated to bed…and not for fun.

He pushed himself to a sitting position and eased up the leg of his work-worn jeans. He was relieved not to see bones protruding, but the persistent, shooting pain from his ankle confirmed the injury was more than a bruise. Gritting his teeth against the ache, he inched himself backward to lean against a sapling and swat at gnats until he heard the rumble of two four-wheelers heading toward him.

Kendall came into view first, his face a mask of concern. Marcus followed a few yards behind, his mouth pulled down in annoyance. Porter waved to get their attention. They pulled to a stop a few yards away. For all his irritation, Marcus was the first one off his ride, and the first to reach Porter.

"You okay, little brother?"

"Peachy," Porter said through clenched teeth.

Marcus glanced up at the water tower, then back to Porter. "Damn fool. Did you think you could fly?"

Anger flashed through Porter's chest. "Yeah, Marcus, I did a swan dive off the platform."

"We know it was an accident," Kendall soothed, crouching to inspect Porter's leg.

"Doesn't matter whether it was on purpose or not," Marcus grumbled. "Outcome is the same—you're probably out of commission for the whole damn summer!"

"Why don't we wait to see what a doctor says?" Kendall suggested.

"What doctor?" Marcus said with a snort. "One of us will have to take him to Atlanta. As if we didn't have enough to do today."

"Maybe we should call for an airlift," Kendall suggested.

"It's not that serious," Porter protested. "Marcus, if you'll let one of the workers drive me to Atlanta, I'll find an emergency room and be back before you know it."

Marcus gave a noncommittal grunt.

Kendall strode back to the four-wheeler and opened the storage compartment. "I brought a neoprene wrap from the first-aid station, but it's going to be a bumpy ride on the way down." He knelt to fasten the wrap around Porter's ankle, boot and all, then waved for Marcus to get on the other side. When they heaved him to his feet, the flood of pain took Porter's breath away, covering his face with a sheen of sweat.

"Think about something else," Kendall urged.

Porter tried to smile. "I'm thinking…about…all the women…waiting…in town."

"Marcus mentioned you saw some cars headed this way."

"Dozens of cars," Porter said, exhaling loudly. "All carrying…hot, young women. We'll get down the mountain…just in time…to say hello."

"You're going to make a hell of an impression," Marcus offered. "No one's going to want a busted-up man to take care of."

"I beg to differ," Porter said, setting his jaw against the pain. "Women will be…lining up…to take care of me. In fact…that was my plan…all along."

Marcus handed him a small stick. "Here, bite down on this."

"For the pain?"

"No, so you'll stop talking."

Porter tried to laugh, but getting settled on the four-

wheeler was more painful than he'd anticipated. Ditto for the trip down, although Kendall tried to take it easy.

By the time they rolled into the center of town, Porter was ready to be horizontal—and drugged. But the sight of cars of all makes and models pulling to a stop in front of the boardinghouse and diner and all along the narrow paved road sent a shot of adrenaline coursing through his veins. Blondes…brunettes…redheads…it was a veritable smorgasbord of female deliciousness.

Countless feminine faces peered at them questioningly through windshields and open windows. And from their four-wheelers, the Armstrong brothers peered back. Apparently the workers had noticed the caravan of cars passing by because a rickety supply truck chugged up behind them, with men packed in the back like cattle. The tension in the air was palpable, as if both groups knew the importance of this moment, each side sizing up the other.

Porter shot a glance at Marcus and at the panicked look on his older brother's face. A pang of sympathy barbed through him. Poor Marcus. He hated situations he couldn't control. By comparison, Kendall's expression was anxious. He panned the sea of faces, willing… but wary.

Porter decided it was up to him to show these beauties what Southern hospitality was all about. Summoning his strength, he ignored the excruciating pain and pushed himself to a standing position on the four-wheeler.

"Ladies," he shouted, lifting his arms, "on behalf of the Armstrong brothers and our friends, welcome to Sweetness, Georgia!"

Suddenly everything started to go dim. He vaguely heard the sound of whoops and car doors slamming

just as he tumbled headlong from the four-wheeler. At least this fall wasn't as far…but damn, his pride would be busted all to hell. Before he hit the hard clay ground, though, something broke his fall…Kendall. He heard Marcus's voice, cursing, as always, coming to him through a tunnel.

"We need help!" Marcus shouted.

Porter was being laid on the ground. He felt the warm, baked dirt beneath his shoulder blades, sensed the crush of bodies closing around him. His leg was on fire.

"Is anyone a nurse?" Marcus repeated. "My brother fell off the water tower and might have broken his leg!"

Porter felt his equilibrium returning, blinked his eyes open, tried to bring the faces of the circle of women who surrounded him into focus. Alien female scents assailed his nostrils…fruity shampoos, floral perfumes… heaven.

"Will a doctor do?" a female voice said, distant, but strong.

Even flat on his back and fighting unconsciousness, Porter's pulse spiked in anticipation of seeing his angel of mercy. Would she be blonde? Leggy? Busty? Tall?

The circle of onlookers parted to let her in and when she stepped into his line of vision, Porter fought a stab of disappointment.

None of the above.

3

Dr. Nikki Salinger had wondered how long it would take before she truly regretted this arduous trek to Sweetness, Georgia.

"That would be now," she muttered under her breath as she crouched to study the rather large man who had delivered a magnanimous welcome to this so-called town in the middle of nowhere, then dropped like a sack of potatoes. She thought she'd imagined the flutter of movement she'd seen at the top of the water tower when she was driving in. Little did she know it was this fool testing gravity.

The day-long drive from Broadway, Michigan, had left her tired, dusty, hungry and irritable. If the travel conditions weren't wearisome enough, the prattling of the three women who had ridden along in her van was enough to drive her completely mad. Traci, Susan and Rachel could recite the newspaper ad they were respond-ing to by heart: *The new town of Sweetness, Georgia, welcomes one hundred single women with a pioneer-ing spirit looking for a fresh start!* Blah, blah, blah. The women were particularly excited about the part promising lots of single, Southern men. In fact, Rachel

Hutchins, whom Nikki'd had to sidestep to reach the ailing man, seemed to view their adventure as one big manhunt.

Nikki pursed her mouth. She was probably the only woman in the caravan who wasn't in the market for a husband, and here she was, the first one paraded out in front of the herd of men.

Not that it mattered. Next to most of the tall, curvaceous, ultra-feminine women like Rachel, she was boyish and plain in comparison. With her small stature, she knew she came up short, in more ways than one. A fact born out by the faint look of disappointment in her patient's blue eyes when she'd walked into his view. No matter—she'd never been the prettiest girl in the room… but she was usually the smartest. And that would have to do for the big, strapping man lying flat on his back in need of her services.

"Please give us some room," she said to the crowd as she set her medical bag on the ground.

Perspiration trickled down her temples, and energy hummed along her nerve endings—just like every time she handled a medical emergency, she told herself. It made no difference that the dark-haired man before her was shirtless and muscle-bound and bronze from working in the Southern sun. His torso was peppered with bloody scrapes and smudges, presumably sustained in his fall.

She reached out to brush aside damp, thick hair to feel his forehead, but dismissed the expected warmth to the day's blazing heat—he didn't have a fever. Then she pressed her finger to the underside of his thick wrist to check his pulse…not as strong as she'd like, but steady.

He was conscious and breathing, but his eyes were slitted.

"What's his name?" she asked the two men hovering nearby who had the same cobalt-blue eyes as the injured man.

"Porter, ma'am," the younger-looking of the two responded. "Porter Armstrong. I'm Kendall and this is Marcus—we're his brothers."

Nikki nodded then leaned closer to her patient's ear. "Mr. Armstrong, I'm Dr. Salinger. Where does it hurt?"

"My...ankle."

"Anywhere else?"

He grimaced. "My pride."

That made her smile. "Are you allergic to any medications?"

He gave a laborious headshake.

"Okay, hang in there and I'll try to make you as comfortable as possible."

She withdrew a syringe and a vial of painkiller, even as her gaze darted back to the man's face to check his coloring. During her inspection, she took note of his thick eyebrows, broad nose and strong, clefted chin. She ignored the growing murmur of concern and appreciation moving through the crowd of women, as well as the elevation of her own pulse. Porter Armstrong was a patient. The fact that he was better looking than most of her patients back in Broadway was of no consequence— good-looking bodies were beset with sickness and injury the same as average-looking and below-average-looking bodies.

Still, when Nikki gripped his impressive biceps to swab it with alcohol, then stabbed the smooth brown

skin with a hypodermic, she acknowledged clinical appreciation of a healthy muscle for accepting and disseminating the painkiller more effectively. But her admiration ended there.

Within a few seconds, the tension in her patient's face eased and a sigh escaped his lips. "That…feels… better…little…lady…doc."

Nikki bit down on the inside of her cheek. "Good."

Satisfied the injection was enough to take the edge off his pain, she unfastened the neoprene wrap to survey his ankle. The skin was purple and had swollen over the top of his lace-up work boot. At best, it was a nasty sprain. At worst…well, she'd reserve judgment for now, but the swelling was worrisome. Nikki removed a pair of scissors from her bag and cut his jeans leg up to the knee, eliciting more hums from the crowd.

"Nikki, is there anything I can do to help?" Rachel asked, her cotton-candy pink mouth a bow of mock concern.

With great effort, Nikki resisted rolling her eyes. Rachel seemed to think they had something in common because the woman once had been a receptionist in a dermatology office. She'd gushed about their mutual medical "expertise" the entire drive south.

"No, thank you," Nikki chirped, then turned her attention back to the leg that had all the women atwitter, and loosened the tie of his boot. The swollen joint ballooned into the extra room provided. For now she left the boot on to support his injured ankle. The skin wasn't broken, but a hematoma encompassed the ankle and disappeared into his heavy sock. She palpated the skin gingerly, sensitive to her patient's sharp intake of breath.

"I need to take an X-ray to determine if anything's

broken." She looked up at the other Armstrong brothers. "Where is your medical facility?"

When the two men avoided her gaze, she got a sinking feeling. "You don't have one?"

"We have a first-aid station with basic supplies," Kendall said. "But no X-ray equipment."

"We were planning to drive him to Atlanta," Marcus offered. "Or we could call for an airlift if you think it's serious."

Nikki was starting to realize how primitive this "town" really was. The shrinking multi-doctor family practice she'd left back in Broadway suddenly didn't seem so bad. She swallowed hard. "Does your first-aid station have a place for him to lie down?"

"No," Kendall admitted, then jerked his thumb over his shoulder. "But we can move him to the boardinghouse."

It would have to do. "There's a portable stretcher in the back of my van," Nikki said, "along with a mobile X-ray machine, and other supplies." She nodded toward the workers who were still standing in the back of the supply truck like livestock. "Could some of your friends give me a hand unloading?"

Kendall put two fingers in his mouth and gave an ear-piercing whistle. Men began pouring out of the truck, waiting for direction. Nikki tried to stand, but a tug on her wrist held her back. Porter Armstrong had wrapped long, strong fingers around her wrist. "Little lady doc?"

Unbidden, his touch made her heart race. His lopsided smile grabbed at her. His bright blue eyes, even hazed with painkiller, were riveting and so, so sexy.

"Yes?" she managed to say.

He pulled her closer until his breath brushed her cheek. "Did you bring any pretty nurses with you?"

Nikki blinked at the dig, but was saved from responding when his eyes fluttered closed. With an irritated sigh, she checked his pulse again. The brute had passed out.

Nikki stood and strode to the back of her extended van. At a signal from one of the Armstrong brothers, workers began lining up at the rear of her vehicle, although they were visibly distracted by all the eye candy around them. The men openly ogled the preening women standing around their vehicles, and blonde, hair-twirling Rachel Hutchins was getting more than her fair share of attention. Giggles and elbow pokes ensued. Nikki groaned inwardly at all the coupling to come, then chided herself. The other women had come looking for love, not to escape a cheating fiancé. She couldn't begrudge them their fun simply because she didn't plan to have any.

She'd always wanted to build her own practice, she reminded herself. Here was her chance. While the men unloaded box after box of supplies from her van and headed toward the obviously just-built "boarding-house," Nikki took a minute to look around the town of Sweetness.

Which, as far as she could see, consisted of the boardinghouse and some kind of eatery—both constructed with a patchwork of materials—and a hut the Armstrong brothers indicated was their "first-aid station," all sitting at the crossroads of the paved road they'd driven in on and a red dirt road leading somewhere unknown. The white water tower they'd seen on their long approach, Nikki realized, was a veritable flag warning visitors how

far back in time they were traveling. Even in decline, the manufacturing town of Broadway, Michigan, was a bustling metropolis compared to this place.

She'd been duped by a marketing ploy. The name "Sweetness" conjured up lush shade trees, tall glasses of lemonade and white wicker swings. Instead, it was a hot, sticky, dirty, bleak little spot in the road. On a mountain. And from the way the men and women were looking at each other, Sweetness was about to become one big speed-dating pool. And if Porter Armstrong's reaction to her was any indication, she would be the odd person out.

Which was just as well, since she wasn't looking for a man.

Really, she wasn't.

Nikki was suddenly beset with a pang of homesickness for the town and the people she'd left behind. Hot tears stung her eyes. It was the "looking for a fresh start" part of the ad that had caught her attention. But what had she gotten herself into?

Was this what Southerners meant by the saying "out of the frying pan and into the fire"?

Panic gripped her and Nikki considered jumping behind the wheel of the van and peeling out of there—the little nothing of a town was welcome to the supplies already unloaded. She even took a step toward the driver's side.

Then she caught sight of Porter Armstrong being eased onto a hard plastic stretcher, with his brothers on either side, their body language fraught with concern. And something about the looks that passed between the three men stopped her. It was more than sibling obligation—it was apprehension born of deep affection, an

unbreakable bond. And the way the workers responded to the Armstrong men, it was clear their relationship went beyond that of employers and employees—they were family.

Nikki's heart squeezed. Family—something she lacked. She was all alone in the world. She'd thought her engagement was the first step toward creating her own family, something she craved desperately. It was the main reason her fiancé's betrayal had shaken her to the core. What the Armstrong brothers were trying to do here—bring together disparate people from different regions of the country to build a community from scratch—was a concept that appealed to her on a base level. She wanted to be a part of this grand experiment. This might be her last chance to form her own family, if not in the traditional sense, then a family of friends and neighbors.

From the stretcher, Porter Armstrong lifted his dark head. "Hey, where's our doctor?"

Our doctor.

The man was looped on the painkiller, but when his hooded gaze met hers, Nikki's stomach did a little flip. She blamed the uncharacteristic reaction on her vulnerable emotional state. She had no intention of falling for another man who didn't want her. But meanwhile, duty called.

"Coming," she said, then picked up her physician's bag and strode toward her first patient. The first of many?

Only time would tell.

4

With her heart clicking in her chest, Nikki followed the line of men toward the building they referred to as the "boardinghouse," staying close to her patient who was being transported on a hard plastic stretcher by his brothers.

Porter Armstrong grinned. "Look at me—I'm the Queen of Sheba being carried around by my servants."

"I'm not your servant," Marcus barked over his shoulder.

"Pipe down, little brother," Kendall said, his tone a friendly warning.

From the exchange, Nikki realized that beneath the obvious affection between the three men ran an undercurrent of discord. "It's the painkiller talking," she offered. "He doesn't realize what he's saying."

"Dr. Salinger, our little brother talks out of his head most of the time," Marcus said drily, "with or without medication."

Porter turned his head in her direction, his eyes glassy and his smile lopsided. "Marcus and Kendall are sticks in the mud," he slurred, then thumped himself on the

chest. "Tell all your pretty friends *I'm* the fun Armstrong brother." He was looking past her to Rachel Hutchins, who had found a bag of cotton balls to daintily bring along under the guise of helping to transport supplies.

Nikki tried not to react to being excluded from the "pretty" group, but his words cut deep. Academically, she knew that her ex, Darren Rocha, cheating on her said more about his shortcomings than hers, but it was hard not to feel deficient in the looks department—and otherwise—when your fiancé strayed with a stripper.

Her expression must have given her away because Kendall flashed an apologetic smile, then leaned over Porter and said, "Shut your pie hole. Dr. Salinger is here to try to patch you up, not *hook* you up."

"I was only—*ow!*" Porter's protest was cut off when, like a snake striking, Kendall boxed his brother's ear.

Nikki blinked. This was how Southern men treated each other—punching at will? It occurred to her suddenly they were all probably armed, too. Was this a renegade town? Would she be treating gunshot wounds? She wasn't a surgeon, hadn't dealt with serious trauma cases since her residency. And she hadn't noticed a police station or a jail along the road coming in. So who was keeping order in this would-be town of Sweetness, Georgia?

Behind her, she heard two men carrying supplies whispering. "I don't know about you," one of them said, "but I'm not going to a female doctor."

"Me, either," the other man said. "Too embarrassing. Riley can fix me up if I need it."

"You got that right."

She forced herself to keep moving forward, her mind

churning with questions that would have to wait until after she stabilized Porter Armstrong's ankle.

The multicolored wood-plank siding—some planks bare, some painted, some weathered, some new—gave the two-story boardinghouse a decidedly cottage feel. But upon closer inspection, it was huge. A long, deep wraparound porch lined with rough-hewn rocking chairs welcomed them into a spacious great room that was warmly, if sparsely, furnished. The pungent scent of sawdust filled her nostrils as footsteps echoed off the bare wood floors and freshly painted white walls. She walked past a large kitchen and dining room, then lifted her gaze to the second floor. Behind a bright red railing that stretched for days on both sides were numerous doors, presumably bedrooms. Nikki swallowed hard. She hadn't planned on sharing a kitchen and living area with dozens of other women. She only hoped each room had its own bath facilities.

Assuming she stayed.

The wide hall crossed another hallway with more rooms stretching on both floors to the right and to the left. At last the group emptied into a large room spanning the rear of the house that appeared to be another great room of sorts, with bays of tall windows shepherding in slanting rays of the southern sun. The room was largely empty and almost the size of a dance hall. Crazily, she had visions of square-dancing accompanied by much hooting and hollering.

The older Armstrongs deposited their brother, who was now singing at the top of his lungs, on a long, sturdy table.

"Will this do, Dr. Salinger?" Kendall asked her, wincing at Porter's off-key rendition of "Crazy."

She nodded, then directed workers where to set the boxes of equipment and supplies. Rachel stood prettily in everyone's way. Not surprisingly, Porter Armstrong was angling his melodramatic delivery toward the statuesque blonde.

"…and I'm crazy for luh-uh-ving…yooooo…"

Marcus clamped his hand over Porter's mouth, reducing his lyrics to a muffled protest. "Dr. Salinger, we'll start building a proper clinic right away," Marcus told her while his brother squirmed under his pressing hand. "And when everything calms down, we'd like to talk to you about an employment contract."

Nikki merely smiled, unwilling to commit to staying long enough to inhabit a brick-and-mortar building— or whatever strange materials these men would use for construction.

"What can we do to help you now?" Kendall Armstrong asked.

Nikki put her hand to her forehead. Since medical school, the gesture had helped her switch into crisis management mode. "Clear everyone out of here."

"I can assist you, Dr. Salinger," Rachel offered brightly.

"Everyone," Nikki repeated evenly. "I need to get an X-ray of this leg and see what I'm dealing with."

Kendall started shepherding everyone, including the reluctant Rachel, out of the room. Then he turned back and glanced at Porter, who was shouting, "Hey! Where is everybody going? We finally have women in this town…let's have a party!"

"He can be a pill," Kendall said. "We'll check back to see if you need a hand."

Nikki nodded.

Kendall hesitated, then said, "Dr. Salinger, I know the women are probably looking forward to getting settled, but…" He looked sheepish. "Let's just say while we hoped our ad would elicit a response, this is all a little…uh—"

"Overwhelming?" she supplied.

"Yes, ma'am. Is there a particular lady you'd suggest I talk to who would help to coordinate the rest of the group?"

Nikki mentally reviewed the faces and names of the nearly one hundred women who'd traveled from Broadway that she knew—a good number of them, in fact, since many had been patients of hers. Nice enough women, all of them, with different talents and strengths. As much as she resisted, her mind kept going back to one woman.

"Rachel Hutchins," she said finally. "The tall blonde who offered to assist me." She resisted adding that Rachel was no "lady," instead offering, "Rachel spearheaded the trip down here. She has a record of everyone in the group." The woman was vain and haughty, but she could get things done.

Kendall inclined his head. "Thank you, ma'am. I'll leave you to your patient." He flashed a smile. "Good luck."

When the double doors closed, Nikki looked back to said patient, who was now singing a song she didn't know, but it had something to do with trains, pickup trucks and mama. Nikki inhaled for strength, walked over to him and removed his work boot and sock. He wailed throughout.

"Mr. Armstrong," she said loudly, poking one finger

in her ear, "as much as I'm enjoying your singing, I need for you to be quiet while I X-ray your ankle."

He stopped. "Mr. Armstrong is my brother Marcus. Call me Porter." A frown pulled at his mouth and he glanced around wildly. "Why did everyone leave?"

"I asked for some privacy," she murmured, then pushed a button to power up the hand-held X-ray scanner.

He wagged his dark eyebrows. "You wanted to be alone with me, little lady doc?"

Nikki rolled her eyes. "For professional reasons only, Mr. Armstrong. Now I'm going to remove your pants."

"Porter," he corrected, then grinned and clasped his hands beneath his head, as if he were getting comfortable. "And if I had a nickel for every time a woman took my pants off—"

"Spare me the calculation," she interrupted, lifting her scissors. "I'm only cutting open your jeans so I can X-ray your entire leg. You might want to be still so I don't snip something I shouldn't."

That did it. For the time being, at least, he lay unmoving. If only her hands would be as still, she thought with consternation as she laid open the fabric to reveal the rest of his leg.

It was a fine leg. Corded with thick muscle and covered with dark hair except where it had been rubbed off in spots, presumably by tall boots. Small jagged scars started below his knee and grew larger in an arcing pattern moving up his thigh, ending just below the edge of his black boxer briefs.

Nikki winced inwardly—shrapnel scars. She'd completed her residency at a veterans' hospital, so she'd seen

her fair share of the ravaging war wounds. Her respect for Porter Armstrong rose a notch—the man was no stranger to pain.

He squirmed. "Uh, little lady doc?"

"Dr. Salinger," she corrected.

"This is a little embarrassing." His cobalt blue eyes were sheepish as he lowered his hand to cover the growing bulge in his underwear.

It wasn't the first time she'd seen it in her medical career, but it was still unexpected. She averted her gaze and said, "It's okay, Mr. Armstrong."

"Don't take it personally," he slurred. "It's been a long time since I've been this close to a woman."

Nikki pursed her mouth. "I don't take it 'personally,' Mr. Armstrong. It's simply a physiological reaction." And even though his erection obviously wasn't meant for her, she took a moment to note its impressive size out of clinical curiosity.

If pressed, she'd have to say the man's sex organ was above average.

"I'm trying to think of something else," he said, "but it's hard—" He stopped. "I mean, it's *difficult* to think of something else with all those good-looking women outside."

"Keep trying," she said wryly, then pulled the lead-lined apron she was required to wear while operating the X-ray machine over her head.

He made a face at the bulky garment. "I never had a woman want to get me alone and then put more clothes *on*."

Nikki rolled her eyes and picked up the hand-held scanner. "Mr. Armstrong, if you keep talking, I'm afraid

this is going to be very painful." Painful for *her,* but he didn't have to know that.

"Porter," he muttered, but fell quiet.

Nikki had to smother a smile while she held the scanner close to the skin, then ran it slowly over his foot and leg.

She hit a button to tell the machine she was finished, then waited while the image appeared on the eight-by-ten-inch black-and-white screen.

"Is my ankle broken, doc?"

Nikki studied the X-ray and took her time responding. "The ankle is simply the joint where your leg bones meet your foot bones." She turned the screen and pointed to the skeletal image. "Looks like the tibia, which is the larger leg bone connected to your foot, is intact. But the smaller bone, the fibula, is broken, and I'm guessing you have some torn ligaments, too."

"Can you fix me up?"

"I can set the bone and apply a cast to your ankle to support it while everything heals. The bone had a clean break, so it should be fine. But the ligaments are less predictable, and your ankle could be dislocated. You really should see an orthopedic surgeon sometime in the next few weeks to make sure it's healing properly."

"How long will I be laid up?"

"At least six weeks."

He frowned. "That long?"

"More if you have complications."

He looked devastated. "Are you sure?"

She set down the X-ray machine so he could see the screen. "I'm only telling you what I see," she said, arching her eyebrow. "You're welcome to get a second opinion."

A sheepish expression crossed his face. "Okay, do whatever you need to do, little lady doc."

She pulled out a syringe and filled it from a vial.

"Except give me another shot," he protested, pushing up on his elbows. "I already feel…loopy."

She flicked the syringe. "Trust me, Mr. Armstrong, you don't want to be awake while I set the bone."

"Porter. And I can handle pain."

"No doubt," she said, nodding to his scars. "But there's no need to be a hero here. Besides, my job will be easier if you're under."

"Okay," he grumbled.

"While you're out, I'll clean your cuts." She leaned over his arm and swabbed it with an alcohol pad.

"You smell nice," he murmured, his voice husky.

The remark caught her by surprise, sending a shiver along her shoulders. She forced a little laugh. "I smell like the road I came in on."

"You smell good to me."

He smelled good to her, too. A mixture of perspiration, sun and a woodsy scent that didn't come from a bottle. All male.

She sucked in a breath, then stabbed his arm with the syringe and dispensed all the painkiller, for both their sakes. He relaxed noticeably. Nikki leaned down to hold his eye open to check the pupil.

The man had a high level of concentrated pigment in the iris—in other words, his were the bluest eyes she'd ever seen.

"It sure is nice to have women around," he slurred. "It's been a long…long time."

"So you said, Mr. Armstrong," she murmured, then

leaned over to check his other eye, satisfied the medicine was doing its job.

"Porter," he whispered.

Suddenly his hand reached up to clasp her neck, and
before she realized what was happening, he'd pulled her
mouth down on his for a long, wet kiss.

5

Nikki lost her balance and fell against Porter's chest. In those few seconds, she wished she wasn't a doctor and this man wasn't her patient, because it was…a…very…good…kiss. His lips were firm, his tongue seeking. Unbidden, fire streaked through her chest, and an alien sensation—lust?—flowered in her midsection. The realization made her stiffen. The man was sex-starved and under sedation.

She planted her hands against his chest and pushed hard to escape his embrace. "Mr. Armstrong, let go of me," she said, although her voice sounded breathy and weak, even to her own ears.

"Porter!" Marcus shouted from the door. When Nikki turned to see both the older Armstrong brothers charging toward them, she realized they'd returned and witnessed the kiss. By the time the men had reached them, though, Porter had released her and his head lolled to the side. He was out cold.

"I'm sorry, Dr. Salinger," Kendall said. "Are you okay?"

She nodded, but she was still shaken—more by her reaction to the kiss than the kiss itself. After Darren's

betrayal, she'd promised herself she'd be immune to the charms of men, yet here she was trembling like a virgin.

"My little brother has the manners of a mule," Marcus said, his voice thick with disgust.

"It's probably the medication," she murmured, trying to gather herself, but not succeeding. She pressed her fingers to her mouth in an attempt to erase the imprint of Porter Armstrong's lips on hers. Her face burned. The brothers studied her, as if they suspected she might bolt.

Indeed, she was considering it.

"How can we help you?" Kendall asked hopefully.

She touched her hand to her forehead, forcing herself to focus. "His lower leg bone is broken. You can provide some leverage so I can set it."

With their help, she set the bone relatively quickly and confirmed its position with another X-ray. Then she bathed her patient's leg and swollen ankle with antiseptic, and wrapped cotton strips from his instep to just below his knee. Next came wet lengths of fiberglass cloth over the cotton, which dried quickly to form the cast. She'd hoped the rote movements would allow her to distance herself from the man she was administering to, but the amazing kiss kept flashing in her mind like a stuttering synapse, and the adhesive mixture made her light-headed. She felt flustered throughout and was never so glad to be finished with a procedure.

But then she had to bathe the scrapes and scratches on his chest and arms, which required even more contact, to areas that were even more…pleasing. Porter Armstrong's physique was lean, with long, well-developed muscles—a very nice specimen. His pectoralis major and rectus

abdominis were particularly appealing, but his deltoids were noteworthy as well. It was nerve-wracking to administer to him under the scrutiny of his two concerned brothers, but at last she was satisfied he wasn't going to be infected by whatever branches and stones he'd come into contact with during the fall. She snapped off her rubber gloves.

"He's going to be okay?" Marcus asked.

She smiled. "As far as I can tell, although he should be monitored overnight for a fever or pain that might indicate internal bleeding. He should wake up within an hour or so," she said, dousing her hands with sanitizing gel. "I saw the water tower driving in. He's a very lucky man to have sustained such minor injuries from a fall like that."

Marcus frowned. "One day our little brother is going to push his luck too far."

Kendall elbowed Marcus, as if he didn't want him airing family squabbles. "It's kind of you to do this after such a long day, Dr. Salinger. You must be tired and hungry."

"I am," she admitted.

"The men are planning a barbecue tonight in the meadow to welcome our guests," Marcus said. "We hope you'll come."

After her unsettling encounter with Porter Armstrong, she needed some time alone to assess her decision to come to Sweetness. In hindsight, she hadn't thought through the emotional ramifications of picking up and moving across several states to literally build a practice from scratch. And from the conversation she'd overheard earlier, it seemed as if everyone in Sweetness wouldn't be exactly welcoming of her services. She was

starting to think she wasn't ready for a fresh start—not in a place where it seemed her ego was doomed to take a beating.

"If you don't mind," she said, "I'm going to skip the barbecue and get settled in for the night."

"We saved one of the nicer rooms for you," Kendall said, his voice eager. He handed her a key with the number 225.

"Your bags have been carried up," Marcus added.

Both of them were looking at her like hopeful little boys.

"Thank you," she said. "I'm going to freshen up, then I'll be back to check on your brother. He seems like the type who will fight coming out from under the sedation. You should stay with him so he doesn't hurt himself."

"We will," Kendall said. "Thank you, Dr. Salinger."

"Yes, thank you, Dr. Salinger," Marcus said, pumping her hand. "I can't tell you how happy we are that Sweetness has a physician."

Nikki wet her lips. "I heard some men talking earlier about a Dr. Riley?"

"Riley Bates," Kendall said. "He's not a doctor. He gives the men home remedies for minor ailments."

Great. She'd be competing with a witch doctor.

"There's no conflict," Marcus assured her. "Everyone is glad you're here."

But from the brothers' forced smiles, she got the feeling they'd also heard unhappy rumblings among the men about having a "female doctor."

"Don't hang my shingle just yet, gentlemen. Now that I've seen your town, I have some thinking to do." Nikki

picked up her doctor's bag and trudged toward the door. Maybe she'd feel better after a long, hot shower.

Assuming this place had hot water.

This place had no hot water.

Nikki shivered under the shower head, her teeth chattering uncontrollably. After a long, sweaty day, the icy blast had felt refreshing…for about five seconds. Then the cold needles had penetrated her skin and stabbed down to her bones. She hurriedly shampooed her hair and lathered her skin, but it was far from the leisurely bathing experience she'd been looking forward to. She jumped out and wrapped herself in a towel. Still shivering, she walked out of the bathroom into the bedroom she'd been assigned to.

Admittedly, it was a beautiful room, simply decorated with a new black wooden bed and matching wardrobe, plus a red upholstered couch and two cream-colored upholstered chairs around a simple black coffee table. It was a corner room, with two large windows. The sun was on a slow descent into the western clouds, spilling pink and orange tones over a mountain range. When something akin to awe began to bleed into her chest, Nikki turned away. She didn't want to fall in love with anything about Sweetness. Romantic sunsets did not make up for the lack of basics, like hot water and a medical facility.

And her encounter with Porter Armstrong had affected her more deeply than she wanted to acknowledge. For most of her life, she'd been overlooked as a desirable woman, but she'd found acceptance as a medical professional. She'd hoped she was coming to a place where she could start over as a physician and make a

difference. Instead, she'd immediately been reminded she didn't measure up in the dateable department.

And why was she surprised? The Armstrong brothers, after all, were hoping to attract women who wanted to settle down with their workers…and probably with the Armstrong brothers themselves. So if she decided to stay in this place, she'd have to make peace with the idea that she would be immersed in, surrounded by and inundated with besotted women and hormone-crazed men pairing up like animals headed for the Ark…and that in the midst of the chaos, she would stand alone.

She thought she was okay with the idea of throwing herself into her career and giving up the idea of meeting a man to share her life with. But upon closer inspection, Sweetness was possibly the most unfortunate choice of environment she could've made. Considering the comments she'd overheard from the male workers, her ambition of building her own medical practice in Sweetness might be an uphill battle.

So the only practical reason to stay would be if she thought she might be able to achieve…that other thing.

That *meeting a man to share her life with* thing.

Porter Armstrong's incredible kiss taunted her, stirring forgotten urges. Nikki inadvertently licked her lips—she could still taste him, could still feel his strong fingers cupped around the nape of her neck and the warmth of his bare, muscular chest beneath her splayed hands.

Then she gave herself a mental shake. The only reason Porter Armstrong had kissed her was because she was *there*. The man was the exact kind of oaf she'd come here to escape!

Nikki touched her forehead, then checked her watch. She needed to get back to her patient, who most likely wouldn't even remember the kiss that was messing with her ability to make a rational decision about staying in Sweetness, or getting out—as Southerners were fond of saying—while the getting was good.

6

Porter smiled…he was in the old swimming hole he and Marcus and Kendall had played in when they were boys. He was the best diver and the fastest swimmer. It was the one place he could out-do his older brothers, and he loved to show off. But now no matter how much he kicked, he couldn't seem to surface. The harder he tried, the more murky the water became, and the more the sticky mud at the bottom pulled at his legs.

As frustration swelled in his chest painfully, he thrashed and clawed at the water, as afraid of embarrassing himself in front of his brothers as losing his life.

"Stop fighting it," came Marcus's voice, and suddenly Porter's arms were rendered to lead. Which only made him work harder.

"Dammit, Porter, stop fighting us and open your eyes."

As much as he hated doing anything Marcus told him to do, Porter opened his eyes, cringing against the light. He was disoriented, but slowly realized his brothers were holding him down. He grunted and strained against them, his mind reeling.

"Settle down, little brother," Kendall soothed. "You fell off the water tower and broke your leg. Dr. Salinger put you under sedation to set the bone and apply a cast."

Porter relaxed as the events of the afternoon flooded back to him. From the shallow angle of the sun coming through the windows, he realized dusk was approaching. He'd missed most of the day. He winced. His head was pounding and every muscle in his body ached, no doubt a result of his fall.

"Dr. Salinger?" he repeated, squinting as the serious face of a tiny, mousy woman came back to him. "Little lady doc?"

"You owe her a big thank-you," Kendall said, helping him to a sitting position. "If not for her and her van full of supplies, we would've had to take you to Atlanta."

"And you owe her an apology," Marcus barked.

Porter gave the fiberglass cast on his left leg beneath the split in his work jeans a cursory knock. "What for?" he asked absently, still a little woozy.

"We walked in on you kissing her. She was struggling to get away," his older brother bellowed. "Are you such a hound dog that you couldn't keep your hands off the damn doctor?"

Porter squinted. There was a distant recollection of a very nice kiss. He grinned. "What can I say?"

Marcus's face turned crimson. "You can say you're sorry, you idget!"

"It was just a kiss," Porter protested.

"It was inappropriate," Kendall admonished.

"She's already skittish about being the only doctor in town—with no facilities," Marcus said. "We can't

afford to lose her because you can't keep your hands to yourself."

Porter scoffed. "Come on, Marcus. She probably enjoyed it. From what I remember of the little lady doc, she looked like she hasn't been kissed all that much. The woman probably has her nose stuck in a book most of the time, and sleeps with her cat."

At the sound of a door closing, Porter swung his head around to see the topic of their conversation standing there. The woman was tiny—five feet two inches, max—with a figure as slim as a weeping willow branch in stiff khakis and a white button-up shirt. Her mousy-colored hair was falling into her eyes, still damp from a recent shower. The black medical bag she held in one hand looked like it might topple her over. In the other hand, she held a pair of crutches that were almost as tall as she was. Her pale face was free of makeup, highlighting the rings of exhaustion under her eyes. And from the bright pink tinge in her cheeks, she'd obviously heard his comment.

Remorse barbed through Porter's chest. He opened his mouth to apologize, but she straightened and moved toward them like a miniature steamroller.

"How's my patient?" she asked cheerfully.

"Fine," the brothers answered in three-part harmony. Porter shot his brothers an annoyed look.

"I'm fine," he said more forcefully.

Kendall cleared his throat meaningfully.

"Thank you," Porter added, "for…everything."

She gave a curt nod and handed the crutches off to Kendall. "Let's get you on your feet, Mr. Armstrong."

She positioned herself on one side of him and Marcus stepped on the other side.

Porter surveyed her slight frame. "No offense, little lady doc, but maybe Kendall should do this instead of you."

Her pointed chin came up. She had green eyes—rather pretty green eyes. "I'm stronger than I look, Mr. Armstrong."

Feeling put in his place, Porter lifted one arm around Marcus's shoulders, and settled one arm around hers. A jolt of awareness ripped through his body at the feel of her skin beneath his, catching him off guard. She was a tiny thing, with the bone structure of a songbird. She barely came up to his armpit, but true to her word, when he eased to his feet, she bore his weight as well as his big brother. She smelled like wildflowers, fresh and clean. Her hair brushed his chin with the satiny caress of a butterfly wing. His body started to respond, but the memory of a similar reaction when she'd cut his pant leg flashed back to him. He hardened his jaw to get his body under control. Marcus was right—the woman deserved more respect. When he was standing, albeit awkwardly, Kendall grabbed the crutches and gave them to him, allowing Marcus and the doctor to step away.

But when she slipped out from under his arm and took her womanly aromas with her, Porter felt her absence acutely.

"Take a couple of steps," she encouraged.

Maybe it was because he felt like such a heel for the comment he'd made, but he suddenly wanted to please this woman.

He shifted his weight to his good leg, then moved the crutches forward and swung his body to catch up. It was an awkward movement, but muscle memory kicked

in from years before when he'd been on crutches for an injury he'd rather forget.

"Looks like you got the hang of it," Dr. Salinger said. She opened her bag and removed a bottle of pills. "Stay off your feet for the next couple of days. These are for the pain. You should take them with food."

"I'm famished," he admitted.

"The men are having a barbecue in the meadow for our visitors," Kendall said, then jerked his head toward Dr. Salinger when she wasn't looking. Porter, not understanding whatever his brother was trying to tell him, lifted his hands in confusion.

She picked up her bag. "My work here is done."

"Dr. Salinger," Marcus said into the silence, his voice solicitous. "Have you had time to unpack?"

"Not yet," she said, her voice hesitant.

"I hope your room is satisfactory," Kendall added in a rush.

She gave him a little smile. "Yes, it's very comfortable. If you'll excuse me, gentlemen, I think I'll call it a night."

Her slim shoulders drooped as she walked toward the door. Guilt washed over Porter. The woman was a long way from home, and her first day in a strange place had been spent taking care of him. Yet he'd been no gentleman. If his mother were privy to his behavior, she'd give him a good tongue-lashing.

Porter felt the expectant gaze of both of his brothers on him, but he couldn't conjure up any flattering praise to assuage his earlier slight. Instead, he resorted to an approach more familiar to him—flirting.

"Hey, darlin', it's way too early to call it a night," he said, using the voice he reserved for thirty minutes

before a bar's closing time. He winced—his words sounded cheesy even to him, an opinion seconded and thirded by his brothers' withering looks.

Dr. Salinger turned back and kept moving, but pinned him with her intriguing green eyes. "Maybe so, but I have a book to finish, and I wouldn't want my cat to get lonely."

Porter's mouth opened, but he seemed to have lost his ability to speak.

The thud of the door closing behind her mirrored the impact of his heart dropping to his stomach. He was an ass.

"Porter, you're an ass," Marcus confirmed.

"What are we going to do?" Kendall asked, uncharacteristically flustered. "She's probably on her way upstairs to pack and hightail it off this mountain!"

"*We* aren't going to do anything," Marcus said, then reached forward and thumped Porter on the chest. "Fix this, or I might be tempted to break your other leg."

Porter winced and rubbed his sore pectoral muscle. He had no doubt Marcus would do it.

"If Dr. Salinger leaves Sweetness," Kendall added, pacing the floor with agitation, "the rest of the women will probably leave, too. They won't want to live where they can't get medical care." He jammed his hand into his hair. "If word gets out how primitive the conditions are on this mountain, we might never get another woman to set foot in Sweetness."

It shook Porter to see his middle brother so rattled. Sure, the town would grow more quickly with women, and Kendall had been the one who decided to place the ad in Broadway, Michigan, but…he was acting as if he had an *emotional* stake in these women staying—

"Porter!" Marcus shouted. "Are you hearing us? You were the one so gung-ho about bringing a bunch of females here. We spent a damn fortune building this boardinghouse and fixing the water tower for them. Now they're here and you've managed to maul *and* insult the only doctor on her first day!"

"You do need to make this right," Kendall admonished.

"Oh, no, don't put this all on me," Porter said, then an idea occurred to him. "Unless…you want to sweeten the pot a little."

Marcus frowned. "What do you mean?"

"If I can convince the doctor to stay…the homestead gets deeded to me." The Armstrong homestead, where once stood the house they'd grown up in.

"That piece of property belongs to all of us," Marcus said.

"But Porter keeps it cleaned off," Kendall countered. "And face it, Marcus, if we can't get this town off the ground, owning a piece of isolated property on Clover Ridge is going to be a moot point."

Marcus lifted his hands. "Okay. If you can get the doctor to agree to sign a two-year employment contract, you can have the homestead property, little brother."

Porter grinned. "You got yourself a deal."

A rap on the door made them all turn. "Doc" Riley Bates stood there, his soiled work hat in his hand, his grizzled face apprehensive. The man was the oldest worker they had, and even though he pulled his weight, the brothers always tried to find light duty projects for him. Since he had no family, Porter suspected Riley hung around more for company than because he needed or wanted the work. Porter had a soft spot for the man,

who got along well with the workers and gave them teas and compresses for sore throats and black eyes.

"Hey, Riley," Kendall said. "What can we do for you?"

The man gestured toward Porter. "I heard about the accident. I brung something that might help." He held up a small jar.

Marcus grunted. "Thanks, Riley, but we're good—"

"What is it?" Porter cut in, waving the man forward.

"Wintergreen oil," the man said, offering a toothy grin as he handed Porter the grubby jar. "It's good for pain and for swelling."

The man took an "earthy" approach to bathing, too— his body odor was breathtaking. Porter held his breath. "Thank you kindly, Riley. I'll try it."

"Good," the man said, then planted his feet and looked at Porter expectantly. "Go ahead."

"He'll try it later," Marcus said.

Riley looked wounded. "It works better the quicker you rub it in."

"Then let's get to it," Porter said, knowing the man wouldn't be satisfied otherwise. Besides, what could it hurt? He opened the jar and gave it a sniff. The strong minty scent burned the hair in his nose and made his eyes water. He dipped his fingers into the oil and dabbed it on the skin around the top and bottom of his cast. Then he looked at Riley. "Feels better already."

Riley grinned, clearly pleased with himself. "Guess I better get back to work. You let me know, Porter, when you run out."

"Will do," Porter promised.

The old man backed out of the room. When the door

closed, Marcus exhaled and waved his hand in front of his face. "I don't know what smells worse—the man, or his concoctions." He frowned at Porter. "You shouldn't humor him."

"He's harmless," Porter said with a wave.

"Okay," Kendall said. "But he's your problem if he starts making trouble for the new doctor."

"I got it covered—the doctor, too. Consider that employment contract signed."

"Don't get too cocky," Marcus said. "This woman seems immune to those boyish charms of yours."

Porter grinned. "I'll grow on her."

Kendall frowned. "Just don't do anything stupid."

Marcus pointed to Porter's cast. "He means *more* stupid."

As his brothers walked out, a couple of cute girls walked by and gave Porter coy waves before moving on.

Porter smiled. His broken leg gave him the excuse to visit the doctor, which would put him in proximity to all the other single women. And once he convinced the little lady doc to stay, he'd get the family land.

Who was the stupid one?

7

Nikki maintained her composure on the trek back to her room by concentrating on putting one foot in front of the other. But Porter Armstrong's stinging remark reverberated in her head, resurrecting old insecurities and self-doubt her ex-fiancé's betrayal had reinforced.

It hurt to be rejected, darn it.

The women were settling into the rambling boarding-house. Smiling faces passed by and happy feet skipped up and down the stairs. Chatter filled every corner, billowed by bursts of laughter and squeals of delight. But the merriment grated on Nikki's raw nerves—everyone seemed so happy to be here...and she'd never felt more alone.

"Dr. Salinger," called a shrill voice behind her. "Dr. Salinger!"

Rachel Hutchins. Nikki turned and forced a smile up at the towering blonde. "Yes?"

Rachel was holding her pug, Nigel. The wrinkly dark-faced pooch looked uncomfortable, as if he were being squeezed. "How is Porter?" the woman asked, her doe eyes welling with concern.

Nikki pursed her mouth. "He'll live. It's only a broken leg."

"Will he be bedridden?" Rachel looked hopeful.

"Not unless he wants to be," Nikki chirped. "When I left him, he was getting around pretty well on crutches." Nikki turned to go, but Rachel refused to be mollified.

"Is he in a lot of pain?"

She turned back, her ire flaring. "You'll have to ask him."

"Oh, I will," Rachel promised in a singsongy voice. "He's very handsome, isn't he?"

Exasperated, Nikki lifted her hands. "I didn't notice."

Rachel tilted her head. "Really? Gosh, Dr. Salinger, your boyfriend back in Broadway did a horrible, lowdown thing to toss you aside for a stripper, but you shouldn't let it sour you on men altogether."

Nikki bit down on the inside of her cheek. "Fiancé."

"Pardon me?"

"He was my fiancé," Nikki said evenly.

"Ouch—even worse."

Nikki closed her eyes, but when she opened them, the woman and dog were still there. "I'm tired, so if you don't mind, I'm going to my room." She turned and started climbing the stairs. Her feet felt like bricks.

"The men are having a barbecue to welcome us to Sweetness," Rachel said behind her.

"I think I'll pass," Nikki replied over her shoulder.

"Do you suppose Porter will need my help getting there?"

Nikki rolled her eyes, but didn't turn back. "Sounds

like a plan." At the top of the stairs, she veered toward her room at the end of the hall.

"Dr. Salinger?"

Nikki sighed, then turned back and leaned on the railing. "Yes, Rachel?"

"Do you like it here?"

Surprisingly, the woman seemed pensive, as if Nikki's response actually mattered. The dog yelped, and Rachel loosened her grip.

"I...don't know yet."

"Okay, thanks."

Nikki turned back toward her room and pressed her lips together. It looked as if Rachel and Porter Armstrong would be the first couple to pair off. Granted, they did seem suited to each other in terms of physical beauty...and tact.

She wished them well.

As Nikki passed other rooms, she was appalled to find most of the doors standing open. Inside, women were sprawled on the beds and floors, painting toenails and doing each other's hair. Had everyone regressed to college dorm behavior?

"Hey, Dr. Salinger," called Traci Miles, one of the women who'd ridden down in the van with Nikki. She was smearing something gooey on a seated woman's eyebrow. "Want me to wax your brows?" Traci pressed a white strip of cloth to the goo, then ripped it off. The woman in the chair grimaced in pain.

"Um...no, thanks," Nikki said. All the way down the hall came offers for hair highlighting, makeup airbrushing and manicures. She declined as graciously as she could, considering how alien all that girly stuff was to her. She self-consciously touched her never-plucked

eyebrows and bare face and curled under her stubby fingernails. She was the only woman in the building with
a medical degree…so why did she feel lacking?

By the time Nikki closed the door to her own room
and leaned against it, she had made a decision.

She was leaving Sweetness.

She'd wait until everyone had left for the barbecue,
then make her escape to avoid any drama. She'd leave a
note for the Armstrong brothers, and by the time anyone
noticed she was gone—probably tomorrow sometime—
she'd be back in Broadway. She wondered if she could
get her old job back at the family medical practice…
and if the apartment she'd rented after moving out of
Darren's house was still available.

Since she was only a few hours from Atlanta, Nikki
toyed with the idea of driving there to take her chances
in the sprawling metropolis. But she still had some
friends in Broadway, like Amy Bradshaw, a yoga partner and Southern girl whom Nikki had hoped would
come with them to Sweetness. Amy hadn't even considered leaving her civil engineering job to relocate, but
had asked Nikki to stay in touch.

On impulse, Nikki went to her purse and rummaged
for her cell phone to call Amy—maybe she would have
some words of advice, something wise and…*Southern* that would help Nikki see things from a different
perspective.

But at the "No Service" message on her phone screen,
Nikki dropped her head and released a strangled cry of
frustration. The fact that she couldn't reach anyone in
the outside world was a sure sign she needed to leave
this no-cow town, pronto.

Thank goodness she hadn't fully unpacked yet, she

thought as she moved to the one open suitcase on her bed. She refolded the clothes she'd worn earlier and placed them on top, then began to gather the toiletries she'd used. Her movements were furtive, which was ridiculous, she realized. It wasn't as if she was doing anything wrong. In fact, she was correcting a mistake. Coming here made her realize how good she'd had it in Broadway. And if she went back, no one could say Darren Rocha's public disposal of her had humiliated her so much she'd had to leave.

Even though it was true.

She was so deep in thought, a knock startled her. With her heart thumping, Nikki made her way to the door and, in deference to her nearly repacked suitcase on the bed, opened it only a crack. She didn't want to tip off any of the women that she was leaving.

Only it wasn't a woman on the other side.

"Hi," Porter Armstrong said with a pained smile. His cobalt-blue eyes were a little hazy, and he was leaning heavily on his crutches. He had, she noticed, found a shirt—a pale blue T-shirt that stretched agreeably across his biceps and shoulders.

Nikki's pulse picked up. "Is something wrong, Mr. Armstrong?"

"Nope. I came to talk to you. Can I—er, *may* I come in?"

She shifted uncomfortably in the three-inch wide opening, trying to shield the suitcase from his view. "I'd rather you didn't. Did you come up the stairs on your crutches?"

"Thought it would be good practice." Then he made a rueful noise. "Guess I didn't realize how much it would take out of me."

Nikki felt contrite, then opened the door and waved him inside. But she left the door open as he settled himself, of all places, on her bed next to her suitcase.

An acrid aroma filtered into her lungs. "What's that smell?"

"Oh." He grinned. "It's wintergreen oil. Doc Riley says it's good for swelling and pain."

After she'd given him legitimate medical care, he'd sought a second opinion from the resident aromatherapist? Nikki set her jaw. "So are the prescription medications I gave you."

"I know, but the oil can't hurt, can it?"

Nikki dabbed at the corners of her watering eyes. "Only the sensibilities of the people who have to be around you."

His eyes danced. "I grow on people, kind of like this smell."

Beyond frustrated by his mere presence, Nikki folded her arms. "What's on your mind, Mr. Armstrong?"

He surveyed the full suitcase on her bed, then took in the one sitting next to her empty closet. "Going somewhere?"

She bristled. "I just haven't unpacked yet. I've been busy, if you recall."

He nodded. "Sorry about that. I really appreciate you patching me up, little lady doc."

"I took an oath to 'patch people up.' You didn't have to come all the way up here to thank me, Mr. Armstrong."

He was glancing all around. "Nice room. Do you like it?"

She wet her lips. "Yes."

"Any complaints?"

"Hot water would be nice."

He looked offended. "There should be plenty of hot water."

"Well, there wasn't a drop when I took a shower."

He pushed to his feet and hobbled to the bathroom on his crutches. "Are you sure? Did you turn the knob to the left?"

Nikki stuck her tongue into her cheek as he invaded what was supposed to be a private space. "You mean toward the big red 'H'? Yes, I figured that one out."

But he apparently didn't believe her because he opened the glass shower door, reached in and turned on the water, twisting the knob all the way to the left. He leaned on one crutch, and stuck his large hand under the stream. Unbidden, Nikki's thoughts went to being naked in the shower with this man. She gave herself a mental shake, and congratulated herself for making the decision to leave. The last thing she needed was a crush on a gorgeous man who made her feel bad about herself.

His frown deepened. "I calculated carefully for how many and the right size of water heaters to install. Up to two women in a room times ten gallons of water."

"Ten gallons of water?" she asked, confused.

He nodded, then gestured to the fixtures. "We installed low-flow shower heads that deliver about eight gallons of water for a five-minute shower. I used ten gallons in the calculations to make sure there would be enough hot water for a hundred showers in a short period of time."

He looked so proud of himself Nikki almost hated to burst his bubble. But when she could no longer hold it in, she laughed into her hand.

"What's so funny?" he asked.

"I don't know any woman who takes a five-minute shower."

"Really?" He looked panicked, and in the space of a few seconds, Nikki realized how clueless this ladies' man was about ladies. Obviously he had no sisters and had never been married, had never cohabitated with a girlfriend…and apparently, had never even taken a shower with a woman.

"Really," she said, unable to hide her amusement.

He scratched his head. "This isn't good."

Nikki almost felt sorry for him…but didn't. "Well, I'm sure you'll figure it out." She didn't add she wouldn't be around to observe the outcome. Nikki walked back to the main room and stood next to the open door, hoping he would follow. He did, slowly, navigating around the woven throw rugs on the bare wood floors. Every time he swung his body forward on the crutches, the thick muscles in his arms contracted.

Nikki had to avert her gaze.

He stopped next to her bed and leaned over, then used the rubber tip of his crutch to lift the muslin bed skirt. "Is your pussycat hiding?" he asked, craning his neck.

Nikki crossed her arms. "Goodbye, Mr. Armstrong."

The hallway was filled with the sounds of the women leaving their rooms, presumably for the barbecue. Their voices were high-pitched, punctuated with giggles and the *click-clack* of sandals and high heels.

Porter glanced toward the hallway, then back to her with those piercing blue eyes. "Actually, doc, I came to ask if you'd walk down to the barbecue with me. I'm sorry for the things I said earlier—it was a bad

joke. I'm really not such a terrible guy once you get to know me."

Nikki hesitated, allowing her imagination to indulge in the fantasy of spending the evening "getting to know" Porter Armstrong. Any red-blooded woman would relish being in the company of this big, good-looking Southern boy for a few hours, and she was human. And the intensity of his kiss still teased her mouth like a mischievous shadow. But warning bells sounded in her head. That kiss hadn't been intended for her—her mouth had simply been within reach. And she'd heard the man's unflattering opinion of her when he thought she wasn't listening. Her relationship with Darren had taught her to beware of charming kisses and the men attached to them…and Porter Armstrong had confirmed that lesson.

Reminded of her resolve to leave, Nikki lifted her chin. "No, thank you."

Porter's smile fell. He seemed to be at loose ends, obviously unaccustomed to being turned down, especially—she speculated—by someone who looked like her. It was probably more common for women to melt into a puddle of ooze at his feet. "Oh…okay."

Suddenly Rachel Hutchins appeared in the doorway, with Nigel at her feet at the end of a pink leash. The woman was stunningly sexy in a short denim skirt and tight yellow T-shirt, her golden hair flowing around her shoulders. "I thought I heard your voice, Porter. What are you doing up here?" Her voice had a suspicious lilt. Even Nigel glanced back and forth between Porter and Nikki.

"Mr. Armstrong was checking the hot water in my bathroom," Nikki said quickly.

"Oh, it's perfect in my room," Rachel gushed. "I took the longest, hottest shower. It was amazing."

Porter seemed mesmerized. And since even Nikki was visualizing Rachel standing naked under a spray of steaming water, she could only imagine where his mind had gone.

"Rachel," Nikki said brightly to interrupt the uncomfortable moment, "Mr. Armstrong is heading to the barbecue—maybe you could walk with him to make sure he doesn't fall?"

Rachel beamed. "I'd be happy to."

Porter took one swinging step forward, then looked back to Nikki, as if he suddenly remembered she was there. "Come with us, doc."

"Maybe later," she lied, shutting the door to move him along. He looked as if he might protest, but she succeeded in shepherding him into the hall and closed the door on the happy couple. Nikki stood with her ear to the door and listened until the *thump, thump* of his crutches meeting the floor faded. Rachel's tinkling laughter reached back and curled under the door, mocking Nikki. *I'm just like you…only prettier.*

Nikki indulged a barb of envy, then sat down and penned a note to the Armstrong brothers saying she'd decided Sweetness wasn't for her after all, and propped it on the table. When silence settled over the house, she gathered both pieces of luggage, opened the bedroom door and stuck out her head to make sure all was quiet. When she was convinced she was alone in the house, she carried her suitcases into the hall, closed the door and stole downstairs.

Moving stealthily, Nikki exited through the front

door, crossed the shadowed porch and hurried in the direction of her extended van.

Darkness was settling quickly. A light high on a pole in front of the boardinghouse illuminated fluttering moths and guided her footsteps to the side of the road. Then she picked her way down the row of vehicles to her van. Insects chanted in rounds, the noises swelling, then falling away to build again. The unbearable heat of the summer day had given way to a breezy evening. She attributed the wide swing in the temperature to their altitude.

She swallowed hard at the thought of descending the mountain road with nothing more than her headlights and the glow of the three-quarter moon to guide her. Maybe she should wait until morning....

Across the road and beyond a tree line, voices, music and the radiance of a fire indicated the barbecue was getting underway. The good-time sounds pulled at her, but the suitcases in her hands propelled her forward. If she waited until morning, there would be confrontations, explanations, excuses...drama she didn't want or need.

Especially when it came to a certain pair of cobalt-blue eyes.

After loading her suitcases in the back, Nikki climbed into the driver's seat that was uncomfortably warm from the build-up of the day's heat. She zoomed down the window to let the stale air escape.

In the side mirror, the amazing watercolor sunset was melting onto a distant mountain range. Nikki paused a few seconds to drink in the matchless scenery. If this

town ever took root, it would blossom in the most glorious of surroundings.

Then, nursing a tiny pang of regret, she started the engine, turned the van around and pulled away.

.

8

From a rocking chair in the shadows of the porch, Porter observed Dr. Salinger pulling away in her long van. Damn it, Marcus and Kendall had been right about her hightailing it back north at the first chance. Sneaking out when everyone was preoccupied, without so much as a "nice to know you."

Truth be known, his feelings were a little hurt.

Porter pulled at his chin and waited, counting off the seconds the way he and his brothers used to do when they were little, trying to figure out how far away storms were by measuring the time lapse between a flash of lightning and a rumble of thunder. *One Mississippi… two Mississippi…three Mississippi…*

The van's brake lights came on before *four Mississippi,* then the engine sputtered and died.

Porter positioned his crutches and pushed to his feet. His leg was aching from crawling under the van to disconnect the fuel pump, but it was a quick way to safely disable the vehicle.

Marcus had charged him with keeping the little lady doc here. He hadn't specified the methods had to be *aboveboard.*

The van slammed into Park, and the sound of the engine trying to crank floated on the evening breeze. By the time Porter reached the driver's door, Dr. Salinger was banging on the steering wheel and cursing like a longshoreman.

"What's up, doc?"

She startled and screamed, then turned her head to look at him through the open window. "You scared me to death!"

He grinned. "Sorry about that. Going somewhere?"

She opened her mouth, then seemed to cast about for a plausible explanation. "I...was just...exploring."

He craned his neck to look over her shoulder into the backseat. "With your suitcases?"

She looked away, then back, and lifted her hands. "Okay, you got me. I was leaving."

"I guess we didn't make a very good first impression," he conceded. He was struck by the perfection of her profile in the low lighting. The woman had exquisite bone structure. She was really quite pretty...not sexy by any stretch of the imagination, but pretty.

"I shouldn't have come here in the first place," she said quietly. "I...I don't belong here."

No surprise, he thought, Sweetness wasn't good enough for her and her medical degree. "So you're going back home?"

Her small hands tightened on the wheel. "If I can get out of here. I don't know what's wrong with the van." She peered at the dashboard. "The gas tank is almost full and I bought a new battery a couple of weeks ago."

"Let me take a look under the hood," Porter offered magnanimously. "Do you have a flashlight?"

She rummaged in the glove compartment and came up with one. "Can I help?"

"Uh, no. Stay inside in case I need you to turn the key."

He hobbled to the front of the vehicle, then made a big production of lifting the hood and putting the hood's prop arm in place. He pinged the light around, pretending to inspect various pieces and parts, but craned in the direction of the barbecue site with longing. The voices and music were louder, beckoning. Damn, all those hot, single women were being sociable and he was stuck trying to convince the one woman who wanted to leave Sweetness to stay.

"Try turning it over now," he called idly.

She did, but of course, deprived of fuel, the engine didn't catch.

He tapped the flashlight on an engine support, then called, "Again."

She turned over the ignition but again, nada.

After a respectable pause, he slammed down the hood and wiped his hands on his jeans. "Sorry. Looks like you're stuck for a while."

She thrust her head out the window. "What's wrong?"

He shrugged, careful not to lie…too much. "Could be a lot of things. Hard to say in the dark. Best to have a mechanic take a look in the morning."

Her jaw dropped. "In the morning?"

"Everyone is at the barbecue," he said, jerking his thumb over his back toward the commotion through the trees. "Except us."

She frowned. "I thought you were going with Rachel."

As if he needed to be reminded that he'd had to cut

the leggy blonde loose. "My ankle was hurting, so I told her to go on ahead. I was resting on the porch when I saw you sneaking out."

"Did you take the pain pills I gave you?"

"Sure did."

She climbed out and slammed the door. "I wasn't sneaking out."

"Do you need help with your suitcases?"

"You're on crutches," she reminded him, then opened the back door and yanked out her luggage. "Is it safe to leave my van sitting in the middle of the road?"

"It's not like we have a lot of traffic."

But she didn't seem amused as she turned and headed back to the boardinghouse.

"I'll have a couple of the guys come back and roll it to the shoulder," he promised as he hurried to keep up with her. She marched into the house and down the long hallway. For such a small woman, she was sure man-handling those suitcases. At the bottom of the stairs, she whirled around.

"Why are you following me?"

He drew back. "Since you're staying until morning, I thought we'd go to the barbecue together."

"You should be in bed."

Porter's mouth went dry because standing this close to the little lady doc was messing with his senses. The scent of the lemony soap she used filtered into his lungs. Why was he suddenly thinking about her lithe body straddling his on a big, soft bed? Porter shifted on his crutches as a dozen responses to her comment came to mind, innuendos that would've entertained or tempted most women. But he was already in trouble for pushing

things too far with this one, and he couldn't afford to nudge her over the edge.

"I don't want to miss the party," he said finally, then grinned. "But I'd feel better if I were under medical supervision."

"I told you I don't care to go!"

When her eyes filled unexpectedly with tears, Porter almost bolted. Tears were beyond even his skillset. The reasons men cried could be counted on one hand: a Superbowl win, a Superbowl loss, too much hot sauce and losing a favorite spinner bait. The reasons women cried were limitless and mysterious, running the gamut from hormones to clearance sales. He was at a loss.

Besides, he was a modern guy—the woman had a right to do whatever she pleased. Homestead or no homestead, who was he to try to change her mind? After she stomped upstairs to spend the evening alone, he'd go outside and reconnect her fuel pump. She could leave in the morning as planned and forget all about Sweetness. They'd find another doctor.

But, damn…those tears. They made her eyes glisten like huge emeralds against her pale skin. She looked small and vulnerable standing there with her little chin stuck in the air. Unbidden, protective instincts welled in his chest.

And his brothers' words came back to him. From the broken leg that needed tending to the stolen kiss to the cold-water shower, he hadn't exactly been the Welcome Wagon. He couldn't be sure of the exact cause of her tears, and he was limited in his remedies, but there was one thing that always made men feel better.

"You should have something to eat," he announced.

On cue, her stomach howled like a wild animal.

Taking advantage of the opening, he rushed to add, "There's a guy on our crew from Memphis who makes the best barbecue you ever tasted." She didn't react, but she didn't flee, so he went for the close. "Besides, I'm sure my brothers would like to say goodbye."

She looked away, then back, wavering. Porter gave her a little smile of encouragement. Her chin dipped. "Okay." She sounded utterly defeated. "Give me a few minutes to stow my suitcases in my room, and I'll be back down."

Feeling frustrated because he couldn't help her, and for other reasons he couldn't quite put his finger on, Porter watched as Dr. Salinger struggled to carry her luggage up the stairs. Her shoulders drooped and her feet dragged. Porter frowned. Usually women who were going to spend the evening with him acted a little happier about it.

He exhaled loudly. Entertaining the mousy little lady doc all evening was going to be a major bummer.

Then those amazing green eyes flashed into his head and Porter pursed his mouth.

He reckoned he could take one for the Armstrong team.

9

Nikki pushed open the door to the corner room she'd left only minutes before, felt for the overhead light switch and flipped it on, then carried in her suitcases and set them down.

A wave of defeat washed over her. Academically, she knew she wasn't stranded here forever, that she could leave as soon as her van was repaired. But emotionally, she felt as if she was being thwarted at every turn. And that cosmically, she was being punished for doing something so wildly out of character as leaving the family practice in Broadway and coming to a Southern town in the middle of nowhere with the fantasy of starting over.

She pressed her palms to her temples and shook her head. Coming here was easily the dumbest thing she'd ever done. It served her right to be stuck.

Out of nowhere came her grandmother's words of advice that things would look better in the morning. Considering the setting, it wasn't so unusual she'd think of her Grammy, who had raised her family in a dense auto manufacturing city in Michigan, but who had spent her own childhood in a small town in Tennessee.

Grammy had been full of commonsense sayings with country roots. For the first time, Nikki wondered if some part of her had been attracted to the idea of coming here because her grandmother had made rural life sound so idyllic.

It suddenly occurred to her that Grammy might have embellished the truth a bit for the sake of her only grandchild.

Nikki walked into the bathroom to splash her face with cold water—the one thing that Sweetness had plenty of. She patted her skin dry with a hand towel, then peered at her face. Pale, pale, pale, with bluish circles under her eyes and splotches of red on her cheeks. But she didn't have time to do anything about it...not that her inept skills with makeup would make a difference. The best she could do was run a brush through her fine hair to fluff it a bit. Then she chastised herself.

It wasn't as if this was a date.

That...*thing*...that had sprung up between her and Porter Armstrong earlier, that thick, palpable pressure hanging in the air after she'd made the comment that he should be in bed...it hadn't been sexual tension. It couldn't have been. The more likely explanation was... humidity.

That was it—she simply wasn't used to the barometric pressure at this altitude.

And she had agreed to accompany Porter Armstrong to the barbecue simply because the irreverent man needed to be monitored over the next several hours in case he developed complications from his fall.

Her stomach growled.

And because she was famished.

She retraced her steps to the stairs and ignored the

little jump in her pulse at the sight of Porter Armstrong waiting for her. The man was ridiculously handsome, and she knew when she was out of her league. But she was only going to be in Sweetness, Georgia, for a few more hours, and there were worse ways to spend it than on the arm of a good-looking man, even if he'd only extended the invitation out of...

Nikki frowned. Why *had* he extended the invitation?

He smiled and, if possible, grew even more handsome.

The reason didn't matter, she told herself as she walked downstairs. She could pretend over the next few hours that he saw something in her no other man had ever seen. Sweetness owed her a fantasy evening.

"Ready?" he asked.

"Ready," she said.

Porter was grateful the weather was holding. "Doc" Riley had announced all week that his forecasting bunions were hurting, which meant rain was on the way. But the last thing the Armstrongs wanted was for their guests to see the ugly mud hole this place turned into when driving rain met bare red clay.

He was aware of the small woman walking next to him, and tried to imagine what this place looked like through her eyes. It was a glorious Southern night, steeped with the scent of freshly mowed grass and the hum of insects.

Dr. Salinger sneezed violently, then smacked at something on her neck.

He winced. Maybe it wasn't so glorious if you were allergic to freshly mowed grass and attracted mosquitoes.

"God bless you." He stopped and balanced himself to fish a clean handkerchief from his back pocket, then handed it to her.

"Thank you," she said, giving her nose a wipe. "Why do Southerners say that?"

"Say what?"

"'God bless you' after someone sneezes."

He laughed. "Is that a Southern thing?" Then he shrugged. "I never thought about it. Didn't mean to offend."

"You didn't offend me. I just think it's curious how different people are, and how different the customs are in different parts of the country."

She sounded so clinical, as if she were conducting a study. Little lady doc sounded…lonely. "Do you have family back in Broadway?"

"No."

"Another part of the country?"

"No."

An orphan. "I'm sorry."

"It's not your fault," she murmured. "I was an only child. My father passed away when I was very young, and my mother died when I was in high school. But I was loved."

Loved. Past tense. Porter's chest tightened. And she'd pulled herself through college and medical school—impressive. "As much as my brothers and I butt heads, I couldn't imagine a world without them in it."

"You're lucky to have each other. Are your parents still living?"

"Pop has been gone for a while now. But Mom is as feisty as ever—she lives just north of Atlanta."

"Is that where you grew up?"

Porter stopped and blinked at her in the semi-darkness. "You don't know?"

She stopped, too. "Know what?"

"Sweetness is where my brothers and I grew up. A tornado destroyed the town ten years ago."

The moonlight caught her face as those amazing eyes widened. "So that's why you're rebuilding this town—it's…it's your *home*."

Something about the tone of her voice—she sounded awestruck…and almost envious. Unbidden, a lump formed in his throat, catching him completely off guard. "Th-that's right."

"I only decided at the last minute to come with the rest of the group. I guess I didn't read the fine print."

As they started back down the path, Porter tucked away that nugget of information. Dr. Salinger did not seem like the kind of woman to make a last-minute decision. Something had forced her hand. A lost job, a foreclosed home…a bad breakup?

I was loved.

A hasty departure would also explain why most of the women had come with trunks and trailers of personal possessions, and Dr. Salinger had arrived with only two small suitcases. Lucky for him she'd been more concerned about packing her portable X-ray machine than her extra case of high-heeled shoes.

Not that she seemed like the type to own a closetful of high-heeled shoes.

He pursed his mouth. And consequently—not his type at all. He liked the trappings of femininity—heels, hosiery, skirts, cleavage, long hair, perfume, painted fingernails, jewelry—

"The materials used in the rooming house were re-covered from tornado debris?"

Dr. Salinger's question jarred him out of his musings. "Right. We want to build the town's economy on recycling. There are still piles of debris all over this mountain, and we plan to reclaim as many things as we can."

She didn't respond, seemed to turn inward.

"This path is lined with rubber mulch from recycled tires," he added, driven by a sudden compulsion to impress her. "These fixtures along the path are solar lights. And the road you drove in on was paved with recycled materials. There's something rewarding about rebuilding this town with little pieces of its own history."

Porter caught himself—he hadn't meant to wax poetic. Dr. Salinger made a thoughtful noise, but he had the feeling she was bored. It occurred to him that she probably didn't care about the Armstrong brothers' master plan for the town of Sweetness because she was planning to leave first thing tomorrow.

They topped a tree-lined rise and the meadow lay before them. The high school and gymnasium had once stood on this spot, with countless outbuildings. The tornado had obliterated this patch of land so extensively even the footers of the buildings had vanished. The brothers had found rusted basketball hoops in trees and yellow school buses nose deep in three feet of dirt. Once cleared, the plateau had become a gathering place for their men.

The barbecue was contained in an area the size of a football field outlined with tiki torches. Rows of wooden tables and benches extended from end to end. Enormous smoking grills sat at one side, emitting delicious aromas

of beef and pork. Country music played from a couple of elevated outdoor speakers. It had all the makings of a good party.

Except the men of Sweetness, who outnumbered the women of Broadway more than two to one, stood to one side and conferred as if they were planning a covert mission. And the women congregated on the opposite side, as if trying to decide if they were going to put up a fight.

The women did not look happy, and based on her body language, their ringleader was letting Marcus and Kendall know why.

But what a body Rachel Hutchins had. She stood holding her little pooch with one hand, and making a point with the other hand. The woman's tanned legs went on for miles. Porter lamented leaving her side earlier, then reminded himself that entertaining the little lady doc was for the greater good. Being in the military had trained him for self-sacrifice.

"Let's get this party started," Porter said loudly to interrupt.

When Rachel looked his way, her expression softened. "Porter…you made it."

"Under doctor's supervision," Porter said, deferring to Dr. Salinger, who hung back.

Rachel gave Dr. Salinger a suspicious glance, then turned her attention back to the Armstrong brothers. "So…what are you going to do about it?"

"We have a few problems," Kendall announced to Porter.

Porter almost felt sorry for his brothers—they were totally inept when it came to dealing with women. He turned a charming smile on Rachel. "Like?"

"Like the women are getting eaten alive by mosquitoes," Rachel said, her head weaving. The woman was accustomed to getting what she wanted.

"Marcus will round up bug spray," Porter offered. "See? Problem solved. Let's turn up the music and get everyone dancing."

Her pretty nose wrinkled. "We don't like this music."

Porter's smile wavered. "You don't like country music?"

"If that's what this is," Rachel said, gesturing to the speakers playing a Toby Keith song, "then no."

Porter balked. That could be a problem. But he tried to remain cheerful. "I'm sure we can round up some other CDs, something more...contemporary."

Rachel held up her iPod. "Is there a dock for this in your sound system? I have some fantastic playlists with Lady Gaga."

Porter exchanged anxious glances with his brothers. If they thought they were facing mutiny from the men before the women arrived, a Lady Gaga song would send the men stampeding.

"Kendall will check for you," Porter assured her. With no small amount of relief, he remembered the ace up their sleeve—good Southern food would calm the savage females. "I know everyone must be hungry—just wait until you taste Bubba King's ribs."

Rachel crossed her long shapely arms, inadvertently pushing up her cleavage. "I hope you have something on the grill other than cow and pig. At least half of us are vegetarians."

Porter dragged his gaze away from her chest. "V-vegetarians?"

"Some are vegan."

"Vegan?"

"And we have a few fruitarians."

Porter was hit with the sudden and awful realization that the Armstrong boys had gotten in way over their heads. He'd made a big mess of things by injuring himself and almost scaring off their only doctor in one fell swoop. Because of his miscalculations, hot water would have to be rationed. And he'd grossly underestimated the logistics of folding a group of women into their primitive, rural environment.

Marcus and Kendall looked at him with expressions that said, "Now what?"

Porter looked to the heavens, hoping for divine inspiration. Instead he got a fat raindrop in the eye. Within seconds, a deluge descended, extinguishing the torches and sending the women squealing and running for cover, slipping and sliding in the instant mud that formed when water met the red soil.

A small hand touched his arm. He looked up to find Dr. Salinger standing there, drenched. "Let me help you back to the trail!" she shouted over the pounding rain.

Porter was rooted to the spot, and his tongue seemed paralyzed. Her green eyes were huge in her fine-boned face. Her white shirt had turned transparent, clinging to her slender curves and leaving little to the imagination. Little lady doc was…hot.

"We got him, doc," Kendall shouted, as he and Marcus positioned themselves on either side of Porter and literally lifted him off his feet. "Save yourself!"

She turned and was soon lost in the confusion of fleeing bodies crisscrossing the field. Shrieks filled the air and mud was flying. It was ugly.

As Porter watched the bedlam, Marcus's comment about unleashing another natural disaster on the town by importing women came back to him with clanging clarity.

At this rate, the town of Sweetness would be a ghost town before it even opened for business.

10

"You disconnected her fuel pump?" Marcus asked, his eyes bulging. "That was the best idea you could come up with?"

"Shh!" Porter leaned heavily on his crutches and looked around as they stood in the rear of the dining hall. Dozens of perturbed women were in the breakfast line in front of them, and everyone knew that women's ears were as keen as a bat's. He lowered his voice to a whisper. "The doc's still here, isn't she?"

"Well, her van is," Marcus said. "After the reception she got yesterday, I wouldn't blame her if she parachuted out of here at first light."

"Knock it off, both of you," Kendall said, chopping his hand in the air. "We've got bigger problems. Last night's fiasco at the barbecue proved we have to get this situation under control. We can't even feed these women."

"We have plenty of food," Marcus said with a frown. "It's just not gourmet."

A commotion at the front of the line seemed to bear out Marcus's statement. Rachel Hutchins, armed with

her impertinent little dog, appeared to be having some kind of confrontation with Colonel Molly.

By silent consensus, the men headed to the front, with Porter trying to keep up. "By the way, my leg hurts like hell, thanks for asking."

"Good," Marcus tossed over his shoulder.

They skidded to a halt in front of the cafeteria-style serving line at what appeared to be just in time. From the body language of the tall, lithe Rachel and the short, solid Molly, they were on the verge of hand-to-hand combat.

"Good morning, ladies," Kendall said smoothly. "Is there a problem?"

Molly waved her wooden spoon at Rachel. "Miss Uppity here wants proof that the fruit cup is *organic*."

Rachel glared. "Judging from the slop you're trying to pass off as oatmeal, I don't think it's out of line to ask if the fruit has been washed in pesticides before I put it in my mouth."

The women behind Rachel chorused agreement.

Molly's face turned red and she balled up a fist. "I've got something for that mouth of yours!"

"How dare you threaten me!" Rachel shrieked. The little dog barked at Molly in rapid-fire yelps.

"And there are no varmints allowed in my mess hall!" Molly bellowed, pointing to the door.

"Ladies, ladies," Kendall soothed. "Let's talk this through like rational adults."

Porter winced at his brother's word choice and took a step back.

Rachel and Molly both turned on Kendall. "Are you saying I'm not rational?" demanded Rachel.

"Inviting these women here was irrational!" Molly boomed.

Rachel's eyes narrowed. "Believe me, we're all starting to regret coming!"

The women backed Rachel up, then began chanting, "We want yogurt! We want yogurt!"

Porter glanced at Kendall, who seemed at a loss for words. Then he glanced at Marcus, who looked as if he was ready to levitate out of there. Porter had to do something—quick.

He put his fingers in his mouth and gave a loud, piercing whistle.

Everything stopped.

"Ladies," Porter said, leaning heavily on his crutches for effect and spreading his smile around like warm cream cheese. "The Armstrong brothers would like to invite everyone to a town meeting. You can air all your grievances, and we can share all our plans for rebuilding the town of Sweetness, which, you'll be glad to know, include an organic garden."

Rachel's body language loosened toward him. "When and where is this meeting?"

"Uh…here…this afternoon." He flashed her a proprietary smile. "Pets are welcome, of course."

She gave him a reluctant smile. "I guess it can't hurt—we've come this far."

"Good," Porter said. "For now, trust me, ladies, eating canned fruit for one day isn't going to wreck your lovely figures." Winks all around and a salute for Molly smoothed ruffled feathers. Everyone got back in line for breakfast and played nice…for the time being.

Marcus and Kendall pulled him aside. "What was all that?"

"How can we expect these women to stay and help us build Sweetness if they don't understand the big picture? They don't know what we've already done, and what's coming down the pike. We need to get everyone together and have a dog and pony show, like when we convinced the communications company to install the cell tower, and the state park system to buy our mulch."

"Planting an organic garden is way down on the list," Kendall reminded him.

"I didn't even know it was *on* the list," Marcus interjected.

"We have a hundred extra hands," Porter reminded them. He gestured to the women standing in line for food—the irritable, sour-faced bunch was a far cry from the excited, smiling group that had arrived the day before. "We hooked them with a clever ad, but now we're going to have to reel them in on the idea of Sweetness as their home and get them invested in the work we have to do."

Marcus closed his eyes and massaged the bridge of his nose. At that moment, Porter was pretty sure his brother was entertaining the idea of leaving the mountain himself. Finally, Marcus opened his eyes and heaved a sigh. "In for a penny, in for a pound."

"That's the spirit," Porter said, clapping him on the shoulder.

Marcus frowned. "Make sure Dr. Salinger is at the meeting."

"We can get her input on the clinic we're going to build," Kendall said.

Porter was looking past them to Rachel Hutchins, who had carried her breakfast to a nearby table and

was giving him the look saying she wouldn't mind if he joined her. She crossed her long, tanned legs.

Marcus boxed his ear. "Porter, are you listening?"

He dragged his gaze back to his brothers. "I heard you. I'm going to look for the little lady doc now."

"You might want to dial up the enthusiasm a notch," Kendall said.

"Yeah, what happened to that lady-killer charm of yours?" Marcus asked.

Porter sighed. "She's a bit of a cold fish."

"Too much of a challenge for you?" Kendall asked.

Porter's pulse spiked. "No. I got this."

He left the dining hall in an ill temper. So far nothing was going as planned.

As he hobbled across the road, he checked to make sure the doctor's white extended van was still on the shoulder where two of the workers had pushed it. He told himself he was relieved because of what his brothers would do to him if the good doctor left…and not because of anything else.

Like how good Nikki Salinger had looked the previous night when she'd stopped to ask if she could help him find cover. The image of her standing there, rain-soaked and luminous in a transparent shirt, had kept him awake long after his aching body wanted to surrender to sleep.

Again, nothing was going as planned.

Thank goodness the rain had stopped sometime during the night. The sun was on its climb, but the downpour had left everything saturated and steamy. Marcus had ordered a crew of men to spread sawdust and gravel in the muddy walkways between the rooming house and the dining hall.

Clusters of women were leaving the boardinghouse, heading toward the diner. "Town meeting in the dining hall this afternoon," Porter said as he passed them. "Town meeting, everyone welcome."

As he entered the house, he kept an eye out for Nikki, but didn't see her in the great room, the kitchen or the laundry room where women were spreading out muddied clothing and shoes to dry. He decided against telling them they were better off just to burn the clothes or relegate them to the rag bag—the red Georgia clay was more permanent than dye. Instead he told them about the town meeting and kept moving.

Porter lumbered through the hallway and on to the back room, where he found Nikki sorting through boxes of supplies. She wore chinos and a pink polo shirt and her hair was pulled back into a ponytail.

"Good morning," he called.

She looked up, but didn't seem particularly glad to see him. "Maybe if I'd gotten a hot shower."

"I'm working on that," he fibbed.

"Are you also working on getting my van repaired?"

"Soon," he promised.

"How soon?" she pressed. "Today?"

"The mechanic who takes care of our work vehicles is going to make it a priority."

She seemed satisfied, if not pleased.

"I came to tell you about the town meeting."

She turned back to a box. "What town meeting?"

"There's a town meeting in the dining hall this afternoon."

"Why would I want to be there? I'm not staying, remember?"

Alarm blipped in his chest. "Does anyone else know that?"

"No." She looked up again. "Why would it matter?"

"Having a doctor in town will make everyone feel safer about living up here."

"You'll find another physician. Someone more...suitable." She stopped and dusted her hands on her pants. "How are you feeling?"

He was tempted to man up and tell her he was feeling fine, but it occurred to him that she might feel compelled to stay if she thought her services were needed.

"Not so good."

Her concern was immediate. Boxes forgotten, she walked toward him. "Do you have a fever?" She put her small cool hand to his forehead.

"I don't know...I feel warm." Not a lie, considering how close she was standing to him. The image of her breasts outlined in a wet shirt was imprinted on his brain.

"Have a seat," she said, removing a box from a chair. "I want to take your temperature."

He lowered himself into the chair, conceding it felt good to get his weight off his injured leg. Nikki came back and thrust a thermometer in his mouth, then leaned over to listen to his lungs with a stethoscope. To get his heart racing, he dropped his gaze to her chest.

"Your pulse is elevated," she murmured, then she took out a penlight and shined it in his eyes.

"Look straight ahead, please."

He did. She smelled good, like something he'd like to lick...or nibble...or taste—

"Any dizziness or nausea?"

"No." Then he remembered his plan to exaggerate his symptoms. "Not at the moment."

She pulled back, her eyebrows furrowed. "But you did before?"

"Um…some."

Her mouth tightened. "I think you should go to a hospital for a full workup."

"It's not that bad," he said, backpedaling.

"Still…you could have a concussion, or other injuries I don't have the equipment to detect. Your health isn't worth the risk."

The intelligence and the compassion in her eyes was a heady combination. He marveled at the encyclopedia of information that must be filed away in her quick mind. The long hours of studying and the dedication necessary to become a physician were staggering to him. At first glance, Nikki Salinger seemed too fragile for such an undertaking, and such a demanding job. But upon closer inspection, the woman was as tough as a reed.

And as gentle as a morning glory.

"I'll go to a hospital," he agreed, "if I start feeling sick again."

Her mouth flattened. "Are you taking your painkillers with food?"

"Maybe that's the problem," he offered. "After the barbecue got rained out, I went back to the barracks and crashed. Haven't had much food on my stomach."

She made a chiding noise. "You need to stay nourished so your body can heal."

"I haven't had breakfast yet. Why don't you join me?"

"I had a protein bar. Mr. Armstrong, would it be possible to borrow a vehicle?"

He panicked. "What for?"

She lifted the hem of her shirt to tap a phone clipped to the waist of her pants. Porter was riveted by the glimpse of a flat stomach and nipped waist.

"I was planning to drive down the mountain until I get cell service."

"We have a cell tower here and coverage from several carriers."

She grimaced. "It's my phone— I've been having trouble with the antennae, so I don't have much range."

"You're welcome to use my phone," he said, wondering who she needed to call. A colleague? A boyfriend? A taxi?

"Thanks, but I need to check my text messages, too... and my email. Never mind. I'll borrow a car from one of the girls."

Porter's mind raced. If Nikki left Sweetness, would she just keep driving? That seemed like a good possibility. He pulled at his chin, then brightened.

"I have an idea, little lady doc. Come with me."

11

Nikki was apprehensive about following Porter Armstrong anywhere, but curiosity got the better of her. So she followed him out a side door into the June morning sun, but hung back while he awkwardly climbed on what looked like a riding lawnmower, one of the all-terrain vehicles he and his brothers had been riding yesterday. He settled on the seat and stashed his crutches next to his injured foot, then looked up and patted the space on the seat behind him.

"Jump on."

Nikki hesitated. "Where are we going?"

He grinned. "To get you a cell phone signal."

Her pulse jumped crazily at that smile. The man was too good-looking for her own good. But she didn't have to worry about being here long enough to fall for Porter Armstrong—she was leaving as soon as her van was repaired.

"Are you sure you can drive with your leg injured?"

"No problem. The controls are on the handlebars."

"What about helmets?"

He seemed momentarily irritated, but turned and

lifted the rear of the seat to reveal a storage compartment and removed two helmets, extending one to her.

Nikki conceded she'd run out of excuses...and it did look kind of fun. And she was eager to make a couple of phone calls. She took the helmet and pulled it down on her head as she moved to climb onto the four-wheeler. She straddled the seat behind him, looking for a handhold.

"Just hang on to me," he said over his shoulder.

And before she could argue, he'd started the engine and goosed the gas. She put her arms around his waist out of self-preservation as the ATV lurched forward.

But she had to admit having her arms around his external abdominal oblique muscles wasn't unpleasant.

He steered off the mulched trail then headed into the woods, following a rocky path barely wide enough for one car to navigate. On both sides, the trees were tall and the underbrush was thick. The temperature was a few degrees cooler under the canopy of leaves.

He turned his head. "Having fun?" he called over the hum of the engine.

"So far," she responded, some part of her unwilling to admit she was enjoying the unbridled freedom of having the wind on her face.

Earthy aromas of grass, moss and soil filled her lungs as they ascended at a steady elevation. As gravity pulled at her, she tightened her grip around Porter's waist, conscious of the thin layer of cotton between the warm skin of his flat belly and her hands.

They rode for about twenty minutes before slowing and leveling onto a clearing. Ahead Nikki recognized the supports of a water tower—no doubt the one she'd seen from the road when driving into Sweetness.

The one from which Porter had taken his spill.

He pulled the four-wheeler to a halt, then turned off the engine. Nikki climbed off first and removed her helmet, then helped Porter find his footing and arrange his crutches.

"Back to the scene of the crime," he joked.

She tipped her head back to see the top of the water tower through the trees. "How far up were you when you fell?"

"All the way to the top."

She shook her head in wonder. "You're lucky you didn't break your neck."

He grinned. "I know."

For some reason, she thought of the man's mother and felt a pang of sympathy for her. How many times had Porter escaped serious injury when he was younger and flashed that same heart-bending grin?

He gestured to the phone at her waist. "See if you have service now."

She pulled out her phone and was gratified to see two bars out of five…then it dropped back to one. Her "message waiting" indicator was zero. "I have some reception, let me try to make a call." She punched the button to dial into her voice mail, but the call failed. She tried two more times, with the same result.

"The signal isn't strong enough for a call to connect, much less check my email." She gave him a little smile. "But it was nice of you to bring me up here to try. Guess I'll be driving down."

He pursed his mouth. "Or you could go up."

Nikki lifted an eyebrow. "You mean climb the water tower?"

"Are you afraid of heights?"

"Not really."

"Then you're bound to get a better signal up on the platform." His blue eyes danced. "I promise the view alone is worth the effort."

Nikki bit her lip and considered the climb. The last thing she needed was to fall, too. "Is it safe?"

"As long as you take it slow." He looked sheepish. "I saw your caravan coming and got in too big of a hurry to get back to town."

"I saw you up there," she said. "When we were driving in."

"You did?"

Nikki nodded, then tipped her head back and shielded her eyes from the sun dodging in and out of the treetops. She'd been a city girl all her life, so there was something irresistibly charming about the thought of climbing a water tower. She would be leaving this place soon—why not take back one exciting memory? "I'm up for it."

The smile he gave her warmed her to her toes. It was as if she'd passed some kind of test. He walked with her to the base of the ladder, coaching her. "About every twenty feet is an extrawide ladder rung you can stop and sit on if you need to rest."

"Okay."

"Once you get to the top, be extra careful stepping off the ladder onto the platform."

"Okay."

"And don't worry. If you fall, I'll be right here to catch you."

She gave him and his crutches a withering look. "Right."

"I'll boost you up," he said, pointing to the bottom rung that was just out of her reach.

"I think I can get it," she said, then jumped to clasp the metal rung.

Nikki pulled herself up, and quickly realized she didn't have the upper body strength to get to the next rung. Just when she was afraid her arms were going to give out, a firm hand lodged under her butt and gave her a push. Having his hand in a private place was a shock to her system and her first instinct was to protest, but she couldn't deny she needed his help. So she just reached for the next rung and scrambled up until her feet caught and she could support herself. Nikki climbed a few steps up the ladder and when she started to feel more stable, she glanced down to see Porter waving and smiling.

"Take your time," he called through cupped hands. "I'll just hang out down here and commune with nature."

She kept climbing, taking a break about halfway. It was a surreal feeling being among the majestic trees as the wind sent branches swaying and leaves dancing. She wondered what kind of trees they were. The frothy evergreens were easy to distinguish, but she knew there were as many different kinds of evergreens as there were bones in the human body. Her head was full of facts from medical tomes, but she knew next to nothing about nature. She had no idea what kinds of birds were swooping between limbs, what kinds of insects were singing back and forth.

Nikki was struck by the empty sensation of having an incomplete education.

"You okay up there?" Porter called.

She looked down and gave him a thumbs-up, then continued climbing until she reached the platform of the enormous white water tower. Heeding his words

of caution, she moved carefully from the ladder to the floor of the metal platform, exhaling in relief at being on firm footing again.

The water tower was enormous, shaped like a time-release capsule on its end, with a metal hat on top. It appeared to have been newly whitewashed, and she could only imagine the layers of paint underneath. She placed her hand on the metal tank, still cool on this side shaded from the sun, and marveled at the strength and history of the structure. Nikki followed the chest-high handrailing around to the front of the tower that faced the valley and inhaled sharply at the panoramic sight before her.

She hadn't known so many different colors of green existed. Mountain ranges in the distance were covered with thick foliage that moved in waves reminiscent of the ocean as the wind whipped over the landscape, circling back to the water tower. Her fine hair was pulled loose from its ponytail holder, sending the stray strands dancing around her face. She lifted her face toward the sun and inhaled deeply, registering how fresh the air was at this height—unpolluted and further cleansed by natural filters like grass and leaves. It was an intoxicating perfume.

Beneath her, the wooded terrain fell away from the water tower to the floor of the gorge where the road leading into Sweetness was a man-made black band cutting through the seemingly impenetrable expanse of red soil. From here, Porter Armstrong had surely had a good vantage point to see the caravan of cars arriving.

A movement on the handrail caught her attention. The tails of a blue denim work shirt folded over the handrail were being teased by the wind. Her mind went to the bare torso of Porter when she'd first seen him

yesterday—this must be his shirt. She could picture him trying to catch a breeze after his climb, ridding himself of the garment. Nikki lifted it from the handrail. The cotton was softly worn, still a little damp from last night's rain before being dried in the morning sun.

She pulled the neck of the shirt to her nose—it still smelled of his manly scent. The pleasant association sent a tug of longing to her midsection that surprised her in its intensity.

Then Nikki realized her phone was vibrating.

Remembering why she'd made the climb in the first place, she removed the phone from its clip. The reception signal was strong and two-way arrows indicated voice mail and email messages were being delivered to her inbox. Nikki was bemused at how relieved she felt at being reconnected to the outside world. She'd never considered herself dependent on technology, but coming to this remote town had made her feel so incredibly lonely. Being cut off from everything familiar had only exacerbated the feeling.

Her heart hammered as she dialed in to pick up her voice mail. Had Darren called? Had he discovered she'd left Broadway and realized how much he loved her? Was he sorry for breaking her heart? Would he beg her forgiveness and ask her to come back?

No. She listened to the voice messages—most of them having to do with shutting off utilities for her apartment—with an increasing sense of disappointment. She knew Darren wasn't the man she'd thought he was, but she'd loved him and had planned a future with him. It was going to take a while to retrain her heart. And she yearned for some kind of confirmation that she hadn't

fabricated his feelings for her. She hadn't imagined the tender moments they'd shared, had she?

Yes. Or else how could he cheat on her with a stripper and, when confronted with the rumors, act so cavalier?

The last message was from Amy Bradshaw. Her friend's lyrical voice brought a smile to Nikki's face. She didn't know Amy that well. She'd only gotten to know her since she'd moved out of the house she'd shared with Darren and into the apartment complex near Amy's neighborhood. But when they'd met in yoga class, they had seemed like kindred spirits. And despite being a successful civil engineer and stunningly beautiful with a quick wit, Amy was a homebody and had seemed grateful to find a friend who shared her quiet interests.

When Nikki had told her she was thinking of joining the group of women who were moving to Sweetness, Georgia, Amy had been cautiously supportive. She'd seen the ad, she said, and could see why women would be intrigued by the promise of free room and board for two years and lots of strapping, single men. But when Nikki had asked Amy if she was tempted by the offer, her friend had laughed it off, saying she'd grown up in a place very much like Sweetness, and had no intention of going back to that kind of life.

"Just checking to see that you made it to your destination," Amy's voice sang. "Call me when you get a minute."

Nikki punched in her friend's number, her mood buoyed when Amy answered on the first ring.

"Amy Bradshaw."

Nikki pictured her friend at her desk, scrutinizing a set of blueprints. "Amy, it's Nikki."

Amy exclaimed in surprised. "Hi, there. Where are you?"

"You wouldn't believe me if I told you."

"Try me."

"I'm on the water tower above the tiny town of Sweetness, Georgia."

Amy was silent for a couple of beats. "I don't believe you."

Nikki laughed. "It's true. I had to climb up here to get reception on my cell phone."

"That place sounds like it's lost in time."

"It is," Nikki said. "But it's beautiful. Trees and mountains as far as the eye can see."

Amy made a noise that almost sounded envious. "What about the people?"

"The men who placed the ad, the Armstrong brothers, are likable enough, but I think they've bitten off more than they can chew. They weren't prepared for a hundred women to descend on the town."

"I take it the Armstrong brothers are single, and like most single men, clueless about dealing with women?"

"Right. I think they were all military men at some point. And apparently they grew up here. I knew a tornado had wiped the town off the map, but I didn't realize the men were trying to rebuild their hometown. It makes me wonder if they're letting sentimentality get in the way of common sense."

"Southern men seem to think they can steamroll their way through just about any situation," Amy agreed. "So...speaking of Southern men—have you met anyone interesting?"

"*No.*"

"That was quick. Are you sure?"

"Yes. Get this—the youngest brother fell off this water tower, so the minute I pulled into town, I had to treat a broken leg."

Amy laughed. "That had to be some fall. Is that all he broke?"

"Yes, can you believe it? Anyway, I've been stuck taking care of him."

"Hmm. Is he cute?"

Nikki ran her fingers over the soft fabric of Porter's blue work shirt. The shirt was the same color as the man's eyes. "Only if you like muscles, piercing blue eyes and a cleft chin."

"Whoa—sounds promising."

Nikki laughed. "I'm not interested. Besides, he and Rachel Hutchins are already circling each other."

"Oh, yes. Rachel. How is she making it without a hair salon?"

Nikki laughed. "Actually, she seems to be in her element, bossing everyone around. In fact…I'm the one who's decided not to stay."

"Why not?"

She hesitated. "I thought by coming here I'd be able to forget about Darren and all the plans we'd made. But somehow, it only feels worse." Tears pricked her lids and she fought to control her voice.

Amy sighed. "I thought that might happen. There's something about being in the country, free of the distractions of technology and the hustle-bustle of a city that can make a person feel…emotional. It's hard to explain to someone who's never experienced it, but the mountains have their own way of seducing a person."

"I'm starting to realize that," Nikki said, gazing over the blue-green splendor before her.

"But don't be deceived," Amy said. "Rural life isn't as romantic as it seems. And neither are those country boys."

Cold showers, no medical facility. "I'm starting to realize that, too," Nikki said drily. "This just isn't the life for me."

"So when are you coming back?"

"As soon as my van is repaired. It broke down just as I was trying to make my escape, can you believe it?"

"That is hard to believe," Amy said, her voice suspicious.

"But Porter said he'd have someone look at it, so if it's something minor, I might get started back today. Tomorrow at the latest."

"Porter?"

"The youngest Armstrong brother."

"Oh. Mr. Cleft Chin?"

Nikki laughed. "Yes. He's waiting for me on the ground, so I guess I'd better wind this up. Is everything okay back in Broadway?"

"Fine as frog hair," Amy said brightly. "At least you planned your trip with perfect timing."

Nikki frowned. "What do you mean?"

"Uh-oh… I thought you knew."

"Knew what?"

"I'm sorry to be the one to tell you, but there was an engagement announcement in the newspaper today. Darren and his woman are tying the knot."

12

Nikki felt as if she'd been kicked in the stomach. She gripped the phone tighter. "Darren is…engaged?"

On the other end of the line, Amy Bradshaw made a disgusted sound. "Yes. But if it's any consolation, the photo of them is ridiculous. They look like they're going to the midlife crisis prom."

Nikki's head spun. She gripped the handrail of the water tower to steady herself.

"Nikki, are you okay?"

She wet her lips, found her voice. "I'm okay. I just didn't… I mean, it's so soon…"

"The jerk probably gave her the ring you gave back to him."

"Threw."

"Pardon me?"

"I actually threw the ring back at him."

Amy laughed. "That a girl."

Nikki laughed, too, but it was bittersweet. "Wow, I can really pick 'em."

"Don't blame yourself. It happens to the best of us. Maybe it would be better for you to hang out in the

mountains for a few days before coming back, clear your head."

"Hey!"

Nikki's head turned at the sound of a distant voice. Porter.

"Are you okay up there?"

"I should go," she said into the phone. "Thanks for the advice, Amy."

"No problem. Take care."

Nikki disconnected the call, then made her way back around the platform to the ladder and looked down.

Porter waved up at her. "Everything okay?"

"Yes," she called. "Just a few more minutes."

"Take your time," he said through cupped hands. "I'm having a blast down here with the bugs." He swatted at the air like a windmill, nearly falling off his crutches.

She smiled and her heart lifted—a little. Then she reminded herself that Porter Armstrong was only trying to make up for the things he'd said about her yesterday.

Things about the sad state of her love life that were more true than even he knew.

Nikki turned away and quickly checked her email account. The only message of significance was from her former employer Dr. Hannah, saying how much they missed her in the practice and reminding her that the door was always open if she wanted to come back. Good to know. Nikki didn't respond, but saved the message.

She started for the ladder, then remembered the forgotten work shirt and went back to get it. Without a place to stuff it, and afraid it would be in her way if she tied it around her waist, she pulled on the shirt and rolled up the sleeves, then began her descent.

The climb down seemed to go faster, and before she

realized it, she was out of rungs. She was planning to drop to the ground, but suddenly a strong arm wrapped around her waist and lowered her to the ground. She tried to disentangle herself from Porter Armstrong as quickly as possible, but a full-body slide was unavoidable.

And the friction between her pliable frame and his hard physique was not unpleasant.

"Hey, that's my shirt," Porter said.

"I figured as much," she said, shrugging out of it.

"Keep it. It looks good on you," he said with a wave.

"It swallows me whole."

"It looks…cute," he said, reaching forward to pluck a small blossom out of her hair. "Windy up there?"

"Yes," she said, warming under his touch. "What kind of flower is that?"

"Mountain laurel," he said, handing it back to her. It looked like a small umbrella in her palm. "It's all over these mountains."

"It's pretty," she murmured. "Like the view up there."

He nodded. "It's grand, isn't it? And did you get a good cell signal?"

"Yes. I was able to make a phone call and check my messages."

"Everything okay?"

She looked up, wondering if the fact that she'd been delivered an emotional blow was written all over her face. "Everything's fine," she lied.

His eyes narrowed slightly, but he didn't question her. "Ready to head back?"

"Yes. I'd like to talk to that mechanic about my van."

"Sure thing," he agreed, then led the way back to the four-wheeler.

"You are very proficient on those crutches," she remarked.

"This ain't my first rodeo," he said with a little laugh.

Nikki pressed her lips together, debating whether to pry. She wasn't going to be here long enough for details about this man to matter. "I noticed the shrapnel scars when I examined your leg."

He didn't respond, and it was hard to decipher his expression.

"In what branch of the military did you serve?" she pressed.

"Army."

"Iraq?"

"Afghanistan."

"I'm sorry," she murmured.

"I'm not. I was proud to be there."

"I'm sure you were," she said. "I meant I'm sorry for what you must have gone through. I've worked with veterans."

"It was bad," he agreed. "But not as bad as what the people who live there deal with. Every day I'm grateful to be here on this land."

"I'm sure," she said, with a growing appreciation for the attachment Porter Armstrong and his brothers had to these mountains. Nikki caught sight of something glinting through the dirt and leaves at her feet, and crouched to investigate.

"What've you got there?" Porter asked, stopping.

She brushed away bits of debris and used her fingers

to dig out the dirt-covered item that was attached to a chain.

"It's a pocket watch," Porter said with a smile. "Good eye."

"Someone must've dropped it while they were walking around up here." She handed it to him.

"Maybe," he agreed, rubbing at the dirt and peering closer. "Or maybe it was carried up here by the tornado. We find things every day that were scattered by the storm—jewelry, tools, furniture, sometimes even photographs."

"Is there any way we can find its rightful owner?"

He gave her a smile. "We can try. It's time you met Colonel Molly. Let's go."

During the ride back down on the four-wheeler, Nikki tried to hold herself away from Porter's broad back, but gravity pressed her against him. She didn't want to like the feel of her hands around his waist. She didn't want to like anything about this man—or any man, for that matter. The news of Darren's engagement to the young dancer he'd cheated on her with reverberated in her head, returning the echoes of *How dumb could you be? Men don't fall for women like you. Men want a sex bomb by their side and in their bed…*

She'd never had time to date when she was in medical school, or during her residency. She'd become accustomed to eating alone and sleeping alone. When attorney Darren Rocha had stopped by the practice where she worked in Broadway with flu symptoms, they'd connected on an intellectual level and their relationship had slowly developed from there. The night Darren had proposed, she distinctly remembered lying awake next

to him thinking how happy she was, and feeling as if it was all too good to be true.

In hindsight, it had been.

Suddenly Porter's hand covered hers. "You okay back there?" he called over his shoulder.

She instinctively pulled her hand out from under his. "I'm fine," she said, more sharply than she intended.

To have someone you trusted betray you so thoroughly and so publicly, was excruciating. But far worse was knowing she couldn't trust her own judgment where men were concerned. They all had an angle that would be revealed in time.

After a few minutes, the slope of the terrain leveled out and the roof of the boardinghouse came into view. Porter steered the ATV back into its parking place and killed the engine. Nikki climbed off, relieved to be away from him. But her mind still reeled and her hands were shaking from Amy's pronouncement, leaving her fumbling with the strap on her helmet.

"Let me help you with that," Porter said.

She protested, but he brushed her fingers aside and, leaning on his crutches with his elbows, deftly unfastened the strap. She avoided eye contact, staring studiously at the cleft in his chin. A cleft chin was actually a bone deformity, resulting from the imperfect fusion of the left and right sides of the jaw during fetal development.

But it was an appealing deformity.

"Thank you for the ride," she said stiffly, then pulled off her helmet.

"No problem, little lady doc." He lifted her chin with his finger. "Did something happen on the water tower?"

His voice sounded gentle, but she reminded herself that this man felt sorry for her. He'd basically admitted to his brothers that he'd kissed her out of pity.

She yanked her chin away. "Nothing to concern yourself about. You were going to introduce me to someone named Molly?"

"Right," he said, then headed in the direction of the dining hall. "Colonel Molly McIntyre grew up here, but left to join the Army. She retired after thirty years and when she heard we needed someone to feed our crew, she signed on to run our diner."

"So the men take every meal here?" Nikki asked, gesturing to the long, industrial building.

"Unless we do something special, like the barbecue last night, which we try to do as often as we can." He winced as he held open the door with a crutch. "Molly runs an organized ship—but she's a terrible cook."

That made Nikki smile. "So you're bringing me here for a bad meal?"

"Molly's been doing one other thing for the town," he said, following her inside.

Nikki took in the no-frills dining hall—a long serving counter up front where food was chosen or served cafeteria style, and rows of hand-hewn wooden tables and benches. Inside were a few stragglers who looked less than enthusiastic about the breakfast they were eating.

"This doesn't look like a diner," she felt compelled to say.

"We have big plans," Porter said with a grin. "Which you'll hear all about if you come to the town meeting."

A stocky woman wearing a camouflage apron stood

behind the serving counter, checking an enormous conveyor dishwasher. Porter waved to get her attention.

Molly walked toward them, drying her hands, a stern look on her face. "Kitchen's closed until lunch, soldier."

Porter gestured to his leg. "Come on, Colonel. I'm wounded here—and starving. You can't rustle up something special for me?"

"No. And don't go winking those big blue eyes of yours. You know your sweet-talkin' ways are wasted on me."

Nikki smothered a smile. She was inclined to like this woman.

Porter sighed, then turned to Nikki. "Molly, I'd like to introduce Dr. Nikki Salinger. Dr. Salinger patched me up."

"Nice to meet you, Dr. Salinger. I'm Molly McIntyre." Molly stuck out a sturdy hand, which Nikki shook.

"Nice to meet you, too."

"You're not one of those vegetarians, are you?" the woman asked suspiciously.

"Er…no," Nikki said, then turned over the woman's hand and pointed to a red rash. "Contact dermatitis, I'm guessing from the dish soap. Are you treating it?"

"Doc Riley gave me a lotion he made out of blueberry leaves."

Nikki pursed her mouth. "If the itching continues, you might want to see a real doctor for a steroid cream."

Molly was unfazed. "I'll take that under advisement."

"Dr. Salinger made an interesting find this morning up by the water tower," Porter said, then pulled out a bandanna he'd wrapped around the pocket watch and

handed it over to Molly. "Do you mind if I show her the property room?"

Molly's face lit up as she inspected the watch. "Go ahead. I'll get this piece cleaned up."

Porter led the way through a rear exit of the dining hall. A few yards away sat a large, long metal building with a combination lock on the door. He punched in a number, then pushed open the door and flipped on a light.

It was, Nikki realized at a glance, a warehouse.

To the right of the entrance was a work area with a desk, tables, file cabinets, utility sinks, a water hose, rags and various cleaning supplies. The rest of the building resembled one enormous swap meet—furniture, lawn statues, quilts, clothing, musical instruments, tools, even a couple of motorcycles.

"Here's where we keep all the valuables we find." He opened a file cabinet to reveal tagged plastic bags. He lifted a random bag that held a shiny silver picture frame, with a stained, but legible black-and-white wedding photograph inside. "Molly cleans and repairs everything and matches it to a list of items residents declared missing after the tornado. If she's able to locate the former resident, she ships the item to them. If not, she tags it, bags it and stores it here."

Nikki stared at the wedding photo, thinking of how much that picture had meant to the people in it, and to their children. "Until when?"

He shrugged and returned the picture frame, then closed the file cabinet. "We haven't decided. One of our ideas is to get a website going so it's easier for former residents to contact us."

"There are at least a couple of techie-types who came in our group," she offered.

"Kendall will be glad to know that."

Surveying remnants of the people who had once lived in Sweetness was almost overwhelming. She could picture people sitting in these rocking chairs, eating around these tables. These people had loved and laughed and cried and raised their families here. A tornado had obliterated their histories, which might have gone unrecorded if not for the Armstrong brothers trying to resurrect an entire town with their bare hands.

It was mind-boggling.

Nikki walked over to a group of odds-and-ends furniture cordoned off in a corner, drawn to a massive wood headboard with the distinctive curve of a sleigh bed. It was an aged piece, but the finish gleamed.

"How beautiful," she breathed, running her hand over the satiny wood.

Porter came up behind her. "My mother thought so."

She turned. "Your mother?"

He nodded. "These are all things that came from our home. This was the bed she and my dad shared. Over there's the coffee table Marcus made her one year for Mother's Day. And there's the cabinet she kept her good dishes in, minus the glass. But we did find a few of the dishes intact. We're keeping everything for the day we can bring our mother back to Sweetness."

Myriad emotions played over his handsome face, and his deep blue eyes brimmed with affection. Nikki could only imagine how many memories washed over him every time he looked at his family heirlooms and keepsakes. The loss of her own family felt acute at that

moment. Her heart welled, but at the same time, she didn't want to know these personal stories, didn't want to become emotionally invested in a place she was planning to leave. Suddenly, returning to Broadway was preferable to staying here and being lulled into a fantasy. The Armstrongs were operating on a wing and a prayer, trying to recapture a sense of home and family that were long gone. Rebuilding Sweetness was going to take a Herculean effort by people who truly cared.

And she didn't want to care.

Nikki drew herself up. "This is all very nice," she managed to say. "But if you don't mind, I'd really like to talk to that mechanic about getting my van repaired so I get on the road back to *my* home."

She turned and strode out, before she could think too hard about the definition of "home."

13

Porter watched Nikki march out of the property room, uncertain what had caused the about-face in her mood. One minute she'd been admiring the keepsakes of the town's former residents, and the next minute, she couldn't get out of there fast enough.

He wondered again about the phone call she'd made on top of the water tower. Had the situation she'd left back in Broadway changed? Did someone there want her to come back?

He cast another look at the recovered pieces of his mother's furniture—it always gave him faith that they would reach their goal of restoring the town of Sweetness and relocating their mother back to the place where she'd met their father, raised her children and laid to rest members of her family, his dad included. He needed to do whatever it took to grow the town. And right now that meant convincing the Broadway women to stay.

Including Dr. Salinger.

She stood there waiting for him, arms crossed, looking off in the direction she wanted to go—away from Sweetness. Damn, if she didn't look good in his shirt.

"I'm calling the mechanic now," Porter said, pulling out his cell phone.

"Good," she chirped.

Did anyone care that his leg was throbbing like a toothache? Porter stabbed in Kendall's number.

"Porter?" Kendall answered. "Where are you? And why aren't you helping me and Marcus get ready for this meeting you roped us into?"

"I'm calling to check on the doctor's van," Porter said, exaggerating his tone so Kendall would know something was up.

"Oh, brother. Is Dr. Salinger standing there?"

"You got it," Porter said.

"You're pathetic."

"Whatever it takes," Porter said cheerfully.

Kendall laughed. "I think this woman is getting the best of you, little brother."

Porter hardened his jaw. "Keep me posted." He disconnected the call before his brother could say some other fool thing.

"What did the mechanic say?" Nikki asked, her face hopeful.

Porter hesitated. If she wanted to go home that badly, maybe he should just reconnect her fuel pump and let her go. The woman's talents would probably be wasted in a place like this, where most of her cases were likely to be pulled muscles and bee stings.

Then he reminded himself of the enormous challenge he and his brothers had before them. And like it or not, this woman could be the linchpin.

"He said it looks like the problem is your fuel pump."

"And?"

"And…he's ordering a new…thing."

She looked pensive. "A new fuel pump? How long will that take?"

He shrugged. "A few days maybe."

"Will it be delivered?"

"Yeah."

She looked around. "Where's the post office?"

"Uh…we don't actually have a zip code yet."

Her eyebrows arched. "How will a replacement part be delivered?"

"Let me worry about that," he said breezily. "You fixed me up, so I'll fix up your van."

She looked dubious, but he could tell she was weighing her options and coming up with none. "You should get some food in your stomach," she said finally, then turned and skirted the dining hall, heading for the rooming house.

He felt a twinge of remorse for deceiving her, but told himself that there must have been a good reason for her to answer their ad. Maybe if she stayed here long enough, she would remember why.

"Don't forget the town meeting!" he called after her.

But if she heard him, she didn't respond.

Porter frowned, then backtracked through the dining hall. He found Molly standing next to a window, scrutinizing the newly shined silver pocket watch under a magnifying glass.

"Find any identifying marks?" he asked.

Molly handed him the magnifying glass. "Three initials. First two are *C* and *A*, I think. Can you make out the last one?"

Porter balanced himself on his crutches, took the

magnifying glass and allowed her to hold the piece. "Maybe a *W?* Hard to tell." He whistled low as he ran a finger over the heavily embossed silver. "Great piece, though, huh?"

"It's a beauty," Molly agreed. "Hope we can get it back in the hands of the rightful owner." She looked around. "Speaking of beauty, where did Dr. Salinger get off to?"

Porter gave a little smile. "She'd had enough of me, I guess—and the town. She wants to go back where she came from as soon as her van is repaired."

"Really? Too bad. She seemed like the sensible kind we need around here."

"She is," he admitted. "Although I wouldn't exactly call her a beauty."

Molly shook her head. "Open your eyes, soldier. That girl has the kind of beauty a man would never get tired of."

Porter scowled. "Maybe I'm looking for the kind of woman I *will* get tired of."

"I won't tell your mother you said that," Molly said with a disapproving expression.

Contrite, he muttered, "Sorry. My leg is killing me and I'm starving. Little lady doc says I should take my painkillers with food. Can you help me out?"

"I'm not a short-order cook."

"Come on, Colonel." Porter angled his head. "Be the only woman in town who isn't causing me grief right now."

She worked her mouth back and forth. "I guess I could scramble a few eggs."

He grinned. "Atta girl."

"Watch it, soldier."

Porter straightened and saluted, which garnered him a smile. He glanced out the window and watched Dr. Salinger's whip-slim figure move toward the boardinghouse slowly, as if she had the world on her shoulders.

She didn't know it, Porter thought, but she certainly carried the fate of Sweetness on them.

Nikki idly sorted through supplies, her mind torturing her with images of Darren and his young stripper fiancée in all kinds of acrobatic positions. She and Darren had never set the sheets on fire, but she'd been satisfied with their sex life, and assumed he was, too.

That, obviously, had not been the case.

Fresh tears pricked her eyelids. In the distance she could hear sounds of the women talking and laughing in the kitchen, the chug of washing machines churning. She felt so removed. How did she get here? Her life was a train wreck—fleeing one place, trapped in another. Choosing between the lesser of two evils.

At the sound of footsteps, she wiped her eyes. When Rachel came into view, Nikki tamped down her irritation. It wasn't the woman's fault that her feminine gorgeousness played to the insecurities Nikki was wrestling with.

"Am I interrupting something?" Rachel asked.

"No, come in. Do you need more Benadryl?" The women were plagued with bug bites and allergies—her included. Nikki had doled out ointment and antihistamines all morning. It wasn't exactly the life she'd dreamed of in medical school.

"No, I'm fine," Rachel said, scratching idly at her

bite-riddled arms. "I just came to get you for the town meeting."

"Oh." Nikki hesitated. "I'm not going."

Rachel frowned and crossed her arms. "Why not?"

Should she tell the woman she wasn't planning to stay? No. She didn't want to deal with the questions. No doubt the women had called back to Broadway to talk to family and friends. If one or two people had heard about Darren's engagement announcement, then most likely everyone knew. They'd think she was pathetic, maybe returning to try to win back her man.

The truth was much more pathetic—that as many bad memories as she had in Broadway, this little place with its big expectations scared her more.

"I...I'm busy, that's all," Nikki said, but her excuse sounded thin, even to her own ears.

Rachel frowned. "We need you to be there, Nikki, to ask questions and back us up. We want to make sure this town is ready to provide everything a doctor needs."

Nikki conceded the wisdom of Rachel's argument. Even if she left, the next town physician would have similar needs. It was only fair that she help set the stage for someone else to step in. It was part of the Hippocratic Oath, to be a responsible member of society. She had special obligations to her fellow human beings to safeguard their care.

Besides, it wasn't as if she had anything better to do.

Nikki noted the mood in the dining hall was expectant—and a little suspicious. The women were already starting to miss the creature comforts of home, of having things at their disposal. The weather, the bugs and the

seeming lack of compatibility with the single men they'd been promised would welcome them with open arms did not help.

Marcus Armstrong started the presentation by describing the way he and his brothers remembered Sweetness growing up. Pictures of small-town life were projected on a large white overhead screen. The people looked simple and happy, Americana at its best—high school football games, Fourth of July parades, watermelon-eating contests.

"But the economy was failing," Marcus explained. "The town was isolated and our young people were leaving in droves. With a dwindling population, companies weren't willing to bring technology this far up the mountain and conditions continued to worsen. When the tornado hit ten years ago this summer, it wiped out what was left of our town."

Pictures of the devastation flashed onscreen to audible gasps. Nikki's heart squeezed—very few things in the footage were even recognizable. The town had been reduced to a pile of rubble.

"The federal government offered disaster recovery funds, but it wasn't enough. The local government was too bankrupt to rebuild schools. Residents and business owners simply abandoned their property."

Nikki's thoughts flashed to the items in the property room Porter had shown her—no wonder the residents hadn't been able to find their belongings. And no wonder they had decided to leave.

"After a few years," Marcus continued, "the state took ownership of the mountain, and it was left to grow wild. Wildfires that went unchecked only made the area more uninhabitable. Several months ago, my brothers

and I were granted a federal grant to reclaim this land and turn it into a green community with a viable tax base. We have two years to meet program minimums, and so far, we're on track."

Kendall Armstrong, whose credentials included a master's degree in environmental engineering, took over. He presented the overall vision for the town of Sweetness: an economy based on recycling and generating alternative energy. All businesses, schools, municipal buildings and manufacturing plants would be powered by solar energy, and the meadow where the barbecue had taken place would become a windmill farm. To encourage hybrid and electric vehicles, recharging stations would be installed. Computer-generated drawings helped the audience envision what the town might look like.

"For now," Kendall added, "we believe diesel is better for the environment than gasoline, so all of our work vehicles are diesel-powered. Both this building and the rooming house were built from reclaimed materials. We've installed energy-saving appliances and water systems. In short—we practice what we preach."

He handed the presentation over to Porter Armstrong, and Nikki wasn't surprised to learn he was the marketer of the family. He was, after all, a natural salesman. But she *was* surprised to discover how articulately the man was able to convey his vision of Sweetness becoming a tourist destination for outdoorsmen, and even its own brand.

"We want the name of Sweetness to mean something to consumers," he said. "If we can capture their attention with our recycled products and our trees and streams, then we can educate them, too."

Marcus, the businessman of the trio, took the podium again to explain the town of Sweetness would be an incorporated community, with all residents registered and invested in the stock. "We'll give you room and board for two years and provide all the basics. In return, everyone will contribute in some way, and we'll all profit as the town grows."

Kendall joined him. "This is a chance to help mold the place where you'll live and raise your families."

"Sweetness will be a true cooperative," Porter chimed in. "But we can't do this without you." He looked directly at Nikki, pinning her with those amazing blue eyes. "All of you."

She almost expected music to start playing. It was an impressive presentation, no doubt, and the brothers were convincing in their conviction to rebuild the town. But from what she had seen, there was a huge gap in logistics. And from the lack of applause, she had the feeling the other women were thinking the same thing.

"Where are the police?" a woman shouted. "Are we safe here?"

"Where's the internet access?" someone else asked. "Unless you have a smart phone, you're screwed."

"What about cable TV?"

"How do we get our mail?"

"Where is the nearest grocery?"

"The nearest mall?"

"The nearest pet store?"

"I had to take a cold shower this morning."

"What's up with this red stuff you call dirt?"

"Is it always this hot?"

"Is it always this humid?"

"Can you do something about the bugs?"

The women kept firing questions. The men looked as if they were ready to run for cover, until Marcus Armstrong waved his arms and asked for quiet. "Ladies, we don't have this all figured out yet, but we're willing to work with you to address the things first that are most important to you."

Rachel, who was sitting next to Nikki, stood up. "You're asking us to take a big leap of faith here."

Marcus nodded. "Yes."

Rachel turned to Nikki. "I want to know what Dr. Salinger thinks."

Nikki was horrified as every eye in the room turned in her direction. Rachel sat and elbowed her, encouraging her to stand. Reluctantly, Nikki pushed to her feet, her mind and heart racing. Porter Armstrong stared at her, imploring her to give them her endorsement.

She broke out in a sweat, then wet her lips and prayed for coherency. "I'm very impressed with what the Armstrong brothers are trying to do here. But I, too, have considerable concerns about day-to-day needs being met. I'm particularly concerned about the lack of medical facilities and personnel."

She averted her gaze from Porter's intense eye contact. "And I have to be honest—I worry that your collective sentimentality for rebuilding your childhood home is clouding your judgment, obscuring the hundreds, if not thousands, of decisions that have to be made for Sweetness to be a safe, desirable place to live."

A murmur of consensus traveled over the room. Heads nodded and women began conferring among themselves.

"Dr. Salinger," Porter asked, his deep voice cutting into the room noise, "why did you come here?"

The room fell quiet again. Nikki's face heated. So many people in this room thought the reason she'd come here was to escape a cheating fiancé…and she admitted the breakup was the impetus for her decision to leave Broadway. But she wasn't about to admit that aloud, and especially not to Porter Armstrong. "I came here, like your ad said, looking for a fresh start."

He nodded slowly, then hobbled off the podium and made his way on his crutches over to the large double doors. Every eye followed him—and rightly so. He was fairly bursting out of the T-shirt he wore, his jeans hanging loose and low on his waist. When he reached the doors, he used a crutch to push them open wide. Sunshine rolled into the room. Porter leaned into the dancing rays and closed his eyes, inhaling deeply. His broad chest expanded and a look of rapture crossed his face. Then he exhaled noisily and opened his eyes. "It doesn't get any more fresh than this."

Nikki pressed her lips together. The man had a flair for drama…but his effect on the women was undeniable. Eyes were soft, mouths were bowed, and, if she was any indication, darn it, hearts were pounding.

Rachel stood up again. "The women would like some time to discuss our decision. In private."

The brothers exchanged glances, then nodded and headed toward the exit. As Porter was leaving, he locked gazes with Nikki. She looked away.

When the doors closed, a healthy debate broke out among the women that went on for some time. Nikki was quiet, wishing she hadn't come to the meeting, uncomfortable with voicing her opinion when she wasn't planning to stay.

"I trust Dr. Salinger," Traci Miles said, then turned to Nikki. "I'll do whatever you say."

"Me, too," another woman said. "If Dr. Salinger stays, I'll stay."

To her dismay, other women chorused agreement. Rachel angled her head toward Nikki. "Looks like it's up to you, Doctor. Should we stay…or should we go?"

14

"What do you think's going on in there?" Porter asked his brothers, staring at the dining hall. He sat on a bench with his aching leg propped up. Over an hour had passed since the women had asked them to leave so they could discuss whether or not to make Sweetness their home.

Kendall was pacing. "I think they're raking us over the coals."

"They made some good points," Porter felt obligated to say.

"I know," Kendall snapped. "We still have a long way to go. But we've achieved a lot here, and we'll really be in the hole if they all decide to just up and leave."

"I just wish they'd make up their minds," Marcus said, looking at his watch. "We've already lost most of the workday. With Jennings and Mason getting injured this morning on the mulch line, we're down a couple of bodies."

"If the women leave, we can run the ad again in a different town," Porter offered, wiping his neck in the oppressive heat. "Maybe somewhere south of the Mason-Dixon Line this time. Is it just me, or are Northern women bossy?"

"They're bossy," Marcus confirmed, then scowled at Kendall. "Whatever possessed you to bring a bunch of Yankees to this mountain, I'll never know."

Kendall stopped pacing. "I got news for you two— the fact that those women are bossy has nothing to do with the fact that they're Northern and everything to do with the fact that they're *women*. I just assumed that women living in a county where the unemployment rate approached twenty percent would be a little less picky about the conditions here."

Marcus gave a harsh laugh and lifted his hands. "Look at us. We're idiots. None of us are married, or have even had a serious girlfriend since high school. We've pretty much spent our whole lives avoiding relationships with women. Big surprise that we can't get into their heads."

"I thought we made a good case in there," Kendall said.

"We're not dead in the water yet," Porter said. "I've never had any experience with it, but I've heard it takes some women a while to get to 'yes.'" He grinned to lighten the mood.

Kendall rolled his eyes. "Yeah, Porter, you're the man. You have Dr. Salinger so impressed, you had to sabotage the woman's vehicle to keep her from leaving."

Porter was hot and irritated, and the mere mention of the woman's name made his temper flare. "I seem to remember you not being able to keep a woman from leaving Sweetness a few years back."

Kendall blanched, and Porter knew he'd gone too far.

Before he could apologize, the sound of the doors creaking open caught their attention. The women stood

there, with stoic faces. Rachel Hutchins, obviously the group's spokeswoman, stepped forward. Dr. Salinger hung back, avoiding Porter's gaze.

Not a good sign.

He used the crutches to push to his feet, a knot in his stomach.

"What have the women decided?" Kendall asked.

Rachel crossed her arms. "We're leaving first thing tomorrow morning."

Porter's shoulders fell.

"To buy supplies the town will pay for," Rachel added.

He caught his breath in relief as his mood rebounded.

She handed Kendall a yellow legal pad of paper. A list of items had been written on the page. Porter looked over Kendall's shoulder to scan the list. Food items, dehumidifiers, gardening supplies, bug zappers, computer equipment.

"This looks reasonable," Kendall conceded with a smile.

Rachel nodded. "There are ten pages."

Kendall's smile froze. "O…kay."

"We want a clinic built immediately," Rachel said. "We want to have a say in what's on the menu served in the dining hall. And we want titles."

"Titles?" Marcus asked.

"We want roles assigned," she clarified. "City Planner, Director of Technology, Director of Safety, Director of Communications, that kind of thing. If Sweetness is incorporated, we need the structure of a business."

Marcus pursed his mouth. "We'd planned on getting to all of that."

Rachel smiled. "We expect it sooner rather than later. Also, we want regular town hall meetings. And we've come up with a set of rules."

"What kind of rules?" Kendall asked. He was starting to look worried.

A woman Porter remembered as Traci stepped forward with another list on a legal pad. "No men in the boardinghouse overnight, for example. And we want quiet hours."

Marcus frowned. "Quiet hours?"

No operating machinery, no building activity or anything else that causes loud noises in the evening, early morning and on weekends."

"That's ridiculous," Marcus sputtered. "We have a town to build!"

"And no setting other rules without our input," Rachel continued as if he hadn't spoken. "We want authority to help decide how the town moves forward."

Marcus's face turned red. Before he could say something Porter was sure the women wouldn't like, Kendall cut in. "These are all very good suggestions. We do want your feedback and we need your help on every aspect of rebuilding Sweetness. Thank you."

Out of the corner of his eye, Porter noticed Dr. Salinger had separated from the group and was trying to slip away. He saw his chance to put her on the spot again. "Dr. Salinger!"

She stopped and turned back. "Yes?"

"We hope we can count on your input to the clinic we're planning to build."

Her eyes communicated supreme annoyance, but under the pressure of an audience, she finally gave a

curt nod. "Of course." Then she gestured toward the rooming house. "I need to get back."

He smiled wide. "I'll walk with you."

Porter made his way over to her, but could tell from her body language she wasn't pleased. She walked ahead of him, but he managed to catch up.

"Your group had us on pins and needles back there."

"It's not my group," she said in a clipped tone.

"We're glad you're all staying."

"You know I'm not staying," she admonished.

"But they don't, do they?"

Her mouth tightened. "No. Not yet."

"So until your van is ready, will you help us get the clinic underway?"

"I guess I don't have anything better to do," she said without enthusiasm.

"Meanwhile, we're going to move all your supplies into one of the empty bedrooms on the first floor so you'll have privacy to see patients."

"Speaking of which, I heard some workers were injured this morning. Why wasn't I called?"

He didn't want to tell her the men hadn't wanted her to be called and had instead asked Doc Riley to tend to their cuts and bruises. "Their injuries weren't serious— just some scrapes."

"Right," she said in a disbelieving tone.

"These men are strong, and they're accustomed to sucking up small injuries."

They had reached the rooming house. She paused at the door, obviously expecting him not to come in. Her nose wrinkled. "How's that evergreen oil working for you?"

He felt contrite. "Not as well as the painkillers you gave me."

Her eyebrows arched. "Imagine that. Now if you don't mind, I'm going to make a list of the basic items this new clinic of yours will need."

"Can I help?"

"No," she said bluntly.

As she started to turn away, he said, "Dr. Salinger, I'm sorry for putting you on the spot."

The look she gave him said she didn't forgive him. It made him wonder again what situation she'd left in Broadway, the situation she now wanted to get back to.

Nikki gestured to his cast. "You really should take your weight off your leg." She walked into the boardinghouse and closed the door behind her.

On the way back to the dining hall, Porter passed Rachel, who stopped to give him a flirtatious smile. "Would you like to accompany us on our shopping trip to Atlanta tomorrow?"

For a moment, he was happily distracted by the woman's sunny beauty. He'd like nothing better than to spend the day with a pretty woman who wanted to spend time with him. But he had to keep an eye on Nikki in case she decided to make a run for it.

"Thanks, but I'm not particularly mobile at the moment," he said with a little laugh. "Rachel, how well do you know Dr. Salinger?"

She frowned slightly. "We're friends, I guess. Broadway isn't a big place, so everybody sort of knows everybody."

"What's her story?"

"Nikki wasn't even planning to come with us until the last minute. She was engaged."

Porter was surprised. "Engaged?"

"To an attorney. Seemed like a nice guy. Then she found out he was cheating, so they broke up. I think she just wanted to get away from all the gossip, you know?"

So she'd come to nurse a broken heart…and now was having second thoughts. Had she talked to her ex on the water tower yesterday? Had he asked her to come back?

"Thanks," Porter said absently.

"Do you have plans this afternoon?" Rachel asked, touching the front of his T-shirt. "I thought maybe we could get to know each other."

Two minutes ago he would've said yes. So why was the idea suddenly less appealing? "Maybe some other time," he heard himself say. "My brothers and I have a lot to discuss."

She pouted. "Okay, some other time then."

Porter watched her walk away, admiring the swing of her rounded behind. The woman had more curves than a mountain road. When he got things under control with the doctor and got rid of this cast, he'd like to take that trip. He sighed. For now, duty called.

The women were dispersing, leaving his brothers standing alone in front of the dining hall. They looked utterly defeated.

"Cheer up," he said, limping up to them. "They're staying, aren't they?"

"At a pretty price," Marcus snapped, pointing to the lists.

"It's the cost of doing business," Kendall said calmly. "It has to be done."

"Is our doctor staying?" Marcus asked Porter.

"She's balking," Porter hedged. "But she agreed to help with the plans for the clinic until her van is ready."

"So the longer we deceive her," Kendall said drily, "the more work we can get out of her."

"Or the longer I have to convince her to stay," Porter added.

Marcus jabbed his finger at Porter. "You work with the doctor, get her invested in the clinic. If we put a crew on it, we should be able to get the footers dug and poured tomorrow. Kendall thinks he can get the modular units delivered by the end of the week. Maybe once she has a building to practice in, she'll be more inclined to stay."

Porter made a rueful noise. "If she has patients. She asked why she hadn't been told about the men who were injured this morning."

"So you have another job," Marcus said. "Finding her patients." Then he turned to Kendall. "And *you* are going with the women tomorrow to round up supplies. Make sure they don't bankrupt us buying hair spray and tofu. You two got us into this drink. Start swimming."

15

Nikki was in the room on the first floor that had been designated as her office, sitting at a small desk and tapping on her laptop keyboard, adding to the growing list of supplies needed to put together a basic medical facility. The few supplies she'd brought with her had been arranged to her satisfaction on bookshelves. A twin bed had been brought in and chairs for patients sat out in the hall.

Not that she had any patients.

Which was, she kept chiding herself, a good thing. But she felt so antsy.

The house was relatively quiet this morning since the contingency of women who'd left to purchase supplies also constituted some of the most boisterous residents. Nikki had considered hitching a ride with them to Atlanta, then getting a rental car to drive back to Broadway.

But she'd be adding eight hours to the already long drive, and then how would she reclaim her van? Plus, she'd given her word that while her van was being repaired, she'd do what she could to help get the clinic off the ground.

And this morning something occurred to her—what better way to assuage her guilt of leaving Sweetness without a physician than to find her own replacement? She wished she knew the way to the water tower because she needed to make a private phone call.

She glanced to Porter's worn denim work shirt folded over the back of a chair and impulsively picked it up. She shouldn't have kept it. It made her curious about what caused the jagged tear on the shoulder and the green-ish stain on the cuff. It was a lived-in shirt. There was something very sexy about a man who wasn't afraid to get dirty and work with his hands. By comparison, Darren had been pristine.

A beeping sound filtered through her thoughts. It wasn't a car horn, but similar. And it was insistent. She went to the window and peered out to find Porter sitting on the four-wheeler, waving to her. He gestured for her to come out.

Nikki's stomach did a little flip that made her hesi-tate. Last night she'd lain awake thinking about Darren, aching with loneliness…and then her thoughts had crept to Porter Armstrong and that misplaced kiss, his mis-chievous smile and how he seemed so eager to make up for his careless words. She didn't want to like him so much, so soon.

He beeped again and gestured that he'd meet her out front. She looked back to her laptop and decided a ride on the four-wheeler was preferable to being shut in her office working on such a pretty summer morning. So she closed her computer and grabbed her phone, hoping he'd give her a ride to the water tower.

She hurried into the hall, locked the door, then checked her pace and walked outside.

Porter gave her a big grin. "Thought you might like a tour of the town."

"You mean there's more than this?" she asked, gesturing to the two buildings and the first-aid shack.

"There will be," he said, extending his hand to help her on.

"Do you have helmets?"

"We're going to the clinic site first—it's just around the bend."

She settled onto the seat behind him, putting her arms around his waist loosely. He felt so…familiar. And the man could wear a T-shirt.

"How are you feeling?" she asked him.

"Fair to middling," he said breezily. "How about you?"

"I'm…fine," she said, suddenly realizing how few people asked her how she felt. She supposed everyone simply thought doctors were okay all the time. "But I had to take an ice-cold shower this morning."

"I'm working on that," he said lightly. "Isn't it a beautiful day, little lady doc?" He goosed the engine and they took off.

His enthusiasm was contagious. It was a shimmery June morning, with birds singing and insects chirping and flowers blooming. Mother Nature was bursting with vitality, giving the impression that every living thing was having sex. From the lush surroundings, it was easy to see how the term "the birds and the bees" had evolved. There was something very sensual about the pervasive foliage and the steamy humidity. Her friend Amy's remark about the mountains' power of seduction came back to Nikki.

But her friend had also said it was a deceptive seduction.

Nikki smirked. Was there any other kind?

As Porter had promised, the ride to the site that had been staked off for the clinic was just around the curve of the road, on the same side as the dining hall. At least two dozen men swarmed over the site operating machinery and using shovels to dig a trench for the building footer and foundation. Nearby another group of men added water to a concrete mixer whose drum was spinning slowly.

When they climbed off the ATV, Porter retrieved blueprints from the storage compartment and spread them over the seat. "I know it looks pretty uninspiring at the moment, but it'll go up quickly. We're bringing in prefabricated units for the individual sections."

He pointed to the plans. "There will be a waiting room, exam rooms, procedure room, lab, pharmacy, secure drug room, offices for staff, a filing room and a small lounge. Oh, and your office, of course."

Nikki was impressed with the efficient layout, but felt compelled to add, "Not my office, Mr. Armstrong. But this does look like a workable layout."

"Porter," he corrected. "Here's the front elevation," he said, turning to a computer-generated rendering of what the finished building might look like. For a utilitarian building, it was rustic and homey.

She lifted her head and visualized the building on the site. It would sit in a natural curve of foliage. Nearby was a huge tree with a giant trunk. It would be picturesque…a beautiful place to come to work every day. She couldn't help but compare it to the family prac-

tice she'd left in Broadway that occupied an abandoned strip mall.

"We're situating the building here because there's a nice plateau a few hundred yards behind this site that will accommodate a helipad for a Medevac."

They were thinking ahead, she conceded. "How does modular building work?"

"The sections are built in a factory, then shipped here on trucks and assembled on-site. There's a factory two hours away, so we can do business locally. It's faster, and there are fewer building materials to discard. Kendall worked with modular buildings in disaster recovery efforts overseas when he was in the Air Force, and in New Orleans after hurricane Katrina."

"Will it be obvious that the structure is basically boxes set in place and welded together?"

He smiled. "You tell me—the boardinghouse is a modular building."

She pursed her mouth. "No, I can't tell. It looks... traditional. Is it as strong as a conventionally built structure?" She thought of the destruction in the pictures of the aftermath of the tornado. Lightning usually didn't strike twice, but...

Porter nodded. "Since they have to withstand being transported from factory to site, the framing is actually sturdier than building codes require."

She was impressed, both by the process and by the men's dedication to new construction techniques. "You'll have to recruit trained professionals to work in the clinic—a pharmacist, for example, and at least one nurse."

"We want to apply to join the Federal Rural Health Clinic network, which requires us to have certain

personnel on hand. Kendall's been reading the women's bios. He said someone in the group is a recruiter?"

"Regina Watts," Nikki confirmed.

"He's going to work with Ms. Watts on getting the word out about any job we can't fill from current residents. But I'm hoping you'll help us get started with the paperwork for certification and licenses to operate in the RHC network." He rolled up the blueprints and returned them to the storage compartment, then removed a fat accordion folder. "I have the federal manual for getting started, and all the forms."

Nikki blinked. She'd underestimated the Armstrong brothers. And how could they know that she'd dreamed of being a part of this very kind of medical establishment ever since she'd graduated med school? "I'll do whatever I can while I'm here."

Porter's grin made her tingle. The sensation jarred her—like the road leading into Sweetness, that direction was a dead end. Darren had once made her tingle like that. She averted her gaze.

"Ready for the tour?" he asked.

"Would it be possible to take me back to the water tower first so I can make a phone call?"

"Let's go," he said, stowing the folder and retrieving the helmets.

The ride to the top of the mountain was invigorating. Nikki closed her eyes and inhaled the grape-soda scent of the mountain laurel Porter had identified yesterday. Two rabbits jumped into their path and hopped ahead in a zigzag pattern before bounding off into the underbrush.

When they reached the base of the water tower, Nikki dismounted the four-wheeler, handed Porter his

crutches, and made her way to the ladder. She jumped up to grab the bottom rung, telling herself she didn't enjoy the boost Porter gave her to send her on her way.

But she did, darn it. Which was ridiculous, considering he probably didn't think twice about it.

The climb to the top was sweeter than the day before because she was more relaxed, had more time to take in her surroundings. When Nikki reached the platform, she allowed herself a few minutes to take in the spectacular emerald- and violet-hued view before pulling out her phone to check email and voice messages. She had none, a fact she digested with a pang of loneliness. Then she dialed Dr. Hannah's office, relieved when her mentor answered, delighted when the woman seemed pleased to hear from her.

"How are things in the country, my dear?"

"It's…different," she said, trying to sound cheerful.

"What was the name of the town again?"

"Sweetness. Sweetness, Georgia."

"Sounds quaint."

"It's that," Nikki agreed.

"We miss you here."

She toyed with the idea of telling Dr. Hannah she was coming back to Broadway, then decided to hold off. It might be difficult to attract other medical professionals to Sweetness if she admitted she was leaving. "I miss the pace," Nikki finally said. "This isn't exactly a hotbed of activity."

"It sounds like a vacation. I'm envious."

"Speaking of which, do you know of a physician who might be willing to come here and help run a Federal Rural Health Clinic?"

"They have an RHC?"

"Not yet," Nikki said. "But they're applying for certification and a clinic is underway. They'll also need a Physician's Assistant, a Nurse Practitioner and a Certified Nurse Midwife."

"I'll put out feelers," Dr. Hannah said. "Do you have an address for this place?"

"Not in front of me," Nikki stalled. It didn't sound good to say the town didn't yet have a zip code, so she gave Dr. Hannah basic directions from the nearest interstate and told her if she found anyone who was interested in the positions, to call her.

"How's the scenery?" Dr. Hannah asked, her voice singsongy.

"It's picturesque," Nikki said with a little frown.

"I meant the eligible men. I read the ad in the newspaper, too, you know."

Nikki's face burned. Dr. Hannah knew Darren from the times he'd stopped by the office to pick her up for lunch or bring her flowers. Deceitful cad.

"I wouldn't know about that," Nikki said breezily.

"Darren was in the office today," Dr. Hannah said, her voice quiet.

Nikki's pulse jumped. "Oh?" Maybe he'd been asking about her.

"He and his new honey came in to get blood tests."

For their marriage license…at the place where everyone knew her. Her heart crimped and her eyes filled with tears.

"I'm sorry, Nikki. I always thought Darren was a nice guy, but he's obviously lost his mind."

Nikki couldn't speak. How many more hits could she take? As she stalled, a loud whistling noise floated up to her.

"Oh, I'm a birdwatcher," Dr. Hannah said. "What is that in the background?"

Grateful for the change in subject, Nikki made her way around the platform back to the ladder and glanced down, wiping her eyes. On the ground Porter Armstrong was puckered up, warbling, while dropping something from a paper bag into a bird feeder. To her amazement, a pair of brilliantly colored blue birds appeared and swooped down to pluck something out of the feeder, uncaring that Porter was close enough to reach out and touch them. Nikki gasped in awe. The man could literally charm the birds out of the trees.

"Nikki, are you there?"

Nikki yanked her attention back to the phone conversation. "I'm here. I'm no expert, but it looks like bluebirds?"

"Oh! They're the most beautiful creatures."

She was taking in Porter's large athletic frame, and the simple joy on his handsome face watching the birds dance around the feeder. "Yes, they are," she murmured. Unbidden, desire fluttered in her stomach, but it sent something akin to fear rushing through her veins. She couldn't do this again…become infatuated with a man who was out of her league.

"Nikki, are you still there?"

"I should go, Dr. Hannah. I'll call again soon."

"Okay. Take care, dear."

Nikki disconnected the call, then clasped the handrail to get a grip on her emotions. She felt so unlovable and so lonely. If only she could stay on this water tower, far above the complications of people on the ground.

"Hey!"

She looked down to see Porter shading his eyes, staring up at her. "You okay up there?"

She nodded and waved, then took a deep breath and began to descend the ladder. She didn't have to be in this place much longer. She could get through this.

When Nikki reached the bottom of the ladder, Parker was there to help her to the ground. His touch was like fire on her skin. She stepped away as quickly as she could, her face burning. Could he see how he affected her? Of course he could. Men like Porter Armstrong knew their power over women, and enjoyed it. He probably felt as if he was doing his good deed for the day, giving the plain girl a thrill.

"Were you able to make your call?" he asked.

"Yes."

"And is everything okay?"

Instead of answering, she gestured to the bird feeder. "I saw you calling the bluebirds—do you talk to animals, Mr. Armstrong?"

He laughed. "No. The birds just know when they hear me whistle, they'll get mealworms."

She made a face. "Mealworms?"

"We use them in our compost bins behind the dining hall, and the worms are a treat for the birds."

She followed him back to the four-wheeler and reached for a helmet. "What other kind of wildlife do you have around here?"

"The usual—possums, raccoons, deer…the occasional bear."

She stopped cold. "Bears?"

"Don't worry. Black bears are more afraid of you than you are of them."

She gave him a flat smile. "I doubt that." One more

reason to get out of here. "Not to change the subject, but any update on my van?"

He made a rueful noise as he lowered himself onto the ATV and stowed his crutches. "Sorry, no."

She secured the strap on her helmet. "Where are we going next?"

He grinned. "To my favorite place on the mountain."

Nikki fought it, but his excitement pulled at her. She climbed on behind him and tried to hold her body away from his. But as soon as the four-wheeler jumped forward, she was jammed up next to him. Nikki was too drained to resist, so she closed her eyes and pretended he enjoyed it as much as she did.

16

Porter guided the ATV halfway down the mountain, then veered right and rode a ridge around to familiar surroundings. He located an overgrown, crumbling paved road and geared down to make the steep climb, inexplicably pleased when Nikki's hands squeezed tighter around his waist. They passed mounds of rubble along the way, the remnants of former homes now covered with kudzu vines. Porter silently ticked off the last names of the families who had once inhabited Clover Ridge...the Trundles, the Boyds, the Maxwells, the Russells...the Armstrongs.

He pulled the four-wheeler to a halt next to a cleared and freshly mowed piece of land. Even as he waited for Nikki to climb off, he was second-guessing himself for bringing her here. He'd told himself he was just trying to find ways to occupy her time and delay her departure, hoping she'd form a bond with the town, but he could've taken her to countless other landmarks in Sweetness. Why did he choose this one?

Because he was feeling soft toward her after Rachel had told him yesterday that Nikki had come here to escape a cheating fiancé. No wonder the woman was so

prickly and had that deer-in-the-headlights look. She'd had her little heart broken. Was she going back to Broadway because her ex had asked her to come home? It seemed likely.

His hands tightened on the grips of the ATV. He didn't know the man she'd been engaged to, but he already disliked him. It was one thing to play the field before settling down, but it was something else entirely to sleep around after making a commitment. Nikki struck him as the type who took things seriously, including her relationships with men. She'd probably given her heart entirely, and was left reeling. For some reason, he felt compelled to keep her from going back to the man who'd treated her so carelessly. Plus, he wanted to show her that some things lasted…that some things could weather any storm.

"Armstrong," Nikki murmured, pointing to a newly painted mailbox at the end of what had once been a gravel driveway, but was now mostly choked with weeds. She scanned the plot where the concrete foundation outlined the home his father had built with his own hands. Then she glanced at Porter, her green eyes wide. "This is where you grew up?"

He nodded, his chest filled with longing and nostalgia. "It's funny. The storm leveled our house and carried away everything in it, but when it was over, that mailbox was still standing."

She set down her helmet and wandered into what had been their front yard, then turned and looked back over the valley. Her face transformed. "What a gorgeous view."

He turned to take in the scenery, so familiar, yet different. Some areas had grown up in the last decade,

others still reflected the path of the storm that had shorn trees like a giant chain saw. No matter—it remained spectacular, sitting in a bowl surrounded by terraced levels of evergreen and hardwood trees, rimmed by peaking mountains, bright orangey-red from the clay content in the soil and rocks.

"It's why my dad built here. He was a military brat and had never really had a home. When he met my mother, they used to drive all around and look for the place where they wanted to put down roots and raise their family. He'd said he knew this was the spot as soon as they saw it."

"I can see why." She gestured to the property. "You keep it cleaned off. Do you plan to rebuild here?"

"Someday," he admitted. "I have a lot of good memories here."

"I'm sure you do," she said, then stared at the outline of the house. "It must have been devastating to see it all wiped away. Where were you when the tornado struck?"

"Here," he said. "It was just me and Mother. Marcus and Kendall were both overseas. I was home on leave from the Army for a few days with a buddy. I was helping Mother pick green beans for supper." He pointed to a vine-covered field to the right. "Our garden was over there, and it produced enough to feed an army. But instead of scaling back as she got older, every year she thought of something she wanted to add. She gave extras to neighbors and friends."

He smiled at the memory, then frowned and lumbered over to the door of the storm cellar built into the side of a grass-covered mound. "I saw the twister coming, then heard the alarm." He tapped the door with the end

of his crutch. "We took cover in the storm cellar. The ground shook and it sounded like a freight train was rolling over top of us. It seemed to go on forever."

"Were you scared?" she asked quietly.

Porter looked at her. No one had ever asked him that question. The memories from that day still raised the hair on the back of his neck. "Yeah, I was scared plenty," he said, surprising himself. "Before my father died, my brothers and I promised him we'd take care of Mother. All I could think, while we were crouched in the cellar, is that I'd failed him—and her. I was sure we were going to be sucked out of there and blown clear to Atlanta."

Her expression softened. "But you weren't."

"No, we weren't. When the storm blew over, I climbed out, not knowing what to expect. I couldn't believe what I was seeing. The house—it was just…*gone,* along with everything in it. Our vehicles were tossed over the side of the ridge. I didn't want Mother to come out. I was afraid she wouldn't be able to handle it."

Nikki smiled. "But she did."

He nodded. "She shed a few tears, but said we should be grateful to be alive. And when we saw the widespread destruction, but learned that no lives had been lost, it was hard not to feel lucky."

She looked wistful. "You still had each other."

"Right." His chest tightened. He couldn't imagine being all alone in the world like she was. She looked so small and so vulnerable, her sagging ponytail a little worse for wear from the helmet, her cheeks pink from the unaccustomed sun exposure. He was overcome with the sudden urge to fold her into his arms.

Thank goodness for the crutches.

"Does this land still belong to your family?"

He gave himself a mental shake. "Yes. The incorporated town limits have been drawn up, but the land outside those boundaries still belongs to the families whose names are on the deeds as long as taxes are paid. My brothers and I located the families who owned the parcels around ours and made them a fair offer for their land. The Armstrongs now own about three hundred acres."

"That's nice," she said with a faraway look in her eyes. "It must feel good to know where you belong."

The lump that formed in his throat kept him from responding. Little lost sheep.

"What color was your home?" she asked. "What did it look like?"

He gripped the handles of the crutches and swung forward. "Come in, I'll show you around."

She squinted, but followed him as he made his way toward what had been the front of the house. "My father wanted a log home, but Mother had her heart set on a white house, so they compromised and he did it her way."

Nikki laughed. The sound of it was so unexpectedly contagious, he lost his train of thought.

"They sound like a lovely couple," she said.

"They were," he admitted. "My dad was a rough-and-tumble guy, but when my mother walked into a room, his eyes followed her everywhere." Porter checked himself—why had he said that? And why was he having trouble pulling his gaze away from the little lady doc?

He cleared his throat. "Step up five stacked stone steps onto the shadiest porch you can imagine. Mother had hanging flower pots everywhere, and hummingbird feeders." He nodded to the right. "Over there was a

swing painted red, that she sat on every evening to watch the sunset." Then he pointed left. "Over there hung a hammock that I snagged many a nap on." He stopped at the edge of the concrete foundation and swung himself over.

"Open the front door with the stained-glass window into a hallway with hardwood floors and a coatrack that held Mother's gardening smock, and my favorite fishing vest and Daddy's old flannel shirt that Mother just liked to touch."

He lurched forward and turned to the right. "Here's the kitchen where Mother always had something in the oven, something in the canner, something hanging up to dry, something setting out to cool."

He watched as Nikki closed her eyes and appeared to inhale. Why was he suddenly seized with the thought that he wished his mother could meet her? The first thing Emily Armstrong would do is set a plate of gravy and biscuits in front of the slip of a woman to fatten her up.

But Porter's gaze skimmed over her slight curves with appreciation. He preferred women who had something to get his hands around, but Nikki was…appealing. And those eyes of hers were like the greenest grass after a summer rain.

Porter blinked and resumed the "tour." "Over there was our dining room with a big round table and a chandelier my mother bought in Atlanta. She was so proud of it. The china cabinet I showed you the other day sat in that corner."

"I'll bet you had big Sunday dinners."

"We did—after church, of course. Looking back, I have no idea how Mother managed to feed all of us and

the stray friends we brought home." He felt a twinge of sadness and guilt that his mother had made a big production out of Sunday meals while he and his brothers had grumbled about missing out on daylight hours of fishing and swimming.

"Sounds fun," Nikki said.

He turned to the rear of the house. "This whole back area was our family room, with a big fireplace and comfy couches. Poor Mother always had to put up with us watching sports all the time and roughhousing."

"I'm sure with three boys, she was used to that."

"Yeah, but rest assured, when Mother put her foot down, we listened."

Nikki smiled. "I can tell you're fond of her. How often do you see her?"

He laughed. "To hear her tell it, not often enough. She talks to one of us a couple of times a week, but I owe her a visit."

"Does she know about your injury?"

"What she doesn't know, she can't worry about."

Nikki laughed this time. "I'm sure that doesn't stop her from worrying."

"You're probably right," he agreed, then pointed. "There was a set of stairs here that led to the bedrooms on the second floor—my parents' room and the two rooms my brothers and I shared. Marcus had his own room and Kendall and I doubled up until he left home. Mom decorated the guest room with frilly, feminine curtains and bedspreads and kept her sewing machine in there." He grinned. "I guess it was her only reprieve in a house full of testosterone."

He swung the crutches forward, but hit a sinkhole in the ground and lost his balance. He pitched forward, but

was saved from falling by the grace of one crutch—and Nikki shoring him up on the other side. Her touch made his body leap to attention.

"Are you okay?" she asked, her eyes wide, her face mere inches from his.

Maybe it was all the reminiscing and the sentimental setting, or the fact that he'd become accustomed to having her body snug up behind him, but Porter suddenly wanted to kiss her—on purpose this time, and not under the influence of mind-bending drugs. He slanted his mouth toward hers and since he hadn't given her a choice the first time, hesitated to see if she'd resist. Her breath escaped to brush his lips. With her eyes half-closed and her mouth parted, he was struck by how incredibly sexy the little lady doc was. Blood rushed to his midsection.

The ringing of his phone broke the moment. Nikki pulled back and stepped away. Porter bit back a moan of disappointment, then retrieved his phone to see it was the foreman on the clinic dig calling. He connected the call. "Hello?"

"Porter, there's been an accident. Nelson's hand is cut pretty bad."

Porter set his jaw. "Hold on." He looked at Nikki, who was standing several feet away. "One of the workers cut his hand."

"Wrap it tightly with something to stop the bleeding," she said, instantly all business. "And have him hold his hand above his heart."

Porter relayed the message. "The doctor and I will be there in a few minutes." He hung up the phone and moved toward the four-wheeler where Nikki was already putting on her helmet. It struck him what a comfort it

was to have her around in an emergency. Kendall was right—if she left, the rest of the women would probably also leave en masse.

She helped him get settled, their movements hurried, neither one of them alluding to the near kiss. Porter was grateful for the interruption—he'd lost his head for a moment. The last thing he needed was a woman on the rebound.

He continued to berate himself on the ride down. From the wistful look on her face when he'd described his family life, she definitely wanted the entire package. And while he, too, wanted to settle down and have a family someday, he wanted to have a little fun first. In hindsight, he should've gone with Rachel Hutchins on the shopping trip to Atlanta and let the little lady doc get started on the forms for the Rural Health Clinic.

Behind him, Nikki's body felt rigid and unyielding, but he reasoned she was probably thinking ahead to whatever situation waited for her at the clinic site. And she sneezed several times—the fresh mown grass and infamous Georgia pollen was getting to her. He went as fast as safety would allow and within a few minutes, they rolled onto the paved road that curved around to the clinic site. A clump of workers surrounded the injured Nelson Diggs.

But Porter's stomach filled with dread when he saw that Doc Riley was already tending to the man.

This did not bode well.

When he stopped the four-wheeler, Nikki was off in a flash, discarding her helmet. She dispatched one of the workers to get her medical bag, and approached Nelson. Porter clambered off the ATV, grabbed his crutches and tried to catch up.

But by the time he reached the group, the lines were drawn in the sand. Nelson shunned her attention, instead holding his hand to his chest and deferring to Doc Riley, who had apparently bound the wound on the man's palm with—were his eyes deceiving him?

Silver duct tape.

"Duct tape?" Nikki asked, her body language incredulous. "Did you even clean the cut first?"

"I put honey on it before I taped it up," Riley said, equally defensive.

Porter winced.

"Honey?" Nikki asked. "This man might need stitches. There could be nerve damage." But the fact that she suddenly sneezed several times in succession broke her momentum. Porter handed her his handkerchief.

"It wasn't that deep," Riley said with a dismissive wave. "It was just a lot of blood."

"I'm okay to keep working," Nelson offered. "I'll just wear a work glove."

"It's your call," Porter said to the man. "We'll talk later about how this happened."

Nelson got up to return to work, and the other men followed, except for Riley. "Let me know when you need more wintergreen oil salve for your leg," he told Porter. He tipped the bill of his work hat to Nikki and sauntered off.

The man she'd sent to fetch her medical bag came running up and handed the black bag to her. Nikki wiped her watering eyes and thanked him, but Porter could tell it was a slap in the face in light of the fact that Nelson had preferred Doc Riley's care.

"It's no big deal," Porter said to Nikki. "The men are accustomed to him patching them up for minor stuff.

Sweetness needs you around to handle serious medical issues." He gestured to his cast and gave her a cajoling smile. "Riley couldn't have set my leg."

Nikki studied him, her expression unreadable. "I'll get started on those forms," she said finally. "Thanks for the tour—and the handkerchief." She sneezed twice, then blew her nose. Then she walked over to the four-wheeler, removed the accordion folder from the storage compartment and set off toward the boardinghouse. He pondered the wisdom of sticking the two-year employment contract in the folder along with the RHC forms. Maybe he should've mentioned it.

"I'll give you a ride," he called, but she waved him off.

Porter watched her, the set of her shoulders, the angle of her chin. They were losing her. He needed to find the little lady doc some patients…fast.

17

The next morning, Nikki was stowing her toothbrush and smothering a yawn when a knock sounded on her bedroom door. She glanced at the dark circles under her eyes and sighed—she'd gotten next to no sleep last night, churning over the fact that her life was in limbo. Spending time with Porter Armstrong yesterday at what remained of his homestead had stirred a deep-seated longing for the kind of family life he'd described. She'd been so mesmerized that she'd almost let him kiss her, for real this time. Thank goodness fate had intervened in the form of a phone call before she'd done something that would've only mired her mind and body in another complication. She'd lain awake watching the moon fade into daylight before dragging herself out of bed this morning. And the nasty case of allergies that had hit her wasn't helping. If not for the ice-cold shower she'd taken, her eyes would probably still be glued together.

She washed her face and blew her nose, then opened the door to find Susan Sosa, one of the women who'd ridden down in the van with her, standing there. Susan was a prettily rounded woman with short blue-black curls, but she looked older than her thirty years. Nikki

knew from the tidbits she'd learned on the drive down that Susan's family life had mirrored her own until college. While Nikki had buried herself in her studies and pushed through eight years of school, Susan had taken another route, getting a factory job right out of high school, spending the last twelve years on her feet in front of an automaker's assembly line before being laid off the previous year. She'd been so animated about the move to Sweetness, she'd chattered all the way down about meeting a nice man with Southern manners.

It struck Nikki that the women were looking to her for solidarity to stay in Sweetness. And if she left, she'd be poking holes in the dreams of those who'd uprooted their lives to move here.

"Hi, Susan. What's up?"

Susan bit her lip. "I'm sorry to bother you, Dr. Salinger, but you have a patient waiting downstairs at your office."

Nikki raised an eyebrow. "I do? Who?"

The woman dimpled. "It's Kenny Stapleton, the really cute guy who came to get your medical bag yesterday."

She was inordinately pleased to hear that one of the men was finally seeking her out to be treated. "Is it an emergency?"

"No, he said to take your time."

Nikki pursed her mouth, then grabbed her black bag, stepped out into the hall and closed the door behind her. It was probably hay fever or bug bites. If not for the extreme pollen and the Jurassic mosquitoes, she'd have nothing to tend to.

"I brought you some coffee," Susan said, extending a steamy mug.

"Thank you," Nikki said, taking the cup. She had a feeling the woman had something else on her mind.

Susan tucked a stray curl behind her ear. "Dr. Salinger, I wondered if you could use someone to, you know, help out with patients and stuff. Like a secretary."

"I don't exactly have a stampede of patients."

"I know I'm not the most qualified person, but I'll work really hard."

Nikki was moved by the woman's sincerity. She realized that if one or two things had gone differently in her life, she could've easily been in Susan's shoes. "I'd like that," Nikki said, "but I'm afraid I don't know how this is all going to work yet." She thought of the two-year employment contract she'd found among the forms Porter had given her yesterday—subtle. "I haven't signed an agreement with the Armstrongs, so I can't even pay you."

"That's okay," Susan said in a rush. "I just want the chance to prove myself until a real job is available. Between you and me, I'm a little bored."

Nikki hesitated, not wanting the woman's hopes to be dashed when she left Sweetness. On the other hand, Susan had a point—there wasn't much to do until the town was better organized. "Okay by me, but we'll have to take it day by day."

Susan smiled wide. "Great. Thank you. So what can I do?"

Nikki found the key to the office on her ring and handed it to Susan. "The new patient forms are in a folder in a blue file box on a bookshelf. Get one for Kenny and have him fill out the top."

"Okay." Susan jogged ahead, leaving Nikki smiling at her enthusiasm. She passed another woman in

the hall, Regina Watts, the recruiter Porter had mentioned. "Regina, did the group return from Atlanta last night?"

"No," Regina said with a little laugh. "Rachel called and said they'd be back sometime today. She was hiring a delivery truck to bring everything here."

Nikki pressed her lips together, wondering if the Armstrong brothers had yet grasped what they'd agreed to when they'd sent Rachel on a shopping trip.

"I know you're working with the Armstrongs to recruit professionals to come to Sweetness. I wanted to mention that I asked my former boss to put out feelers for medical personnel."

"Good to know," Regina said. "Thanks. I have my work cut out for me. Imagine trying to convince an attorney to come here." The woman suddenly looked stricken. "I'm sorry, Dr. Salinger. I didn't mean to—"

"Don't worry about it," Nikki cut in, nixing her allusion to Darren Rocha. "Let's talk again soon."

The woman nodded and went on her way.

Nikki proceeded downstairs, trying to shake off the comment. It was true that attorney Darren Rocha wouldn't be caught dead within a hundred miles of a place like this.

She frowned. Was that a good thing…or a bad thing?

When she arrived at the temporary office, Susan had found the form and a clipboard and was hovering over Kenny, who seemed pleased by her attention.

Nikki said good morning and told him to come in when he was ready.

She went inside and downed some antidrowsy antihistamine, donned a lab coat, then hooked her

stethoscope around her neck and disinfected her hands. She'd never wish an illness on anyone, but she hoped Mr. Stapleton's case, if not challenging, was at least interesting.

It wasn't.

Nikki tamped down disappointment a few minutes later as Kenny described his infected ingrown toenail and removed his shoe and sock. She squinted. "Is that... bacon?"

He grinned. "Yeah. Doc Riley told me to tie a piece of raw bacon around my toe to draw out the infection. And it worked some—see where the bacon turned green?"

She swallowed hard. "I see." She snapped on gloves, then unwound the offending piece of bacon and disposed of it. Kenny's big toe was greasy and red. She carefully cleaned the area, then inserted a small piece of cotton gauze under the edge of the nail to lift it from the inflamed skin and gave him a tube of antibiotic ointment.

"Should I get another piece of bacon from the dining hall?" he asked, rolling on his sock.

She rolled her eyes. "I think it's safe to retire the bacon cure."

"Okay," he said, but he looked doubtful. Why did she have the feeling he'd do it anyway, and then give "Doc" Riley the credit once the infection had run its course?

She walked him out and said goodbye, startled to see that five other men occupied the chairs in the hall. Susan was fluttering around, tending to them. She'd set up a coffee station and a folding table for herself nearby. She handed Nikki a new patient form. "Joe Griffith is next."

Nikki smiled, reenergized to be busy and glad the

men were warming to the idea of seeing a "female" doctor.

Not that their ailments were all that serious, she noted as the morning wore on. A sore back muscle, halitosis, ear wax buildup, a cold sore and...

"Dandruff?" Nikki asked, staring at the man sitting in front of her who had a military buzzcut. "You're concerned about dandruff?"

He shifted uncomfortably. "I've noticed a few flakes when I comb my hair."

Nikki gave his scalp a cursory examination, then handed him a tube of lotion.

"What's this?" he asked.

"Sunscreen. You don't have dandruff—your scalp is peeling from a sunburn. You might try wearing a hat."

"I will. Thanks a bunch, doc." And he continued to thank her as he backed out into the hall. "You're the best doctor ever."

Nikki gave him a tight smile. She was starting to get the feeling that something was up, especially when she walked out and saw four more men sitting in her "waiting room," all offering toothy smiles.

"Business is booming!" Susan said, her cheeks flush with excitement.

"So I see," Nikki said, then held up her finger. "I'll be right back." She took off down the hall, following her last patient at a discreet distance. He exited the boardinghouse, then he looked all around and ducked into a copse of shade trees just off the path. Nikki followed, picking her way as quietly as possible and slowing when she heard voices.

She parted the branches of a bush and saw Porter

Armstrong a few yards away sitting on the ground, his back against a wide tree trunk, his crutches lying nearby, talking to Dandruff Man, who stood over him nodding. Then Porter removed a roll of cash from his shirt pocket, peeled off a couple of bills and handed them up to her "patient." When the other man walked away, Porter looked pleased with himself, pulled a bill cap down over his eyes and slouched back against the tree.

Nikki gritted her teeth and charged through the bushes toward him. He heard her coming, lifted his hat, his eyes wide. "Taking a walk, doc?"

She skidded to a halt. "You! You're *paying* your workers to come to me with piddly little complaints?"

"Whoa," he said, holding up his hand. "It's not what you think. I only offered to give my men paid time off to see the doctor if they had any ailments for you to check out."

"Dandruff?" she shouted. "Bad breath?"

"Hey, those are legitimate concerns," Porter insisted, "especially now that women are here." He reached for his crutches and struggled to push to his feet. "Can I get a hand here?"

She begrudgingly reached down to help him up. Which was a mistake because when he got on her level, she couldn't avoid contact with those intense blue eyes. Her stomach quivered and the air left her lungs, like yesterday when he'd almost kissed her. Worse, he looked like he was about to try again. She wet her lips, then remembered why she was here in the first place. She drew her head back. "Don't even try to change the subject."

He pouted. "Come on, little lady doc—I wanted to help. I thought if I could convince the guys to come see

you about small stuff, they wouldn't be so uptight when it came to something more serious."

She jammed her hands on her hips. "That's *so* patronizing! Don't you dare do me any favors, Mr. Armstrong. The only reason those men should be coming to me is because of the medical degree that has my name on it."

"I know," he said with a sigh. "But these men are macho, Southern boys. They have their pride. They're going to have to ease into letting someone as pretty as you see them in pain."

The "someone as pretty as you" comment struck her like a slap. He was mocking her. All of his flattery, the near kiss yesterday—and today—was only to manipulate her.

"No," she said evenly, "they're not going to have to *ease* into seeing me as their doctor because I won't be here, remember? By the way, I found the contract you slipped into the folder yesterday. You could've mentioned it." She sneezed violently, then blew her nose.

"I wanted to give you time to look over it, hoped you'd changed your mind. Are you okay?"

"Allergies," she muttered, dabbing at her eyes. "And I haven't changed my mind. In fact, I called my former boss yesterday and she's looking for my replacement."

Porter seemed surprised. "Well, I appreciate the fact that you're trying to help us out."

She crossed her arms. "By the way, how are the repairs on my van coming along? Did the new fuel pump arrive?"

"Uh…Kendall is supposed to bring one back from Atlanta, if he has room."

She squinted. "I didn't realize fuel pumps were so large."

The loud sound of a deep horn blasted into the air over and over, growing louder each time. Porter frowned, then moved in the direction of the noise, and Nikki followed. They emerged from the trees to see two thirty-foot-long delivery trucks pull up in front of the boardinghouse. Rachel waved from the passenger side of the first behemoth truck.

"Good God almighty," Porter muttered.

Nikki turned a smile on him. "Looks like he had room."

18

Porter tensed as Marcus paced their office behind his desk. Kendall sat next to Porter, looking straight ahead, apparently prepared to take whatever Marcus was going to dish out regarding the two enormous truckloads of stuff he'd escorted back from Atlanta. Porter somehow knew, even though he hadn't been part of that outing, he was going to get lumped into the tongue lashing that was to come.

Instead of calming down, Marcus seemed to become more irate, like a penned bull. His face grew redder, his hands fisted. Finally, he stopped and planted his hands on his desk. Steam was practically streaming out of his nose. "I don't even know where to start."

Kendall threw up his hands. "Just say whatever high and mighty thing you have to say so we can get back to work."

Porter glanced at his brother, surprised. Kendall rarely provoked Marcus. Come to think of it, Kendall had been uncharacteristically irritable since the women had arrived, as if he were…disappointed.

Porter pulled on his chin. He and Kendall had both

underestimated the amount of work it would take simply to convince the women to stay in Sweetness.

Marcus's eyes bulged. "Get back to work? You mean unpacking knickknacks for the ladies, don't you? Because from where I stand, there's not much real work getting done around here!"

"We're making good headway on the clinic," Porter added.

But wished he hadn't, because it only shifted Marcus's focus onto him.

"Fat lotta good that's gonna do us with no doctor to run it!"

"She's still here, isn't she?"

"But has she signed the contract?"

"Not yet," Porter muttered.

"Our application for an RHC won't even be considered if we don't have a physician on staff. We've put this clinic in motion, we can't stop now."

He didn't want to mention that Nikki had put out feelers to find a replacement— He wasn't giving up on having the homestead land. "I just need some more time to convince the little lady doc, that's all."

"So you're going to continue to hold her hostage and lie about the van?" Kendall asked.

"Absolutely. By the way, I told her you were supposed to bring a new fuel pump back from Atlanta, so if she asks you about it, play dumb."

Kendall frowned. "That's your role. I heard you paid some of the men to make up reasons to go see her?"

Marcus rolled his eyes.

"They all had legitimate conditions," Porter argued. "Small…things."

"And how'd that work out?" Kendall asked.

Porter frowned. "Not as well as I'd hoped."

Marcus pointed to Kendall. "You talk to Dr. Salinger about staying." Then he pointed to Porter. "*You* stay away from her."

Porter drew back. "What about our deal?"

Marcus gave a wave. "Kendall and I were going to give you the homestead anyway, Porter."

He looked back and forth between his brothers. "You were?"

Kendall nodded. "So why don't you let me work on Dr. Salinger. She might respond to sanity."

Porter's momentary pleasure about the land deed was strangely overshadowed by the knowledge that he no longer had an excuse to be with Nikki. "But I'm the only patient she has!"

"Maybe we should break something else of yours to keep her busy," Marcus suggested in a tone that indicated the subject was closed. Then he zeroed in on Kendall. "Back to the matter at hand. I specifically asked you to accompany the group to Atlanta to supervise the spending." He picked up a stack of receipts and shook them. "What happened? Did you let those females flirt you out of a fortune? Porter can't help but be an idiot when some woman bats her eyelashes, but I thought you were immune to all of that nonsense."

"Why?" Kendall shouted, jumping to his feet. "Because I've lived like a monk most of my adult life?"

Porter blinked at Kendall's outburst.

Marcus retreated, apparently just as surprised. "No."

But Kendall was fired up. "For your information, I think the women made sound choices in technology and

equipment that will move this town forward by leaps and bounds!"

They were still staring at him.

"Okay," Marcus murmured, having had the wind knocked out of his sails.

Kendall seemed to catch himself. "I have to go now," he said in an odd voice. Then he hesitated as if he'd lost his train of thought, before striding out of the office trailer.

Porter exchanged glances with Marcus.

"What was that all about?" Marcus asked.

"I don't know," Porter said. "If you ask me, he's been acting strange since the women got here."

"Has he developed an attachment to any of them?"

Porter couldn't help but notice that Marcus referred to the women as if they were aliens. "Not that I've seen. In fact, it's as if he's gone out of his way to make himself scarce."

Marcus stared after Kendall, then scratched his head. "Funny, because I only remember him being distracted and irritable one other time in his life."

Porter made a rueful noise. "I know. When I razzed him the other day about Amy leaving town, maybe it stirred up bad memories."

"You think? That's been, what—ten years?"

"More like twelve," Porter said. "But you know how serious Kendall is. I wouldn't be surprised if he's still holding a torch for her. Which is why you shouldn't have come down on him like you did."

"Excuse me?"

"Come on, Marcus. You know Kendall would never do anything foolhardy. It's just not in his nature."

"I know. That's *your* role."

"Nice," Porter said drily. "All I'm saying is if Kendall thought it was worth spending money on all that stuff, then we should trust him."

Marcus's cell phone rang. He glanced at the screen. "It's Mother."

Porter winced. "She doesn't know about my leg… or that Kendall went to Atlanta and didn't stop to see her."

Marcus frowned. "Anything else we're keeping from her?"

"She doesn't know I was the one who broke her blue vase when I was fourteen and glued it back together."

Marcus punched a button and set his phone on the desk. "Hi, Mom. Porter's here with me."

"Oh, good." Emily Armstrong's lilting voice floated into the room. "Hello, Porter."

"Hi, Mom."

"How are things, boys?"

"Bumping along," Marcus said.

"Fine and dandy," Porter said.

"Where's Kendall?"

"Working," they said in unison…too quickly?

"Is he all right? The last time we talked, he didn't sound like himself."

Porter and Marcus glanced at each other.

"He's fine, Mom," Marcus said. "We're just busy, that's all. How are you?"

"Missing my boys. What does a mother have to do to get a visit from one of her three sons?"

"We'll come soon," Marcus promised.

"That's what you always say. Porter, I had a dream about you last night, that you were hurt…or something was broken."

He shook his head. The woman's intuition was uncanny.

"He's fine, Mom," Marcus answered. "He's just been
wanting to tell you he's the one who broke your blue vase
when he was fourteen and glued it back together."

"Thanks a lot," Porter mouthed.

"Oh, I knew that," their mother sang. "How's the town
coming along? Kendall told me a caravan of women arrived from Michigan."

"Yeah," Marcus said, unable to keep the sarcasm out
of his voice. "That's why we've been so busy."

"Any love matches for my boys?"

"No," Marcus and Porter said in unison.

Too quickly? Porter wondered again. "But we have a
doctor now," he offered. "And we're building a clinic."

"It's good to know I won't have to worry about a
doctor when I move back to Sweetness," she said. "I
can't wait until that day comes."

Porter waited for Marcus to say something, but when
the silence stretched on, he said, "We're looking forward
to that day, too, Mom."

"I'll let you boys get back to work. I love you."

"We love you, too," they chorused, then Marcus disconnected the call.

Porter reached for his crutches and pushed to his feet.
"I should get going. I have some hot water heater issues
to sort out, and I promised Kendall I'd oversee the stak-
ing of the colossal garden the women are so gung-ho to
plant."

"Porter?"

He looked back.

Marcus jammed his fingers into his hair, then sat on

the edge of the desk. "I'm starting to wonder if we can pull this off."

Porter was dumbstruck. Marcus was asking for reassurance from him? He struggled for words. "Of course we can. We'll rebuild this town and bring Mother back, just like we promised."

"That day seems so far away."

Porter cast about for an analogy they could both relate to. "It's like when we were deployed. You can't get bogged down thinking about the war—you just have to take it one battle at a time."

Porter waited for Marcus to tell him he was full of crap or make some other dismissive big-brother remark.

"You're right," Marcus conceded. "The Armstrongs have never backed down from a challenge. We'll figure this out." Then he straightened and nodded to Porter's cast. "How's the leg?"

"It's not slowing me down…too much."

"I noticed that blonde Rachel giving you the eye. Anything happening there?"

Porter felt compelled to defend his reputation as a playboy, and wasn't about to admit that he was more interested in getting a real kiss from the little lady doc. "Maybe. I'm keeping my options open. How about you?"

Marcus scoffed. "I'm not looking for a woman."

"Famous last words," Porter said with a grin, then left the office. But when he got outside, he had a knot in his gut.

It was unsettling to see Marcus unsure of himself, no matter how fleeting. Porter hadn't realized, until this moment, how much he relied on his big brother as a

life compass, especially since their father had passed away. Marcus carried a mountain of responsibility on his shoulders. They were talking about building an infrastructure and economy that could make or break future generations.

Porter swallowed hard. For months now, the reconstruction had consumed his waking hours, but day-to-day tasks had distracted him from the big picture of what they were trying to achieve. When considered in its entirety, the mission of rebuilding an entire town was...

Daunting.

He wouldn't have dreamed of attempting it without his brothers. Knowing that Marcus felt the same way bolstered his confidence and worried him at the same time. He suddenly felt the mantle of obligation settle around his own shoulders. Maybe the stress of it all was getting to Kendall, too.

Porter rode one of the four-wheelers to the boardinghouse to consult with the plumbers who were reassessing the hot water system. Unfortunately, there were no short-term solutions. Hot water would continue to be scarce, which he knew didn't help their case when it came to convincing Nikki to stay. He made his way to the room that had been turned into Nikki's temporary office and noticed, with a cringe, that four of his men were sitting in the chairs lined up in the hallway.

"Why are each of you here?" he asked.

"Razor burn."

"Hammer toe."

"Backache."

"Baldness."

Porter sighed, pulled out his wallet, and started

peeling off bills. "Here's twenty bucks. Get back to work. And spread the word that my offer for paid time off to see the doc has expired. Don't come unless you're bleeding or something is falling off, got it?"

The men took the money and left. Porter dropped into one of the chairs, and scratched at the skin under his cast. He'd had to mutilate most of his work pants, cutting off the left leg at the knee to accommodate the cast. His ankle still throbbed at times. And it itched like a sonofabitch. He pulled a pen out of his shirt pocket and stuck it under the cast to try to get some relief. He moved it back and forth, but it fell short of the area that was driving him crazy. And when he pulled out the pen, the cap didn't come back out.

"Shit."

The door opened and Kendall stood there with Nikki. She looked so…*competent* in that lab coat, it was sexy as hell. Kendall gave him a suspicious look. "What are you doing here?"

"Besides paying off my patients," Nikki added drily.

He noticed her eyes were red-rimmed—still suffering from allergies…or crying over her cheating fiancé?

"I, uh…came to see if the doctor could give me some lotion or something for the itching," he improvised to Kendall. "What are *you* doing here?"

"I wanted to say I'm sorry to Dr. Salinger for dropping the ball on bringing back the fuel pump for her van," Kendall said pointedly. "And to say how grateful we are that she's agreed to prepare the RHC application."

"I explained I had nothing better to do until my van is repaired," Nikki said, gesturing to her empty "waiting room."

"What about me and my itch?" Porter asked hopefully.

"I do have something for that," she admitted. "Excuse me."

She disappeared from view. Kendall frowned and whispered, "Marcus said for you to stay away from her."

"I don't listen to everything Marcus says," Porter whispered back.

Kendall lifted an eyebrow.

"But don't tell him," Porter added.

"I think you have a thing for Dr. Salinger," Kendall whispered.

"That's crazy," Porter whispered back.

Nikki reappeared at the door. "This should work." She handed him a wire clothes hanger, then sniffed the air. "You might also want to lay off the wintergreen oil—you could be allergic." She gave them both a flat smile. "I'll let you know when the RHC application is done, and I trust you'll keep me posted on my van?"

"Sure thing," he mumbled.

"Good day, gentlemen." She closed the door and all the joy went out of the room.

Kendall looked at him. "It's a good thing you don't have a thing for her...because I think she kind of hates you."

"Shut up," Porter muttered.

Kendall clapped him on the shoulder. "Don't worry. You don't have time for courtin', little brother. You have a garden to plant, a media room to put together and a clinic to finish...by the end of the week. Let's go."

19

Nikki sneezed violently and bit back a curse. Despite her effort to stay inside with the windows closed, her allergies had only worsened as the week wore on. Whatever allergen was in the air, it had permeated the house and her body, and was impervious to nasal washes and antihistamines. It was embarrassing when she couldn't even cure herself.

The best thing about being holed up in her office the last few days was that she didn't have to interact with Porter.

Nikki frowned.

And the worst thing about being holed up in her office the last few days was that she didn't have to interact with Porter.

She wiped her watery eyes and blew her nose, then tossed the crumpled tissue in the trash on top of a mound of others. Because her head was foggy, she'd made slow progress on the application for the RHC, but was nearing the end. With no prepaid male patients in her waiting room, her foot traffic had been curtailed to taking care of the women's needs—mostly insect bites and migraines.

And the ever present allergies.

She sneezed again and moaned at the pressure on her raw sinuses. The rumbling sound of big trucks arriving and voices raised outside caught her attention. She pushed to her feet and looked out the window. Two flatbed eighteen-wheelers carrying what looked like shrink-wrapped buildings crawled past the boardinghouse. Nikki smiled and her heart beat faster. The modular sections for her clinic had arrived.

Then she caught herself—it wasn't *her* clinic. There was no reason to get excited about a building going up in a place she was going to leave. Porter drove by on a four-wheeler, escorting the trucks to their destination. Unbidden, her pulse picked up again. She straightened and stepped away from the window, feeling thoroughly miserable. She needed to get away from this place.

Get away from that man.

She dabbed at her eyes and blew her nose, then rummaged in her desk drawer for more antihistamine.

A knock on her door was a welcome distraction—Susan, no doubt, who was probably finished sorting and pricing the list of supplies Nikki had assembled for the clinic. After that, she had no other tasks to give the woman.

"Come in," Nikki called.

The door opened and Nikki blinked. "Doc" Riley Bates stood there with a smug smile on his grizzled face. His ripe body odor permeated even her swollen nasal cavities. "Hiya, doc."

"Hello," she said, wary. "How can I help you, Mr. Bates?"

"I came to help you," he said, nodding to her trash can overflowing with tissues. He walked to her desk,

then reached inside a pocket on his cargo work pants and withdrew a plastic baggie full of some dark substance. He extended it to her and when she hesitated, he shook the bag. "Take it, it's homemade licorice."

Confused, she took the bag, studying the strips of dark rubbery candy inside.

"It's the genuine article," he said. "Made from licorice root, not like the mass-produced packaged stuff that gets passed off as licorice." He grinned. "It's for your allergies. I noticed the other day they were getting the best of you."

She stiffened. "I'm sure they will pass."

"Sure they will. But they'll get worse before they get better, which will be the first hard freeze, along about November."

His grin irked her. "Thank you, Mr. Bates, but I'm treating my allergies with proven medication."

"If it's proven, why ain't it working?"

She tucked her tongue firmly into her cheek.

"The licorice will help," he insisted, "and it tastes pretty good, if I do say so myself."

"Thank you," she said, setting it on the far corner of her desk.

"You're welcome," he said, although the tone of his voice said he knew she had no intention of trying his home remedy. He tipped the bill of his cap, then backed out of her office and closed the door.

Nikki managed to stifle a sneeze until the door closed, then erupted into a tissue three times in a row before dropping back into her chair. She frowned at the bag of candy, then picked it up between two fingers and dropped it into a bottom desk drawer.

Another knock sounded. Nikki sighed, hoping the

self-proclaimed medicine man hadn't returned, or one
of Porter's patients-for-hire.

"Come in."

The door opened and Molly McIntyre stood there,
shoulders back, her square face stoic. "Is this a bad time,
Dr. Salinger?"

"No," Nikki said. "Please come in. What can I do for
you, Ms. McIntyre?"

"Call me Molly." She closed the door, then lifted her
hands, palm up. "It's this rash—it just won't go away."

Nikki hesitated. "Did Porter Armstrong put you up
to coming here?"

"Excuse me?"

"Did he pay you to see me for treatment?"

Molly frowned. "No. Why would he do a fool thing
like that?"

Nikki believed her. "Have a seat and let me take
a look." She walked to a cabinet and withdrew latex
gloves, then pulled a chair close to Molly's and examined the angry red bumps between her work-worn fingers. Her hands also had a faint bluish stain.

"The blueberry lotion Riley Bates gave me worked for
a while, but then the rash got worse. The lotion smelled
good, though."

Nikki made a rueful noise. "It's definitely contact
dermatitis. You might switch detergents, and wearing
rubber gloves will be a big help." She smiled. "Meanwhile, a steroid cream will reduce the itching and allow
your hands to heal. Unfortunately, it won't smell as good
as your blueberry lotion, but the good news is you won't
turn into a Smurf."

"I don't care, as long as it helps with the itching."

Nikki pushed to her feet and walked over to a cabinet,

fished through a bin of samples and removed a tube. She walked back and handed it to Molly. "If you don't feel better soon, I can write you a prescription for something stronger, but I can't fill it."

Molly nodded. "Thank you." Then she opened the tube, squirted out some of the white cream and rubbed it in, the instant relief showing on her face. "That's better already."

"Good."

"What do I owe you?"

Nikki waved. "No charge. That's only a sample."

"What about your time?"

"I'm biding it until my van is repaired," Nikki said, thinking it wouldn't hurt to tell the woman she was planning to leave.

"I'm sorry to hear that," Molly said, then stood to leave. "But I understand. This place is a waste of your talents."

"I didn't say that," Nikki said, feeling petty. "It was a mistake for me to come here." She gestured vaguely toward the door and the outside. "The rest of the women came to Sweetness looking to settle down and have a family. It feels…disingenuous for me to be here."

"You think there's no place here for someone who doesn't want to get married and have kids?"

Nikki realized Molly was referring to herself. "No," she said quickly. "I just think this town deserves a doctor who's committed to the goals of the community. All this home and hearth stuff…it's more than I signed up for."

"Ah. It seems hokey to you."

Nikki bit her lip. "I meant no disrespect."

"None taken," Molly said. "Stereotypes exist about

Southerners for a reason—we tend to be more sentimental about things that people in other parts of the country think is old-fashioned. We feel deeper and laugh louder and cry harder. I understand why that makes people uncomfortable, especially Northerners."

Nikki was both surprised and disturbed by the woman's analysis. "It doesn't make me uncomfortable."

"It's nothing to be ashamed of," Molly said, moving toward the door. "It just is what it is." She smiled. "Much obliged for the cream."

"No problem," Nikki said, feeling self-conscious. "Um, Molly—were you able to locate the owner of the pocket watch I found?"

Molly grinned. "I did. It belongs to Cletis Arnold Maxwell. He was a neighbor of the Armstrongs up on Clover Ridge. Cletis moved to Florida after the tornado. He was mighty glad to hear his watch had been found. It was a gift from his father. Said to thank the woman who found it most kindly."

Nikki's heart welled with pleasure. "Mr. Maxwell is very welcome."

"Actually, it's *Dr.* Maxwell. He was the physician here in Sweetness for many years. He was so pleased to hear the person who found his watch is our new physician— said it was a sign. Hope that doesn't make you uncomfortable." Molly winked, then left.

When the door closed, Nikki suddenly felt empty... and shallow. She hadn't meant to imply that the people here in Sweetness were too...much. She saw her inability to immerse herself in the efforts of the town as her own weakness, not the other way around. Hot tears filled her eyes. She'd underestimated what would be expected of her, didn't realize how much the breakup

with Darren had taken out of her and how little she had left to give.

Loneliness engulfed her, leaving her chest aching. She groaned. And the misery of her sinus headache wasn't helping matters. She blew her nose to relieve some of the pressure, then was overcome with the urge to consume something comforting, like warm tea or chocolate cake.

Or warm chocolate cake.

Her mind went to the licorice candy Riley Bates had brought her. She didn't believe for a minute it would help her allergies, but it might at least satisfy her sweet tooth. She pulled out the bottom desk drawer where she'd relegated the candy and pulled out the baggie. The ropes of dark candy were lumpy and uneven, the ends jagged. It looked a little…unsanitary.

She swallowed and opened the baggie. The bittersweet aroma of licorice had to be strong if it was able to infiltrate her swollen sinuses. Her mouth watered. She withdrew a piece of the candy and cautiously bit off a small piece, prepared to spit it out if the taste was revolting.

It wasn't revolting.

It was soft and melty and chewy, flooding her mouth with sweet and savory cherry flavors that made her jaw lock in appreciation. "Um," she moaned. "Mmm." She took another bite and savored it as well, softening toward Riley Bates for the moments of pure pleasure. She finished a finger-sized portion, then tucked the rest of it back into her drawer, feeling like a naughty child.

Suddenly restless, Nikki walked to the window to see if she could catch sight of any activity. Men and women streamed toward the clinic site, obviously curious. Nikki

was curious, too, and while her body strained to go, something held her back. She didn't want to become more invested in this place. And she didn't want to run into Porter and deal with his intense eye contact when she was already feeling physically weak.

Molly's words reverberated in her head—the assertion that Northerners were afraid of how deeply Southerners felt about things. Despite Nikki's protests, Molly's insinuation that Nikki was afraid of developing emotional attachments hit close to home.

But she had a right to protect herself from more hurt. She ran her thumb over her empty ring finger where a slight indention betrayed how thoroughly she'd been deceived. She'd learned the hard way that no one else was going to look out for her.

Nikki turned away from the window and went back to her desk. The sooner the RHC application was completed, the sooner she could leave Sweetness with a clear conscience.

20

"What do you think of our clinic?" Porter asked Marcus and Kendall, his chest puffed out as far as he could get it while balanced on his crutches. "Looks good, doesn't it?"

"It does look good," Marcus conceded, surveying the newly assembled clinic that workers were painting khaki green. "It's a good-looking, expensive, big, *empty* building." He looked at Kendall. "What's the status on the RHC application?"

Kendall jerked his thumb over his shoulder. "I'm on my way to see Dr. Salinger. She said she'd have it ready this morning."

Porter's pulse rocketed higher. Every day this week he'd been hoping Nikki would come to see the clinic going up. Every day this week he'd been disappointed.

Not for himself, of course, but for the town that was on the verge of losing a doctor with such pretty eyes—er, with such potential.

"I'll go with you," Porter offered to Kendall.

"I don't think so," Marcus said. "Let Kendall handle this."

Porter frowned. "Maybe I need to see the little lady doc about my leg."

"Do you need a refill on the coat hanger?" Kendall asked drily. "I think she made it pretty clear that she didn't want to see you again unless it was a legitimate medical issue."

Porter could only watch his brother walk away.

"I know that look," Marcus said.

Porter straightened. "What look?"

"That 'I want what I can't have' look."

He frowned. "I have no idea what you're talking about."

"Uh-huh." Marcus looked over Porter's shoulder. "Don't look now, because here comes a woman who's looking at you like you *could* have her."

Porter turned his head to see Rachel Hutchins walking toward him. She was scorching hot in a pair of cutoff shorts and a pink T-shirt, her body language loose and inviting—a far cry from Nikki's sterile lab coats and crossed arms.

Porter pursed his mouth. Dr. Salinger wasn't his responsibility anymore. He was free to turn his attention in other, more promising directions. When Rachel smiled at him, he smiled back.

"Hi, there," she said.

"Hi, yourself."

"Congratulations on getting the clinic up so quickly."

"Thank you," he said, noticing her bra strap had slipped down her arm. Strangely, though, instead of imagining what lay underneath the blonde's pink T-shirt, an image of Nikki's transparent wet shirt flashed in his mind.

Rachel gestured to his cast. "How's your leg?"

"Great," he said, even though at the moment it was throbbing. "I'm not letting the cast get in my way."

She reached forward to trace the small John Deere logo on his T-shirt with a pink-tipped finger. "Of doing anything?"

He swallowed hard. "That's right."

"That's good to know. Could I interest you in a picnic lunch today?"

As he surveyed her tall, curvy figure, a strange feeling came over him—it was as if the *idea* of being with Rachel was more appealing than actually being with her. She had a hard edge that makeup couldn't soften...and her voice was shrill to his ears, like a dog whistle.

Then Porter shook himself. He was going soft—literally. There were worse ways to spend time than being fed by a sexpot. "That would be...great."

She beamed. "I'll pack sandwiches. Noon?"

"Sure. I'll bring the ATV around and pick you up at the boardinghouse."

"It's a date," she sang.

Porter watched her sashay away and considered the possibilities of a long, lazy afternoon on a blanket under a shade tree.

Marcus walked over and clapped him on the shoulder. "Don't do something to run her off, too, okay?"

Porter scowled. "Since everything is under control here, I think I'll take the riding mower up on the ridge. I was up there the other day and the homestead could use a trim."

"Why were you up on the ridge?"

"I took the little lady doc on a tour."

Marcus's eyebrows shot up. "Really."

"I was just showing her around. I thought if she connected with the area, she might stay."

"Uh-huh." Marcus grinned. "Face it, Porter. Dr. Salinger is the only woman in the world unaffected by that dented chin of yours."

"I'll catch you later," Porter said sourly.

He climbed on one of the four-wheelers and drove to the large garage where they kept the work vehicles. After parking the ATV, he made his way to a tractor with a riding lawnmower strapped on the trailer hitched to the back. He arranged his crutches, then hoisted himself up and fired up the tractor. Then he steered it toward Clover Ridge and tried to relax for the long, slow drive. He was looking forward to some fresh air to clear his head.

For some reason he couldn't put his finger on, he already regretted telling Rachel he'd meet her for lunch. After all, Marcus was right—they couldn't afford to lose the ringleader of the women. What if she became clingy, expecting something from him? Sure, things could go well—at first. But considering his short attention span when it came to women, there was a better chance that things wouldn't end happily. Besides, the women had just arrived. It was way too soon to form an association with just one of them. Rachel was easily the most striking and the most sociable of the women, but there could be a sleeper in their midst…someone who didn't necessarily stand out, but when awakened, could fuel a man's passion higher than any siren.

Like Nikki, he thought irritably. He suspected the pint-sized pent-up practitioner would be a wild thing in bed if she'd let down her guard.

Had she been like that with her ex-fiancé—wild and

uninhibited? And why did the mere thought of her being intimate with some faceless man bother him?

Something large darted across the road and Porter slammed on the brake with his good foot. Despite his efforts, the animal collided with the front of the tractor with a sickening thud—a deer, he realized with a sinking feeling as it scrambled into the underbrush, and from the way it hobbled, obviously injured. A few yards off the road, the bushes along the path it had taken stopped shaking—the animal was down.

Porter shifted gears and let the tractor idle, then climbed down and grabbed his crutches. He picked his way carefully through the brush, afraid of what he was going to find. He was relieved to hear the animal breathing hard and snorting. When he reached the deer, he saw it was a young doe. The animal's eyes rolled and it tried to stand, but fell back to the ground due to the ugly, bloody break in one of the lower hind legs.

Porter winced and approached the animal with soothing noises, but acknowledged the only reason it allowed him to lay his hands on it was probably because it was in too much pain to move. He surveyed the situation and the distance back to the tractor. His mind made up, he removed his work shirt and tied it around the deer, then tugged.

It was slow going, moving forward on one crutch and dragging the injured animal with his free hand. He finally made it back to the road where he lowered the ramp on the back of the trailer and half pulled, half lifted the deer into place behind the mower and secured it by crisscrossing soft cotton ropes over its body. It was still breathing, but its chest heaved.

He smoothed his hand over its furry ear. "Hang in

there…the little lady doc will fix you up, just like she did me."

Porter didn't take the time to analyze how good it felt to know that Nikki was in Sweetness…and how bad it might feel after she left.

21

"Thank you, Dr. Salinger. I can't tell you how much my brothers and I appreciate all the hours you put in on this RHC application."

Nikki accepted Kendall's handshake. "You're welcome. Once it's submitted, you should have approval within thirty days."

"That doesn't give us much time to stock the clinic... or hire staff."

"Susan has the list of basic equipment and supplies you'll need. As far as staffing, I'll help you all I can—remotely." She extended the unsigned employment contract.

He held up his hand. "You can toss it if you've absolutely decided to leave."

She nodded. "Do you know when my van might be ready?"

"Uh...can't say that I do."

"Do you know if the replacement fuel pump has even arrived?"

Kendall looked uncomfortable. "Uh...no. Porter was sort of taking care of it."

Nikki crossed her arms. "Mr. Armstrong, I'd like to leave as soon as possible. I need my van."

"Are you sure there's nothing we can do to change your mind? Have you seen the clinic?"

"I haven't seen it," she admitted. "But I won't change my mind."

He nodded. "I'll have a talk with Porter. We'll get you back on the road as soon as possible."

She smiled. "Do that. Now that the application is completed, I don't have much to do—unless your brother hires more patients for me."

The middle Armstrong brother had the good grace to squirm.

"I haven't seen him around the past few days," she said casually. "How is his leg?"

Kendall pursed his mouth. "Between you and me, I think it bothers him more than he lets on."

"I've told him over and over to stay off it."

"If it makes you feel better, he's been through worse, and didn't listen to the doctors then, either."

"Your younger brother seems to have a rebellious streak," she agreed.

"I know. But it's served him well in life." He grinned. "And women seem to love it."

Nikki gave him a deadpan look.

"Er…not *all* women," Kendall corrected hastily. "Maybe his methods are a little unorthodox, but when he puts his mind to something, he makes it happen. Like rebuilding this town, for example. If something happened to me and Marcus tomorrow, I have no doubt Porter would still meet the federal deadline."

"You and your brothers seem so close," she murmured. The whole family dynamic was alien to her.

"For better or worse," Kendall said with a little laugh.

"Your brother showed me where your home once stood."

Kendall's eyebrows shot up. "Porter took you up on Clover Ridge?"

She hesitated, wishing she hadn't said anything. Kendall was obviously reading something into a simple gesture. "I think he was trying to entertain me. It's a beautiful place."

He nodded, but was looking at her strangely. "I guess I'd better let you get back to work, Dr. Salinger."

They both knew that was a laughable statement, but she was starting to feel awkward about the direction of their conversation, so she didn't protest. Kendall thanked her again, then left.

When the door closed, Nikki pondered Kendall's comment about his younger brother. Porter Armstrong planned to get this remote mountain town off the ground and spend the rest of his life here…get married here… raise a family here. Based on the population predictions for the town on the paperwork for the RHC, the Armstrongs had big plans for Sweetness. But all she could visualize was living in a fishbowl, where everybody would know every move she made. Where she would be expected to participate in everyone else's lives and allow them into her life in return.

She started to toss the employment contract in the trash can, then changed her mind and stuck it in a desk drawer.

To save it for the next doctor who came to town.

She paced around her office, feeling caged, fighting the urge to run outside and start walking toward the

interstate. She was tempted to ask one of the women to drive her back to Broadway, but she wanted to leave with as little disruption as possible. They were all so… *pushy,* constantly inviting her to come to their rooms after dinner to listen to music and gossip. But it felt invasive because she was afraid they'd want to talk about her scandalous breakup with Darren. And even if they didn't ask, she knew they were thinking about it when they looked at her. They pitied her.

It made her want to tuck in her edges and keep to herself.

Nikki massaged her temples and the bridge of her nose to relieve the pressure caused by the allergies that seemed to have taken up residence in her head. The pollen alone was enough to send her back to Michigan where the bitter winters zapped allergens that thrived in hot, humid temps. She went to her desk drawer and removed a chunk of the black licorice candy Riley Bates had given her—not because she believed in its medicinal qualities, but because the act of chewing would relieve some of the compression in her ears.

And she was starting to crave the sharp, cherry flavor.

She was moaning with pleasure when a rap sounded on the door. Before she could respond, the door burst open. Porter Armstrong stood there, taking up the entire door frame with his large physique and crutches.

The jump in Nikki's pulse at the sight of him sparked her ire. She swallowed the mouthful of candy. "Why knock, Mr. Armstrong, if you're going to barge in?"

"Sorry," he said, moving to get out of the way of the men following him. "It's an emergency."

That's when she noticed the blood on his shirt. Nikki

was on her feet instantly. "Someone's injured?" She was already performing a mental checklist for trauma treatment. But when they deposited the bloody patient on the twin bed and stepped away, Nikki came up short.

"It's a…deer."

Porter gestured for the other men to leave, then looked up. "Right…a doe, actually. She ran out in the road, jumped into the side of the tractor I was driving."

Nikki held up her hands, incredulous. "Mr. Armstrong, I'm not a veterinarian. I don't know how to treat animals, especially wild animals."

He seemed surprised. "What does it matter? A broken leg is a broken leg. Can't you just put a cast on it?"

"And give the deer crutches to use while its leg heals? It's not the same as treating a human. It's not even close."

Porter's face fell. "C'mon, little lady doc, surely you can do *something*."

His expression pulled at her. Defeated, she stepped forward to assess the animal's condition. Its furry chest shuddered up and down, but it didn't open its eyes. She pulled her stethoscope from her coat pocket and gingerly placed it on the deer's chest. The pelt was thick and silky, its body temperature warm—warmer than a human's, which, she remembered, was normal for many creatures. Its heartbeat was rapid, but weak, and its lungs sounded normal.

Nikki frowned. As far as she could tell.

The deer's eyes opened, rolled wildly, and it struggled to rise. Porter's crutches went crashing as he lunged forward to hold it down. He stroked the deer's neck and made soothing sounds and the animal quieted. Nikki remembered the scene at the water tower where he called

the bluebirds to him. The man had a way with wild creatures.

And with tame creatures.

"What do you think?" he asked, his face anxious.

She removed the ear tips of the stethoscope. "I think I'm not qualified to help this animal."

"Just do what you can. I don't want to have to put her down."

He implored her with those intense blue eyes and she felt helpless to refuse. She nodded, then put her hand to her head to force herself to focus.

The animal needed to be sedated—that she could do. The strength required to put an animal to sleep would be higher than for a human, but she could probably ensure the deer didn't bolt for long enough for her to examine it more closely. She went to a locked cabinet, withdrew a vial and a syringe, and drew a dosage.

"Hold it still," she said, then injected the sedative into the deer's hip muscle on the uninjured side.

"I can feel her relaxing," Porter said as the animal's eyes slitted.

Nikki pointed to a cabinet. "Hand me a few gauze pads. I need to see where this blood is coming from."

She retrieved antiseptic and began cleaning the blood from the deer's fur. Luckily the cuts and abrasions were minor. But she couldn't say the same for the broken leg. She booted up the hand-held X-ray machine and was alarmed by just how fine the leg bones were—they looked too delicate to even support the animal, much less bear the impact of running and jumping.

"Can you set the bone?" Porter asked, looking over her shoulder at the image on the screen.

Nikki lifted her shoulders in a slow shrug. "I don't

know. I can try, but that means the deer will have to be confined somehow while its leg heals and be hand-fed. It still might not make it, especially if an infection sets in."

"I'll take care of it," he said.

"You're not exactly one hundred percent mobile yourself."

"Just do your thing, Nikki."

It was the first time he'd called her by her given name, she realized. The casual intimacy was unsettling, as was the confidence in his voice that she could save this animal. And the way he looked at her…it made her believe, too.

It was tedious work, setting the delicate bone and wrapping it with cotton strips to hold the bone in place while fiberglass for a cast warmed to liquid to apply the outer layer. Despite his own cast, Porter was an able assistant. He followed her lead and they worked well together, hands moving in tandem. Although Nikki was focused on the task before them, she was aware of him physically at every turn, every brush of their hands and shoulders.

His concern for this animal tugged at her heartstrings. It revealed how connected he was to this land and everything on it. His intensity moved her. How did one develop that kind of bond with a place? With other people? What was missing in her that not only did she not possess that kind of connection, but she didn't want to?

A dark realization descended over her. Did she tell herself she didn't want to have that kind of connection so she didn't have to face the fact that she didn't have the capacity for that kind of connection?

Had Darren picked up on that aspect of her personality? Is that why he'd turned to someone else?

Her hands kept moving even as she felt a chasm in her heart cracking open to expose an abyss. It was a terrifying moment of self-discovery.

"It looks great," Porter said, examining the narrow cast that encompassed most of the deer's leg. He looked up, but his smile suddenly dropped. "Are you okay?"

Nikki started to nod, then realized her cheeks were wet. Mortified, she turned away, her mind reeling. What must he think of her? She walked to the sink to strip off her gloves and wash her hands with more zeal than necessary.

She felt him come up behind her, then his breath was on her neck. "Hey...talk to me."

Nikki glanced up and locked gazes with Porter in the mirror. She couldn't identify all the emotions pinging around in her chest, much less vocalize them...especially not to Porter. She wiped at her cheeks and tried to smile. "I'm sorry, this is so unlike me. For some reason, a lot of things seem to be converging today."

"Don't apologize," he said, his deep voice caressing her.

Then before she realized what was happening, he'd turned her around. At his closeness, desire flared and consumed her body, leaving her breathless.

He leaned on one crutch and used his other hand to brush the tears from her cheek. "I know you came here to forget someone who betrayed you."

Nikki blinked. So word had gotten around.

"And I know that Sweetness isn't exactly what you expected," he continued, his eyes burning into hers. "But you're wanted here."

The sheer power of his words made Nikki's throat convulse. His nearness was electrifying, his big frame made her feel scared and safe at the same time. His body pulled at hers as if there was a magnetic field between them. Nikki's mouth opened to draw more air into her quaking lungs. Porter would not let her look away—his gaze held her captive, challenging her. He cupped his hand around the nape of her neck and lowered his mouth to hers so slowly she thought he might never get there.

But he did, covering her lips with his so thoroughly and so tenderly, her eyes filled again. The kiss deepened as he explored her mouth with his tongue, rousing sensations buried in her womb. Her breasts grew heavy with need. When she pressed against him to satisfy the hardened tips, he groaned into her mouth and smoothed his hand down her back, pulling her to him awkwardly, but fervently. Nikki lifted her hands to his chest, reveling in the feel of hard muscle beneath the thin T-shirt.

In a heartbeat, the kiss went from tender to passionate. Porter devoured her mouth, then dipped his head to kiss her neck.

"Damn crutches," he muttered, and backed her into the sink. Despite his injury, he lifted her onto the vanity and wedged his hips between her knees. Nikki's body was on fire, her hands moving along his shoulders and arms. His eyes were hooded as he fumbled with the buttons on her shirt. His male scent filled her lungs and her heart pounded in her ears as she strained into him, whipped to a sensory height she'd never known before. She felt like a runaway car. She couldn't stop, and she didn't want to.

"Hurry," she murmured, afraid she was going to change her mind. Her words seemed to flip a switch in

him. His mouth and hands became more insistent. He unclasped the front closure of her bra and uncovered her breasts. He moaned his appreciation and her nipples hardened in anticipation. He drew a tip into his mouth, sending shockwaves through her body.

Nikki cried out, jamming her fingers into his hair, urging him on. He gave the other nipple equal time, hungrily suckling her in response to her whispered commands, pushing his hand between her thighs. Nikki grew weak, gasped with pleasure. When he lifted his head, he kissed her fiercely and guided her hand to the bulge at his zipper. Nikki stroked his erection, eliciting a sharp intake of breath. Emboldened, she wet her swollen lips and reached for his belt.

A sharp knock on the door shattered the moment.

"Nikki?" came Rachel's voice from the other side. "Are you in there? I'm looking for Porter."

Nikki crashed back to earth. At the guilt in Porter's eyes, she stiffened and pushed against his chest. He stepped back and dragged his hand down his face.

Nikki refastened her bra and shirt with shaking hands, righting her clothes as she walked to the door.

Another knock sounded. "Nikki?"

She took a deep breath and opened the door. Tanned and leggy and carrying a picnic basket, Rachel looked every inch the country-girl pinup.

"Hello," Nikki said.

Rachel craned to look in her office. "Have you seen Porter? Someone told me he came to see you and his tractor is still parked out front. We're supposed to go on a picnic."

Nikki's blood ran cold. Too bad the cad hadn't mentioned his date with Rachel before he'd stuck his tongue

down her throat. Beyond mortified, she opened the door wider to reveal Porter.

"Oh, good, you're here," Rachel said with a flirtatious smile. Then she frowned at the sight of the animal lying on the bed. "What happened?"

Porter looked everywhere but at Rachel, Nikki noticed. "Deer jumped into the side of the tractor, broke her leg. I brought her to the doc here to patch up."

"You take care of animals, too?" Rachel asked Nikki. "Wow, with you the town gets a two-fer. Nigel's been having digestive problems—maybe you could examine him and figure out what's wrong."

Nikki gave her a flat smile. "We'll see."

Porter gave her what might have been an apologetic look, but Nikki averted her gaze. Her body was still warm and tingling from his insistent mouth and hands—an apparent warm-up session for his private lunch date with Rachel. How could she have been so stupid?

"Are you ready?" Rachel asked him, lifting the basket.

He looked contrite. "Sorry, I'm going to have to cancel to take care of my little buddy here."

"Oh, don't do that," Nikki said cheerfully. "I'll keep the doe sedated until you get back. It probably shouldn't be moved for a while anyway. You two go, have fun." She waved them toward the door, Rachel beaming, Porter's face unreadable.

At the door, he turned back. His eyes searched her face, then he said, "It's just lunch, we'll be back soon."

"Oh, take your time." Nikki smiled, then shut the door.

Nikki closed her eyes and covered her face with her

hands. What had she been thinking? She'd almost had sex with Porter. She would have had sex with Porter if Rachel hadn't interrupted. And now he was probably off to have sex with her.

For men like Darren Rocha and Porter Armstrong, women were interchangeable. She had to leave this place…and she was seriously rethinking a move back to Broadway. Maybe she needed to start over in a big, anonymous city, like Atlanta.

From the bed, the deer snorted softly. Nikki walked over and stroked the animal's silky neck. The doe opened her big coal-black eyes briefly and looked at Nikki, as if she knew Nikki was helping her. Nikki softened.

"Don't worry," she whispered on a sigh. "I'll stay until you're well."

The trick would be staying out of the reach of Porter Armstrong.

22

"I'm glad you didn't mind Nigel coming along," Rachel sang, nose to nose with her pug. She had the dog in a chest carrier, its legs spread-eagle, hanging out of four different holes.

Porter gave her his best attempt at a smile. As if he'd been given a choice. "No offense, but he looks uncomfortable in that contraption."

"No, he wuvs it," she said in a baby voice, still nuzzling her pooch. "He's been having some tummy problems, so I didn't want to leave him a-wone."

Porter decided not to suggest that a dog with digestive issues might be happier in a horizontal position. He led the way to the base of a shade tree next to Timber Creek and lowered himself to a rock, setting his crutches next to him. His mind was still on Nikki, whom he'd left reluctantly after they'd come so close to making whoopee right there in her office…in broad daylight. If Rachel hadn't come looking for him, he and Nikki might still be going at each other. Instead, Nikki probably thought he was an ass—at best.

And he would have to agree.

If he were honest with himself, his attraction for her

had been building since she'd arrived. Something about the tough little woman pulled at his heartstrings...and other parts of his body. He respected her independence and what she must've had to overcome in order to be a physician. While caring for the injured deer, his admiration for her had flared into passion, and to his surprise, she'd responded. And he'd been so diverted by Nikki's eyes...and mouth...and hands, he'd completely forgotten about the time, and that he'd agreed to a date with Rachel.

Porter hardened his jaw. Although Nikki had tried to hide her humiliation at the untimely interruption, the expression on her face when she told him to have fun was seared in his mind.

Rachel set down the picnic basket, then pulled her dog out of the carrier and put him on the ground. After lifting the carrier from her shoulders, she stretched her arms high and arched her voluptuous figure. Porter averted his gaze. He *so* didn't want to be here.

"This is a great spot," she said. "How did you find it?"

"My brothers and I used to come here to swim," he said, trying to shake his preoccupation and be in the moment. He owed Rachel that much for accepting her invitation. "Timber Creek is mostly wide and shallow, but this is one of the deepest pools."

"It's a good thing I wore my suit," she said, and before Porter could blink, she'd stripped off her T-shirt to reveal a pink-and-white polka-dot bikini top.

Overflowing with tanned flesh.

Porter cleared his throat, then gestured to the tree above them. "This oak used to be twice as tall. It got clipped by the twister."

"There's still plenty of shade for a picnic," she said, then bent over to retrieve a blanket out of the picnic basket, sending her shorts into unmentionable places.

Porter pulled his hand down his face. Why did he have the gnawing feeling he was being disloyal to Nikki by simply being here? It wasn't as if they had any kind of understanding or...anything. In fact, the woman had gone to great lengths to let him know she wasn't impressed with him. What had happened back in her office was probably just her reaction to being lonely... and maybe a little revenge thrown in for her cheating fiancé. Maybe she wanted to sleep with someone else before she went back to him.

Why did that thought bother him so much?

"Earth to Porter."

He jerked his attention back to Rachel, who stood with her hands on her hips giving him a questioning look.

"Am I boring you?"

"Sorry," he said, feeling contrite. He grabbed his crutches and pushed to his feet. "What can I do to help?"

She gave him a coy smile. "Take a bite and tell me how good it is."

Porter stumbled, but caught himself on one of his crutches.

Rachel laughed and held up a sandwich. "Of my chicken salad, silly."

Porter gave a little laugh of relief, feeling foolish as he lowered himself to the blanket. When he'd accepted Rachel's invitation, hadn't he been hoping they'd roll around on the ground most of the afternoon? But that had been before Nikki...before he'd known how quickly

the little lady doc could go from cold to smoldering, like a piece of dry tinder. Before he'd known how her small, supple hands could send his body temperature soaring like the sun...that her mouth would leave him breathless.

"You don't like chicken salad?"

He turned his head to see Rachel extending a sandwich. He gave himself a mental shake and smiled. "I like it fine," he said, then took the sandwich. "Thank you. I'm happy to get a break from Molly's cooking."

She made a face. "Things at the dining hall are improving. She agreed to let some of the women help her with the food preparation and make the place a little more attractive, more like a restaurant."

"Really? That's good." He accepted a chicken salad sandwich and took a bite. He smiled until a strange flavor hit his tongue, but maintained his expression until he swallowed. "Um, that's...different. But good," he added quickly.

Rachel beamed. "I add cinnamon to the mayonnaise. I'm glad you like it."

He kept nodding and took a bigger bite. Best to get it eaten as quickly as possible. He noticed she wasn't indulging in her "secret ingredient" chicken salad, instead picking at a fruit cup in deference to being vegetarian.

Today, he wouldn't have minded being vegetarian.

In between bites, he asked, "So how's the media room coming along? I saw the TV antenna going up."

Rachel nodded. "And the new computers are hooked up. A router is being installed. Hopefully, Sweetness will be fully wired within a few days. The women can't wait to be connected with the outside world again."

It suddenly occurred to him that this woman, too, had left a life behind. "Do you miss Broadway?"

"Not now that I've decided to stay."

"Just like that?"

She shrugged. "Why spend your life second-guessing decisions? It gets you nowhere. I'm here and I'm committed to helping you and your brothers turn Sweetness into the town you envision. I have all kinds of ideas."

Porter finished eating his odd-tasting sandwich and listened to the woman describe in detail how she could see the town's retail environment grow—from groceries to hospitality. Porter's mind started to wander when a wet tickle on his foot startled him. The pug was licking his exposed foot as if he might devour it. Porter squirmed and tried to shoo him away, hoping Rachel would notice. But the woman was immersed in her animated monologue. When she reached into the picnic basket, Porter expected her to pull out a binder of business plans. Instead she pulled out another sandwich and extended it to him.

"A big guy like you, I know you have a big appetite to match." She batted her lashes.

Loath to eat more of the strange chicken salad—or acknowledge her innuendo—he held up his hand. "I couldn't."

She looked hurt. "You didn't like it?"

"Of course I liked it," he lied. But he felt like a heel for seeming unappreciative on top of not wanting to be there, so he smiled and took the sandwich. "I just didn't want to seem greedy."

Rachel lit up and continued to talk about the plans she had for the town. Porter listened patiently and got rid of the sandwich by sneaking a few bites to her dog

to divert the pug from his wet, itchy foot. Nigel wolfed down the food like a starved stray.

When another hour passed and Rachel was still talking about building a gondola ride that would take tourists above the mountain views, Porter realized he'd underestimated her. She was more than just a pretty face. The woman had ambition—the kind of ambition the fledgling town needed.

She was beautiful, she was driven and she was dedicated to making Sweetness her home. So why couldn't he get excited about Rachel? Why was he instead tied in knots over the slip of a woman doctor who was here only because he'd sabotaged her van?

Suddenly Rachel stopped. "I *am* boring you now. I'm sorry about going on and on."

"No, it's fine," he said. "I'm glad you're excited about our plans. We're lucky to have you here."

She leaned in and made a doodle on the back of his hand with a manicured fingernail. "There are other things in Sweetness that excite me."

Porter's mouth went dry. The woman packed a powerful physical punch with her golden hair and big blue eyes...but his stomach still churned over leaving Nikki high and dry. A loud bark pierced the air, claiming Rachel's attention.

She turned to her pug. "Do you need to take a walk?" She looked back to Porter and shook her head. "Even in all this wilderness, he has to be on a leash or he can't go." She grabbed a leash and stood, brushing off her short shorts, then cooed to the pooch, who waddled over to be hooked up. "I'll be right back," she said with a promise in her smile.

Porter nodded, then exhaled in relief that the awkward

moment had been interrupted. He jammed his fingers through his hair—he had to think of something to get out of this situation without hurting the woman's feelings. He wanted to check on the injured doe...and he desperately wanted to see Nikki. In hindsight, he should've never left her with the wild animal. If it regained consciousness, it could injure her in an attempt to escape.

Porter began to repack their picnic leftovers. He'd manufacture a work issue or a minor emergency, something that required his attention. He stopped to rub his stomach, which was starting to feel decidedly queasy. Now eager to get back, he pushed to his feet and awkwardly refolded the picnic blanket. He looked up to see Rachel returning with her pug.

"Must've been a false alarm," she said brightly, "but he's acting strange. I've never seen him try to eat grass before." When she noticed their picnic had been packed, her face fell. "We're leaving?"

"I'm afraid so," he said. "Marcus needs for me to check on a work crew."

"Okay. I don't think Nigel is feeling well anyway. Maybe it's the heat."

To punctuate her statement, her pug made an unholy noise, then proceeded to throw up at their feet.

Porter winced and swung back on his crutches. "I'm not feeling so great myself. Did the chicken salad sit out before you packed it? It might have gone bad."

Rachel looked offended. "It only sat out while I was waiting for you. But Nigel didn't have any."

"Yes, he did," he said with remorse. "I fed him some of my sandwich."

She looked distressed, swooped down to cuddle her dog close. "Oh, no."

A wave of nausea shuddered through Porter forcing him to lean on his crutches to stay upright. "Let's get back, pronto."

"Nikki will know what to do," Rachel said, clutching her pet.

Porter was filled with dread that overrode the sickness swirling through his body.

He was sure Nikki would do everything in her power to help the dog, but she just might let *him* perish this time.

He drove back to town in record time, swallowing hard against his roiling stomach every time the four-wheeler hit a bump. When he pulled up in front of the boardinghouse, he urged Rachel to go on ahead instead of waiting for him to get his crutches. But she could see he was weak himself and insisted on helping him inside.

"Nikki!" Rachel shouted, raising the alarm before they reached her office.

Nikki came out in the hallway, her expression wary. "What's wrong?"

"Nigel and Porter might have food poisoning."

"From what?" Nikki asked.

"Chicken salad."

"Nigel in there," Nikki said, pointing to her office. "Write down all the ingredients in the chicken salad. I'll take Porter into the room next door."

When Nikki took Rachel's place under Porter's shoulder, he was relieved, chagrined and embarrassed at the same time. "I'm sorry, little lady doc."

But her body language was all business. "Save your

strength," she said, then ushered him into an adjacent empty bedroom and urged him to lie on the bed.

"I feel lousy," he muttered, happy to recline on the cool sheets.

"You'll feel better once you throw up," she offered, then propped his crutches nearby and positioned a trash can close to the bedside.

"I mean about earlier."

"Can't help you there," she said breezily, still not making eye contact. "But if you have food poisoning, it should work its way through your body in a day or two."

Frustration welled in his chest at his inability to communicate how guilty he felt about putting the moves on her before. "Are you going to stick around that long?"

She finally looked at him, leveling him with a wry stare from those gorgeous green eyes. "Who else is going to take care of your deer?" She adjusted his pillow. "I'll be right back."

Porter watched her leave, and something akin to wonder descended over him. His chest squeezed painfully with an emotion unlike anything he'd ever felt before. But before he could name it, a cramp assailed him.

Good, he thought as he leaned over to empty the contents of his stomach into the trash can. The alien feeling had simply been a symptom of his illness.

It would be gone in a day or two.

23

"I feel well enough to drive you to the water tower," Porter insisted from the doorway of the side entrance of the boardinghouse.

Nikki took in his pale face and how heavily he leaned on his crutches as she tested the feel of the handgrips on the four-wheeler. After forty-eight hours of being in close quarters with Porter Armstrong, nursing him back from food poisoning, she was ready to be away from him. And it had nothing to do with the sickness—*that* she was trained to handle with a clinical detachment. It was the way her pulse picked up when she touched his feverish forehead, the anxiety that gripped her when his body convulsed from the violent retching and the fantasies she spun when she watched him sleep that concerned her. The attachment she was developing to this man felt dangerously familiar...and she wanted no part of it. Not after what had almost happened between them and how it had ended.

"You should rest for at least another day," Nikki said. "And someone has to keep an eye on the animals while I'm gone."

"I'll help," Rachel said, emerging to stand next to

Porter. She put a proprietary hand on his arm. "I was just going to check on my sweet Nigel. I'll make sure that Porter stays in bed."

Nikki took perverse pleasure from seeing Porter squirm. At least the cad had enough of a conscience to feel awkward about bouncing from Nikki's arms to Rachel's the day he'd brought in the wounded deer. Visualizing what they'd probably been doing on their "picnic" before Rachel had accidentally poisoned him made it easier for Nikki to keep her distance. She gave the couple a cheerful smile. "Sounds like everything is under control. I'll be back soon." She pulled on a helmet and buckled it under her chin.

"How are you going to get up the ladder?" he asked.

Remembering how he boosted her to the bottom rung before sent unwanted sensations through her midsection. "I'll manage."

Porter took a half step closer. "Go slow. And tackle that last climb on a diagonal rather than head on."

She nodded, then pushed the ignition button to fire up the engine.

"Use the two-way radio if you run into trouble," he shouted. "And be careful climbing the ladder!"

Nikki ignored him and goosed the gas. After a couple of lurching false-starts, she steered the four-wheeler toward the path that would take her up to the water tower.

Her adrenaline climbed as the vehicle ascended the incline. The vibration of the engine resonated through her body, keening her senses. The dank scent of moss and soil permeated her lungs, along with the fragrances of grass and flowers. Her allergies seemed to have

calmed a bit, although she was sure it had nothing to do with the licorice candy she'd been ingesting and everything to do with the massive doses of antihistamines she'd been taking. The fresh air felt good on her face.

The trees on either side of the path were practically pulsating with life—heavy with leaves and nuts and birds and squirrels. Blooming bushes bowed underneath the weight of bumblebees. The sun was high and searing, infiltrating the canopy of trees to spill onto the rocky path in front of her. Heeding Porter's warnings, she slowed her ascent as the climb became steeper, but the thought of the man made her tense in anger.

At herself.

For letting him get to her the day he'd brought in the wounded animal, for believing for one second that they shared a connection or that a physical encounter would make her feel better about anything.

Like being dumped by Darren.

Instead, the encounter had made her feel worse, had reinforced her feelings that men only wanted her for what they could have at the moment. And she'd nearly violated her professional ethics by getting involved with a patient. She needed to get away to clear her head, and she couldn't think of a better place than the water tower.

Besides, she wanted to talk to her former boss, Dr. Hannah, and she was missing her friend Amy. The other women from Broadway were settling into Sweetness and making it their home. She longed to talk to someone from the outside, someone who could reassure her she didn't belong here.

Twenty minutes later, Nikki took the last incline on the diagonal and leaned forward on the four-wheeler,

applying steady throttle as the engine whined to eat up the ground. When the wheels began to spin, she panicked she was going to be stuck, but the tires suddenly caught traction and popped the four-wheeler up over the rise and onto level ground.

She slowed the ATV and pulled it to a stop beneath the ladder, then cut the engine and removed her helmet. The sudden silence was jarring. Nikki had felt alone many times in her life, but she'd never felt quite as isolated as she did at that moment.

Her heartbeat picked up. Hadn't Porter said something about bears? And there were snakes around, too. Just yesterday one of the workers had been bitten. Of course, when she'd arrived onsite, the man wanted "Doc" Riley to tend to his wound. Because the snake was a nonvenomous variety, she'd acquiesced. But from her research, she knew there were at least six types of poisonous snakes in these mountains. Rattlesnakes were charitable enough to issue a warning before striking, but the other species weren't so considerate.

Nikki was suddenly rethinking her quest for solitude.

She glanced all around, but saw nothing except trees and bushes and fallen logs. Eventually, the insects and birds quieted by the sound of the four-wheeler resumed their song, and she relaxed.

To reach the ladder, she stood on the seat of the four-wheeler and pulled herself up. The climb to the top of the water tower was invigorating, just what her body needed. When she reached the platform, her shirt was stuck to her back and her muscles were tingling. Heat emanated from the colossal metal tank, but a tiny breeze cooled the perspiration on her neck.

She moved to the front of the tower and absorbed the sprawling view. She inhaled deeply to fill her lungs, then exhaled, hoping to rid her body of some of the stress that had been building for weeks now. Tears pushed at the back of her eyes over so many things. Her thoughts were jumbled and spinning like a tornado, tossing out hurtful images at will. Thinking of Darren left her almost breathless with grief. She knew she was better off without him if he was going to be unfaithful before they even walked down the aisle, but she mourned the good times they'd shared and the potential of what might have been.

She felt tricked by the universe. She'd rid herself of a happily-ever-after fantasy sometime between starting college and finishing medical school. Darren Rocha had come along and led her to believe she'd been mistaken. And just when she'd allowed herself to be happy, he'd proven she'd been right all along.

Now, here she was, falling under the spell of another man who made her feel unworthy.

Nikki exhaled in frustration. What was broken in her that made her gravitate toward this kind of man?

She pulled out her phone and held it up until the bars climbed, indicating a strong signal. The phone vibrated and a "voice messages waiting" symbol appeared. One message was from Amy, just checking in, wondering if Nikki was on her way back to Broadway. One message was from the manager of the apartment complex where Nikki had lived, asking where to forward her mail. It was a reminder of how quickly and recklessly she'd made the decision to leave town.

And one message was from Darren.

Nikki's stomach dropped when she heard his husky

voice. "Hi, Nikki…it's me. I heard you left town and I was just calling to see if you're all right." His tone was low and fluid, the way it had sounded after he'd had a couple of glasses of wine. "And I wanted to say that if it means anything to you, I'm sorry for the way things turned out. Okay…bye."

Nikki breathed in and out. He was calling to see if she was all right? What if she wasn't all right? What then? And he wasn't sorry for being a lying cheater—he was sorry for the way things turned out? As if he had no culpability in what had happened. She realized her cheeks were wet and swiped at them. How could she have given her heart to someone who'd treated it so carelessly?

She gave in to a few more tears, then wiped her face. Her grammy always said there was no use in crying over spilled milk, and her words had never seemed more appropriate. What was done, was done. She had to keep moving forward.

Nikki punched in Amy Bradshaw's number and smiled when Amy answered. "Greetings from Mayberry," Nikki said.

"Nikki! You're still in Sweetness? I thought you were headed back to Broadway."

"There are…extenuating circumstances."

"Does this have anything to do with a cleft chin?"

Nikki straightened. "No. My van still hasn't been repaired…and I'm caring for a wounded deer."

"You're a veterinarian now?"

"No. But there was no one else to take care of it. And then there's Nigel."

"Nigel?"

She squirmed. "Rachel Hutchins's pug was accidentally food poisoned."

"Don't you have any human patients?"

"At the moment, just Porter Armstrong," Nikki mumbled.

"Ah…he's milking his broken leg?"

"He's suffering from food poisoning, too."

"How did this guy and Rachel's dog both get food poisoning?"

"By Rachel."

Amy laughed. "I guess that's one way to get a man on his back. But no one else gets sick in that town?"

"A lot of the women are suffering from allergies… but the male workers seem to resent a woman doctor. There's an older guy with homespun remedies they turn to."

"Male pride," Amy offered wryly. "Southern men will take a bullet for a woman, but chivalry cuts both ways. No matter how modern they say they are, they're chauvinists at heart. They don't want a woman to see them when they're down."

"All the more reason for me to leave," Nikki said. "My former boss is looking for someone to take my place, but I'm thinking about not coming back to Broadway."

"Where will you go?"

"I was thinking maybe Atlanta, although I've never been there. Any advice?"

"It's a big, hot city. The job market is better than where you are. And I think you'll find the cultural pursuits a little more diversified."

Nikki laughed. "I might check it out since I'm this close."

"And here I was counting on you coming back."

"I'm sorry. What's going on with you?"

Amy sighed. "Still waiting to hear if I'll be assigned to the state reservoir repair job. Keep your fingers crossed for me."

"I will," Nikki said, then told her friend goodbye. When she disconnected the call, she nursed a pang of regret. If she didn't go back to Broadway, she would miss Amy. But after listening to Darren's voice message, she wasn't sure she could go back. She wasn't over him yet, if he still had the power to hurt her.

She called Dr. Hannah and after being put on hold for a short time, she heard the woman's friendly voice come on the line. "Nikki, how are you?"

"I'm fine," she lied, although just saying the words made her feel better.

"I'm glad to hear from you, I was going to give you a call. I might have found a physician who's willing to come to Sweetness to work in the clinic."

Why didn't the news excite her as much as it should have? "That's terrific," she said. "Who?"

"Dr. Jay Cross. He's fresh out of residency and eager to work in a rural clinic where he can make a difference. But he wants to arrange a visit first to see how he likes the town."

Nikki wrote down his contact information and promised to give it to the Armstrongs. "And the town is supposed to be wirelessly connected soon, so communication will be easier." Dr. Hannah said she was still asking around about some of the other clinic positions, and she would be in touch. She ended the conversation by asking Nikki if she was coming back to the practice.

"I haven't decided," Nikki admitted. "But I appreciate the offer. I'll let you know soon."

Nikki disconnected the call and took a few moments to gaze at the peaceful mountain scenery before her. It was a meditative place, to be sure. The majestic peaks, the terraced trees and the rolling foothills...they were unwavering. Nature didn't give a hoot about man's problems, it just kept marching on. A lesson to its inhabitants, she mused. After a few more leisurely moments, she glanced at her watch and decided to head back. For now, at least, she had patients to oversee, even if most of them were of the four-legged variety.

She descended the ladder carefully and stepped on the seat of the four-wheeler, then lowered herself to the ground, feeling oddly triumphant for driving an ATV to the top of a mountain and climbing a water tower—things she couldn't have imagined doing only a couple of weeks prior. She could see how a rural environment produced resourceful individuals, how it had instilled in the Armstrong brothers a will to defy nature and rebuild a town from nothing.

But she could admire their goals without being sucked into them.

Nikki pulled on her helmet and started the engine. When she goosed the gas, the vehicle's wheels spun, kicking up dirt and leaves. She eased off the throttle and glanced at the rear tires. A shiny object stood out among the debris. Remembering the pocket watch find, Nikki put on the brake and climbed off the vehicle for a look.

It was a ring.

The gold filigree band looked delicate against her palm, but in fact, was quite heavy and probably of

considerable value. Was it another artifact carried here by the tornado a decade ago? Nikki was both saddened and filled with wonder—sad for the person who'd lost the ring and amazed that she'd found it by chance. Was the person still looking for it? There were no visible inscriptions in the gold, but the ring might reveal more secrets once it had been cleaned. She tucked it into her pocket, then mounted the four-wheeler and headed downhill, eager to see Porter to show him her find.

And not for any other reason.

Before, the ride down the mountain had always gone more quickly than the ride up, but Nikki drove slowly and it seemed a long time before she saw the roof of the boardinghouse through the trees. After pulling the four-wheeler to a stop where Porter usually parked it, she stashed her helmet and hurried into the building.

Her first stop was by her office to make sure, as she expected, that no one was waiting to see her. She went inside to check on the two animals that had been moved to the bathroom. The deer lay in the bottom of the glass shower stall, still dozing from sedatives to keep it from standing on its cast leg for at least one more day. She watched as its ears flicked and its chest rose and fell rhythmically. The animal wasn't out of the woods yet, but so far, so good.

Outside the shower, Nigel was asleep in the dog bed that Rachel had furnished. He lay on his side, his stubby little legs bicycling occasionally. He was well enough to go back to Rachel's room, but he seemed reluctant to leave the deer, whining and walking back to sniff the animal when Rachel tried to coax him away. For now, she agreed to leave him nearby.

Nikki left her office to go next door to the empty

bedroom where Porter was recuperating. She hesitated, wondering if Rachel was in there with him. Probably. She raised her hand and knocked. "Porter? It's Nikki. Is this a bad time?"

"Come on in," he called.

She turned the knob and pushed open the door. The bed where he'd been confined for the better part of two days was empty. Straight ahead, the bathroom door was open. Porter stood leaning against the sink, shirtless, shaving with a disposable razor. His hair and skin were damp. "I had Kendall bring me a change of clothes and some toiletries so I could at least take a sponge bath."

Her pulse jumped erratically at the sight of his wide shoulders and dark chest hair. "Your coloring is improved," she said to cover the fact that she was staring. "But you still need to rest. Where's Rachel?"

"She left," he said curtly, then picked up a towel to wipe his jaw. He turned to face her. "Listen, Nikki. I want to apologize for what happened the other day in your office."

Her cheeks warmed. "No need. I let things go too far."

He frowned. "I was apologizing for the interruption."

She swallowed hard, assailed by sensual memories. "Like I said—no need. Let's just forget it happened."

"But—"

"Porter," she interrupted, anxious that her body was reacting to him even now. "Drop it, okay?"

He averted his gaze. "Okay." He draped the towel over the edge of the sink. "How was your outing?"

"It was good," she said breezily. "My former boss thinks she's found a replacement for me, so I'm afraid

I'm going to have to insist that my van be repaired as soon as possible."

His expression was unreadable. "I promise I'll get right on it."

"You've said that before," she added.

He pursed his mouth, then nodded. "I mean it this time." He retrieved a light-colored chambray shirt from a hanger, then shrugged into it, leaving the front hanging open to give her a glimpse of his planed stomach. He reached for his crutches, then made his way back to the bed, where he sat on the edge. "So when does your replacement arrive?"

"I don't know." She pulled a scrap of paper from her pocket and extended it to him. "I said I'd pass along his contact information to you and your brothers."

He took the paper. "Your replacement is a man?"

She nodded. "It's probably best for now, don't you think?"

He didn't say anything, just tucked the piece of paper into his shirt pocket.

"Oh, and I found this," she said, pulling out the ring and holding it up for him to see.

All of the "improved" coloring left Porter's face. He took the ring and she noticed his hand was shaking slightly. "You found this at the water tower?"

"Yes, not too far away from the spot where I found the pocket watch. Do you think it was carried up there by the tornado?"

He nodded, turning the ring over and over. "I know it was."

"So you think Molly will be able to find the owner?"

"She won't have to," he said, pinning her with those

amazing blue eyes. "This is my mother's wedding ring."

Nikki's jaw dropped. "Are you kidding?"

"No. She took it off just before the tornado hit, and it blew away with everything else we owned. She cried for days, then resigned herself to the fact that she'd never see it again." He exhaled noisily, visibly moved. "Thank you."

Nikki was almost speechless with incredulity…and the emotional fallout of the find made her uncomfortable. She hugged herself. "You're welcome. But I didn't do anything—it was just there under the wheel of the ATV."

Porter closed his hand over the ring and suddenly a smile broke over his face. "Go to Atlanta with me."

She blinked. "What?"

"Go to Atlanta with me. Someone has to get supplies for the clinic, and you're the best person for the job."

Nikki pondered his offer. It would be a good chance to see the city. "Only if you get an appointment to see an orthopedist to make sure your leg is healing."

He hesitated, then nodded. "Agreed."

"*And* we get a fuel pump for my van."

Another hesitation, another nod. "Agreed. And on the way we'll stop by Mother's to give her her wedding ring."

Panic flooded her chest—she didn't want to know more about this man or his family. "Stop by your mother's?"

"It's on our way. Plus she'll want to meet you to thank you in person for finding her ring."

Nikki bit her lip. How could she say no? Besides, when they returned with supplies for the clinic and

the replacement part for her van, she'd be able to leave Sweetness for good. "I guess that would be okay."

He grinned. "Great. I'll make our hotel reservation."

Her pulse jumped. "Hotel?"

"With everything on our list, we'll have to spend the night."

Nikki swallowed. "Separate rooms," she said pointedly.

"Separate rooms," he agreed, his cobalt-colored eyes serious…and so, so sexy.

"Definitely," she said, nodding.

"Absolutely," he said, nodding back.

24

"I don't like it," Marcus said, then jabbed a finger at the computer monitor on his desk that displayed a profit-and-loss statement. "The last shopping trip to Atlanta almost bankrupted us!"

"Marcus, be reasonable," Porter cajoled. "We have a line of credit to use for planned expenses, and the clinic is useless without basic equipment." He looked to Kendall for support, but Kendall was sitting in a chair chewing on a thumbnail, staring into space. "Kendall—a little help here?"

Kendall jerked his head around. "Sorry, what?"

Porter frowned at Kendall's state of distraction that seemed to be getting worse every day. "I was telling Marcus how important it is that Dr. Salinger and I make a trip to Atlanta to get supplies for the clinic."

Kendall scoffed and pushed to his feet. "If you want to be alone with Dr. Salinger, little brother, you don't have to make up excuses."

Porter's frown deepened. "I'm not making up excuses. I have to go to Atlanta anyway to see an orthopedist, and the sooner we have supplies for the clinic, the sooner we can apply for an inspection to qualify for Federal

Rural Health Clinic status. And don't you want Mother to have her wedding ring as soon as possible?"

"Of course," Kendall said, then gave Porter a mock salute. "Have fun." Then he turned and left the office, allowing the door to bang shut behind him.

"What's eating him?" Porter muttered.

"Damned if I know," Marcus said. "Why don't you ask the doc if she has something for a perpetual bad mood?"

"For Kendall or for you?"

"Funny. And Kendall's right— I thought I told you to stay away from her."

Porter didn't like the look his brother was giving him. "She's already planning to leave, what more harm can I do?"

Marcus arched his eyebrow. "Call me old-fashioned, but since we've been keeping the good doctor here under false pretenses, I feel responsible for her."

Porter glared. "Have you contacted the physician who's offering to replace her?"

Marcus held up the piece of paper Porter had given him. "It's on my list today. Along with a thousand other things."

"Why don't you hold off for now?"

"You're going to try to convince her to stay? You've got something up your sleeve?" He frowned. "Or else-where?"

"No. I mean, *yes*, I'm going to try to convince her to stay…by talking up our plans for the town and her place in it."

Marcus looked dubious. "Okay…go for it."

"So, I'm cleared to get the clinic supplies?"

Marcus scanned the spreadsheet that Porter had given

him and sighed. "*Only* the items marked essential. I'm trusting you not to go crazy."

"Got it," Porter said, relieved. Nikki would never agree to go to Atlanta if they weren't going for business. And despite his assertion to the contrary, he desperately wanted to be alone with her. Kendall, darn him, could read him like a book.

So why couldn't he figure out what was bothering Kendall?

"When are you going?" Marcus asked, breaking into his thoughts.

"Nikki got me an appointment with an orthopedist tomorrow afternoon," Porter said. "I thought we'd head down in the morning and stop to see Mother, then drive into the city for my appointment and spend the night. I'll hire a truck and buy supplies the next day before coming back."

Marcus pursed his mouth. "I can't remember you ever introducing a woman to Mother before."

"I figured Mother will want to meet Nikki because she found her ring, that's all."

"Uh-huh. If I didn't know better, little brother, I'd say you were falling for this woman."

Porter balked, but decided nonchalance was the best way to go. "But you know better."

"Are you sure you didn't hit your head when you took that tumble off the water tower? You've gone soft—first over the doctor and now you're nursing a deer back to health."

"The doe is improving," Porter insisted, skipping over the reference to Nikki. "It's on its feet and walking around with the cast. I had a couple of the guys build a pen for it."

Marcus looked murderous. "Right…because there's nothing else to do around here!" He stood and gestured wildly. "You're out for the whole damned summer, Kendall has fallen into some kind of funk and I'm left to deal with the workers and all those women!"

"Wait a minute. I supervised the clinic on one good leg, and Kendall has been overseeing the media room installation. We've been working, too."

"On things that don't produce revenue!" Marcus boomed. "We're behind on the mulch production line because the men keep getting pulled away for fool things like faking illnesses to see the doctor, or working on a clinic we don't have personnel for or building a pen for Bambi!"

Porter remembered their previous conversation when Marcus revealed how worried he was about meeting their goal. The two-year calendar that papered the office walls with a big circle around their deadline served as a constant reminder, and Marcus was feeling the pressure.

Porter held up his hands, stop-sign fashion. "I know everything seems disjointed at the moment, but it's all going to come together. The men and the women seem to be getting along better—"

Marcus snorted.

"—than before," Porter finished. "And the food in the dining room is improving—"

Another snort sounded.

"—some," Porter finished. "And we're getting our communication lines up and going." He winced, waiting for Marcus to react.

Marcus worked his mouth from side to side. "I guess that's not such a bad thing."

"The garden is growing every day," Porter added. "And the clinic will be ready for business soon. We're making huge strides, Marcus. And we're going to meet that deadline, you'll see."

Marcus pulled his hand down his face, then smirked. "Just come back from Atlanta with a note from that specialist saying how quickly you can get back to work."

Porter grimaced. "I'm more worried about what Mother is going to say when she sees this cast."

Marcus came around the desk and slapped him on the back. "My guess is Mother will be too busy sizing up Dr. Salinger to notice that cast of yours. Is Nikki ready?"

"Ready for what?"

"For Emily Armstrong's sweet-little-old-lady method of interrogation. The CIA could take tips from her."

"We won't be staying that long," Porter assured him. "We have a lot to take care of in the city."

"Right," Marcus said drily. "Just be careful, okay?"

Porter gave a dismissive wave. "I know my way around Atlanta."

"I mean with our doctor." Marcus gave him a pointed look. "Dr. Salinger isn't one of your silly little-girl barflies. While you're trying to convince her to stay, don't do anything to make things worse."

Porter rubbed at the sudden dull pain behind his breastbone. "I won't."

"Are you planning to leave Sweetness?" Rachel asked.

Surprised, Nikki looked up from where she was examining a happy, roly-poly Nigel. "Why do you ask?"

Rachel shrugged. "You're so standoffish around the

other women. It's as if you don't want to put down roots here."

Nikki looked back to her furry patient. "To be honest, I've been thinking about it. I'm just not as committed to this cause as you and the other women are."

"The girls will miss you."

"Don't worry—my former boss thinks she's found a replacement physician for me."

"I mean they'll miss *you*, Nikki."

Nikki blinked. "Why? Like you said, I haven't exactly integrated myself into the house."

"Everyone admires you, and they want to get to know you. But I guess that's not going to happen now."

Nikki continued the examination, her pulse clicking. Rachel's words left her feeling defensive, as if she was letting everyone down. And that was exactly why she hadn't gone out of her way to get to know the women in the first place.

"If you don't mind, please don't say anything yet about me leaving," she murmured, pressing her stethoscope to Nigel's chest.

"Okay. Are you going back to Broadway?"

"I haven't decided."

"What about Porter?"

Nikki froze. "What about him?"

"I hear you two are going to Atlanta tomorrow."

Was that a jealous note in Rachel's voice? Nikki removed the stethoscope from her ears and looked up— she'd never experienced jealousy from another woman. Although it probably had more to do with going to the city than with the fact that she'd be spending time with Porter.

"That's right," Nikki said, keeping her tone light.

"He has an appointment with a specialist to have his leg examined, and I'm going to choose equipment for the clinic."

"If you have a thing for Porter, it's okay."

Nikki stumbled over her words. "I...I don't have a thing for Porter—"

"He has a thing for you, too."

Nikki gave a little laugh. "No...you're mistaken."

Rachel rolled her eyes. "Girl, I was giving out signals a blind man would have picked up on at our picnic the other day. But his mind was miles away—back here with you, I'd venture."

"More likely with the deer," Nikki said wryly. She gave Nigel's head a rub before handing him to Rachel. "He looks fine, just keep an eye on him. If he eats grass again, it might mean his stomach is bothering him."

"Thank you." Rachel shifted to cradle Nigel in her arms. "You know, you shouldn't let that creep of a fiancé keep you from falling in love again."

Feeling exposed, she hugged herself. "That's easier said than done."

"Don't I know it," Rachel said in a sympathetic tone.

"You?" Nikki asked, scanning the gorgeous woman's face and figure. "I can't imagine that you...I mean... you..." She tripped over the words even as Rachel smiled.

"Have been dumped and cheated on more times than I can count," the woman finished. "I've been engaged five times and never once made it to the altar. No one is immune to having their heart broken."

Nikki felt foolish and judgmental for assuming the beauty had fewer problems than the average woman. "I

suppose you're right." She pushed a limp hank of hair behind her ear. "It's just that some of us have fewer opportunities to attract the opposite sex."

Rachel angled her head. "Nikki, you have amazing bone structure, you just need to play it up."

Nikki's cheeks warmed. "I'm afraid I'm not very good with makeup and hair."

Rachel reached forward to touch Nikki's chin. "A few highlights and maybe some bangs would bring out your eyes— Delia would know, the woman's a hair genius. And Traci could define your eyebrows. Monica used to sell makeup in a department store, she knows all the tricks."

Nikki touched her hair self-consciously. "I don't know."

"The perfect time for a new look is after a breakup," Rachel insisted, then gestured to Nikki's khaki pants. "Do you have anything a little more jazzy to wear on the trip?"

She smoothed a hand over the sensible fabric that had become her work uniform. "Not really."

"I'm sure between all of us we could round up something. You should look your best when you go to Atlanta…to buy that equipment."

Her eyes twinkled and Nikki couldn't help but laugh. She felt a rush of gratitude for this woman that she'd previously envied.

"So what do you say. Are you up for a makeover?"

Old habits pulled at Nikki. She didn't want anyone to make a fuss and she was afraid she'd look silly. Plus, she didn't know if she'd be able to maintain a new look. Her hair and scant makeup routine had been the same since her teen years.

Since her teen years. Nikki let that admission sink in. Good grief, she was stuck in a rut the size of the Grand Canyon. She sighed and lifted her hands in submission. "Okay…what do I have to lose?"

25

Porter stopped talking midsentence just to see if Kendall would notice. His brother had offered to drive a work van to meet Nikki at the boardinghouse at the prescribed departure time. She would have to drive the van to Atlanta since Porter's cast had him handicapped. They were parked and waiting, engine running. After almost a full minute of silence, Kendall looked over.

"Sorry, what were you saying?"

Porter shook his head. "What's *with* you, man?"

"What do you mean?"

"I mean you've been in a fog for days."

Kendall ran a hand over his mouth. "I just have a lot on my mind, that's all."

"You've had a lot on your mind since you were ten years old, but you've never acted like this before. Well, except when Amy left town."

Kendall's face went stony. "I don't want to talk about it."

"Marcus and I are worried about you."

"Don't be."

"But—"

"Here comes the doctor." Then Kendall squinted. "She looks...different."

Porter turned his head and did a double-take. Nikki was dressed in a knee-length, pale, sleeveless dress and high heels. Her hair was lighter and cut in a new style—bangs, he realized as she walked closer, carrying an overnight case.

"I'll get her suitcase," Porter murmured and almost fell out of the van before he caught himself and realized he couldn't manage his crutches and her suitcase. Luckily, Kendall came to his rescue, meeting Nikki on the walkway to take her bag. Porter couldn't take his eyes off her. The dress skimmed over her slight curves and the heels highlighted her shapely legs. The new hairstyle and color set off her eyes and her cheekbones. Her full lips were stained a berry color, emphasizing that smile she didn't share often enough.

It was Nikki, with a shine.

"Good morning," she said to him.

Porter's tongue was tied in knots. Kendall elbowed him, jarring him out of his trance. "Good morning. You look...nice," he managed to get out.

Her smile sent a sparkle to her gorgeous green eyes. "Thank you."

He couldn't think of anything else to say, so he just stared.

"Don't mind him, doc," Kendall said. "He's worried about what our mother is going to say when she sees his busted-up leg."

Nikki laughed. "Did you bring her wedding ring?"

Porter patted his shirt pocket. "Got it right here. She doesn't know we've got it. She just thinks I'm stop-

ping by to say hello. She'll be so excited to have it back again."

"Then maybe she'll be distracted from your cast," Nikki offered.

He remembered Marcus's comment that Nikki would be the distraction of the day...and wow, was that ever an understatement. He stood drinking her in, feeling like a schoolboy admiring his prom date. His heart thudded in his chest and he was transported back to the day when her mouth and hands had set him on fire. The color rose in her cheeks. Could she sense what he was thinking?

Kendall cleared his throat indiscreetly, then put Nikki's bag in the van.

Porter couldn't get his fill of her—her finely chiseled features were absolute perfection. She wore the tailored dress as elegantly as any model.

Nikki gestured vaguely toward the horizon. "We should get on the road if we're going to make your appointment."

Porter nodded. "I'm sorry you have to drive."

"It's no problem, as long as you'll navigate."

"Sounds like we make a good team," he agreed.

The silence stretched on.

"Okay, team," Kendall broke in, clapping his hands, "have a good trip, be safe, give Mother my love and don't break the bank."

"Do you want a ride back to the office?" Porter asked.

"I'll walk back," Kendall said drily, then tapped his temple. "Try to clear the fog." He turned and strode off in the opposite direction, his body language tense. Porter watched his brother go, feeling helpless.

"What was that all about?" Nikki asked.

"I have no idea," he murmured. "Kendall goes deep when something is bothering him. I guess he'll come up for air when he's ready."

At first the atmosphere in the van was strained. To keep from staring at Nikki's profile, Porter rattled on about landmarks and boundaries they passed...until he realized she was only listening out of politeness. Because, of course, she wasn't planning to stay, so why would she care where the mercantile had once stood? Or that the covered bridge over Timber Creek had been blown away and would likely be their next big endeavor to reconnect a huge chunk of remote farmland to the road leading to Sweetness?

"That's nice," she remarked.

He decided to give it a rest for the time being and turn on the radio. At this altitude, it picked up mostly static, but he finally found a country music station.

"Is this okay?" he asked.

"Fine as frog hair."

He laughed. "That sounds like something someone from Sweetness would say."

The look on Nikki's face said she didn't want to be categorized as "someone from Sweetness." "It's a saying a friend of mine back in Broadway uses. She's from a small town."

Her eyes were glued to the rural road, her small hands positioned on the big steering wheel at ten and two o'clock. She looked so diminutive, yet so in control. Porter's heart squeezed with confusing emotions—he respected her strength, yet he felt compelled to protect her. But since she'd arrived in Sweetness, she'd taken care of *him*. She wasn't the kind of woman he was normally attracted to, yet she'd dominated his thoughts and

kept his body on notice, especially since the encounter in her office. He shifted in his seat and vainly tried to think of something more mundane.

"Does your leg hurt?" she asked.

"Uh…some," he lied.

Her hands tightened on the wheel. "Do you have any painkillers left?"

"I took one this morning," he said. "I'm just feeling a little stiff…and itchy. I can't wait to get this cast off."

"You still have a few weeks to go," she said in her doctorly voice. "But I'm glad you're getting X-rays today to see if the bones are healing properly. That was quite a fall you took."

"Uh…about that. I wasn't planning to tell Mother I'd fallen off the water tower."

A small smile quirked her mouth. "What were you planning to tell her?"

"I'll think of something a little less…hair-raising."

"I would think with three sons, she'd be accustomed to hair-raising. But she's your mother. Does she live alone?"

"She moved in with her sister Elaine in Calhoun after the twister hit. They're a lot of company to each other, but Mother makes no bones about the fact that she misses Sweetness. Sometimes I think her wanting to come home puts more pressure on Marcus than the federal deadline." He smiled. "You know how family can be."

When she bit into her lower lip, he regretted his careless choice of words—Nikki didn't have family. "I'm sorry. I wasn't thinking—"

"It's okay," she cut in. "You don't have to walk on eggshells. I realize that most people have relatives."

"You don't have aunts or uncles, cousins?"

"My mother told me of a couple of distant female cousins in California who were descendants of my grandmother's sister, but their mother remarried and changed her last name. I wouldn't even know how to go about trying to find them."

"Maybe they'll find you someday," he said, then wet his lips. "Will you be in Broadway?"

She hesitated. "I suppose."

Suddenly her phone, cradled in the console between them, began to chime in successions of threes, as if downloading messages. "I guess my phone has service now," she said with a laugh.

As the chiming continued, it was impossible to ignore. Five messages…ten…fifteen…

"Someone really wants to get hold of you," he observed. Her ex-fiancé?

She shifted in her seat. "I'll check messages when we stop. How long until we reach Calhoun?"

"About three hours."

She nodded. "By the way, the women were lined up to take care of your deer while we're gone."

"That's nice, as long as they don't make a pet out of it."

Nikki laughed. "Don't be surprised if it's wearing a collar and has a name by the time we return."

"Most of the women seem to be acclimating to rural life," he remarked carefully.

She nodded, but made no comment.

"Sweetness will be a great place to raise kids," he said, now officially feeling like an infomercial.

"I can see that," she said softly. "Obviously you

and your brothers have fond memories of growing up there."

"Small-town living seems to have gone by the way-side in the past few decades. But I think deep down, people are eager to get back to simple values."

"Urban living has its advantages, too," she countered.

"I enjoy going to the city and taking in some culture now and then," he conceded, "but I don't think anything can replace growing up in a close-knit community that makes you feel safe. That kind of security instills confidence in a kid to be able to go out in the world and do whatever he or she wants to do."

"The newspaper ad specified no minors. When do you plan to start building a school?"

"Before fall. I believe Marcus mentioned that some of the women are teachers?"

She nodded. "A handful of the women left their children with relatives for the summer, but are hoping to bring them here in a few months."

"We'll accommodate them," he said, although his head spun from all the logistical complications having children living in the community would create. Still, it was inevitable. "Do you plan to have kids someday?"

"No," she said so matter-of-factly it pulled at his heart.

"Mind if I ask why?"

She shrugged. "I don't think I'd be very good at it."

Porter frowned. "Why not?"

"I'm not good with…people," she said, keeping her gaze straight ahead.

"That's ridiculous. You're a doctor, for heaven's sake."

Her throat constricted. "Just because I'm good with bodies doesn't mean I'm good with people."

He opened his mouth to argue, but from the console her phone rang and the screen lit up. With no particular intention of being nosy, Porter glanced down and couldn't help but notice the name "Darren" on the screen.

She noticed, too, and pressed her lips together, although she didn't reach for the phone. The clanging continued to reverberate into the cab of the van.

"Are you going to get that?" he asked lightly.

"No," she said quickly, then added, "not while I'm driving."

The phone finally stopped ringing, but then chimed three times a few seconds later, indicating the caller had left a message. Nikki's distraction seemed to confirm the call had been from her ex. Porter's mood soured, launching him back into his spiel about the virtues of Sweetness, including the proximity to Atlanta with its international airport.

"Of course we intend to have our own airfield someday to go along with the helipad near the clinic. If the town grows enough, I don't see why we couldn't build our own hospital."

To his chagrin, Nikki didn't respond. In fact, she seemed hundreds of miles away. Back in Broadway?

"We might even build a spaceship," he said to see if she was listening at all.

"That's nice," she murmured.

Porter pursed his mouth, then leaned forward to turn up the radio. Nikki still didn't notice. She was obviously lost in thought, pining for that Darren guy. An unfamil-

iar sensation burned in his chest. Jealousy? He'd never been jealous in his life.

Porter slumped in the seat and stared out the window. This was going to be a long ride.

26

Nikki's heart pounded as they walked up on the porch of a darling little yellow bungalow. She had no reason to be nervous about meeting Porter's mother, so she attributed her reaction to excitement over returning the found wedding ring.

"I have to warn you," Porter said as he lifted his hand to knock on the door. "She might cry...a lot."

Before Nikki had time to respond, the door flew open and a plump, angelic face wreathed in smiles appeared. "Porter, you're here!" But when she caught sight of the cast on his leg, her smile turned to dismay. "What's this?"

"Just a little bump, Mom," he said, leaning forward to capture her in a hug.

"How did it happen?" she demanded, squeezing him long and hard around the middle. "And why haven't I heard about it until now?"

"Because it wasn't worth worrying your pretty head about."

Nikki watched the exchange with amusement, noting the way Porter's voice softened to a tone she'd never heard him use before. It was...nice.

When he pulled back, his mother drank him in like she couldn't get enough of her youngest son, then she turned toward Nikki. "Where are your manners, Porter? Who is your lovely friend?"

Nikki's cheeks warmed as she speculated what might be going through the woman's head.

"Mom, meet Dr. Nikki Salinger, Sweetness's new doctor. Nikki, this is Emily Armstrong."

Nikki extended her hand, but the gesture was lost as Emily stepped forward to envelop her in a warm hug. Surprised, Nikki made eye contact with Porter over the woman's shoulder to find him looking as amused as she'd felt earlier. When Emily ended the embrace, she smiled at Nikki with open affection. In that instant, Nikki felt the absence of her own mother's love so acutely, she could scarcely breathe.

"Aren't you the prettiest thing I've ever seen?" Emily gushed. "And a doctor, too? My, my, your mother must be so proud."

"Mom—" Porter started to break in.

"Yes," Nikki said on an exhale, then smiled at the woman. "She's very proud."

"Well, we're letting in the flies. Come in, come in and have a glass of tea. Wipe your feet, Porter."

"Yes, ma'am," he said, then grinned at Nikki as his mother bustled inside the house. Nikki followed, swept along by the woman's effervescence. Porter brought up the rear on his crutches.

"My sister Elaine is volunteering at the library today," Emily said to Nikki, "so we have the house to ourselves. How do you like your tea, dear?"

"Unsweetened, please."

"Unsweetened? Where up north are you from?"

"I'm from Michigan."

Emily nodded. "I thought I detected an accent."

Nikki smiled. Southerners thought everyone *else* in the country had an accent.

"Have a seat in the living room," his mother said, shooing them in the direction of a small but comfortable room with two overstuffed loveseats facing each other over a low wood coffee table. Lining the walls were white built-in shelves crowded with books and picture frames.

One picture in particular caught Nikki's eye—three strapping teenage boys with wide grins and piercing blue eyes. The youngest had a familiar cleft in his chin. She felt compelled to touch the edge of the silver frame.

"You and your brothers?" she asked, lifting her gaze to Porter.

He smiled and nodded, leaning on his crutches. "One of the few pictures we found after the twister."

Seeing him as a boy sent unwanted emotions rising in her chest. She didn't want to know this much about him, didn't want to fall in love with his mother, didn't want to fall in love with—

She dropped her hand abruptly and turned her back on the photograph. "Are you sure we have time for tea? I don't want you to miss your appointment."

"What appointment?" Emily asked, walking in carrying a tray with three glasses.

Porter shifted on his crutches. "With a specialist in Atlanta. Just an X-ray to make sure my leg is healing okay."

Emily set the tray on the coffee table, then glanced at Nikki. "Was that your idea, my dear?"

Nikki nodded.

"So you've been taking care of him?"

She balked at the intimate implication and looked to Porter for help.

"Yes, Dr. Salinger has been taking care of me," he said happily.

Nikki gave him a withering look, which he ignored.

"Thank you for nursing my baby boy," Emily said to Nikki earnestly.

"You're…welcome," Nikki murmured, at a loss.

"I don't want you to miss your appointment," Mrs. Armstrong said, her voice fretful, "but surely you have time to sit with your mama and have a glass of tea?"

Porter looked to Nikki with an arched eyebrow. She nodded mutely and sat on the edge of one of the loveseats. They still needed to give the ring to his mother, after all. But Nikki was already feeling so…*raw*, she wasn't sure she wanted to witness such a personal event.

After hours of close quarters in the van, she was on edge, supremely aware of every inch of Porter's big, muscular body pulling on hers. When he lowered himself to sit next to her on the loveseat and his knee brushed hers, it only made matters worse.

Especially since Emily was eyeing them like a mother hawk.

"Unsweetened for you, Nikki," she said, handing over a cold glass. "And sweetened for you, Porter."

"Thank you," Nikki said, then took a sip, hoping the cool drink would settle her nerves…and lower her body temperature.

"Are you one of the brides, my dear?" Emily asked, her eyes wide with innocence.

Nikki choked on her drink, then swallowed. "Brides?"

"One of the brides who came to Sweetness looking for a husband?"

Her tongue was paralyzed. Luckily Porter's voice was still working.

"Mom," he chided, "the women who answered the ad weren't looking for a husband…not all of them anyway." He cleared his throat. "Dr. Salinger has been seeing patients and helping us to get our clinic underway. She's been a huge asset to our efforts."

Emily beamed. "So you're helping my boys rebuild Sweetness." She looked wistful. "It's such a special place. I made so many good memories there, and of course my wonderful Alton is buried there." Her eyes sparkled with tears, then she angled her head. "When you're ready, it's a wonderful place to settle down and raise children."

Was Porter's knee pressing harder into hers? Nikki gripped the glass tighter. "So I've been told."

"Uh, Mom," Porter said, reaching into his shirt pocket to withdraw a ring box, "Nikki and I have a surprise for you."

Emily's mouth rounded. "You're engaged!" She clapped her hands. "I knew it. As soon as I saw the two of you together, I said to myself, 'Now there's a perfect couple!'"

Nikki almost dropped her glass.

"Mom—" Porter interrupted.

"I must say, Porter, with your reputation for being

such a ladies' man, I didn't think you'd ever settle down—"

"*Mom—*"

"And I certainly never dreamed you'd be the first of my boys to fall—"

"Mom!"

Emily blinked. "What?"

"Nikki and I aren't engaged."

Her brow crumpled as she glanced back and forth between them. "You're not?"

Nikki wanted the floor to open up and swallow her. She shook her head, unable to look at Porter.

"No, we're not." Porter sighed. "Can I finish, please?"

Emily picked up her tea and sipped. "Of course."

He hesitated and Nikki sensed that the moment had been ruined for him. When she glanced over to see his shoulders had fallen, she had the urge to help him smooth over the awkwardness. She instinctively put her hand on his knee.

"Mrs. Armstrong, Porter asked me to accompany him today because while I was out exploring, I found something that belongs to you."

Emily frowned. "Something that belongs to me?"

Porter opened the ring box and held it out to her. The second she realized what she was seeing, her brilliant blue eyes filled with tears. She set down her glass clumsily, and Nikki saved it from spilling. But she was glad for the distraction because she, too, was close to tears.

"My lovely ring," Mrs. Armstrong said in awe, taking the box. "I thought I'd never see it again." She removed the gold filigree band. Nikki knew that Porter had asked Molly to clean it. It sparkled and gleamed as if it were

brand-new. As Emily slid the ring onto her finger, Nikki imagined the woman was remembering her wedding day, when Porter's father had first put it on her hand. The tears slid freely down her cheeks as she held it out to admire. "Alton had this ring made for me. You can't know how much it means to me to have it back." Then she wiped at her face and stood to hold out her arms to Nikki. "How can I ever thank you, my dear?"

Caught off guard, Nikki stood and accepted the woman's embrace. "No thanks necessary." Emily squeezed her and patted her back and it felt so…good. Nikki glanced at Porter, who watched them with a curious expression.

"Mom, you're going to break her in two," he admonished good-naturedly.

Emily stepped back and laughed, still wiping her eyes. Then she leaned down to give Porter a hug, too. "This is the happiest day I've had since the storm. I can't wait to get back home to Sweetness."

"Marcus and Kendall and I are looking forward to that day, too," he said, then planted a kiss on her wet cheek with a loud smacking noise that left Emily giggling like a girl.

Nikki watched the exchange with mixed emotions—unfamiliarity…disquiet…envy. Even when her mother had been alive, there had always been a clinical aspect to their relationship. Hugs were infrequent, and kisses, even less so. She'd never doubted her mother's love, but had longed for pats and cuddles. She caught Porter's eye and wanted to look away, afraid he would see everything she was feeling. But she couldn't drag her gaze from his. After a few seconds, he gave her a wink, then squeezed his mother's shoulders.

"We have to go, Mom. Dr. Salinger was good enough to get me an appointment with a bigwig orthopedist, and I don't want to be late."

"No, of course not," his mother agreed, all aflutter.

He pushed to his feet and gathered his crutches. Nikki stood, relieved to be leaving. She preceded him to the door where she was subjected to one more bear hug before Emily Armstrong would say goodbye.

"I see the way he looks at you," she whispered in Nikki's ear.

When Nikki pulled back, she could only smile at the woman's motherly observation. Of course she was projecting what she wanted to see onto the situation. "I'm glad I had the chance to meet you, Mrs. Armstrong."

Emily scoffed. "You make it sound like we'll never see each other again. But I'll see you when I come to Sweetness, and you're welcome here anytime."

Nikki felt Porter's gaze on her. She wouldn't be in Sweetness when Mrs. Armstrong moved back. She didn't want to outright lie, so she just smiled. "Goodbye."

She walked to the van to unlock it and let mother and son have a private farewell. She took the opportunity to dial into her voice mail and scroll through her messages. Her pulse spiked when she realized most of the calls were from Darren...all hang ups, until the last one.

"Nikki, hi...it's me. I'd really like to talk to you about some things. Call me when you can...please. I hope you're doing okay."

Just the sound of his voice sent anxiety sweeping through her. Her heart pounded and her knees felt loose. What did he want? Her forgiveness so he could feel better about his cruel betrayal? She doubted his conscience was bothering him. More likely, he was starting

to worry about his professional reputation and needed to perform damage control, with her assistance.

Her finger moved over the number keys as she toyed with the idea of calling Darren back. Instead, she listened to a message she'd skipped from Amy Bradshaw, who was just checking in to say hello and to see if Nikki was taking care of any new varmints. Nikki smiled. Her friend's voice always lifted her spirits. She'd call her back tonight once she got settled into the hotel room.

The thought of a long shower with unlimited hot water made her moan in anticipation.

Nikki stashed the phone, then glanced back to the front of the bungalow. Mrs. Armstrong was reaching up to cup Porter's face and saying something that made him smile. The scene tugged on her heart, even if she couldn't relate to it. She felt like a scientist, observing a ritual she didn't understand…but wanted to. At last he turned toward the van and made his way on his crutches to where she waited with the passenger door open. She took his crutches and helped him get settled.

"Sorry about the misunderstanding with the ring," he said. "Mother has an active imagination."

"No problem," she said lightly. "I can see why she made that mistake."

"Because we make a perfect couple?" he teased, his voice husky.

Nikki managed a smirk. "No. Are you in?"

When he nodded, she closed the door with a little more force than necessary, and walked around to the driver's door. She climbed in and started the engine. Darren's voice was in her head, and Porter's big body was in her space.

This was going to be a long drive.

27

Nikki pushed the down elevator button of the Buckhead medical tower. "I'm so relieved that your ankle is healing well."

Porter grinned. "I never doubted it for a minute, little lady doc. But Marcus is going to be disappointed that I won't be back to work as soon as he'd like."

Despite his cheer, she could tell he was leaning on his crutches more heavily, and his face showed signs of strain. "You're tired," she said, and lifted her fingers to feel his forehead before she even realized it. "No fever," she murmured to cover her gaffe, then dropped her hand.

"It's been a long day," he agreed.

"Are we far from the hotel?"

"No. It's just a couple of miles south of here, closer to midtown. We'll have time to rest before dinner. There's a restaurant close by I'd like to take you to, if that's okay."

The elevator dinged and the doors opened. He put his crutch out to hold open the door until she boarded—always the gentleman, she noted. But the day of close quarters and emotional reunions was starting to wear

on her. And Darren's voice message had been looping through her head while she'd waited for Porter to be examined. The elevator doors closed, throwing them into yet another intimate space. Nikki stabbed the button for the parking garage.

"Actually, I'll probably just get room service and turn in early."

He looked hurt. "That's no fun. You're going to make me go out alone? Parts of the city are sketchy— I'd be hard-pressed to outrun a mugger on crutches."

She couldn't help but laugh. "As if I could protect you."

"You've done a bang-up job of taking care of me so far."

At his suddenly serious tone, Nikki sobered. "Just doing my job," she said, partly to remind herself that was the extent of their relationship.

"I won't keep you out late," he cajoled. "And I can't drink an entire bottle of wine by myself."

Nikki squinted. "I didn't take you for a wine drinker."

He leaned in close. "You shouldn't stereotype people."

His voice rasped over her nerve endings, raising goose bumps on her arms. "Maybe you should tell that to your workers who don't want to see a female doctor."

His mouth quirked. "Touché."

But he didn't retreat. Instead, his blue, blue eyes bore into hers, and she knew he was thinking about kissing her. Nikki's mouth opened to drag more air into her lungs.

"Did I mention how good you make that dress look?" he whispered.

Nikki swallowed. As he lowered his mouth toward hers, she was torn—she wanted to indulge in this man, but her mind was spinning in chaos. She wet her lips, but just before their mouths met, the elevator chimed and the doors slid open to an audience of people waiting.

"Saved by the bell," he murmured.

Nikki ducked and walked off, then waited while Porter made his way through the crowd on his crutches. She practically trotted to stay one step ahead of him until they reached the van, and couldn't make eye contact while she got him settled. She was able to mask her restlessness as nerves when she pulled out into bumper-to-bumper traffic to head south on Peachtree Street. It was full-on rush hour across six lanes on the tree-lined road that wound between homes, condo buildings, retail businesses, office high-rises and churches. The sidewalks were crowded with pedestrians and riders whizzed by in narrow bike lanes.

"Impressive, huh?" Porter asked of the activity.

She nodded. "It's a shock to the system after being in Sweetness all this time." She jumped as a driver behind her blasted his horn. "I have to admit I miss the quiet."

"Ah-hah! So there's *something* about living in Sweetness that you enjoy."

"Sweetness has its charm," she admitted. Then she looked over at Porter. "It's just not the right place for me at this point in my life."

He looked back to the road ahead of them. "While you were waiting for me, did you get a chance to return your phone calls?"

"The office had a 'no cell phone' policy. I'll make my calls when I get to the hotel." Besides, she still hadn't

decided if she was going to return Darren's call. She had to admit her curiosity was piqued. But the fact that Darren hadn't hinted at what he wanted to talk to her about smacked of more manipulation.

"Whew, I wouldn't want to deal with this traffic every day," Porter said, as if he knew she was toying with the idea of relocating here.

"I'm sure a person would get used to it."

"Kind of like living in Sweetness... You have to give things a chance."

Nikki didn't respond, just kept her focus on the road. Vehicles were wedged so tightly together, they appeared to move as one mass. The air was thick with haze, and heat undulated off the asphalt and concrete. Her friend Amy's summation of the city mirrored her own observation: Atlanta was a big, hot, sprawling metropolis crowded with busy, distracted people.

The perfect place to lose herself in anonymity. A place where she wouldn't be pressured to have messy, tangled relationships with neighbors, coworkers or patients.

The traffic crawled forward at an agonizing pace, but at last they reached their hotel and valet parked the van. Check-in, at least, was quick, and a bellman took their bags ahead. Nikki's feet hurt in the borrowed high heels, and she was looking forward to that long, hot shower as they walked to their rooms, which turned out to be side by side. There was nothing particularly intimate about the room arrangement, but for some reason, it felt that way as she unlocked her door and he unlocked his.

"So...dinner in two hours?" he asked.

She looked up and started to protest. "I don't—"

"Please? Besides, don't you want to see more of the city?"

She did. And one of the women had lent her a beautiful dress to wear tonight. She wavered. But that close call earlier…

He held up his hand. "I'll behave—scout's honor."

She laughed and relented. "Okay. I'll meet you in two hours." She unlocked the door and walked into the spacious, luxurious room that was exhilaratingly cool from air-conditioning—a welcome respite for her allergies. A king-sized bed beckoned with a satiny white tufted coverlet. She walked over, slipped off her shoes, spread her arms and fell backward on the bed, enjoying the bounce before sighing and sinking into the plush linens. The ceiling was ornate with intricate patterns and gilded curlicues and a sparkling chandelier.

It was a far cry from her simple room in the boardinghouse in Sweetness.

In fact, the lavish hotel room reminded her of the bedroom she'd shared with Darren at his home. He had expensive taste, owned only the best furnishings. She had felt like a princess.

Her mind wandered to the phone message Darren had left while they were driving down. Calling him back seemed like a lose-lose proposition. If he tried to pretend he'd done nothing wrong, she'd be angry and hurt all over again. And if he…

No, her mind couldn't go there.

But she had to deal with it sooner or later—even if she only deleted the message. She sat up and reluctantly reached for her purse. She'd turned off her phone, but now removed it and pushed the "on" button, her heart clicking with dread.

A knock on the door startled her. She looked toward the entrance, then realized the sound had come from another door—a flat door that blended into the wall because it was covered with the same striped wallpaper. The door that connected her room to the one next door.

Porter's room.

The knock sounded again. She pushed to her feet and walked to the door, her tongue firmly in her cheek as she unlocked it. She swung it open to find Porter standing there, shirt hanging open to reveal his muscled chest and stomach, leaning on his crutches. Wounded *and* gorgeous, God help her.

"You got us connecting rooms," she said, deadpan.

"Coincidence," he said with a smile.

"I thought you said you'd behave yourself."

"That's right."

She crossed her arms. "Then why are you knocking on my door?"

He held up a cell phone that she hadn't noticed before. "It's Rachel. She's been trying to reach you on your cell, but—"

"It was turned off," Nikki finished. "Is something wrong?"

"Ask her yourself," he said, extending the phone.

She took the phone, wondering with chagrin if Rachel had overheard that little exchange. "Hello?"

"Connecting rooms, huh?"

Nikki closed her eyes briefly. "Rachel, is there a problem?"

"Yes. You really should turn on your phone."

From the bed where she'd left it, her phone started chiming with downloaded messages.

"Okay," Nikki said, tamping down her impatience. "What's wrong?"

"It's Nigel. He won't sleep."

Nikki exhaled in relief that it wasn't something more serious, although she realized Rachel was probably worried about her pet. "Is he sick again?"

"I don't know. He won't eat, either. Unless he's with Cupid."

"Cupid?"

"The deer. We named her. You know—Comet, *Cupid,* Donner and Blitzen."

Nikki winced and glanced up at Porter. "You named the doe Cupid?"

He rolled his eyes.

"Well, we couldn't just keep calling her 'deer.' The point is, Nigel is obsessed with Cupid. He wants to be with her all the time. Otherwise he whines and refuses to eat or sleep."

Nikki bit back a smile. "He'll eat when he gets hungry enough, and he'll sleep when he gets tired enough. How is, um, *Cupid* faring?"

"Better after we brought her back inside."

"You brought her inside?"

Porter dragged his hand down his face.

"She likes it. The girls are taking turns feeding her and checking the cast. She's doing great, walking around and getting stronger."

"That's good," Nikki agreed.

"So," Rachel said, lowering her voice suggestively, "are you having fun?"

Nikki looked at Porter, who was watching…and listening. "Er…it's been a productive trip."

"Oh, good grief, Nikki, let your hair down a little.

That sexy man wants you, and if you've already decided not to stay in Sweetness, what harm can it do to have a fantastic one-night stand?"

Nikki swept her gaze over his impressive body, and her mouth literally watered. "I'll keep that in mind."

"Look inside the purse I loaned you," Rachel said.

Something told her not to ask for details. "Okay. Thank you and goodbye." She quickly disconnected the call, then handed the phone back to Porter.

"Everything okay?" he asked.

"The women are domesticating your wild animal."

He sighed. "Women have a knack for domesticating wild things."

Nikki's heart skipped a beat. She had the oddest feeling he was alluding to something else.

He craned his neck to look behind her. "How's your room?"

"Great—especially the air-conditioning."

"I prefer an open window myself."

It hit her then—how different and how wholly incompatible they were. Giving in to her physical urges would only leave her feeling more disconnected than before. From the bed, her phone chimed again. "I should get that," Nikki said.

"Okay. See you in two hours," he said, and before she could voice a new protest, he closed the door on his side.

She closed her door, then went to her phone. Darren had called again twice, and the last time he'd left another message. She listened with her heart pounding against her ribs.

"Nikki, it's me...again. I'm worried about you. I un-

derstand why you're angry with me, but I need to know you're okay. Call me. Please. I need to talk to you."

She listened to the message again, but could glean nothing in his intonation or nonverbal clues to determine his motivation for wanting to speak with her.

But the fact that he'd used the word "I" four times was telling.

She set the phone on the dresser and went into the lush bathroom. The bathtub looked inviting, but the large glass-walled shower with two showerheads looked like nirvana. She turned on the hot water to let the steam rise, then turned to the vanity mirror.

Nikki could scarcely believe it was her reflection looking back.

The women had been generous with their time and their supplies. In fact, they'd virtually swarmed on her when Rachel had announced that Nikki had agreed to a makeover. She hadn't been allowed to go near a mirror while they applied chemicals to lighten her hair, then cut and styled it. Ditto while they arched her eyebrows and applied makeup. She'd received her first ever mani-cure and pedicure, and exfoliating scrubs to use in the shower. Shoes and dresses in Nikki's size were scav-enged from various closets.

The results, Nikki marveled, studying the sweep of honey-colored hair across her cheekbones, were noth-ing short of amazing. But more than that, she'd had fun. It was perhaps the first time in her life that she'd felt as if she belonged. The women had buzzed around her, talking about the workers they'd met, comparing notes. Underneath the general feeling of indignation that these Southern men had a long way to go to impress them

was a bubbling sense of optimism that the group had potential.

All of the women had stories of heartache and betrayal. At first Nikki had felt on edge, afraid someone would pry for details about her split with Darren, but it was as if they'd formed an insulating bubble around her. No one mentioned her scandalous breakup, but she'd sensed they were letting her know through the retelling of their own bittersweet romances that she was part of a sisterhood of the brokenhearted.

And that life went on.

As she peeled off the borrowed clothes, Nikki felt a pang of appreciation for the women. And while she admired their tenacity when it came to finding love, deep down, she knew she was different. Since childhood she'd been unusually sensitive—things had impacted her on a deeper emotional level than other people. Over the years she'd developed a good exoskeleton to conceal her soft middle so others assumed she was unfeeling when, in truth, it was the opposite. Opening her heart to Darren Rocha had been a huge risk for her. Having it cut out and handed back to her had been so brutal, there were times when she thought she would die from the pain.

She didn't want to experience that kind of anguish again, ever. Whatever those other women had that made them want to gamble it all again for the chance of love, she was missing. Courage?

Maybe.

Suddenly her chest tightened and her eyes filled with unbidden tears. Grief was sneaky like that—it slipped up on her at quiet moments and reminded her that if she thought she was over Darren's duplicity, she had, as her grammy would say, "Another think coming."

Still crying, she slipped under the showerheads and gave in to the tears. She felt racked with confusion, unsure of her place in the world. It gave her a tiny bit of insight into how the people of Sweetness might have felt when the tornado had ravaged their homes and scattered their belongings, sending them in search of a new place to put down roots. She wished Sweetness could be that new place for her.

Little by little, the hot water relaxed her muscles and the hotel's fragrant soap washed away her troubles for the time being. When she left the shower, she was feeling revived. She carefully applied the makeup and styled her hair like the women had shown her, and was pleased with the results. The teal-colored sundress complemented her skin and eyes, and silver-colored strappy heels gave her a lift. She glanced at her reflection in a mirror on the bathroom door and gave a little twirl.

She was, she admitted, looking forward to having dinner with Porter. He was, by all measures, charming and attentive. The sexual tension that vibrated between them kept things playful and interesting. Rachel's words came back to her and she acknowledged it wouldn't take much to ignite their smoldering passion. But she knew enough about herself to know that a one-night stand wasn't her style. As long as she maintained her distance, she could survive the night with her dignity intact. The man was on crutches, after all.

She could outrun him if she had to.

When it was time to meet him, she scooped up the clutch purse Rachel had lent her, then remembered she was supposed to look inside. At first glance, it was empty, but when Nikki unzipped the little side pocket, she found not one, but *four* condoms. A flush climbed

her neck at the implication. She pushed them back in place, zipped up the pocket and added her wallet, a lipstick and a comb. Then she gave her outfit one last glance in the mirror, and to keep from wrinkling her dress, paced the room waiting for Porter to knock.

Fifteen minutes later, she was still pacing. Thinking maybe he'd fallen asleep, she dialed his cell phone number, but he didn't answer. Worse, she could hear it ringing through the doors that connected their rooms. Worry bloomed in her mind. Had he fallen?

Nikki walked to the door on her side, opened it, and knocked on the door leading to his room. "Porter?"

She pressed her ear to the door and heard his voice, but his words were unintelligible. She knocked again. "Porter? Are you okay?"

His voice sounded again, still unintelligible, but higher—as if he was in distress. Her pulse jumped. She tried the knob, relieved to discover he'd left it unlocked. She stepped into his room, registering that the decor was similar, but in gray and pewter. He wasn't in the big bed that dominated the room, although the coverlet was rumpled.

The bathroom door was closed, but the light shining beneath the door told her it was occupied.

"Porter?"

"Nikki!" he shouted from the other side of the door. "Help!"

She was there in two strides, her head filled with images of him lying in a bloody pool on the floor. She flung open the door...and came up short.

28

Instead of lying in a bloody pool, Porter was immersed in a dissolving bubble bath with his casted leg propped on the side of the tub. He grinned. "Hey, little lady doc."

At the sight of his big nude body, blood rushed to Nikki's erogenous zones. His dark, damp hair hung in his eyes. His shoulders spanned the width of the tub. The hair on his chest merged into a dark rivulet that traveled down his abs and disappeared under the water. One of the few remaining mounds of bubbles covered his privates.

"Wow, you look great," he said, as if nothing was amiss.

Nikki crossed her arms and frowned. "I thought you were in trouble."

"I am. I managed to get in, but now that I'm good and clean, I can't get out." He wriggled his wrinkled fingers. "I'm shriveling." Then he held out his hand. "Help me up?"

She hesitated.

He scoffed. "Come on, doc, I know you're stronger

than you look. And you've seen pretty much all of me anyway."

Not everything, she almost said.

"You can close your eyes," he said wryly, as if he'd read her mind.

He was mocking her. Nikki straightened and sighed. "Okay."

His hand disappeared in the water between his legs. Just when she was starting to wonder what he was doing, a sucking noise sounded, then the water level began to drop—quickly.

In a few seconds, she'd get an eyeful of everything.

"I'll get you a towel," she said, then pivoted to pull a thick bath towel off a rack. While she had her back turned, she gave herself a pep talk and tried to tamp down her racing pulse. She was a physician. She could view his naked body with a clinical detachment. She could. Nikki took a deep breath and turned back around.

Just as all of the water drained out of the tub.

She got a glimpse of impressive equipment before she tossed the towel over him. He unfolded it and arranged it over his waist, then extended his hand. Nikki set down her purse, then clasped his hand and leaned over to allow him to use her body as leverage to push up. She squeezed her eyes shut and braced her feet.

One second she was upright and providing resistance, the next she was tumbling headfirst into the tub.

She landed with an *oomph* on his slippery chest, nose to nose and knees to knees. Only the towel at his waist kept things rated PG-13.

Nikki gasped. "You did that on purpose!"

But he was all smiles and innocence. "Sorry, doc, I slipped. Honest."

She flailed, but couldn't get a handhold on anything except firm, muscled flesh.

"Easy," he murmured, putting his arms around her. "You're going to hurt yourself…or make things worse."

"I'm in a bathtub with you," she said, shaking her head. "How could things be worse?"

He wrapped a hand around the nape of her neck and pulled her mouth to his for an unexpected kiss so hot she could almost feel the steam rising from the tub. He thoroughly explored her mouth, then ended the kiss, but held her face close to his. "I want you, Nikki."

She was still rigid and trying to process where they were and how it was possible that he could elicit such wild responses from her body. Bodies, after all, were essentially the same—two of this, two of that, one of something else. From a scientific perspective, it didn't make sense that this man could make her feel something different or better than another man could make her feel.

Yet here she was trembling, overcome with the sensation that she might die if he stopped touching her. She was intrigued by her own uncharacteristic behavior. Darren's face popped into her head, along with the nagging sense that she shouldn't do anything she'd regret until she called him back.

What if he wanted to get back together?

Nikki pushed aside the thought and attacked Porter's mouth with her own, stabbing her tongue against his. He groaned and ground her closer, deepening the kiss, giving her his breath when she needed more.

He slid his hands down her back to cup her rear and press her against his sex bulging beneath the towel.

Desire shot through her body, setting her on fire. She moved her hands over his chest and shoulders, massaging, caressing and dragging her nails over his skin.

He shuddered and broke the kiss to nuzzle her neck, sliding the straps of her dress down her shoulders and deftly loosening the front buttons until her bare breasts fell forward.

"You're beautiful," he whispered, then rolled the hardened pink tips between his fingers, sending exquisite pleasure shooting through her body. He tasted one point, then the other, laving them with his warm tongue and drawing them into his mouth. Nikki bit into her lip to muffle her moans.

"Does that feel good?" he murmured against her skin.

"Umm."

"I want to make you feel good, baby." He tugged the skirt of her dress to her waist, then lifted it over her head. The sensation of his springy chest hair against her bare skin was electric, sending moisture to the juncture of her thighs. He slid his hands inside her flimsy panties, kneading her buttocks. His eyes were hooded as he teased her secret flesh with his fingers. Nikki gasped and undulated into him. He plied her until she was practically faint, then he pushed down her underwear. Nikki fumbled to rid herself of them, registering dimly that she still wore her sandals as she sat up to straddle him.

"Are you okay?" she asked, concerned the position was putting too much pressure on his leg.

"One problem," he murmured, and when she shifted, he pulled the towel from between them. His erection

strained against her stomach, thick and unyielding. She clasped him, gratified at his sharp intake of breath.

Then he stilled her hand. "We have to stop… I wasn't planning this. I have protection, but it's in the bedroom."

Nikki bit back a smile, then reached for the borrowed purse, still resting on the ledge of the tub. She fished out a condom and held it up.

His eyes widened. "Aren't you full of surprises?"

"Long story," she murmured as she ripped it open.

"Tell me later," he said, exhaling loudly as she rolled it on. He pulled her mouth down on his for a bottomless kiss, then whispered in her ear, "Are you ready for me?"

She sighed. "Yes."

He lifted her hips and settled her down on his sex slowly, staring into her eyes. Nikki's head lolled from the overwhelming sensation of being filled. "You have no idea how good that feels."

"Yes, I do," he said as pleasure played over his face.

Still concerned about his leg, she allowed Porter to set the pace. They found a slow rhythm so incredibly languid and deep, it was almost unbearable. Nikki immediately felt a climax swirling in her womb.

"Is that good?" he asked.

"Umm."

"Come here," he said, and pulled her down for a stabbing kiss as he continued thrusting inside her.

"Umm." An orgasm was gathering…forming… building…

"You're so sexy, baby. You drive me crazy."

"Umm." The pressure in her womb climbed higher.

He flicked his tongue against her ear and suddenly Nikki's body contracted involuntarily. She cried out as she crested, buffeted by some invisible force so powerful she thought she might shatter. The pinnacle lasted for several pulsating, white-light seconds, then she drifted down in long, pleasurable spasms that she didn't want to end.

It was unlike anything she'd ever experienced.

Darn.

Porter watched Nikki's face as she descended from her climax. Being buried inside her felt so amazing, it took every bit of his concentration to hold off, to make sure she was fully pleasured before he took his own release. Even now, he didn't want it to end, wanted to prolong this intense feeling of looking into Nikki's eyes and seeing her so raw and so vulnerable. It was heady to know he was responsible for bringing her to this sensual place…and gratifying to know that his instincts about her had been right.

All that emotion she kept pent up during the day as she went about her business exploded in the hands of the person who knew which buttons to push.

As if to confirm his theory, she leaned down to sigh in his ear, a noise that tapered to a satisfied moan.

The sound of her complete fulfillment sent him over the edge. He gripped her tiny waist and thrust deep into her. Then he came with such intensity, it was as if she were pulling the life force out of him. He released a long guttural groan and held her against him as his body pulsed over and over.

It was unlike anything he'd ever experienced.

Damn.

29

Nikki woke up, startled, and knew instantly something was wrong.

Darren didn't snore.

She turned her head to look at the man lying in the bed next to her and the mystery of the loud rumbling was solved—the man wasn't Darren.

Darren didn't take up the entire bed and sprawl, spread-eagled as if he were lying on some deserted beach, sleeping off a hangover. Darren didn't hog the pillows and kick all the covers from the bed.

Nikki scanned Porter's long, nude body and was bombarded with images of what they'd done last night....

She squeezed her eyes shut. And Darren had never made her feel so indescribably, so deliciously, so incredibly good.

But Porter Armstrong did.

Sleepy street noises wafted through the window he'd left open in defiance of the air-conditioning. Nikki lifted her head to find the clock. It was still early...but not too soon for regrets.

The previous night with Porter had been mind-bending, for sure. They hadn't made it out of the hotel

room, opting for room service and creating their own entertainment. The man was a machine—and that was *with* the encumbrance of a cast. When they'd finally fallen asleep from sheer fatigue they were both utterly sated.

Nikki winced. And now what? They lived happily ever after?

Right. Just because she'd become dangerously attached to Porter didn't mean he felt the same. Even his mother had expressed disbelief that he would ever settle down, teasing Porter for being such a ladies' man.

Nikki bit into her lip. Although…that depiction didn't exactly mesh with Rachel's account that she'd let Porter know she was interested, and he hadn't taken her up on it.

Then a revelation hit Nikki like a thump to the head. The reason he'd slept with *her* was because he knew she was leaving Sweetness. No muss, no fuss. The realization left her chilled…but it also kept her from forming fantasies that would only lead to more heartache down the road.

Nikki eyed the door leading to her room and reasoned the best way to avoid awkward morning-after chitchat was to not be there when Porter woke up. Keeping an eye on his snoring figure, she slowly pushed herself up, grimacing when her body rebelled, reminding her that she hadn't used some of those muscles in…well, never.

She managed to ease from the bed without waking him and stopped to pick up clothes along the way, dodging a room-service cart and plates of half-eaten food, plus two empty bottles of wine.

He didn't stir when she opened the door. Nikki held

her breath and slipped through to her room, then closed the door behind her. Her unslept-in bed mocked her indignant insistence a few days earlier that Porter reserve separate rooms for their trip. She dropped her armful of disheveled clothing on the bed and shivered in the air-conditioning. She went over to switch it off, then noticed her cell phone was flashing to indicate she had voice messages.

Darren. Her stomach knotted with a confusion of feelings. She shouldn't feel guilty for sleeping with someone else after he'd so coldheartedly cast her aside. Chances were, he was only calling to ease his own conscience…assuming he'd grown one.

Feeling antsy, she walked into the bathroom to wrap herself in a towel. When she caught a glance of herself in the mirror, she did a double-take.

Who was that tousled, flushed wanton woman?

Nikki touched her kiss-swollen mouth and had a knee-weakening flash of Porter kissing her fiercely in the bathtub. At that moment, he'd convinced her she was the most desirable woman on the planet. It was in stark contrast to Darren's slow, methodical pursuit of her based more on intellectual interests.

She had to admit that sleeping with Porter made her feel a little triumphant in light of Darren's affair. It felt good to be wanted, even if it was only a one-night stand. It bolstered her confidence and her courage to deal with Darren.

Resolved, she turned on the shower and while the water warmed up, she pressed a button to listen to Darren's latest message.

"Nikki…it's me." He sighed. "I'm worried because you haven't called back. Are you okay? Where are you?

I really need to talk to you… I'm an idiot. I can't believe what I did to you, what I did to us. It's over with Tori. I woke up and realized how stupid I've been. Can we talk?" He made an anguished sound. "Please call me. Please?"

Nikki's heart sprinted in her chest and she closed her eyes. Her heart broken, their engagement over, their life together aborted…all for a woman he barely knew and was now through with. It all seemed so…unnecessary.

And now he wanted to pick up where they'd left off, as if nothing had happened.

Could she?

Nikki took a deep breath, then picked up the phone and dialed.

Porter jerked awake, then realized he'd woken himself up snoring. He only snored when he was dead tired, but that was how Nikki had left him—drained.

He swept his arm to the side of the bed she'd slept on, and came up with nothing. Disappointment gripped him when he realized she wasn't there. He wondered, with chagrin, if his snoring had disturbed her. He glanced to the bathroom, but didn't see a light. She must have gone back to her room.

Which was damned inconvenient since he wanted to make love to her again. And tell her he wanted her to stay in Sweetness.

To give the town a chance.

He massaged the sudden ache behind his breast-bone, wondering if he should mention the pain to Nikki. Coincidentally, it seemed to be worse when she was nearby.

Porter pushed himself up and groaned. His body was

as sore as if he'd put in a full day of jackhammering. He reached for his crutches propped on the nightstand and used one to snag his underwear lying next to the bed. He worked them on, then stood and made his way over to the doors that connected their rooms. She must have collected her clothes along the way…except for her tiny white panties, he noticed with amusement. He stopped to scoop them up, and got a rush remembering taking them off her…every time she'd tried to put them back on.

The door leading to his room was open, the door on her side was closed.

He knocked. "Nikki?"

When she didn't answer, he tried the knob and found it unlocked. He stuck his head inside. "Nikki?"

She wasn't in the room, but the bathroom door was ajar and the shower was running. Porter grinned—he wouldn't mind seeing Nikki naked and wet. His body revved up for it. But as he approached the bathroom, he heard her voice. She was talking to someone…on the phone?

He stopped and held up his hand to knock.

"…I know you're right," he heard her say. "I've been thinking about this nonstop."

Porter frowned. Was she talking to her ex? From the tone of her voice, she was fond of the person on the other end of the line.

"I've decided I'm definitely not staying in Sweetness," she said.

His heart dropped to his stomach. So she *was* going back to her cheating fiancé.

Her laugh tinkled. "Of course I'll call you when I leave…dinner would be great."

Porter could tell she was wrapping up the conversation, so he turned around and made his way back to the connecting door as fast and as quietly as his crutches would take him. When he slipped back into his own room and closed the door, his heart was beating fast from exertion—and anger at himself. After promising Marcus he wouldn't do anything to make things worse, sleeping with Nikki had apparently cemented her decision to leave Sweetness.

It smarted to know that she'd made the decision to go back to her fiancé while the bed they shared was still warm.

Damn, he'd thought she'd enjoyed the night of boundless sex as much as he had. He'd thought that somewhere between the bathtub and the second bottle of Bordeaux, they'd connected on an emotional level. But maybe he was losing his touch. He did, after all, have one leg tied behind him.

Porter lifted a crutch and tossed it across the room.

Nikki emerged from the bathroom wrapped in a towel and bound up with a jumbled mass of emotions. Her conversation with Amy had reinforced her decision to leave Sweetness. She didn't belong there…especially not after what had happened between her and Porter. Things would be awkward, and she didn't want this rebound crush she had on him to develop into something… worse. Been there, done that, had the broken heart to show for it.

But she'd decided not to call Darren. She didn't owe him anything, didn't even know if she was going back to Broadway for good. This morning she'd woken up stronger. Nikki padded to the window and glanced down

at the bustling sidewalk and the pretty streetscape of midtown. She could live here. Maybe she'd return to Atlanta to start over once she tied up loose ends.

She walked back toward the bathroom and glanced at the door that connected her room to Porter's. Was he awake? A white item in the floor caught her eye—her panties. She must've dropped them when she came into the room. Nikki blushed as she stooped to pick them up, remembering how Porter had pulled them off every time she tried to put them on. Her womb tightened at the memory. She'd never laughed so much in bed. Everything with Porter seemed fun and natural and…right.

Nikki glanced at the door and considered walking back into his room and crawling into bed with him, to pretend a little longer. She put her hand on the doorknob and listened to her heart thud in her ears.

No. She should walk away while things between them were good. If his reaction to her this morning was frosty, it would ruin everything. Nikki dropped her hand.

Instead she dried her hair, applied minimal makeup, dressed in a borrowed skirt and blouse, then repacked her overnight bag. She considered calling Porter to see if he wanted to join her for breakfast, then decided against it and descended to the hotel restaurant.

When she walked in, Porter was sitting at a table alone reading the newspaper. He looked so handsome, her pulse instantly ticked higher. But she was glad she hadn't called him. He obviously hadn't wanted her company this morning.

But he glanced up and gestured her over. As she made her way to his table, she tried to determine the reception she'd get. Cold? Flirtatious? Indifferent?

The latter, she realized within seconds.

"Good morning," he said with a flat smile. "Ready to get those supplies and head back?"

"Er...yes," she murmured, then sat in the proffered seat.

"The medical supply warehouse opens in thirty minutes. I asked the hotel concierge to fax our list to their sales department, so I'm hoping they'll have most things rounded up for us when we arrive."

Nikki nodded woodenly and busied herself arranging a napkin over her lap. Was this how a one-night stand worked? No mention of their previous...*activity?*

"That way," he continued, "we can get back on the road as soon as possible."

"Fine," she said, pouring a cup of coffee. "My bag is packed. I'm ready to check out."

"Thought so," he said, his tone dry.

"Excuse me?"

"Because you're so organized," he added mildly. "Do you see anything on the menu that looks good?"

But the slight hadn't been lost on her. Stinging, Nikki picked up the menu with one hand and sipped her coffee. The hot liquid scalded her tongue, sending quick tears to her eyes. She set down the menu. "I'm actually not hungry this morning. Just coffee for me."

He closed the menu. "Me, too. I just want to get on the road."

"Right."

"Right." He massaged the thigh of his cast leg. The woman in her couldn't help but recall the beauty of his muscled leg, and the physician in her couldn't help but be concerned.

"Are you having pain?"

"My old injury…it acts up sometimes." He gave her a pointed look.

Such as when he was up all night having sex.

Her cheeks warmed, but she was saved from responding by the arrival of a waiter. When the man left again, they fell into silence. Nikki sipped her coffee, searching her mind for something to say that was safely neutral.

Porter took a sip of his coffee, too. "Tell me, doc… do you always skip out of bed the morning after a one-night stand?"

She choked on the hot liquid in her cup. "No." When he looked slightly amused, she straightened, realizing her answer made her sound as if she'd had many such escapades. "I mean, I haven't had a lot of experience… in that area."

He lifted his cup. "Then I'm glad I could oblige."

Nikki didn't know what to say. She'd never been good at sexual banter, and last night's hookup apparently hadn't helped in that arena. From her purse, her phone rang. It seemed like a perfect time to answer, so she excused herself and retreated to just outside the restaurant entrance. Darren's name flashed across the screen. She sighed, then decided she might as well get it over with. She connected the call. "Hello?"

"Nikki?" Darren's voice sounded surprised. "Nikki, it's me…Darren."

Her throat convulsed. "Yes, I know. What do you want?"

He stumbled over his words. "How are you?"

She crossed her arms and glanced back toward the table where Porter sat. "I'm fine…and I'm busy."

"Where are you?"

"That's none of your business," she bit out.

"I know, I know," he said. "I'm sorry, I've just been worried about you."

"Darren, my welfare is no longer any of your concern."

He sighed. "I deserve that…and more. I'm sorry for what I did to you, Nikki. I guess I just got cold feet about settling down and I lost my judgment."

She blinked back hot tears at his cavalier explanation, but fought to keep her voice strong. "I'm not interested in your motivation for cheating on me, Darren. Did you call for a specific reason?"

"I…yes." He cleared his throat. "Nikki, I know I don't have any right to ask you this, but I love you and I want us to get back together. Can you forgive me for making a stupid mistake?"

Nikki's heart pounded and her stomach churned. In those first days after he'd broken the news that he'd fallen in love with someone else, hadn't she dreamed of him coming to her and saying just that? Her chest ached with a mixture of anger and hurt that he'd thrown away her love as if it meant nothing. More than anything, she longed for things to be the way they used to be. But could she ever trust him again?

"Darren," she finally said into the phone, "I can forgive you—"

"Oh, thank you, sweetheart! I knew we could work this out."

"But," she continued, "forgiving you doesn't mean I want to get back together with you. Those are two different things."

"Right," he agreed hurriedly. "And I know I've dumped a lot on you in a short time, but please promise me you'll think about giving us another chance."

"I can't do that. Unlike you, I don't make promises lightly."

"Fair enough," he said. "For now, it's just wonderful to hear your voice."

She looked up and saw Porter glancing her way. He pointed to his watch.

"I have to go," she said.

"Okay. I love you."

Nikki hesitated. "Goodbye, Darren." Then she disconnected the call with an unsteady hand.

"Everything okay?"

She looked up to see Porter moving toward her on his crutches.

"Yes," she said, although she still felt shaken as she returned her phone to her purse.

"Not to rush you, but we probably need to get going."

"Of course," she said, trying to compose herself. Thinking about Darren while Porter stood in her personal space was like receiving two radio stations on the same channel—the result was mostly static.

To her great relief, Porter didn't make any other references to their night together on the drive to the medical supply warehouse. They both seemed to have retreated to their respective corners. When they reached the warehouse, the sales manager had gathered a sample of products for Nikki to consider, making the ordering process fast and efficient. Smaller supplies filled the van to its capacity, then Porter arranged for one of the delivery trucks to follow them with the more bulky equipment.

The four-hour drive back to Sweetness was strained and painful. Nikki was uncomfortably aware of the big man next to her, of how recently they'd been intimately

intertwined, and how distant he was now. And her phone conversation with Darren looped through her mind like a break in the pavement on the interstate…*thump… thump…thump.* By the time they pulled up in front of the clinic, Nikki's head pounded, and she just wanted to lie down. She climbed down from the van and retrieved her overnight bag.

"I'll come back later to help unpack the supplies," she said.

After miles of silence, Porter suddenly looked as if he didn't want her to go. "I can get one of the men to drive you to the boardinghouse and bring the van back here."

"That's okay, I'll walk."

"Thanks for going," he said. "It was…interesting."

She gave him a flat smile, then turned toward the rooming house, letting out a sigh. What a mess she'd made for herself. To add insult to injury, she'd been back for mere minutes, and she could already feel her allergies kicking in.

When she walked inside, she deflected inquisitive glances from the women who'd helped with her makeover. She could only imagine what the gossip had been about her and Porter in their absence.

And was confirmation written all over her face?

When she saw Susan Sosa, she asked the woman to meet her at the clinic in an hour to help set up a new office there. Then she hurried upstairs to her bedroom to find some aspirin and lie down for a few minutes to calm her jumbled thoughts.

As she lay there with a cool cloth on her forehead, Nikki began to relax. The night with Porter, the call from Darren… Neither event changed her intention to

leave Sweetness. Her only decision was where to go from here.

Then a realization hit her and Nikki groaned.

She wasn't going anywhere. She'd forgotten to buy the replacement fuel pump for her van.

30

"Nikki didn't say anything about leaving when she got back from Atlanta yesterday," Rachel said.

Porter worked his mouth back and forth—something about the way Rachel wouldn't make eye contact told him she wasn't being completely truthful.

She grimaced at the orange-colored grease sitting on top of the vegetable soup in her bowl. "Honestly, Porter, Colonel Molly needs some cooking lessons. If people had to pay to eat here, they wouldn't."

Remembering Rachel's poisonous chicken salad, he arched an eyebrow.

She blushed. "I'm not saying *I* could run this place."

At her covert change of subject, he was sure she knew something about Nikki leaving Sweetness. "I'm more worried that the town has a doctor than award-winning soup."

Rachel gave him an exasperated look. "Why don't you just ask Nikki when she's going back?" She blanched. "I mean if…*if* she's going back." Rachel glanced at her watch. "Look at the time. We're unveiling the media room today. We're going to download some movies and

invite the men to come over tonight to watch them on the big-screen TV." She gave him an encouraging smile. "You should come. Nikki will be there."

He nodded and lifted his hand in a wave as she moved away. Rachel was right—he should just confront Nikki about her leaving Sweetness. She was probably at the clinic, where she'd been since they'd returned from Atlanta yesterday. He had to hand it to her—the little lady doc was doing everything she could to get the clinic in order before she abandoned him…er, *them*. Abandoned *them*.

He lumbered to his feet and was on his way out of the dining hall when he saw an unfamiliar dark sedan pull to a stop on the road. Porter squinted. Michigan license plate, and the driver was male.

The man rolled down the window and pushed up his glasses. "Excuse me, I'm looking for Dr. Salinger."

Porter's confusion cleared. The doctor Marcus had emailed about replacing Nikki…what was his name? Dr. Jay Cross. Porter frowned, knowing the man's arrival would only hasten her departure.

Then he brightened. Maybe he should let Dr. Cross know what he was getting into. The man didn't seem particularly robust. With the right "introduction" to the area, maybe the man would change his mind about sticking around.

Porter extended a big grin. "Dr. Salinger's been expecting you. Pull over and I'll take you to her."

Dr. Cross looked dubious. "Who are you?"

"Porter Armstrong. My brothers and I own this town."

The man did as he was told, apparently eager to please his potential employer. By the time he alighted from the car, Porter had settled on a four-wheeler.

"Climb on!" he shouted. Dr. Cross, dressed in slacks, shirt, tie and sport coat, was hesitant. "It's the easiest way to get around on this mountain," Porter promised.

The man was barely on the seat when Porter goosed the gas. "Hang on!"

Dr. Cross found the handhold behind his seat just in time to keep from falling off. "Where are we going?"

"Dr. Salinger is at the clinic, but I know a shortcut." Porter steered the ATV off the paved road and tore down a rocky side path. It would eventually wind around to the back of the clinic, but not before rising and falling steeply. "We can see the whole town from up here."

"So there's more to see?" Dr. Cross shouted, appearing to hang on for dear life.

"Not really," Porter said cheerfully. "You might want to duck." He crouched to ride underneath low-lying tree branches, suddenly glad he hadn't been up here lately to clear the trail. Behind him, Dr. Cross bent low, jerking to one side.

They climbed higher and higher, and Porter made sure they hit every rock and rut along the way. When they reached high ground, he stopped the ATV at a precipice and shifted to idle. "Nice view, huh?"

Dr. Cross righted his glasses and looked over the edge, then shrank back. "What exactly happened to this town?"

"Tornado," Porter said matter-of-factly. "An F-5 twister, to be precise. Mowed down everything in sight."

The man's Adam's apple bobbed. "Are tornadoes common up here?"

"Oh, sure," Porter lied. "At this altitude, tornadoes

can spring up out of nowhere. You have to keep one
eye on the sky."

Dr. Cross glanced up warily.

Porter shifted into gear. "Ready?"

Before the man could answer, he tore off, then headed
downhill, gratified when he felt the man bouncing on the
seat behind him. At the bottom of the hill, he slowed to
cross a shallow tributary of Timber Creek, but plowed
through with enough speed to give them both a good
soaking. On the other side, he came to an abrupt halt.

"Uh-oh."

"What?" Dr. Cross said, letting go long enough to
whip off his glasses and wipe the water off the lenses
with the end of his tie.

Porter pointed to raccoon tracks in the soft mud
next to the stream, distorted from the elements. "Bear
tracks."

The man's eyes widened. "Bear tracks? What kind?"

"Grizzly." Porter made a rueful noise as he looked
around. "We'd better get out of here."

Dr. Cross paled, then gave up on the rear handgrip
and threw his arms around Porter's waist. Porter smothered a smile, then peeled off, driving as fast as he dared
over the bumpy, muddy trail until the rear of the clinic
came in sight.

"Here we are," he said, slowing to a halt next to where
post holes were being dug to set the sign for the clinic
that would be going up soon.

Porter cut the engine just as Nikki was emerging from the main entrance of the modular building.
She was dressed in jeans and a dusty T-shirt, holding
a clipboard. At the sight of her lithe figure, his heart
raced. She glanced up and saw the two men. Porter

was disappointed that her gaze skipped over him and lasered in on the man climbing gingerly off the back of the four-wheeler. She stared, crossing her arms over her middle.

"What are you doing here?" she asked.

Porter frowned, confused as the drenched man walked up to her and invaded her personal space.

"Hi, Nikki."

She seemed flustered. "Darren…why are you here?"

Porter's stomach plummeted. Darren? Nikki's ex?

"I came to find you," Darren said. "I had to see you."

Nikki couldn't believe her eyes. If there was one sight she thought she'd never see, it was Darren Rocha and Porter Armstrong side by side.

With Darren looking more than a little bedraggled.

"What happened to you?" she asked, indicating his wet, mud-spattered appearance.

He gestured to Porter. "Mr. Armstrong knew a short-cut." Then his eyes bulged. "Nikki, you can't stay here. There are grizzly bears everywhere. And tornadoes."

Nikki rolled her eyes and looked past him to Porter. "Really?"

From the four-wheeler, Porter gave a little shrug.

Darren was staring at her. "Your hair is different. You look…beautiful."

Nikki warmed under his gaze, pleased by the compliment even as conflicting emotions whipped through her. "Thank you."

"Is there somewhere we can talk?" he asked, his eyes beseeching.

She considered the man before her, so familiar, yet

at the same time, so alien. The last time she'd seen him, he'd casually dismissed her and their engagement, had proclaimed his love for a younger, more exciting woman without any regard to Nikki's feelings. But gone was Darren's cool confidence. He seemed humbled. And the fact that he'd come looking for her showed a determination that surprised her. It broke down her defenses.

She gestured in the direction of the boardinghouse. "My office. You can get cleaned up there."

"Do you need a ride?" Porter piped up.

She leveled a pointed glare on him. "We'll walk, thanks." She was tired of men's behavior in general. Already this morning, two workers had come around asking if anyone had seen Doc Riley because they needed him to treat some ailment or wound. When she'd offered her services, they'd politely refused and left.

She set off walking toward the boardinghouse, maintaining a rapid pace for the man next to her to keep up. "How did you know where to find me?"

His shoes squished as he walked. "Dr. Hannah told me. Don't be angry."

Nikki bristled. "You might've let me know you were coming."

"I left you a voice message."

"My phone doesn't get good reception except on the water tower."

He laughed. "The water tower? What is this place— Petticoat Junction?"

His laughter rankled her. "It's a brand-new town, Darren. There isn't much infrastructure at the moment."

"I understand you answered a newspaper ad? That doesn't seem like something you would do."

Nikki set her jaw. "And yet, I did."

"Looks dangerous to me," he said, peering all around at the rugged landscape. "Do you even have running water?"

"Yes," she said through gritted teeth. "The accommodations are more than adequate."

He gestured at a crew of workers they passed. "What about all these men running around? Who keeps the women safe?"

"The women do."

"And you're the town doctor?"

Nikki wet her lips. "Yes." He didn't have to know that most of the town's residents refused to be treated by her.

"This is beneath you, Nikki."

Irritation spiked in her chest. "I'm a physician, Darren. No place is 'beneath me.'"

"You know what I mean," he said. "The conditions are practically primitive."

"You saw the new clinic. It's nicer than the facility where I worked in Broadway."

"And where is your support staff? What if, God forbid, something happens to *you?*"

"If there's an emergency I can't handle, a Medevac would fly in."

"Because communication on this mountain is so good," he said drily.

"It's improving," she said, feeling inexplicably defensive of the town.

They reached the front of the boardinghouse. Across the road sat Darren's car. She shook her head at Porter's "shortcut." What was he trying to prove?

Darren gestured. "I brought a change of clothes. Let me grab my bag."

She waited while he jogged across the road to retrieve a suitcase from the trunk of his Mercedes. When he came back, she took in his piece of designer luggage and was struck by how out of place he was in this remote wilderness. Porter's work vehicles and leather duffel bag came to mind, but she quickly dismissed the comparison. Contrasting the men was an exercise in futility. It wasn't as if they were both vying for her attention.

Porter had been aloof since their return from Atlanta yesterday. It was clear he'd gotten what he wanted from her, and she couldn't be a hypocrite—she'd gotten what she wanted, too. She'd noticed him talking to Rachel quite a bit since their return. It looked as if he'd already moved on—

"Dr. Hannah said you were only staying long enough to oversee the building of a clinic," Darren said, breaking into her thoughts. "Looks like that's done."

Nikki tamped down her annoyance. "Dr. Hannah misspoke. I…haven't made a decision about my future yet." She turned and walked up to the porch of the boardinghouse, nodding to women they passed who gave them quizzical looks. She led him inside and through the hallway, stopping to pet the deer, Cupid, who was getting around on its cast leg and had adapted amazingly well to human companionship. Around its neck was a glittery pink dog collar.

"So wild animals just roam around indoors here?" Darren asked.

"She's a patient," Nikki said, giving the cast a quick hand check.

The deer gave him a sniff and he pulled back. "You're the veterinarian, too?"

"I do what I can," she said, then led him down another

hall to the room that had been turned into her office. She opened the door and walked in, then pointed to the bathroom. "You can clean up and change in there."

"Where will you be?"

She nodded to the desk next to the window, but her gaze landed on the denim shirt Porter had given her, draped over the back of the chair. "I...I have some paperwork to do." A contract she needed to decide whether to sign or give back to the Armstrong brothers.

To Porter.

He headed for the bathroom. "I'll be right out."

She knew he was eager to shower—Darren didn't like to be soiled. As opposed to Porter Armstrong, who seemed to wear the dust and dirt of this place like a proud second skin.

She sat down and pulled out the two-year employment contract the Armstrong brothers had asked her to sign. She knew each clause by heart, but reread it, as if doing so would somehow present a clear-cut answer to what she should do next in her life. In the bathroom, the shower kicked on, a reminder of Darren's presence. She was still reeling over the fact that he'd driven all the way from Broadway to find her.

Nikki reached into her desk drawer to remove the remaining piece of homemade licorice candy that Doc Riley had given her and ate it slowly while her mind swirled. Hadn't she already decided to leave Sweetness? The workers had made it clear they didn't want her services. So why was she still holding on to this employment contract?

Because deep down, she was holding on to the fantasy that Porter Armstrong would express feelings for her and ask her to stay. The jolt to her heart when she'd

seen him earlier confirmed she wasn't one-night stand material. Instead of scratching a curiosity itch, the night in the hotel had only intensified the feelings she'd developed for him.

And the fact that he didn't feel the same left her smarting.

Nikki closed her eyes briefly. *The fact that he didn't feel the same...* Wasn't that the only answer she needed?

She picked up the contract and dropped it in the trash can next to her desk. Then she busied herself boxing up the remaining supplies in her makeshift office to relocate to the clinic. Her pulse hummed higher when the shower shut off. She dreaded the impending conversation with Darren, yet she knew it needed to happen.

The bathroom door opened and she glanced up, startled to see him standing there wearing only a towel wrapped around his waist. His build was slighter than Porter's, but tennis kept him lean. He was an attractive man.

An attractive man who'd cheated on her.

"Everything okay?" she asked brightly.

"Is there any hot water on this mountain?"

"Very little. Sorry."

His gaze darkened. "After seeing you again, I needed a cold shower anyway." Suddenly he was standing in front of her. "Nikki...I've missed you."

Her heart pounded. She'd missed him, too. So many lonely nights curled up, crying, sleeping in socks because he wasn't there to warm her feet, agonizing over where things had gone wrong and why she hadn't noticed his change of heart.

"Why did you do what you did?" she demanded quietly. "*How* could you do what you did?"

He shook his head. "I don't know. I wasn't thinking clearly there for a while, but I am now. I love you…and I'm so sorry for what I did to you."

She studied his expression and saw genuine remorse. She softened, wondering if most engaged men panicked and did stupid things they later regretted. Wasn't an engagement about trying each other on for size, a trial period? It wasn't as if they were married and he'd broken a vow.

"Let's go home," he said, his voice husky and pleading. "I'll make everything right again. Better than before, I promise."

He reached for her, but Nikki stepped back, trying to gather her thoughts. "I need some time to think, Darren."

"Okay," he said, nodding. "Why don't you sleep on it? Can I at least stay with you tonight?"

She shook her head. "There are no men in the boardinghouse overnight. You'll have to stay in the men's barracks."

He blanched. "O…kay."

But she wasn't looking forward to rehashing things all evening if they were alone. Then she remembered the notice on the dry erase board in the kitchen. "We're having a coed movie night downstairs this evening."

"That sounds fun," he said. In that moment, she realized he truly was making an effort because a group movie night was the kind of thing the old Darren would've looked down his nose at.

He picked up her hand. "Do you still love me, Nikki?"

She swallowed hard. A short rap on the outside door saved her from answering. The door opened and Porter

Armstrong stuck his head and shoulders inside. The man had the most uncanny sense of timing.

"Little lady doc?" He swung his head around and took in Nikki, then Darren in his nearly naked state.

A hot flush climbed Nikki's neck.

"Uh, sorry to interrupt," Porter said. Yet he didn't make a move toward leaving.

"Did you need something?" Darren asked, obviously irritated at the interruption.

Porter glared. "Yes. I *need* to talk to our town doctor. Which is why I came to her *office*."

Nikki pursed her mouth. Apparently, Porter had forgotten that the two of them had almost had sex in her *office*.

"Darren," she said evenly, "will you excuse us, please?"

Darren retreated into the bathroom, but shot daggers at Porter as he closed the door.

Tingling all over, Nikki turned to Porter and exhaled. "Is something wrong?"

He opened the door wider and swung in on his crutches, then lowered himself into a chair next to her desk. He thumped his mud-spattered cast. "My leg is hurting."

Nikki crossed her arms. "Maybe you should stay off the four-wheeler."

He grinned, confirming her suspicion that his "pain" wasn't serious. "But that was fun."

"Uh-huh. Did you have a reason for terrorizing Darren?"

"No. I didn't know he was your ex." Porter's attention was on the wastebasket next to her desk. He leaned forward, reached in and retrieved the employment con-

tract. He was quiet as he eyed the unsigned bottom. "So you're definitely leaving?"

Nikki squirmed as emotions pummeled her. To give her strength, she replayed how coolly Porter had treated her the morning after their sex-studded night at the hotel. "That's right. It should come as no surprise."

He nodded slowly, then tossed the contract back into the trash can. "You're right." He reached for his crutches and pushed to his feet. "I'm not surprised. I knew the minute I laid eyes on you that you don't have what it takes to make it here."

Nikki blinked at the stinging remark, waiting for him to laugh, to say it was a joke and wish her the best. Instead he lumbered out the door and down the hall, his crutches thumping.

Hurt and confused, Nikki stepped out into the hall. "I thought your leg was hurting!" she called out

"I was mistaken," he yelled over his shoulder.

"Porter…wait."

He stopped and looked back, his expression unreadable. Nikki dashed back inside to grab the soft denim shirt he'd given her from the back of her desk chair. She raised it to her nose and mouth to inhale his earthy scent one more time, then she walked out of her office and down the hall to where he'd stopped. "Here's your shirt back."

He stared at the shirt for a few seconds. She wondered if he even remembered giving it to her, and suddenly felt foolish.

Then he reached out and took it, draped it over one shoulder, and without saying a word, hobbled away.

31

"Did they teach you that in the Army?"

Porter leaned his head toward Kendall where they stood in the back of the crowded, darkened media room, but he didn't take his eyes off Darren Rocha, who had slid his arm along the back of Nikki's chair. "Teach me what?"

"How to vaporize the enemy with a hostile stare."

Porter frowned and turned to look at Kendall. "Shut up."

"Shh!" someone hissed from the chairs in front of them.

A high-action flick played on the large flat-screen TV. He'd had his doubts about whether the workers would buy into a group "movie night," but it was standing-room only. Rocha, though, had landed the best seat in the house.

Next to Nikki.

Porter fumed. It was pretty obvious that Nikki had told him she couldn't come back until her van was repaired, so the man had come to fetch her. Like a bone.

That Porter wanted.

"What happened in Atlanta?" Kendall whispered.

"Nothing."

"Is that why you've been as moody as a woman since you got back?"

"You're a good one to talk, Mr. Black Cloud."

"Shh!"

"Do you mind?"

"We're trying to watch the movie!"

Porter felt a familiar sting on his ear, and knew from Kendall's grunt that he'd gotten his ear boxed, too.

"Both of you stop yammering," Marcus said behind them in a low voice, "and follow me."

Porter shot one more glance at Nikki and Darren Rocha, annoyed to see the man had weaseled his arm around her, then turned to follow Kendall and Marcus out of the great room into the wide hallway.

"What's up?" he asked.

Concern lined Marcus's face. "Have either of you two seen Riley Bates lately?"

"No." Porter looked to Kendall, who was also shaking his head. "Why?"

Marcus nodded to the end of the hall. Nelson Diggs, the man who'd cut his hand while working on the clinic site, sat there, his face contorted with pain. He held his duct-taped hand in front of him and as Porter walked closer, he could tell it was swollen. Badly. "That's not good. Let me get Nikki."

Marcus grabbed his arm. "Diggs refuses to see Dr. Salinger. He says he only wants Doc Riley, but I can't find him."

Porter made his way over to Diggs and leaned on his crutches. "Nelson, you should let Dr. Salinger look at your hand. It could be infected."

Nelson shook his head. "Riley can fix me up."

"Nelson, this looks serious. You need to see a real doctor."

"No way," Nelson said, his voice escalating. "My wife went to a hospital with a scratch and came home in a casket. I don't trust doctors, especially women doctors!"

Porter set his jaw in frustration. But the last thing he wanted was to summon Nikki and have the man refuse her treatment in an embarrassing scene—in front of her fiancé.

He ground his teeth. Ex-fiancé.

Porter glanced up at Marcus, who lifted his hands. "No one has seen Riley around the barracks for a couple of days."

"I know where Riley sets up camp when he goes off to collect plants," Porter offered. "It's around Devil's Rock. I'll take an ATV up there to look for him."

"That's a dangerous area to navigate in the daylight," Marcus said. "Much less this time of night, and with your bum leg."

"I'll take an ATV and go with him," Kendall said. "It'll be safer if we drive together, and I can bring Riley back with me."

Marcus gave a curt nod. "Get going."

Porter and Kendall headed out. He cursed the foolish notions of some of the men, the superstitions and the chauvinism. No wonder Nikki didn't want to stay here.

That and the fact that he'd taken advantage of her in Atlanta. He'd known she was vulnerable, on the rebound. And he hadn't cared. He'd just wanted her for himself. He goosed the gas, angry at the circumstances, angry at himself.

Even with the bright headlights, the going was slow and hazardous. There was no trail, per se, just a winding route through trees and over rocks. They had to stop several times to get their bearings. About thirty minutes later, Porter spotted Riley's white tent through the trees and pointed. "There."

When they cut their engines, they could hear the man moaning.

"Riley?" Porter shouted.

"Help," came the feeble reply.

Kendall reached the tent first. It took Porter a while to pick his way through the brush on his crutches. By the time he got to the entrance of the tent, Kendall had found an electric lantern. Riley Bates was lying on a sleeping bag, sweating and clutching his chest. Kendall was leaning close to Riley's ear.

"What's wrong?" Porter asked.

Kendall sat back on his heels. "Chest pains. We have to get him to town—fast."

Dependent on his crutches, Porter was little help situating Riley onto the rear of Kendall's ATV, but he led the way back in record time. When they pulled up to the boardinghouse, he hurried inside to get Marcus to help Kendall, then made his way to the rear great room where the movie was still playing.

"Nikki!" he called, and everyone turned. He caught her gaze. "We have an emergency. Everyone else, please stay seated. Just let the doctor through."

Nikki was already on her feet. To Porter's consternation, Rocha came with her, but she sent him to her office to get her medical bag.

"What's wrong?" she asked Porter.

"Two patients," he said, leading her to the front room where Nelson Diggs sat moaning.

When Nikki asked to examine his hand, he shook his head. "I wanna see Doc Riley."

Nikki sighed and looked up. "Where's Riley?"

The door opened and Marcus and Kendall came in, half carrying Riley Bates.

"There," Porter said. "He's having chest pains."

While Nikki sprang into action, directing his brothers to lay Riley on the floor, Porter explained to Nelson that the man was incapacitated and he would have to allow Dr. Salinger to examine his hand. But the man just tightened his mouth and fell silent.

Rocha returned with Nikki's medical bag and, in Porter's opinion, hovered.

"You can go back to finish watching the movie," Porter offered.

"I'm good," Darren said. "Nikki might need me."

Porter bit down on the inside of his cheek.

"Everyone quiet, please," Nikki said, glaring between the both of them. She knelt over Riley and palpated his chest, then asked him questions. Porter couldn't hear everything, but he got the gist that she was more worried about what he'd taken for his chest pains than the chest pains themselves.

"Mountain laurel," she announced, looking up. "He poisoned himself trying to treat his symptoms—his stomach needs to be pumped. He needs to be moved to the clinic as soon as possible, preferably on a stretcher."

Marcus and Kendall left to get the equipment. Porter noticed that Darren considered going to help his

brothers, yet seemed reluctant to leave Nikki alone... with him.

Nikki left Riley's side long enough to return to Nelson. "Mr. Diggs," she said quietly. "I'm sure you have your reasons for not trusting me. But believe me when I say I only want to help you. I'd hate to see a strong, capable man like you lose the use of your hand from something that could be prevented."

He looked wary. "Doc didn't do anything wrong when he fixed me up."

"I'm sure he didn't," she agreed. "But situations change—your injuries may simply have gotten worse on their own."

Diggs chewed on his lip, then unfolded his hand and extended it to her. Porter winced at the red flesh swollen around the binding of the grungy duct tape.

"Yes, it looks as if it's infected," she said softly. Then she gave him a reassuring smile. "I'll change your dressings and give you some antibiotics." But when she stood and looked at Porter, her expression was grave. "Let's get him down to the clinic, too."

The next hour was a blur of activity. The men were transported to the new clinic where Nikki gave Riley medicine to quiet his chest pains, then scrambled to pump his stomach. Then she turned her attention to Nelson Diggs and convinced him the infection required antibiotics administered through an IV. Once the medicine was flowing, she gingerly removed the industrial tape that had bound his reopened wounds, then set about cleaning and properly dressing the lacerations. Marcus stood nearby, conferring on the welfare of his men. When his body language eased, it was confirmation the men were going to be okay.

Porter observed everything through a glass window. As he watched Nikki work, every movement smooth and efficient, his chest welled with pride and some other emotion he couldn't identify. In the face of an emergency, he had been so grateful, so relieved, to be able to turn to Nikki. How would they fare after she left? They would eventually persuade another doctor to come to their fledgling town, but would that person have the grit of this young woman?

"She's something, isn't she?"

Porter turned to see Darren Rocha standing there, also watching Nikki. Porter schooled his face. "She's a great asset to our community."

The man made a thoughtful noise. "But is this community an asset to her?"

Porter tried to count to ten, but only made it to three. "I don't think you're the best person to decide what's right for Nikki."

Darren raised an eyebrow. "And I suppose you are? You've known her for, what—a couple of weeks?"

"It doesn't take long to figure out a person," Porter said pointedly, scanning the man's preppie outfit and expensive shoes.

Rocha scanned Porter in return, taking in his sweat-stained shirt and dusty jeans, the soiled cast. "I couldn't agree more."

Porter knew these feelings of dislike for the man were unreasonable—Darren Rocha had done nothing to him personally. And the fact that he wore stuffy clothes didn't make him a bad person. He acknowledged the tight ball of anger in his chest for what it was—jealousy. He was jealous that this man had known Nikki first, and

knew her well enough to be able to lure her away from Sweetness.

No...that wasn't fair, Porter admitted. He himself was responsible for Nikki leaving.

"Excuse me." Porter turned and left the new building. He climbed on a four-wheeler and sat there a moment, listening to the crickets and looking up at the stars in the sky. Here in the mountains, they were closer to the heavens. He closed his eyes and inhaled a warm, honeysuckle-scented breeze. How many times when he was in the dry, bleak conditions of the desert had he longed for his childhood home, and thought the world would be a more peaceful place if everyone could live in Sweetness, Georgia.

But apparently, everyone didn't want to live here.

He fired up the engine and drove down to the boardinghouse where the movie was just ending. As the lights came up, Porter made his way to the front of the room and asked for everyone's attention.

"I want to let everyone know, especially the men in this room," he said, searching out the faces of workers who'd been the most vocal about refusing to see a female doctor, "that Dr. Salinger has come to the aid of two of our residents this evening, including Riley Bates, who was on the verge of having a heart attack, and Nelson Diggs, who might otherwise have lost the use of his hand—or worse. And if Nelson had let the doctor tend to him in the first place, he wouldn't be in this position." He let that information sink in. "Dr. Salinger has certainly treated us with more care and respect than we've shown her. I'm sorry to announce that she's leaving."

"Leaving?" one of the women said, sounding distressed. "We can't live here if we don't have a doctor."

The women chorused agreement, many of them on their feet. He let them vent. If the men realized the women wouldn't stay without a doctor, they might treat the next physician—male or female—with more deference.

Suddenly he spotted Nikki walking into the back of the room. She looked small and tired and seemed to be searching for...him. When he caught her gaze, his heart vibrated in his chest, and the realization hit him like a thunderbolt—he loved her. That explained the mysterious pain behind his breast bone every time he was around her. As understanding sank in and his emotions unfurled, his vital signs took flight.

Then plummeted when Rocha walked in behind her and placed a possessive hand on her waist.

Slowly, everyone in the room realized Nikki had appeared. They turned and the room fell silent for a few seconds. Then one of the men stood and began to clap slowly. In waves, everyone joined in until the room erupted into applause and a standing ovation, all for their town doctor. Porter's chest swelled with pride.

Nikki seemed at a loss. Her face turned every shade of red as she lifted her hands to deflect the expression of appreciation. But at last she smiled and nodded her thanks, accepting handshakes as people filed out of the room.

"I hope you'll stay," he heard more than one person say.

"Please stay."

"I hope you'll reconsider."

Only Darren Rocha seemed displeased by the outpouring of affection. When Porter hobbled back to where they stood, the man looked at him with open

resentment. Porter ignored him and turned to Nikki. "You're the woman of the hour."

Her color was still high, her eyes sparkling. "That was very nice—thank you."

"How is everything at the clinic?"

"Stable…and improving. Both men are sleeping. Several people have volunteered to take shifts monitoring the men through the night."

"Good."

She nodded, then looked as if she wanted to say something.

"Do you need anything?" Porter urged.

"I explained to Darren that men aren't allowed to stay in the boardinghouse overnight."

"Right," Porter said in mock sympathy. "He can stay in the barracks."

Nikki gave Porter a little smile. "Will you take him with you and see that he gets settled?"

For that smile, he would've done anything…especially if it meant keeping Rocha out of her bed. "Sure thing." He turned to Darren. "It's not too bad. Have you ever been in the military?"

"No," the man said.

"Oh, okay." Porter tried to think of an analogy the man could relate to. "It's like…summer camp."

Nikki gave Porter a withering look, but Porter just clapped Darren on the back. "Ready to call it a night?"

"Uh…I guess so." He dropped a kiss on Nikki's ear. "I'll see you in the morning."

She nodded, but Porter noticed she put her hand between them and broke eye contact first.

It was a small gesture, but his heart jumped with

hope. Considerably cheered, he gave Rocha a ride to the long, narrow building that served as the men's living quarters. It was utilitarian, but clean and orderly. Still, the man looked around as everyone else stripped down to their skivvies and balked.

"These beds don't look very comfortable."

"They're not," Porter confirmed. "No air-conditioning, either." Then he had an idea. "Tell you what, friend. You can have my bed tonight." He led him to a partitioned-off area where he and his brothers had their cots. "There you go," he said, patting his mattress. "Much more comfortable, and it's cooler in here." It was a bald-face lie. He and his brothers insisted on sleeping in the same conditions as their men. They only slept in a separate area in case they needed to talk amongst themselves.

"But where will you sleep?" Rocha asked.

"I'll make do," Porter said with a self-sacrificing sigh.

Kendall, who was getting ready to lie down himself, shot Porter a sardonic look. Damn Kendall, he could always read his mind.

"Nighty-night," Porter said to Rocha. "Don't worry about the mosquitoes. You've had a malaria shot, haven't you?"

The man paled. "No."

"Oh. Well…it's treatable."

"Good *night,* Porter," Kendall said, punching his pillow.

Porter leaned on a crutch and saluted, then made his way back through the common bunk area, and exited to the shower house. He cursed the cast on his leg for the umpteenth time, but managed to get himself clean. Then he redressed and headed for the four-wheeler. As

he started the engine, he imagined Kendall lying there and hearing it, knowing what Porter was going to do.

He steered the ATV to the boardinghouse. Lights were still on in the great room and the kitchen, meaning some of the women were still up. But the front door was locked. He had a key, but he didn't want to just let himself in. There was, after all, a good reason for the "no men after dark" rule—so the women would feel safe. He knocked, trying to think of a good reason for talking his way inside at this hour.

The door opened and Rachel stood there, holding a dish towel. "Porter…hi."

"Uh…hi." He squirmed. "I, uh…need to talk to the doctor."

"Okay, I'll get her."

"Actually," he said quickly, "if it's okay, I thought I'd just go…up to her room and…knock."

Rachel angled her head. "I wondered if you were going to stand by and let that rotten ex-fiancé of hers take her away from here." She stepped to the side to allow him to pass.

He stopped long enough to drop a kiss on her cheek. "You're a peach."

"Yeah, right," she said with a wave. "Get up there before anyone else sees you."

Feeling like a young buck sneaking into a girls' dormitory, Porter stole down the hallway and up the stairs on his crutches, then sped past the gauntlet of women's room doors before he reached Nikki's.

He knocked and waited, wondering what on earth he was going to say to her. He was a simple man, but realized this occasion called for some fancy words and

smooth talking if he was going to convince her to stay in Sweetness…with him.

He heard a noise on the other side, then a light came on and the door opened. Backlit in a transparent nightgown, Nikki looked sleep-tousled and so sexy, his body surged.

"Porter." She pushed her hair out of her face, her eyes concerned. "Does one of the men need me?"

His heart was pounding so hard, he was sure she could hear it. "Yes," he said finally. "*I* do."

32

Nikki squinted, not sure what Porter meant. He needed her? She opened her mouth to ask for clarification, but suddenly he was kissing her.

And it felt so good.

Her body sprang to life as she opened her mouth to his. One crutch clattered to the floor as he wrapped his hand around the nape of her neck.

"I want to make love to you," he said, backing her into the room.

"Men aren't allowed in the boardinghouse overnight," she murmured.

He kicked the door closed. "It's okay—I own the place."

She fell on her bed with him, waiting for a sense of apprehension or guilt to envelop her. When it didn't, she threw all her inhibitions to the wind. She had longed for him to come to her. He must have felt her body pulling on his.

As frenzied and frantic as their lovemaking had been in Atlanta, this time it was slow and sweet, with thorough kisses and clasped hands. Through the screened window, cicadas serenaded them and the moon

highlighted their naked bodies as they explored each other leisurely. When he finally rose above her to join their bodies, he was so heartbreakingly tender, Nikki felt herself falling into a depth of feeling she'd never experienced before.

She hung there, floating in a liquid mass of sensual impulses until their pendulous climax sent her crashing over an apex, leaving her weak and vulnerable. His heartbeat against hers drew her back to earth. He pulled her onto his chest and ran his fingers over the small of her back, humming his satisfaction.

Even as his breathing steadied and slowed, Nikki resisted sleep. She was falling in love with this man and she wanted to enjoy every delicious second of it. She memorized every sensation of his body against hers—the temperatures, textures and tastes…the facial expressions, musky scents and the guttural noises of fulfillment. She didn't want to go to sleep because she felt as if she'd only just been awakened to the joys of life…

When she awoke, predawn light filtered through the window and Porter was snoring softly in her ear. She wanted more than anything to stay cocooned in his arms, but she knew she needed to check on her patients.

Nikki smiled. Her patients…her town.

She slid from the bed as quietly as she could to dress and brush her hair. She thought Porter was still sleeping, but as she crept by the bed, his hand snaked out to grab hers.

He smiled up at her. "Sneaking out?"

"Going to the clinic," she whispered, wondering if

her newly formed feelings for him showed all over her face. "I'll be back soon."

He squeezed her hand. "Nikki…please say you'll stay."

Her heart expanded. "I'll stay," she said happily.

He grinned. "I'll have that contract ready for you to sign when you get back. Can't have you changing your mind."

She kissed him on the mouth, then slipped from her room. Nikki stared down at the lone crutch lying in front of her door. So much for being discreet. She wondered how quickly word had passed that Porter Armstrong had spent the night in her room.

Pretty quickly, she deduced from the sly smiles she got as she walked into the kitchen to retrieve a cup of coffee.

"Good morning," Traci sang.

"Good morning," Nikki murmured, her face warm.

"Well, for some of us," Rachel said, and everyone burst out laughing.

Nikki was unable to hold back a smile, and felt a rush of affection for these women who had accepted her into their fold.

"Nothing makes your skin look as good as afterglow," Traci said. "We want details."

The women chorused agreement.

"I have to go check on my patients," Nikki said. Groans echoed behind her as she left the room. She smiled into her coffee and gave into the little spring in her step.

She exited the boardinghouse, struck anew by the quiet beauty of this wild place. It was a dew-laden morning, already warm and steamy. The sky was streaked

with pink and yellow ribbons. A bluebird flew by, and two dragonflies. A squirrel scampered ahead of her as she walked down the paved road the short distance to the clinic. She noticed the newly erected sign that had escaped her the previous evening. *Sweetness Family Medical Center.*

She liked the ring of it—family. It seemed to capture all that was to come in this town. And she wanted to be here for it.

To be with Porter.

She inhaled deeply, imbued with happiness. She loved him. She hadn't known it could be like this, to feel as if someone was just so…necessary. She'd cared for Darren deeply, but she now realized the difference in loving someone and being in love. One was a choice and the other was…involuntary. As she struggled to define the giddiness she felt, her gaze landed on a dust-covered compact car parked near the entrance of the clinic. A young man sat slumped in the driver's seat, asleep. His dark-rimmed glasses were askew.

Nikki walked over and knocked on the window. The man jumped, then he righted his glasses and rolled down the window.

"Can I help you?" she asked.

The man's short dark hair stood up at all angles. His clothes were travel worn. "I hope so. I'm looking for Dr. Salinger."

She hadn't been expecting the British accent. "I'm Dr. Nikki Salinger."

His shoulders fell. "Thank goodness. I'm Jay Cross. Dr. Hannah sent me."

Nikki smiled widely. "Welcome, Dr. Cross. I see you found our clinic. When did you get here?"

"A couple of hours ago," he said, fighting a yawn as he climbed out of the car.

To her surprise, he wasn't much taller than she was, and from the looks of his prim suit, maybe he hadn't been forewarned about the rugged conditions. Oh, well, he'd learn soon enough. "Come on in and we'll find you some coffee."

"Tea would be brilliant," he said. "And I'm looking forward to a hot shower."

She sipped her coffee, electing not to tell him how rare both of those things would be. "I have a couple of patients I need to check on if you'd like to join me."

"Absolutely," he said. "I'm eager to learn about mountain medicine."

"Oh, then you're going to love Doc Riley."

"Is he another physician in your practice?"

"Not really," she said, wondering how Riley Bates and the other men would react to this quirky-looking man with his precise speech.

She thanked the volunteers who had kept an eye on the men all night. To her relief, both patients were doing well and were in good spirits. She introduced Doc Riley to Dr. Cross and told him of the young man's interest in learning about natural remedies.

Riley Bates eyed her warily. "I thought you didn't cotton to my homemade concoctions, doc."

Nikki considered the aged man in front of her, recognized the fear in his eyes that he was no longer useful. "I think there's room for both of us on this mountain, Mr. Bates. In fact, I was wondering if you have more of that homemade licorice candy for my allergies."

He grinned. "Does that mean you're sticking around, doc?"

She smiled. "Yes, I've decided to stay in Sweetness."

Riley Bates gave a little laugh. "Well, I gotta hand it to Porter. He told Marcus he'd get you to stay, and he did."

She frowned, suddenly uneasy. "What do you mean?"

"Marcus was afraid if you left, all the women would go, too. So he told Porter to keep you here, no matter what it took." Riley laughed. "Crippled your van on purpose, I heard."

Her mouth went dry. She could've driven out of here long ago?

The old man laughed again, clearly amused. "They wanted you bad. Marcus sweetened the pot, told Porter if you stayed, he could have the family homestead."

The homestead…the place Porter loved most on this mountain. Of course he would do anything to have it, even seduce the doctor into staying. Nikki thought she might be sick.

"So what did that scalawag do to get you to stay? Is he paying you a bundle?"

Nikki swallowed, then found her voice. "No…nothing like that."

Dr. Cross squinted at her. "Are you okay, Dr. Salinger?"

"Yes," she murmured. "I just need to get some air."

"I'll hold down the fort if you trust me," the young man offered cheerfully.

"Actually," she said, taking off her lab coat, "the clinic is all yours."

Dr. Cross blinked. "Pardon me?"

She handed him her coat. "Good luck." Her eyes filled with hot tears. She blindly made her way to the

exit, replaying the most recent encounter with Porter. *I need you…sneaking out?…please tell me you'll stay… I'll have that contract ready for you to sign when you get back…can't have you changing your mind.* There was no mention of love or commitment. She was an idiot.

Again.

She pushed open the door and strode outside, gulping, hoping the flower-scented breeze would cleanse her mind. Instead, the air was stifling and cloying to her lungs. She gasped and kept moving, walking quickly back to the boardinghouse, her mind in turmoil. How could she have been so stupid as to think that Porter Armstrong, a man who could have any woman he wanted, would fall in love with her?

Her skin burned with humiliation. He'd probably gotten a good laugh over how quickly she'd given in to him. She'd been an easy mark, the homely, inexperienced woman who'd just been dumped by her fiancé.

She closed her eyes briefly. *Darren.* How could she face him? Then she swallowed hard. She'd deal with him later. For the time being, at least he could get her out of here.

And right now, she couldn't wait to get out of Sweetness, either.

33

Porter stretched long and tall in Nikki's bed, feeling utterly sated. So this was what it felt like to be in love—tingling head to toe, and already looking forward to the next time he'd see her, caught between wanting to show her off to the world and wanting to keep her all to himself. His mind rolled forward. He couldn't stay here in the boardinghouse with her, and she couldn't stay with him. He'd have to make the time to start building a house on the family homestead.

Only a few weeks ago, he couldn't have imagined thinking about these things, but now he *wanted* to—how was that possible? Porter gave a self-deprecating laugh. His brothers would never let him live this down.

Suddenly he felt a pang for Kendall. So this was how he'd felt about Amy. No wonder he'd been impossible to live with after she'd left. How did a person handle going from such an amazing high to the low of losing that person? He didn't want to know.

He rolled over and inhaled the scent of Nikki from her pillow. He couldn't get enough of her. But he intended to spend the rest of his life trying.

Suddenly the door burst open. He looked up to see

Nikki standing there. He smiled…until he realized she didn't look happy.

"You should leave, Porter."

Alarmed, he pushed up on his elbows. "Did I do something wrong?"

She walked over to the closet, pulled out a suitcase, and carried it to the bed. "No. Apparently, you did everything right."

Porter shifted to avoid the falling suitcase. "I'm confused."

She wouldn't look at him. She began yanking things from the closet and tossing them into the suitcase. "I know everything. I know you sabotaged my van so I couldn't leave. And I know that Marcus promised you the family land if you could get me to stay. Congratulations, you almost pulled it off."

Panic licked at him. "Wait a minute—"

"Are you denying it?" she asked, her voice thick. "Are you denying that you did something to my van?"

He squirmed. "No."

"And are you denying that Marcus promised you the family land if you convinced me to stay?"

Porter was starting to see how bad things looked from her point of view. "That's not why— I mean, my wanting you to stay had nothing to do with…the other thing."

She gave a bitter laugh. "Right."

"Can we talk about this?"

"No." She grabbed the remaining clothes from the closet in one armful, then stuffed them into her suitcase.

He pushed up and reached for the only crutch he had, scrambling to his feet. Damn, where were his clothes?

He pulled a sheet off the bed and wrapped it around his waist while he hobbled forward on one crutch. "Nikki, please listen to me. This isn't what you think."

She stopped. "Really? Then what is this?"

Porter felt paralyzed. He'd never said "I love you" to a woman. He'd never been in love before, didn't know how things were supposed to work. Suddenly, he felt the weight of Nikki's expectations descend on his shoulders. Her decision to stay or leave Sweetness would depend on his feelings for her. And in that moment, he wasn't sure he could live up to that responsibility.

After a long, painful pause, Nikki nodded. "Just what I thought."

"I'm sorry, Nikki."

"It's my fault," she said, zipping her suitcase with jerky movements. "My friend warned me this would happen."

He just wanted to keep her talking while he looked for his clothes. "What friend?"

"My friend Amy Bradshaw, back in Broadway. She's from a small town. She warned me what the men were like, and I didn't listen."

Stunned, Porter's mind raced down a tangent. Amy Bradshaw? Could it be the same person he was thinking of? When Nikki picked up her suitcase and walked out, his attention snapped back to the moment. He followed her, unable to keep up with only one crutch and still clutching the sheet around his waist. A small crowd had gathered in the hallway to gape. He didn't care.

"Nikki, please listen to me," he called after her. "You can't leave."

"Watch me," she said over her shoulder.

34

By the time Porter got dressed and made it downstairs, Nikki was climbing into Darren Rocha's car. He stood in front of the boardinghouse, leaning on his crutches, feeling like his heart was being torn out. Nikki was right that he'd tried to manipulate her...at least in the beginning. He just hadn't planned to lose his heart in the process. She gave him one last glance, then swung into the passenger seat and closed the door. The car pulled away, taking Nikki with it.

Away from Sweetness.

Porter swallowed hard. His heart felt like an anvil in his chest. Suddenly he felt the familiar sting-and-ring of his ear. "Ow." He looked up to see Kendall standing there. "What was that for?"

Kendall nodded at the disappearing car. "You just going to let her go?"

"Hey, brother, you've got some explaining to do."

Marcus walked up, scratching his head. "There's a limey doctor at the clinic. What does Kendall have to explain?"

Porter gave Kendall a pointed look. "How is it that

the newspaper ad ran in the same town in Michigan where Amy Bradshaw now lives?"

Marcus frowned. "What?"

The look on Kendall's face confirmed that it hadn't been a coincidence. And suddenly Porter realized why Kendall had been in such a funk since the women had arrived—because Amy wasn't among them. He'd hoped to lure her back. After all this time, he was still pining for his first love. Porter started to ask Kendall that if he'd known where she was, why hadn't he just gone to be with her after he was discharged from the Air Force. Then it hit him. Kendall had put his commitment to re-build Sweetness above his own happiness. His life was here now. If he and Amy had a future, she'd have to come back.

"Like I said," Kendall murmured, nodding in the di-rection of the dark car rolling down the long paved road they'd built with their own hands, "are you just going to let her go?" Like he'd let Amy go.

But Porter shook his head. "It's not the same."

Kendall looked unconvinced. "Isn't it?"

Frustration and self-loathing boiled in Porter's chest. He couldn't tear his gaze away from the car that grew smaller and smaller. Yet he felt powerless to stop her. He needed to be alone with this unbearable ache.

The water tower.

He glanced down at his cast, then decided he could make the climb. The pain might actually feel good. He could watch Nikki go for miles. Without a word to his brothers, he lumbered toward a four-wheeler. Kendall smiled, as if he thought Porter was going to take off after the car, then frowned when Porter went in the opposite direction.

Porter tore up the winding, hilly path, pushing his speed and the vehicle's endurance to make it to the base of the water tower within a few minutes. The climb up the ladder was a bit more challenging, but he got the hang of pulling himself up while putting as little weight as possible on his bad leg. He stopped once and looked down, conscious of how much damage he might do if he fell again. When he reached the platform, he made his way gingerly to the front, handicapped without his crutches.

Because of the winding path out of Sweetness before leveling into a straight shot to a state road, the black car was still easily visible from the water tower on this clear, hot morning. He could even make out the two seated figures. He wondered what kind of conversation they were having, if they had already reconciled.

Porter banged his fist on the handrail, angry with himself for not taking off after her and telling her how much he loved her. If that oaf of a cheating ex could tell Nikki he loved her and it wasn't even true, then why couldn't he work up the nerve to tell her about these very real feelings thrashing around in his chest?

With a surge of determination, Porter pulled out his cell phone to call her, then remembered her phone didn't get service here. Exasperated, he returned his phone to his belt. At a loss, he waved his arms. Cars approaching and leaving Sweetness could see the water tower for at least ten miles. But could she see him... Was she even looking?

His mind flitted to the tornado sirens mounted on the tower—they would certainly get her attention. He even opened the metal cabinet, although deep down he knew he'd never raise a false alarm.

But wedged inside the cabinet next to the bullhorn sirens was an old can of red spray paint. Porter smiled. Why not?

Marcus and Kendall would string him up for marring the clean, white surface of the water tower, but he didn't care.

His prayers that the paint can still worked were answered, and he was buoyed by the fact that it was almost full. He shook the can vigorously and quickly sprayed "I," then drew a large heart, then wrote the word "Nikki" in letters that were as tall as he was. Then he turned to watch the car getting smaller and smaller, holding his breath.

"Please," he whispered, hoping the brake lights would come on, some indication that she'd seen his message, that she was going to turn around and come back to him. "Please."

But the car kept going…going…and then it was gone over the horizon.

Porter sagged against the handrail and exhaled noisily. His mind raced frantically for other options. He wasn't giving up on her. He'd have her van repaired, then drive it back to Broadway. He'd tell her how much he loved her and make her believe him…

Then a harsh realization hit him. He was in the same boat as Kendall…his life was here in Sweetness. And he'd probably already ruined this place for Nikki.

He threw his head back and shouted in frustration, then listened as the strangled sound echoed back to him as it rebounded off the valley walls.

Totally defeated, Porter started to turn around when something on the horizon caught his eye. A movement… too small to be a car…probably an animal…

He reached for the binoculars always clipped to his belt and lifted them to his face. He adjusted the focus and brought the moving shape into focus.

Nikki.

Walking back, carrying her suitcase.

Walking back to him.

Porter's heart took wing. He whooped and waved his arms. "Nikki! Nikki!"

She lifted her free arm and waved back.

Eager to drive out to pick her up, he made his way back to the ladder and began to descend. Adrenaline pumped through his body and he couldn't stop smiling, but he forced himself to slow down. He didn't want to fall and break his neck. Not now.

He almost made it.

He was about fifteen feet from the ground when his cast caught and he slipped. A sense of déjà vu enveloped him as he tumbled through the air.

35

The flat-back landing jarred Porter's body and drove the air out of his lungs. He lay there for a few seconds and waited for the initial pain to subside before daring to breathe.

When he did, he dragged in enough air to breathe a prayer of thanks that he wasn't dead. Then he moved gingerly. To his great relief, his broken ankle didn't seem any worse for the fall.

His left arm, however, hadn't fared as well.

He grimaced, then laughed into the air as he pulled his phone from his belt and dialed Marcus's cell phone.

"What now?" Marcus asked.

"How do you know something's wrong?" Porter asked.

"It's you, isn't it?"

But even his cranky brother couldn't bring him down today. "I kind of took another tumble from the water tower." He held the phone away from his ear until Marcus's string of curses petered out.

"Did you break your other leg?"

"No…just an arm. But I'm going to need a doctor."

Marcus sighed. "I'll bring the limey."

"Why don't you bring Nikki instead? She's on the road to Sweetness, walking back."

Marcus was quiet for a few seconds, then grunted. "Okay, you get a pass. But this is the last one. We'll be there as soon as we can."

Porter disconnected the call and smiled. It was as close as Marcus would get to telling him he was happy for him.

He pushed himself up with his one good arm and leaned against a rock. A few minutes later, he heard the sound of an ATV coming up the hill, then it came into view. Marcus was driving, and Nikki was riding on the back. Porter's heart catapulted at the sight of her. When they pulled to a stop, Marcus busied himself with the four-wheeler to give them privacy.

Nikki climbed off and hurried to him. Her beautiful face was creased with concern as she crouched down. "This was a little extreme, don't you think? I was already coming back, after all."

"I had to make sure you'd stay awhile," he joked. Then he pulled her face close to his and looked into her green, green eyes. "I love you, Nikki."

She smiled. "I saw that."

"Is that why you came back?"

She shook her head. "I came back because I love you, too."

Porter captured her soft mouth in a sweet, profound kiss that promised all there was to come....

* * * * *

Don't miss book two in the
SOUTHERN ROADS *trilogy,*
BABY, COME BACK.
Kendall Armstrong finally lures his first love,
engineer Amy Bradshaw, back to Sweetness
to build a much-needed bridge...
but can he convince her to stay?